WHAT DID PEOPLE SAY ABOUT THE
BOOKS IN THIS SERIES,

TALES FROM THE DEED BOX OF
JOHN H. WATSON MD

MORE FROM THE DEED BOX OF
JOHN H. WATSON MD

SECRETS FROM THE DEED BOX OF
JOHN H. WATSON MD
&

THE DARLINGTON SUBSTITUTION ?

"Ashton captures the spirit & style of Conan Doyle's heroes in three new original tales. His attention to detail, both in characters & settings, makes the mysteries seem like an extension of the the original works. For this reader, Ashton's stories are like a cool drink of water after a long dry spell."

"In writing new stories about the legendary Sherlock Holmes, Ashton is rubbing shoulders with literary heavyweights - Neil Gaiman, Kim Newman, Andy Lane and many others. How does he compare? Very well, I'm glad to say."

"Hugh Ashton continues to grind out masterpieces very favorably comparable to the original tales by Sir Arthur Conan Doyle!"

"I am not ashamed to admit that I am a Sherlock Holmes snob. I adore the original Doyle works and it takes a great deal to impress me. Ashton writes as if channeling Sir Arthur Conan Doyle himself."

"I HAD BEEN FORTUNATE ENOUGH TO ENCOUNTER A JAPANESE GENTLEMAN ON
THE SHIP ON WHICH I HAD TRAVELLED TO NICOSIA ... HE TAUGHT ME SOME OF
THE HOLDS AND TECHNIQUES OF A JAPANESE SYSTEM OF WRESTLING, KNOWN
AS *BARITSU*. IT WAS ONE OF THESE THAT I EMPLOYED WHEN MY FOLLOWER
UNSUSPECTINGLY ENTERED THE ALLEY IN WHICH I WAS WAITING." (PAGE 331)

The Deed Box of
John H. Watson MD

A Collection of the Untold Tales of

Sherlock Holmes

Discovered by

Hugh Ashton

The Deed Box of John H. Watson MD : A Collection of Untold
Tales of Sherlock Holmes

Hugh Ashton

ISBN-13: 978-0-9886670-0-6

ISBN-10: 0-9886670-0-2

Published by Inknbeans Press, 2012

www.inknbeans.com

www.221BeanBakerStreet.info

Inknbeans Press, 1251 Sepulveda Blvd., Suite 475, Torrance,
CA 90502, USA

Book design and cover by j-views

DEDICATION

 NCE again, I dedicate these adventures to the memory of Doctor John H. Watson, late of the Indian Army, whose friendship with the great detective Sherlock Holmes, and whose keen eye for detail and descriptive powers have given the world so much pleasure for so many years.

Foreword by John Paul Catton

From:
Institute of Intertextual Studies
Deep Dene House
Sydenham Road
Norwood
London SE19

To:
Mr. J. Merryweather
Branch Manager, Coburg Branch
City and Suburban Bank (incorporating Cox & Co.)
Saxe-Coburg Square
London WC2

Dear Sir,

I am writing to you to present my research on Sherlock Holmes, as requested. To recap events, this matter began when a friend of one of your employees, a Mr. Hugh Ashton, was notified of a deed box placed in your vaults almost one hundred years ago. Mr. Gilchrist of Gilchrist and Rao, the well-known firm of solicitors, has informed me of the legal process of how Mr. Ashton obtained custody of the box as a result of his claims to be descended from the original owner of the box, so we need not go into that here.

The metal lid had "JOHN H. WATSON MD" stenciled on it in white paint, with "JHW" and "To be left until called for" on the side. Upon opening the box, Mr. Ashton discovered a large number of foolscap papers, brittle with age, requiring great care in their handling. The papers were covered with handwriting later confirmed to be that of Dr. John Watson of London, and the papers described hitherto unknown cases of the famous detective, Sherlock Holmes. Your bank then contacted me to research background information on this curious matter.

My report is attached.

Yours Sincerely,

John Paul Catton

WHO *WAS* SHERLOCK HOLMES?

VEN though Watson was the chronicler of the detective's exploits, there is a great deal left unrecorded. We know Holmes had an older brother, Mycroft, who held a position of influence in British government; we also know they were both descended from the famous Vernet line of French artists, but I have been able to find no birth or death certificate for Mr. Holmes, and I have found no record of enrollment in any universities or schools of the period. It seems that Watson himself was not aware of many of Holmes' personal affairs, because the detective refused to discuss them, and sometimes *actively discouraged* Watson from writing on certain events or individuals.

What we do know is that Mr. Holmes was a "consulting detective", helping police and private individuals. He accepted payment for his services, but this didn't seem to be his motivation for accepting work; he regarded solving crimes as an intellectual challenge, and often allowed the police to take the official credit. He was also a master of disguise, and could blend in with any social environment, even to the extent that Watson himself couldn't recognize him.

In popular memory, Holmes is regarded as an eccentric genius, with detecting abilities that bordered on the supernatural. He is also known as a forensic scientist, a violinist, and a fighter trained in the obscure martial art of bartitsu. He is the most widely known exponent of the form of inductive reasoning known as the "Holmesian Gaze" – the ability to make a correct conclusion about someone, when meeting them from the first time, from a generalized series of observations about their appearance. Holmes was very fond of employing this skill to impress potential clients. This indicates that Holmes suffered from the medical condition known as "hyper-awareness", and instead of trying to lead a normal life, built a career around his affliction.

Shortly after the first recorded meeting of Holmes and Watson, Holmes mentions he has no knowledge of literature outside of biographies, medical and forensic texts. When Watson explained the basics of astronomy to him, Holmes replied that it was interesting, but he would "do his best to forget it". Holmes maintained a peculiar theory known as the "mind palace" or "memory palace", arguing that the human brain had only a limited capacity, and he needed all that capacity for information relevant to his profession.

He also had no room in his life for romance. Holmes appeared to have been determinedly celibate, never married and had no children. Watson himself writes that Holmes *"...never spoke of the softer passions, save with a gibe and a sneer."*

In my researches, I have tried to find out why Sherlock Holmes still occupies such an enduring place in the public consciousness. One explanation is because his character embodies traits that are seen as quintessentially British. Respect for the enthusiastic amateur, sympathy for the charming eccentric, a healthy disrespect for figures of authority, an unflinching belief in fair play ... all of these are found in the stories of Holmes, and are qualities rarely found today. In our modern world, with our family and work obligations and our private lives all bared on Facebook, the aloofness and audacity that Holmes practiced would be unthinkable. We will never share Holmes' intelligence, or his isolation: so we follow his exploits vicariously, content that there is someone to make a stand against injustice, refusing to be bound by laws of social convention.

What my research suggests, sir, is that Holmes may have been more of an archetype than a human being. It seems fantastic that all these qualities should be embodied in one individual, so I am exploring the possibility that Holmes may have been a false name used by a group of conspirators working together, or a title passed down the generations from father to son. How else can we explain the sightings of Sherlock Holmes during and after World War II; in Washington D.C. in 1943, in the tiny Canadian town of Le Mort Rouge in 1944, and on a cruise ship off the coast of Lisbon in 1945?

There is also the curious case of the man who turned up in New York in 1971, claiming to be the "real Sherlock Holmes"; he was later revealed to be the American millionaire Justin Playfair, who had suffered a nervous breakdown and had concocted a "fake personality" for himself. Most recently, there has been the highly publicized suicide of the individual who adopted the name of Sherlock Holmes and then jumped from the roof of St Bartholomew's Hospital, in Smithfield, London, early in 2012. This dramatic and still unexplained event resulted in the "Sherlock Holmes is Alive" Internet meme that has muddied the waters even more.

In conclusion, sir, I am afraid my research has thrown up more questions than answers. I hope the collection of the deed box stories in the forthcoming hardback volume will stir public debate, and encourage individuals to come forward with further evidence.

Perhaps this will shed some light on the greatest mystery of all, the secret that Sherlock Holmes never revealed to us; himself.

For any further information, please do not hesitate to contact me. If I am not available, my superior at the Institute, Professor G. E. Challenger, will be willing to answer any questions.

John Paul Catton

Researcher, Institute of Intertextual Studies

JOHN Paul Catton is the author of *Moonlight, Murder & Machinery*, a Regency England Steampunk fantasy, and *Voice of the Sword* – Book 1 of the *Sword, Mirror, Jewel* urban fantasy series set in modern Japan. Both are available on Amazon.

Editor's Notes by Hugh Ashton

IT has been my privilege and pleasure to have worked on the papers found in a deed box deposited so long ago in the vaults of Cox & Co. by Dr. John Watson, the friend, confidante, and biographer of the famous detective Mr. Sherlock Holmes.

As we are told by John Watson, there are many cases in which Holmes involved himself, not all of which were published in the lifetime of the principals.

When I discovered that this box was actually in existence (there are, amazing as it may seem, those who did not believe in the box's reality, or even stranger, in the reality of Holmes' and Watson's existence), and that the box was to be delivered to me, my excitement could hardly be described.

The papers within were hardly in a state that could be described as "organised", and reminded me of nothing so much as the chaotic state of Holmes' rooms at Baker-street, as described by Dr. Watson.

As I sifted through these papers, I began to discover some common properties of them. The wax seals impressed with signet rings marked " SH" and " W"; the sprawling, but at the same time legible writing of Sherlock Holmes himself (and the reader may imagine my thrill at seeing this with my own eyes and handling the papers with my own hands); and John Watson's illegible doctor's scrawl, all became old friends.

From the box, I have extracted the eleven complete tales, a few of which are somewhat longer than those recorded in the Canon. The twelfth such complete tale, *The Case of the Darlington Substitution*, is considerably longer than the others here, and has been published separately.

In many cases, there are good reasons which may be assigned to the non-publication of these tales. Some involve matters of State, some are embarrassing to Holmes, and some even to Doctor Watson himself. The length of some of these adventures may also have precluded their publication, being too short to be published as novels, and too long to fit into the canonical framework of short stories.

At some future date, I may examine the jottings that comprise the remainder of the contents of the box, but I fear that these will prove of little general interest, though Sherlockian scholars may find it amusing to discover Holmes' changing taste in eggs over the years; from soft-boiled to hard-boiled, or the fact that he invariably used cloth, rather than leather, laces for his boots (leather hardening and cracking when it becomes wet).

Some of these trivia may also find their way into print at a later date.

NE of the joys of this exploration has been the discovery of Doctor Watson as a fully-fledged character. Too often, in the tales he recounts of Sherlock Holmes, he seems content to remain as a shrinking violet, modest to a fault, and reluctant to reveal his own admirable character.

The John Watson I have discovered is an eminently sensible and intelligent man. He has a realistic estimation of his own qualities in this regard, and he is not above contradicting Holmes and putting him right in matters of social etiquette, or even in matters of deduction.

At the same time, he is loyal to Holmes, standing by him through thick and thin in times of crisis, and ready to defend him and his methods against the attacks of critics, as well as physically defending Holmes against more corporeal attacks on occasion.

He is not without a sense of humour at times, and he can be surprisingly sharp-tongued. Some portrayals of the good doctor on the silver screen have done him less than justice. His good qualities as revealed in these adventures, and his overall sense of justice and fair play amply justify his name in the title of this volume in letters at least as high as those of his more famous friend.

Here, then, are the contents of the Deed Box that John H. Watson MD felt it imprudent to make public during his lifetime.

⋯⟾◉⟾⋯

 HE *Bradfield Push* appears to be the first adventure, chronologically speaking, that is described in this collection. It is obvious, from Watson's unattached state, and roving eye, that this occurred before the *Sign of Four*, when Watson fell in love with Miss Mary Morstan.

Watson makes no reference to this incident in the Canon.

⋯⟾◉⟾⋯

 HE *Odessa Business* introduces a member of the Holmes clan, Sherlock's younger sister Evadne, who would appear to have more in common with their brother Mycroft than with Sherlock. It seems strange to consider Sherlock Holmes as the dunce of the family, but it would appear that this was the case!

Again, Watson fails to record this in his published accounts of Sherlock Holmes' cases.

⋯⟾◉⟾⋯

 HE *Case of the Missing Matchbox* provides us with further details of Holmes' sometimes bizarre lifestyle, as well as an interesting glimpse into the artistic world to which at times I believe he wished he belonged.

This is referred to by Watson in the *Problem of Thor Bridge*.

⋯⟾◉⟾⋯

THE *Case of the Cormorant* is likewise referenced by Watson, in the *Adventure of the Veiled Lodger*, with the threat that it will be used as blackmail against persons unknown who have attempted to purloin the records of Holmes' cases. Given the rather shocking nature of the case, it is unsurprising that it has remained hidden for so long.

COLONEL *Warburton's Madness* is one of the few cases that Watson claims to have brought to his friend's attention (in *The Engineer's Thumb*). Like this other case, it starts as a medical problem, but soon resolves into a crime.

Holmes' skill at disguise and Watson's sound common-sense are both shown to best advantage here.

THE *Mystery of the Paradol Chamber*, mentioned by Watson in *The Five Orange Pips*, is a classic "sealed room" mystery. It is not entirely certain why Watson would have concealed this case, unless it were to protect the reputation of Inspector Gregson, who seems to have been close personally to both Holmes and Watson.

THE *Giant Rat of Sumatra* suffers from no such ambiguity regarding its suppression. The misdeeds of senior Naval officers, one of whom was tipped for Cabinet office, would have caused a scandal had they been publicised. Mentioned by Watson in the *Sussex Vampire*.

ONK-SINGLETON and the associated forgery are referenced in the *Six Napoleons*. Here we see a crime and a scandal that could have caused the collapse of the financial system of the United Kingdom. During the course of the case, Holmes spends a night in the cells at Bow-street—a fact neither he nor Watson would be keen to advertise.

THE *Enfield Rope* involves Royalty. Though Watson hints at the assistance given by his friend to the crowned heads of Europe (and even describes some), British royalty was a subject he probably felt it unwise to describe for publication.

HE *Strange Case of James Phillimore* has long intrigued many Sherlockian scholars, including some who feel that the sudden disappearance of a man must involve a supernatural explanation. The reality is even more shocking, and the horror felt by Holmes and Watson when they first enter the chamber of the murdered man probably account for Watson's repression of the case, and his description of it as an unsolved mystery in *Thor Bridge*.

DESSA makes its appearance in the first story I transcribed from the Deed Box. It also features in *The Case of the Trepoff Murder*, a case about which we know little. For years, it was considered that this reference in *A Scandal in Bohemia* referred to the murder of Dmitri Feodorovich Trepoff, who was reported to have died of angina pectoris, but who may have been murdered.

In fact, the truth has a disturbingly modern feel to it, with Mycroft Holmes playing a shadowy and ambigious role.

S I WRITE THIS, I have just received the exciting news that another box has been discovered in London, corresponding more closely to the dispatch box described in *Thor Bridge*. My informant has let me know that I, whose grandmother's maiden name was Watson, have a good claim on this box in addition to the one which contained these stories that I have set forth here. I look forward to discovering more stories of the world's most famous detective which have remained hidden for so long.

Hugh Ashton
Kamakura, 2012

Acknowledgements

 ANY thanks to all who have assisted in making this book what it is.

First and foremost, I want to thank all my readers—my "physical friends" whom I meet and chat with, and my "virtual" Facebook and Twitter friends around the world on the Internet. Your support and encouragement make it easy for me to continue writing these adventures of the world's best-loved and most famous sleuth, knowing that there are so many of you who will enjoy reading them.

Jo, the Boss Bean at Inknbeans Press, provided encouragement and advice. We worked together on the details of this book to produce a volume which she and I would be proud to produce, and which you, the reader, will be proud to own and happy to read.

And as always, special thanks to my wife Yoshiko, who, despite herself, has found herself sucked into the world of Baker-street and London fogs as Sherlock Holmes and John Watson set off on yet another adventure.

CONTENTS

DEDICATION V

FOREWORD BY JOHN PAUL CATTON VI

WHO WAS SHERLOCK HOLMES? VII

EDITOR'S NOTES BY HUGH ASHTON IX

ACKNOWLEDGEMENTS XIII

SHERLOCK HOLMES & THE BRADFIELD PUSH 1

SHERLOCK HOLMES & THE ODESSA BUSINESS 21

SHERLOCK HOLMES IN THE CASE OF THE MISSING MATCHBOX 39

SHERLOCK HOLMES & THE CASE OF THE CORMORANT 57

SHERLOCK HOLMES & THE CASE OF COLONEL WARBURTON'S
    MADNESS 89

SHERLOCK HOLMES & THE MYSTERY OF THE PARADOL CHAMBER . . 125

SHERLOCK HOLMES & THE GIANT RAT OF SUMATRA 163

SHERLOCK HOLMES & THE CONK-SINGLETON FORGERY CASE 195

SHERLOCK HOLMES & THE ENFIELD ROPE 237

SHERLOCK HOLMES & THE STRANGE CASE OF JAMES PHILLIMORE . 267

SHERLOCK HOLMES & THE CASE OF THE TREPOFF MURDER 301

OTHER BOOKS BY HUGH ASHTON FROM INKNBEANS PRESS: 338

ABOUT THE AUTHOR 339

INKNBEANS PRESS 339

MORE FROM INKNBEANS PRESS 340

THE DEED BOX OF
JOHN H. WATSON MD

Sherlock Holmes &
The Bradfield Push

" Indeed, it was exactly three weeks ago, I remember,
for it was on that evening that I lost my locket, and
Papa was most fearfully angry." (page 12)

EDITOR'S NOTE

This story was the first I discovered in the deed box that came to my hands via a circuitous route, from the vaults of a London bank to my present home in Kamakura, Japan.

Handwritten in a vile, almost illegible, doctor's writing, these brittle yellowing pages revealed a previously unpublished chronicle of Sherlock Holmes as I gingerly turned them.

The timing of this adventure would appear to be some little time after the events described in A Study in Scarlet, *but before those of* The Sign of Four *(given Watson's open admiration of Miss Eileen O'Rafferty, which would seem to argue that Miss Mary Morstan had yet to enter his life). As such, this story is interesting to scholars and followers of the great detective's exploits who can now see the younger Holmes in action.*

F my adventures with the famous consulting detective, Sherlock Holmes, the one I relate here commenced, I believe, in perhaps the most unusual fashion of all.

The events described took place close to the beginning of my friendship with Holmes, at a time when I was still lodging in Baker-street with him, and he had yet to attain the national fame with which he is now associated. Cases were not coming to his door as frequently as he would have wished, and as a consequence I was forced to endure what seemed to my unmusical ears to be endless scrapings on his fiddle as he whiled away the hours. At other times my nostrils were assailed by the odour of mysterious and evil-smelling experiments in chemistry, one of which also assaulted my ears, and left ineradicable brown stains on Mrs. Hudson's carpet, as a glass retort of some nameless liquid that he was heating over the gas shattered with a loud report.

" If I believed in a Divine Providence governing such things, this would be to a sign to me that I should cease this particular analysis," remarked Holmes wryly, as he and I attempted to clean up the worst of the disorder, having thrown open the window in an attempt to clear the noxious fumes that had been released. " Come, Watson, when we have restored some order from this chaos, let us take the air and exercise our critical faculties in the analysis of our fellow-citizens, rather than that of inanimate salts."

I assented readily. The weather was a glorious October day, warmer than the season would suggest, and I felt it would be beneficial to the health of both Holmes and myself if we were to take some more healthful air into our lungs than that which currently filled the room.

Accordingly, in less than thirty minutes, we were promenading along Regent-street, with Holmes' low voice providing a commentary on various passers-by.

" I hope the clerk whom we just passed will be able to locate his young lady in this crowd," remarked Holmes. Thanks to Holmes' tuition, I had been able to remark the double crease on the right sleeve marking a man who spends his working hours in the production of written documents, and the small bouquet of flowers that he carried, while looking anxiously around him.

" That was a simple deduction, even for me," I smiled. " What of this, then ? " indicating as inconspicuously as I could a lady dressed in the height of fashion, holding the hand of a darling infant of not more than four years old, gazing into the window of the famous toyshop that stands at the heart of Regent-street.

" An interesting case," remarked Holmes. " Most interesting," he added, with an inscrutable smile, as the mother and child turned away from the window towards the carriageway and started to walk away from us.

I continued to watch their retreating backs. With no warning, someone in the crowd, unseen by me, jostled the mother, who stumbled against the child.

" Good Lord ! Take care, madam ! " I shouted, and dashed forward to save the infant, who had been thrown down by the impact, and was now lying in the path of an approaching omnibus. I scooped up the squalling child in my arms, and lifted him to safety, with seconds to spare before the approaching horses' hooves crushed him.

" Oh, how can I thank you enough ? " exclaimed the mother, embracing the boy while he was still in my arms. " You have saved my precious little larrikin ! " The child had not ceased his wails and continued to howl at the top of his lungs while she attempted to comfort him. At last, the sounds of woe ceased, much to my relief.

" I am a doctor," I informed the lady, " and it is my strong opinion

that you should take your son home as soon as possible and allow him to rest in order to recover from the shock he has received. I would also advise asking your family physician to examine him at the earliest possible opportunity. Maybe you will allow me to summon a cab for you ? Or perhaps you have your own carriage waiting ? " I suggested.

She thanked me gravely. " We did not take the carriage today. If you would be so kind..." I raised my hand to summon a passing hansom cab, and I helped her and the child into it. Holmes assisted me in handing the lady to her seat.

" Return to Baker-street now," he hissed at me as the hansom trotted off in the direction of Regent's Park. " Ask me no questions," he added, hailing a cab himself. As he sprang into the hansom, I heard him rap on the roof with his stick and instruct the cabbie to follow the vehicle into which we had just placed the lady and her child.

I was not yet as accustomed to Holmes' fancies as I was to become later in our friendship, and I stood in astonishment as I watched the retreating cab bearing my friend. I guessed that it was now time for my return to Baker-street, regardless of Holmes' mysterious instruction, and reached for my watch to confirm this, only to find that I was seemingly in possession of the chain alone, with the watch apparently having slipped from its mounting, and now nowhere to be found in my pockets. Not a little angry at this mishap, for the article in question had been an inscribed presentation from my regiment when I retired from the Army, and apart from having this sentimental value, was a costly timepiece in its own right, I examined the end of the chain to see how the watch might have been lost. I was more than a little astonished to discover that the links had been cut through, and there was no question of the watch's having accidentally become detached from the chain.

Obviously I had been the victim of a skilled pickpocket, and I took the opportunity of checking my other belongings to ensure that all was in its appointed place. Happily, it appeared that the watch was my only loss, but I rapidly abandoned any thought of the police being able to locate and apprehend the thief. Holmes and I had passed literally hundreds of people in our walk along the crowded streets—any of whom might well now be sporting my watch or handing it in to a pawnbroker in exchange for a sum well below the value of the piece.

It was with a heavy heart that I resigned myself to the loss of my valued timepiece, and turned back to retrace my steps towards Baker-street.

 WAS still brooding over my loss some two hours later when Holmes returned.

" Do you have the time ? " he asked me, and chuckled as he watched me unthinkingly pull the chain out of my waistcoat pocket, having temporarily failed to remember that my watch was no longer attached to it.

" It is not amusing," I told him, more than a little irritated by his laughter. " The chain was cut and my pocket picked while we were on our walk this afternoon."

" I know," he replied calmly. " I observed it."

" You observed my pocket being picked, and you took no action ? " I replied with some heat. " Even for one of your detached nature, Holmes, this is going too far ! "

" I never claimed that I took no action," he smiled, drawing his hand out of his pocket and displaying my watch resting in the palm.

" Holmes ! " I exclaimed. " How on earth did you... ? "

" I flatter myself that my skills as a pickpocket are at least equal to those of she who took it from you originally," he laughed.

" 'She' ? " I asked, somewhat taken aback.

" Yes, the woman with the child whom you saved from the wheels of the omnibus."

" I cannot believe it ! " I retorted. " The mother of that sweet little child ! "

" That was not her child. As you saw, I hired a cab and followed her cab, which stopped, with the child leaving it, it a little after it reached the Park. A woman, dressed in a style not in keeping with the child's clothing, met it and led it away by the hand. I was more interested, as you can imagine, in the woman, and continued following her cab, which drove on, passing Baker-street, and then turned down the Edgware Road, dropping its fare at Marble Arch. I alighted, and followed her to her house in Upper Grosvenor-street, where the door was opened for her by a liveried footman."

" But my watch ! " I cried. " What of that ? "

" I had observed her while she embraced the child. She had a small pair of strong scissors which she used to sever your watch chain before removing the watch itself from your pocket."

" How did you come to observe that ? "

" I was expecting something of the sort. It was obvious to me that she was not the mother of that child," he replied enigmatically. " Her action in pushing the child into the roadway hardly makes her appear a loving parent," he added in explanation.

" Holmes, you cannot be serious in making that accusation ! That would have been murder if the results had been other than what they were."

He shrugged in reply. " I believe she chose her time to carry out her deed precisely in the expectation that there would be time for an active man, such as yourself, to rescue the child. I believe she could have performed the rescue herself had you been a little slower."

" And the watch ? " I asked again.

" I marked the location in her clothing where she secreted it, and retrieved it from there when I helped her into the cab. In my early days, I acquired a certain small skill in picking pockets from a man who was a true master of the art. Sadly, he is no longer plying his trade. He has reformed his ways, and is currently the pastor of a small evangelical church in the Midlands, where his flock have no knowledge of his past. This means that I am now unable to call on his services as I used to do in the past."

" Thank you," I replied as he handed my watch to me, somewhat bewildered by this latest addition to my knowledge of Holmes' skills and his acquaintances. " What do you make of the woman who took this from me ? "

" She is unfamiliar to me," admitted Holmes. " She appeared to me to be dressed fashionably, but I lack your interest in such matters, Watson." His eyes twinkled as he said these words.

" She was indeed dressed in the height of fashion," I declared. " The hat was of the very latest style, and I could not help but remark the gloves that she was wearing, with the coral buttons, which are a very recent trend."

" So you would assume that she is a lady of some standing ? " asked Holmes. " I would concur with that judgment, given what I observed. Since the front door was opened to her, and she had no occasion to ring, I think it is safe for me to assume that 45 Upper Grosvenor-street is her abode." He strode to the bookcase and pulled down a thick reference volume—a directory of central London.

" That address is given here is that of the Marquess of Cirencester," he declared. " But, if I recall correctly, the Marquess is of advanced years, and is childless. Be so good as to reach me that *Debrett's*," he requested. " As I thought, the Marquess and Marchioness are both over seventy years old and are childless. The woman we saw is known to them and the household, however, or the servant would never have opened the door to her."

" A guest who is currently residing there" I hazarded.

" Obviously that must be the case," replied Holmes. " Tell me, did you notice anything strange about the woman's speech ? "

" She hardly said anything."

" Even so, there was a distinct timbre to her voice that was not entirely English. Something of the Antipodes, if I am not mistaken. And that word, 'larrikin' that she employed," he mused. " I believe that is chiefly an Australian term of affection. It has much the same meaning as our term 'hooligan', I believe, but though it comes from an English dialect phrase, it is my understanding that Australians use the term much more frequently than do we. Furthermore, it is not the kind of vocabulary I would expect to be employed by a woman of the class that was suggested by the dress of our acquaintance."

" I have met very few Australians," I confessed, " and I would not undertake to identify the way of speaking."

" Tomorrow I shall find out all there is to know about this woman, never fear."

" How will you achieve that ? " I asked, full of curiosity.

Holmes failed to respond to my question, but merely commented upon an article in the evening paper describing the theft of some jewellery at a ball the previous evening. " This is the fourth such case in as many weeks," he remarked. " I am somewhat surprised that Lestrade has not yet contacted me regarding his failure to solve the problem. It may be that we can expect a visit from that quarter in the near future."

N the event, Holmes' prophecy was fulfilled the next day. I awoke to discover on the breakfast table a note in the familiar writing of Sherlock Holmes, " Will be out all day. Expect me for dinner. S.H."

I fell on the waiting bacon and eggs with a good appetite, and had barely finished my meal when Mrs. Hudson announced the arrival of Inspector Lestrade.

The little Scotland Yard detective entered the room with a cheerful greeting on his lips, which died as he peered about the room and failed to discover my friend. " Where is he ? " were his words, not taking the trouble to name the object of his inquiry.

" To be frank with you, I am not entirely certain," I replied. " He left the house before I awoke, and will not be returning until the evening."

Lestrade's face fell a little at the news. " I was hoping that he might be able to lend us some assistance with a problem whose solution seems to be temporarily beyond

our grasp," he said, seemingly more than a little embarrassed at the confession of the failure of the official guardians of law and order.

" This is in connection with the jewel thefts from the society balls and parties ? " I asked. The effect of my words upon Lestrade was remarkable. His mouth dropped open, and he stared at me. Then he started to laugh heartily.

" Dr. Watson," he exclaimed, between his fits of merriment. " I would have sworn to you that no-one except Sherlock Holmes, and maybe not even he, could have guessed my errand, and almost before I have opened my mouth, you tell me my own business ! By all that's remarkable, I feel that Sherlock Holmes will soon meet his match in the business of impudence and nerve, in the person of John Watson ! " He made an ironic bow in my direction.

" If you relate the facts to me, I shall be happy to present them to Sherlock Holmes upon his return," I offered, amused despite myself at Lestrade's reaction.

" That's very decent of you, Doctor," answered Lestrade, accepting the cigar I offered him and settling himself comfortably in an armchair. " You probably know that there have been four such robberies reported over the past month or so. A fact of which you may not be aware, however, is that there have been several more losses, sustained under similar circumstances, which have remained unreported in the Press for reasons of discretion."

" All occurring at society functions, then ? " I enquired.

" You are correct there. And none of these losses is valued at under three hundred pounds," he replied. " The thief, whoever he may be, obviously has an eye for quality."

" And those attending the functions ? " I went on. " Is there no one person who has attended all these functions, and who therefore can be regarded as a suspect ? "

Lestrade threw back his head and laughed once more. " My dear Doctor," he informed me. " Those who attend are what is sometimes known, I believe, as 'the Smart Set'. The same group moves from ball to ball, and from party to party, and retains essentially the same composition, no matter where the event is held, or who is acting as host. To make matters more difficult for us, these people are typically of the highest rank, and do not take kindly to the sound of police boots echoing in their hallway. Even the act of questioning is regarded as an outright accusation, and we are shown the door pretty smartly under these circumstances, I can tell you."

" I begin to see your difficulties," I replied. " Have you not attempted to place some of your plain-clothes men at these functions, as waiters or as other servants ? "

" Police detectives do not usually make the best footmen or servants, we have discovered. We did attempt such an operation, but with a lamentable lack of success."

" And your request, then ? "

" Is for you and Sherlock Holmes to attend these functions in the future, as guests."

" We do not move in such exalted circles," I protested. " I scarcely think that we would find ourselves invited as guests to these parties and balls and so on."

" It could easily be arranged with a word from the right quarter," smiled Lestrade. " Please consider the matter and put it to Holmes when he returns. The purpose, of course, is for you and he to keep your eyes and ears open for any thefts or suspicious persons and report them to us."

" Do you have a list of the missing items, together with their owners and the circumstances surrounding them ? " I asked. " I think that Holmes would appreciate such information."

" I guessed that request would be made, and I have accordingly prepared such a list," replied Lestrade, pulling a piece of paper from his pocket and handing it to me. " There is one other thing I would like to mention while I am here," he went on. " There have been several reports of pickpockets operating in the West End recently. If you or Holmes were to see or hear anything relating to this outbreak, believe me, Scotland Yard would be more than grateful for such information."

I mentioned yesterday's incident to Lestrade, but omitted Holmes' actions in retrieving the watch, or his subsequent following of the woman who had purloined the article. Lestrade thanked me, and commiserated with me on my loss.

" This is all very good of you,

Doctor," replied Lestrade, rising to his feet and reaching for his hat. "As you know, Mr. Holmes has been very close to solving a number of cases in the past where we have reached an impasse, and his hints have enabled us to bring a number of villains to justice."

Lestrade's vanity, as Holmes had remarked to me on several occasions, was such that he was unable to admit the value of others' work in the solution of the puzzles to which he sought answers. Far from being offended by this attitude, however, Holmes regarded it with a detached amusement, seeing the satisfaction of solving these puzzles as its own reward, without seeking public recognition or financial gain.

I pondered the prospect of Holmes and myself making an entry into the layer of society that Lestrade had named as the "Smart Set", and smiled to myself at the thought of the celebrated detective waltzing with Society beauties. For myself, I rather welcomed the prospect, as it had been some time since I had experienced such an amusement.

⋅⋗═◉═⋖⋅

 N the afternoon, I left the house for a constitutional stroll, remembering, as I had promised Lestrade, to keep watch for the pickpockets that he claimed were infesting the metropolis, but saw nothing to engage my attention in that regard.

On my return to Baker-street, Mrs. Hudson stopped me as I was going up the stairs.

"I hope you don't mind, sir, but there's a man waiting outside your rooms. He wouldn't go away, and he's just standing there on the landing."

"How long has he been there?" I asked.

"A good thirty minutes, I'd say, sir."

"A gentleman, would you say, Mrs. Hudson?"

"Oh no, sir. Quite the opposite, if you want my opinion."

I mounted the stairs to our rooms to discover a somewhat dishevelled elderly man standing outside the door, with his most distinctive feature being a shock of white hair standing out from his head in all directions. He was dressed in garments that might have been smart once, but had certainly seen better days when they belonged to someone other than their present wearer. The disparity between the dimensions of the legs of the trousers and the length of the legs of their current occupier, despite his stooped posture, informed me that they had not been purchased by our visitor.

"Beggin' your pardon, guv'nor, but you must be Mr. Sherlock Holmes?" he demanded of me in a strong Cockney accent.

"I regret to inform you that I am not. I am a friend of Mr. Holmes, whom I believe to be absent at this moment, and whom I am expecting to return soon. May I enquire your business with him?"

"That's for me to say and him to hear," replied the other truculently. "If you let me in, I'll wait for him."

I was somewhat reluctant to allow him access to our rooms, but I judged that should he attempt anything untoward, I was younger and stronger than his appearance suggested, and I would come off better in any potential physical encounter. I therefore acceded to his request, unlocking the door and inviting him to enter.

Once in the room, he seemed slightly ill at ease, moving from foot to foot restlessly. " You don't mind my sitting down ? " he asked, moving to place himself in the chair usually occupied by Sherlock Holmes.

" I would rather you chose another place to sit," I admonished him, turning away to indicate the preferred location. " That chair—"

" —is my usual seat," he replied in a completely different voice. I turned and looked, astonished. The white hair had gone, as had the bent posture, and Sherlock Holmes was sitting in the place of my aged unkempt visitor, his wig now in his hand, laughing at my surprise.

" Holmes ! " I exclaimed. " Why on earth... ? "

" There are occasions, Watson, when Sherlock Holmes is not an identity with which I necessarily wish to be associated. Today, Enoch Masterton has been exercising his trade and assisting the grooms of Upper Grosvenor-street with currying the horses and cleaning out the stables. And many interesting things he learned, too, while he was so engaged. Allow me to resume my usual attire and appearance," he added, rising, " and I will tell you all."

Holmes reappeared in a few minutes, dressed in his usual style, and with all traces of the grime and dirt that had previously disfigured him now washed away.

" Before you start, I must tell you some things," I said to him, and proceeded to tell him of Lestrade's visit, handing him the list that had been presented to me.

Holmes scanned it and frowned. " This upsets my theory," he said. " I was almost certain that I was on a strong scent, but this throws me back to the start." He noticed my look of puzzlement and continued.

" Let me explain. The object of today's little masquerade was, as I am certain you realise, to determine the identity of the woman who took a fancy to your watch yesterday. To that end, I assisted the grooms and coachmen of the house where I saw her enter, as well as some of the neighbouring houses—in order to divert attention away from my main object. I discovered that the woman in question is, as we surmised, from Australia. However, she is a niece of the Marquess, and comes from a wealthy family. Miss Katherine Raeburn arrived about six weeks ago on an extended visit to her relations and has impeccable credentials."

" Miss Katherine Raeburn ? Unmarried ? " I asked. " So the child is definitely not hers ? "

Holmes shook his head. " None of the servants seem to have seen any child at the house. The child we saw yesterday seems to have been borrowed as a property, to use a theatrical term, for an occasion such as the one that transpired."

" And you say that she is from a wealthy family ? Why, then, would she wish to engage in acts of pilferage and theft such as yesterday's ? "

" That makes little sense to me also. In cases of the condition known as kleptomania, the afflicted person typically acts on impulse, seizing the object on display in an almost spontaneous, somewhat magpie-like action. Such was not the case here. There was evidence of forethought and planning, as evidenced by the use of the scissors—which must be of a particularly sturdy construction, given that they cut through your watch-chain so readily—and the use of the child. These would appear to be the work of a dedicated thief, and there is no apparent necessity for this, given that she is by all accounts independently well-off, and further-more is a guest of one of the wealth-iest peers of the realm. I confess to suffering from some mental confu-sion here."

" And I suppose there is still a possibility that this Miss Raeburn is not the woman that relieved me of my watch yesterday ? "

Once more, Holmes dismissed my suggestion with a motion of his head. " There is no doubt whatso-ever. No other person remotely an-swering to that description appears to have entered the house in the past few days. Furthermore, as I was engaged in cleaning the wheels of the landau, the woman in ques-tion was pointed out to me as she departed the house, and she was, without a shadow of doubt, our ac-quaintance of yesterday."

" It seems most mysterious," I said.

" Indeed it is. But notwith-standing these factors, I remained convinced that somehow there was some connection between her and the thefts that have taken place of which we talked last night, and con-cerning which Lestrade paid his visit this morning. But it appears that I was mistaken." He waved Lestrade's list in his hand. " This wretched piece of paper has upset all my calculations."

" How so ? "

" One of those who reports a missing diamond bracelet, valued at three thousand guineas, is a Miss Katherine Raeburn."

" That would certainly seem to argue her innocence."

" As regards that particular series of crimes," he admitted. " But the fact remains that I discovered her red-handed, Watson, in the theft of your watch. Can she be both perpe-trator and victim ? "

" We have a chance to find out," I pointed out to Holmes. " Should you accept Lestrade's invitation to the ball, if I can put it that way."

" Hmph. I can imagine more en-joyable and productive ways of pass-ing the time," he remarked. " Still, these functions may prove to be of some interest if there are to be law-breakers as well as the nobility pres-ent. And of course," he added with more than a touch of cynicism and a twinkle in his eye, " the two groups are not necessarily distinct from each other."

 T was two days later that Holmes and I set out for Lady de Gere's ball to be held at her Park Lane res-idence. The ball was a glittering af-fair, and though I was introduced to many guests whose names were fa-miliar to me from the newspapers, only a few were known to me person-ally. There were two Royal person-ages present, to whom Holmes and I were presented, and I noticed with some amusement Holmes' pride in his name being recognised by them. The ladies were splendidly dressed, in the height of fashion, and I no-ticed many glittering ornaments which would undoubtedly constitute a temptation to any thieves such as those whom we were seeking.

When the dancing began, I was presented to a charming young girl blessed with glorious auburn hair and eyes of emerald green, the daughter of an Irish aristocrat. We chatted together happily as we cir-cled the floor, almost as old friends rather than acquaintances of a few minutes' standing. While danc-ing, I was struck by Holmes' skill as he escorted his partner around the floor. He moved with a grace that I had previously only ascribed to habitués of dance-halls and similar establishments. My fair partner and I danced the next few dances together, after which I led her to the supper-room, where we availed ourselves of an ice apiece and retired to an ante-room away from the crowds. To my astonishment, Holmes was already there, partnering the purloiner of my watch as he helped her to refreshments.

I could not help being fascinated by the sight, and I fear my interest must have been obvious, because my partner broke in on my reflections.

" Do you know that lady ? Or that gentleman ? " she asked me. " You seem most interested in that couple."

I saw no reason to dissemble my acquaintance with Holmes, but somewhat to my disappointment, I confess, she appeared not to recognise his name or his reputation. " The lady," I concluded, " I do not know. Are you acquainted with her ? "

" She is the cousin or niece or some such relation of the Marquess of Cirencester. She is visiting this country from Australia, I believe. She was introduced to me first about three weeks ago. Indeed, it was exactly three weeks ago, I remember, for it was on that evening that I lost my locket, and Papa was most fearfully angry."

" I am sorry to hear that," I replied. " Was it a valuable piece of jewellery ? "

" Papa tells me that it was, and he scolded me for being so careless. But indeed," she assured me, with an attractive fluttering of her eyelashes, " I was not careless in the least little bit. The locket was securely fastened by a chain around

my neck, and the chain broke, and the locket must have dropped to the floor without my realising it. Though we searched after the ball, and we made enquiries of the servants, the locket was nowhere to be seen. I wish you had been with me to help me find it, since you tell me that you are a friend of a great detective." She appeared almost kittenish as she made her innocent appeal to my limited powers of detection.

I was intrigued by her story, which had a somewhat familiar ring to it. " This may appear a somewhat unusual request," I said to her, " but do you perhaps have the chain of the locket with you at this moment ? "

She looked at me strangely, as well she might. " I suppose this is a result of your acquaintance with that man," she replied. " Do you know, I may possibly have it in my reticule, for it is the same as I was carrying on that occasion." She opened her bag, and withdrew a slim golden chain, which she passed to me.

I moved over to a spot under a gasolier, by whose light I examined the chain closely. As far as I could make out without the benefit of a lens, the chain had been cut in the same fashion as had my watch-chain a few days earlier.

I returned the chain and thanked her. " Did you inform the police of your loss ? "

She flushed slightly. " Oh, no. Papa has a strong aversion to publicity and seeing his name in the newspapers."

We returned to the ballroom, and spent the next few dances agreeably discoursing of trivial matters, before she excused herself, telling me that she had to take an early Holyhead train the next morning. I bade my fair companion a good night, and handed her into a cab, before returning to the revels.

On my way to the ballroom, I nearly collided with a large man blocking the entrance, whose corpulence and red face spoke eloquently of his taste for the good things of this life.

" By Gad, Watson ! " he exclaimed. I was somewhat dumbfounded by this sudden greeting, but looked a little closer at the speaker.

" It's Brookfield ! " I cried as I recognised an old Army comrade. " I thought you were still in India with the regiment. Fancy meeting you here ! "

" The same might be said of you, you old dog. No, no India for me, old boy. A touch of the old malaria did for me, and I came home," he answered, digging me familiarly in the side with his elbow. " By the way, I saw you with that charming little Miss Eileen O'Rafferty. An elegant filly, is she not ? "

I particularly detest such talk, but there appeared to be no escape from the man, who now seized my arm and dragged me to the supper-room where he loudly demanded two brandy and sodas.

" Here you are, sir," answered the footman, handing over the glasses. Something in the inflection of his speech attracted my attention, and I spoke to the man.

" Excuse me, my man, are you in Lady de Gere's employ ? "

" No, sir. I work for the hotel kitchen providing the catering for this occasion."

" You're not a Londoner ? " I asked him.

" No, sir, I am not. My home's in Sydney, Australia. I arrived here some six weeks back. Now, if you'll excuse me, sir, there are others waiting." He turned to another

guest and started to open a bottle of champagne.

" I say, Watson," said Brookfield, who had been listening to the exchange. " Do you always chat to the servants in that way ? Dashed bad form, if I may say so, at a 'do' such as this."

I bit my lip against the possible retorts I could make to his words, and instead asked him what he was doing in civilian life.

" Insurance," he sighed. " Fire, loss, damage, or theft. Y&L Insurance. Best in London. Come and see me some time and buy a policy. Special rate for old comrades in arms." The brandy he was drinking was obviously far from being his first of the evening, and the drink was having its effect on him. " Extraordinary thing," he remarked to me in an over-loud voice. " You wouldn't believe the amount of villainy that goes on in this town. Even in places like this, it's amazing the amount of jewellery and things like that going missing. Mysterious business, wouldn't you say ? "

Before I could reply, Holmes was at my elbow. " Can you persuade your oafish friend to keep his mouth shut ? " he hissed at me. His mouth was smiling, but there was anger in his eyes. " Let us get him outside." Holmes and I took an arm each, and assuming as friendly a manner as we were able, escorted my acquaintance to the door. A footman followed us, bearing Brookfield's hat and coat, which we handed in to him after we had installed him, with surprisingly few complaints on his part, in a hansom cab.

As the cab clattered away, Holmes turned to me. " I apologise, Watson," he said to me. " I do realise that you are not responsible for the actions of your friends, and I understand you well enough, I hope, to know that the fat fool now making his way home is not the kind of companion with whom you would choose to spend an evening. My ill temper comes upon me, though, at times and lashes the undeserving. My sincere apologies."

" Accepted without reservation," I replied, touched by this manly confession of his weakness.

" I fear, though, that we have outstayed our welcome somewhat, and it may be as well for us, too, to depart. Come, let us collect our hats and coats, and make our way back to Baker-street on foot. It is a good night for a walk, do you not think ? "

Our way home took us along Upper Grosvenor-street, and Homes paused for a moment outside number 45. " Only the servants are awake, waiting to admit Miss Raeburn, I assume," he remarked, looking at the darkened windows.

" I noticed you dancing with her," I replied. " And remarkably skilfully, I might add. I had no idea of your terpsichorean expertise."

" Pah ! The trivial exercise of dancing presents no fears to me. Fencing and boxing are good training for the dance-floor," he retorted. " But yes, I was indeed dancing with the lovely picker of pockets. She had no opportunity to exercise her skills while she was with me, I can assure you. As soon as I saw her eyes fix on some bauble adorning another dancer, I was able to direct the dance to another part of the room." He chuckled. " How she must have hated that series of seemingly accidental movements around the floor, forever removing her from her quarry."

" So there is no question at all of the identity of the thief ? "

" None at all in my view. In addition, while we were refreshing ourselves she unintentionally allowed me to observe that her reticule contained a piece of paper—a telegram, in fact. I managed to extract it without drawing her attention to the fact that I had done so. Before replacing it, I made a copy of the wording and other information. You may read it for yourself." He passed his notebook to me.

" Sydney, NSW, 14 October 189–," I read. " That was two days ago," I remarked. " Addressed to Miss Katherine Raeburn. 'GLEBE PUSH SALED LAST NIGHT STOP SUGEST COME HOME NOW STOP JAY'. Do you understand this, Holmes ? "

" At present, no, but I intend to do so tomorrow. What did you learn ? " he asked me in his turn.

I told him of the fair Irish maid's loss of her locket and my examination of the chain, and his eyes shone. " Well done, Watson ! Bravo, indeed. More grist to the mill, would you not say ? "

" I agree, given what you have just told me. And there is one other point which may or may not be significant." I informed him of the Australian footman, who had come to England at the same time as Katherine Raeburn.

The effect on Holmes was electrifying. He clapped his hands together and stood on his tiptoes in a seeming ecstasy. " Watson, you have solved the whole problem for me ! That was the link that was missing and you have found it. You have exceeded my expectations ! "

" I fail to grasp your meaning," I said.

" Never mind," replied Holmes, more soberly. " Tomorrow night, Lestrade has secured us an invitation to the dance given by Sir Geoffrey and Lady Marchmont, has he not ? Good. I foresee an excellent evening's entertainment ahead of us."

HE next evening, we both dressed for the occasion, with our only departure from formal evening attire being a revolver, which I carried in an inside pocket of my dress coat, and a weighted life-preserver, which Holmes bore in a similar place of concealment. Each of us also carried a police whistle.

"It would be foolish to be unprepared for opposition," Holmes had remarked to me when suggesting the adoption of these accessories. "I am not anticipating any such, but one never knows."

"Will your little Irish friend be here tonight?" asked Holmes as we entered the house.

"Alas, no," I replied. "She informed me that she had to travel to Ireland today, and left for Holyhead by an early train this morning." However, to my great delight, for I had much enjoyed the company of the pretty maid of Erin on the previous evening, I discovered I was mistaken, for she was standing in the ante-room, and, to my greater pleasure, came towards me smiling.

"Doctor Watson," she said to me. "You mentioned your friend Mr. Holmes, the famous detective, last night. This is he?"

"I am indeed," replied my friend courteously, as I introduced them. "But Doctor Watson informed me you were to be in Ireland today."

"We were to travel today, it is true," she replied, "but Papa was feeling unwell, and we have put off our journey for a day or so."

"I am delighted to hear that your father is unwell," I replied, before I fully realised the meaning of what I had said. "What I mean to say is that I am very pleased to have the opportunity to meet you again, even considering the circumstances," I blurted out in my confusion. I noticed Holmes smiling to himself at my gaffe, but my pretty companion thankfully took my meaning rather than my actual words.

"A word with my friend, if I may, Miss O'Rafferty?" Holmes requested. He drew me aside and spoke in a low voice. "I spoke with Lestrade earlier today while I was at the Yard. His men are surrounding this place, and are ready to enter as soon as you or I blow our whistles. If you see anything untoward—you know my meaning—do not hesitate, but blow three blasts on your whistle. If you hear me do the same, no matter what you are doing at the time, come to me, as I will to you."

"I understand," I replied, though in truth I understood little.

The ball proceeded along its course, and after a few dances with Miss O'Rafferty, I suggested that we adjourn to the supper-room and partake of champagne and some light refreshment. She assented gladly, and I gave her my arm as we left the ballroom. Not altogether to my surprise, I saw Miss Katherine Raeburn in the almost deserted supper-room. She appeared to be in conversation with the footman with whom I had spoken the previous night, whose company had obviously been engaged for this occasion. Neither appeared to have noticed me, as I disengaged myself from my partner, and moved forward as quietly as I could, motioning to Miss O'Rafferty to remain silent. I was now close enough to overhear their conversation.

" ...more than you did for the last one. That was worth eight hundred, and you only got seventy-five for it," she said to the servant.

" It's not up to me, Beckie," whined the footman. " I get what I can from those d—ed Amsterdam sheenies. What do you want me to give you ? I can't give you what I don't have."

" If you can't do better than you have been doing, I'm out of it." She spoke in a low voice, and there was menace in her words. " I'm going to pack it all in and go back home tomorrow, and you can swing, for all I care. The Glebe Push is coming this way, and we've not got that long before they're on our backs and then we're going to have to pack it in, anyway."

" You wouldn't peach on me, would you, Beckie ? "

" I'd peach if I b— (and here she pronounced a word that I had never previously heard used by a woman) well like, you b—. I know you're getting more for the swag than you're telling me, and I want you to know that I'm not going along with it any more. "

" You can't—" and the man stopped in horror as he realised my presence.

" What have you been listening to ? " asked the woman, turning and looking at me aghast. " I know you, don't I ? " as she scanned my face. " You were the bloke with the jerry in Regent-street the other day, weren't you ? And then the jerry went missing when I got back. Some b— had twigged it. What the h— are you doing here ? No, Jem," she said to the footman, who was advancing towards me. " You can't do anything here. In any case,

she's watching us," pointing at Miss O'Rafferty.

" Stay where you are and do not move," I ordered them, taking the whistle from my breast pocket and blowing three sharp blasts. Within a minute the music in the ballroom ceased as the dancing stopped, and the guests peered cautiously into the supper-room.

" Rebecca Sudthorpe and Jeremy Atwood, I order you to stay. Do not attempt any escape ! " cried Holmes in ringing tones, as he pushed his way through the crowd to stand by my side. The two appeared stunned and frozen, but Atwood's hand made a sudden move towards the inside of his livery coat, which was checked by Holmes' advance on him, brandishing the life-preserver above his head. Sudthorpe's face froze in a mask of horror as she recognised her erstwhile dancing partner of the previous evening.

At that moment, Inspector Lestrade arrived at the head of a squad of uniformed constables.

" Put the derbies on them, lads," he called to his men, and in a trice, the woman that society had known as Katherine Raeburn and the footman, who was speedily relieved of his pistol, were securely handcuffed. " That was a mighty fine piece of work there, Mr. Holmes, I don't mind telling you. Maybe you can tell us how you came to make these discoveries."

" I would sooner that we were without an audience," replied Holmes, waving a hand at the crowd of immaculately dressed onlookers who were thronging the entrance to the room, some with their mouths literally hanging open.

Lestrade ordered the room cleared and the doors to be closed, but my dance partner, Miss O'Rafferty, clung to my arm and murmured to me, "It's all so terribly exciting. Do you think that I might be allowed to stay and listen?"

Holmes, with his keen hearing, overheard this, and smilingly nodded his assent, with (I am ashamed to say) a knowing wink in my direction.

"It was a few days ago in Regent-street," he explained to us, "that Sudthorpe picked the pocket of my friend Dr. Watson, severing the chain of his watch with a stout pair of scissors, which, I have no doubt, will be on her person at this moment."

"So that's what happened to my locket!" exclaimed Miss O'Rafferty.

"I believe that to be the case," acknowledged Holmes to my partner, who was now blushing prettily, seemingly at her temerity in interrupting. "It was obvious to me that the child was not hers, even before the 'accident' that pushed the child into the roadway. This was confirmed when I followed her cab and saw her give the child to another—"

"You are a cunning b—, aren't you? So it was you following me!" broke in the Australian.

Holmes bowed ironically to her. "I had that honour," he replied.

"How did you know that the child was not hers?" I asked. "Forgive me for interrupting."

"When we were walking behind her and the child, who was walking on the outside?" Holmes asked me.

I recalled the scene in my mind. "Of course. The child was walking on the outside closest to the carriageway. No mother would expose her child to the danger of the passing traffic in that fashion." I noticed Sudthorpe shaking her head ruefully at Holmes' observation.

"When I read the list of the items stolen at the balls and dances, it appeared to me that all of them could have been removed by the same method, other than the bracelet that was reported stolen by Miss Katherine Raeburn. That was an anomaly, Lestrade, a glaring exception, that should have alerted you immediately."

"Never mind that," replied the Inspector gruffly. "Why did she report a theft that never took place? And where is Miss Katherine Raeburn?"

"As to your first, Inspector, it was dust thrown in our eyes. It blinded you successfully, Lestrade, and it nearly blinded me. As to the second, I believe that Katherine Raeburn was murdered by the members of the Bradfield Push—'Push' is an Australian colloquialism meaning 'Gang'—and Sudthorpe took her place. Her hands are not those of a lady—I am unsurprised that she habitually wears gloves, but I noticed the redness and roughness when she removed the gloves to partake of the refreshments. Your table manners, Miss Sudthorpe, if I may venture a personal remark, are also hardly those of a lady."

"That's a lie about the murder!" cried the woman. "Thief I may be, but murderer never. I was maid to Miss Raeburn, working as an indentured servant. She was a good mistress to me, but on our journey from Australia to England she suddenly took sick and died of a fever in Cape Town, where we had only just arrived and we were completely unknown. She had told me that no-one in England knew what she looked like, so it was easy for me to take her body, dress it in the clothes I wore as her servant, and lay it in my bed. She took my place, as it were, and I took hers, dressed in her clothes, and copying her voice and her ways, and took my opportunity to lead a good life here in England. She had a decent burial in Cape Town, in case you're wondering. Her gravestone has Rebecca Sudthorpe on it, and I paid for it all with her money. The ship for England sailed the week after she died, and none on board knew me from Adam's wife Eve, except Jem here, who by pure chance happened to be on the same boat."

" Ah yes," replied Holmes. " Jeremy Atwood, the leader of the Bradfield Push, as I discovered from the records in the Colonial Office earlier today. How did you come to know Rebecca Sudthorpe ? "

It was the woman who answered. " My father was under Jem in the Push, and Jem had been close to our family. I swear to you that I was going to lead a good life here, and then go back to Australia, but Jem came up with this idea that you have discovered. He was to dispose of the jewels I stole at these dances and we would split the proceeds."

Holmes nodded. " I knew that there had to be some way of disposing of the loot. No pawnbroker or jeweller had ever reported any items being offered to them—I must congratulate you, Lestrade, on your thoroughness and tenacity in verifying this—and it was obvious that the jewellery was being passed to a confederate at the very events where it was being purloined. There was too great a risk of discovery if Sudthorpe were to retain them on her person, let alone in Upper Grosvenor-street. Either the goods were being held by a third party, or, as I judged more likely, they were being sold abroad."

" Amsterdam, I believe," I added.

" Indeed ? " asked Holmes. Atwood nodded sullenly in confirmation. " Amsterdam, then. Given the diamond trade there, I should not be surprised, I suppose. So Atwood, in his intervals of serving at the gatherings to which the supposed Miss Raeburn was invited, slipped across the Channel and raised the cash by selling the loot passed to him. And with the Glebe Push arriving in London in a month or two, it was obvious that they would have to work fast before the competition, as it were, arrived on the scene. For now, I would be interested to see what is concealed on their persons in the form of tonight's takings."

" I have a woman here who will search Sudthorpe if a room can be provided," announced Lestrade. " Atwood will be searched by the constables."

The two were led away by the police officers, and Lestrade turned to Holmes. " Well, Mr. Holmes, maybe there is something to these methods of yours, though I dare say I should have reached the same conclusion in the end."

" I dare say," commented Holmes absently.

" All this excitement has made me quite hungry," complained my little companion. " Doctor Watson, may I presume on your kindness," she smiled up at me, " and request that you take me to supper at a restaurant somewhere ? "

" I will be more than delighted to do so," I replied, taking her arm. " I am sure that Mr. Holmes and Inspector Lestrade have many points of the case that they wish to discuss."

WAS informed later by Holmes that the search had revealed three pendant brooches, valued together at over ten thousand guineas, as well as the stout pair of scissors used by Sudthorpe to acquire the items. The other stolen items, apart from one that had been abstracted on the previous night, were never recovered, and my little Irish lass had to be resigned to the loss of her locket.

" The moral of the story is, Watson," Holmes remarked to me with more than a touch of cynicism, " that one should never trust the fair sex."

I objected to his misogyny at the time, but had cause to remember his words a few weeks later, when Miss Eileen O'Rafferty announced her engagement to Captain Lucan of the Connaught Rangers.

SHERLOCK HOLMES & THE ODESSA BUSINESS

"I NOTICE THE BOTTLE IS SEALED, AND THE SEAL IS UNBROKEN. MY
GUESS IS THAT IT IS SOME SORT OF POISON." (PAGE 29)

EDITOR'S NOTE

This tale, which is not mentioned at all in any of the stories that Watson released to the world, came as a complete surprise to me when I first deciphered it from Watson's handwriting. Without a doubt, this is one of the more extraordinary revelations about the personal circumstances surrounding the great sleuth that I have so far encountered in the stories contained in the deed box. There were more to come.

*We know little of Holmes' family life, other than the existence of brother Mycroft (*The Greek Interpreter *and* The Final Problem*). This story sheds an unexpected light on this aspect of the detective's existence as well as showing him capable of hitherto unsuspected depths of family feeling.*

Y friend, the famous consulting detective Sherlock Holmes, was reticent about his family and his early life. Occasionally, indeed, as in his description of the affair of the *Gloria Scott*, he gave an account of his doings before he and I became acquainted, but my friend's family remained for the most part an enigma to me.

Nothing, it seemed, was of import to Holmes other than his pursuit of the solutions to the puzzles and mysteries that came to our door. It was one summer morning, when the metropolis seemed almost deserted, that I became aware of yet another side to the remorseless logician that had up to that time remained unsuspected by me.

For the previous two weeks, London had been what Holmes described as "plaguey dull", by which he signified that no major outbreak of criminal activity had occurred recently—a source of satisfaction to most law-abiding citizens, but a fount of frustration for Holmes, whose mind thrived on the crimes committed by the felons of the land and whose energies seemed replenished by the villainies of others. We were finishing an excellent breakfast, I remember, when the post was brought in by Mrs. Hudson, our housekeeper, and deposited by Holmes' elbow, where it remained unopened as he devoted his attention to toast and marmalade.

At length he threw down his napkin and crossed to the large armchair, flinging himself into it.

" Ah, Watson," he remarked, " if only you could begin to guess at the ennui that afflicts me. Yesterday, I solved the mystery of the bisulphate of bismuth. My monograph on the regional differences in bootnails, which should be of great service to the official police when they come to examine any footprints following the execution of a crime, is at the printer's, and I now have that Bach partita almost by heart. If you would be good enough to open the post, and provide me with a verbal précis of each item, I would be much obliged." So saying, he lounged back in his chair, and lit his foul-smelling pipe.

I picked up the first envelope.

" A ducal coronet," I observed.

" This letter appears to be from His Grace the Duke of Shropshire."

" He will want to know about his son's losses at cards," replied Holmes, his eyes half-shut in that peculiar fashion of his, before I had even opened the envelope. " It is, of course, Colonel Sebastian Moran who has been cheating him, but the cunning devil has so many tricks and ruses that it would be almost impossible to prove it without my personally taking part in the game. And that, Watson, is something I am not prepared to do at this time."

" Astounding ! " I exclaimed after having opened the envelope and read the contents. " You are absolutely correct in your guesses as to His Grace's wishes."

" Hardly guesses, Watson," he reproached me. " Put the letter on one side. We may decide to assist in this matter, if nothing more interesting or amusing comes to light." My friend's ideas of what events fell under those two headings were, I need hardly add, somewhat at odds with those possessed by the average Londoner. " I have long had my eye on Colonel Moran, and it would be a positive pleasure to remove him from the gaming rooms of the London clubs. Next letter, please."

I scanned the contents. " A Mrs. Henrietta Cowling suspects her husband of a dalliance with an actress at the Criterion, and requests—"

" Next, Watson. I do not dabble in these petty affairs."

I picked up the next envelope, which gave off a faint scent that I was unable to place. I glanced at the back. " From St. Elizabeth's Academy for Young Ladies, Brighton," I remarked.

" Read it," commanded Holmes. He had not altered his position as he lounged in the chair, but to someone who knew him as intimately as myself, here was a subtle change in his attitude. " Extraordinary ! " I burst out, when I had finished perusing the epistle. " The lady who wrote this has the same surname as yourself. Miss Evadne Holmes."

" Indeed ? " replied my friend. A strange sort of half-smile, almost unnoticeable, played about his lips. " Perhaps you would be good enough to inform me of its contents after ascertaining some more information about this establishment ? " He waved a lazy hand towards the shelves of reference works.

I reached for the Almanac, and proceeded to ascertain the facts regarding St. Elizabeth's.

" Of course." I summarized the contents of the entry I had just read. " The lady is the principal of this academic institution, where nearly one hundred young ladies are educated, founded by her to provide young ladies with a sound general education on Christian principles, in the year—"

" Enough, Watson. Proceed with the letter."

I turned to the sheets of stiff paper that comprised the epistle. " Among the pupils there is the young Russian Archduchess Anastasia, who is completing her studies in this country. A few nights ago, three to be precise, the young lady was disturbed by a noise at the window of the room shared with ten other girls, and she saw what she described as a hideous bearded face peering through a gap in the curtains. She was, not unnaturally, frightened by this, as were the other girls in the room, and the alarm was raised, but a search by the principal and the mistresses of the academy discovered no trace of the intruder."

" No trace ? " remarked Holmes. " I had thought better of Evadne."

I looked at him sharply, but he

gave no clue as to the meaning of that utterance. " She requests your help in investigating this matter," I concluded. " Shall I put this on one side with the Duke of Shropshire's epistle, or consign it to the rubbish with Mrs. Cowling's ? "

" Neither, Watson. I believe that the sea air at Brighton will do us both good. Let us start this morning. But before we set off, what do you learn from this letter ? "

" Little, I fear. There is a strange smell about the paper that I cannot, for the life of me, place. It is written in violet ink—unusual, but not that unusual. There is little I can deduce from this."

" The smell, I would guess, is carbolic soap."

I put the envelope once more to my nostrils and inhaled. " Indeed it is, Holmes ! " The smell was now familiar to me. " How— ? "

" I doubt if Evadne's habits have changed with middle age," he remarked, somewhat enigmatically. " My dear fellow, you have missed many of the important points. The writer is left-handed, no ? " I used what little skill in graphology I had acquired to examine the letter, and was forced to agree with Holmes' guess, if that is what it was. " But I think you have missed the most significant point of this letter." His smile was now plain to see. " What is the superscription ? "

I examined the letter once again. " ' My dear Sherlock'," I read. " This seems a most intimate form of address for a client to use. The lady is a relation of yours ? "

" My sister," he replied, enjoying my obvious surprise.

I had met Holmes' brother Mycroft, in the matter of the Greek interpreter, but Holmes had never alluded to any other brothers or sisters.

" She is, without a doubt, the intellectual equal of my brother Mycroft, and, but for the accident of her sex, would no doubt occupy the same place in government he currently holds. As it is, she advises the Treasury on matters of finance and the Foreign Office on diplomacy under a male pseudonym through Mycroft while maintaining St. Elizabeth's Academy to occupy her idle moments. She is also, as you may or may not be aware, a contributor to various mathematical journals, again using a male alias. She recently achieved something in the nature of an academic triumph over Professor James Moriarty, in her rebuttal of his treatise upon the binomial theorem. I must confess, however, that Evadne and I have not seen each other for a number of years, not on account of any animosity between us—indeed, as children we were remarkably close, and that attachment has never entirely disappeared—but simply through indolence, chiefly on my part, I fear. It is time for me to strengthen the family bonds again, Watson, and, as I mentioned, the change of air will do us good, trapped as we are in the metropolis. Be so good as to look up a convenient time in Bradshaw."

Before I could fulfil this request, there was a knock at our door, and Mrs. Hudson announced the arrival of Inspector Lestrade of Scotland Yard. The small man almost bounded into the room in a state of excitement.

" Halloa ! " exclaimed Holmes. " What brings you here straight from your home ? Help yourself to coffee, and sit yourself down in that chair. But how did your small change come to rest in the right-hand pocket of your trousers ? Do you not find it inconvenient to have

Mrs. Lestrade arrange the contents of your pockets of a morning ? "

Lestrade looked from Holmes to me and shrugged. " Another of your conjuring tricks, Mr. Holmes ? "

" Hardly, my dear Inspector. I have had occasion previously to notice that you are left-handed, and the present mild disarray of your garments indicates to me that you have reached across to extract something from the right-hand pocket, thereby disarranging your clothes. The object would hardly be your watch, that I see is placed in a place convenient for your left hand, and I scarcely imagine that you would need your keys when you have come to pay us a visit. I therefore deduce that you found it necessary to reach into that pocket to extract some money for the purpose of paying the fare of the hansom I heard draw up a few minutes ago."

" And how did you know that I had come straight from my home ? "

" Tut, man. I cannot imagine Inspector Lestrade entering the hallowed precincts of Scotland Yard with flecks of shaving soap behind one ear, and one boot improperly laced. But when you are visiting the humble abode of Sherlock Holmes, such matters are presumably of no importance..."

Lestrade laughed ruefully. " You are too much for me," he confessed. " But I admit that your assistance would be most useful in a case that was brought to my attention by a telegram brought to my house this morning, followed by a longer dispatch from the Yard."

As he spoke there was another knock on the door, and Mrs. Hudson presented a telegram to Holmes.

" Ha ! " he ejaculated, ripping open the envelope, and scribbling a few words on the reply form. " Take this to the post-office, if you would, Mrs. Hudson. You were saying, Inspector ? " as Mrs. Hudson left the room.

" Yes, Mr. Holmes. I would greatly value your knowledge of European matters in helping me with this affair. It concerns an educational establishment for young ladies in Brighton—"

" St. Elizabeth's, I believe ? " smiled Holmes.

Lestrade gave a visible start in his seat. " How the deuce do you know that ? " he said.

Holmes smiled. " I believe we have received telegrams this morning referring to the same incident. Maybe you have a little more information from the report to which you alluded than do I at this present time ? Perhaps we could travel to Brighton together, and you could occupy the time by recounting the facts as you know them ? Oh, and if you wish to remove that shaving soap to which I alluded previously, feel free to avail yourself of this establishment's ablutionary facilities."

 E arrived at Brighton at about midday. Lestrade had informed us of the events at St. Elizabeth's as we sat in our first-class carriage. It seemed that the mysterious bearded visitor mentioned in Miss Holmes' letter had been seen again at ten o'clock the previous evening, again by the young Archduchess, in the same way as before, peering through the curtains. Again the alarm had been raised, and a search party sent out, aided this time by several of the male teaching staff and the gardener, who had been requested to stay on the premises that evening by Miss Holmes, contrary to usual custom.

This time, the search had not been fruitless. A body whose countenance, as far as could be ascertained, resembled that seen by the girls earlier in the evening had been found by the French master, Monsieur Leboeuf, lying in a flowerbed, on the opposite side of the building to the window where the face had been observed. Firmly implanted in the chest of the dead man, and seemingly the cause of his death, was a long paperknife, subsequently identified as the property of the principal herself.

" Intriguing," Holmes had remarked, listening to Lestrade's narrative, his eyes closed, and his fingers steepled in that characteristic pose of his. " And what does the owner of the knife have to say about this ? "

" Miss Holmes," replied Lestrade, " insists that although the knife is hers, it had disappeared from the desk in her study some two or three days before—she cannot be exactly certain—and that she had no idea where it was until it reappeared as the apparent murder weapon. By the by, it is curious, Mr. Holmes, that you and she should share the same name."

" I believe it is common," replied Holmes sardonically, " for a brother and sister to share a name."

Lestrade stared at Holmes in astonishment, and the notebook from which he had been reading dropped from his hand. " I had no idea..." he stammered. " You have a personal interest in this case, then ? "

" You requested my assistance on this case," replied Holmes coldly. " I shall give it to the best of my ability, regardless of any family ties that may be present."

" Just so, just so," muttered Lestrade, obviously embarrassed.

I was anxious to restore some semblance of social ease to the gathering. " Perhaps you can tell us what is known about the murdered man ? " I suggested to Lestrade.

The police inspector retrieved his notebook and started reading from it, with an obvious sense of relief at being delivered from his gaffe. " From papers found on him, the dead man appears to have been a Russian, by the name of Plekhoff. His passport shows he entered England a week ago. As of this morning, the Sussex police have been unable to discover where he has been staying."

" Of course, there is no reason for them to assume that he was staying locally," remarked Holmes. " The train service to London from Brighton is a particularly good one, and the last trains leave a little before midnight, I believe."

" True, true," agreed Lestrade.

" Have any arrests been made ? " asked Holmes.

" If you are concerned for your sister," replied Lestrade, with an obvious attempt at reconciliation, " I am happy to tell you that the Sussex police saw no grounds for her arrest simply as a result of the murder weapon having belonged to her."

" Thank you," replied Holmes, and gazed out of the window. Without turning his head, he addressed us both. " May I trouble you both to remain silent until we reach Brighton ? I wish to consider this matter." So saying, he pulled out his pipe and proceeded to almost asphyxiate both of us until we arrived at the Brighton London Road station, and were able to pull fresh air into our suffering lungs.

E were greeted by Inspector Steere of the Sussex Constabulary, a ruddy-faced guardian of the law of the old school.

" Well pleased to have you with us," he said to Lestrade. " These foreign doings to do with Russia are somewhat out of our league, and we welcome help from London on these matters."

" You suspect that the Russians are involved, then ? " asked Holmes.

Steere looked inquiringly at Holmes, and Lestrade hastened to introduce us.

" Well, I've heard of you, Mr. Holmes, and you too, Dr. Watson, and I am well pleased to see both of you here, too. In answer to your question, it stands to reason, doesn't it, that it's all connected with the Rooskies ? That young Archduchess and all that ? "

" Quite so," replied Holmes, though I knew from his expression that his words belied his true feelings on the matter. " May we visit the scene of the crime ? "

" The cab's waiting, sir. The body is just where it was found."

When we arrived at St. Elizabeth's, a handsome red-brick mansion, I was somewhat surprised that Holmes made no immediate attempt to meet his sister, but allowed himself to be led immediately to the scene where the body had been discovered and still lay, covered by a tarpaulin cloth, that was withdrawn by two constables as we approached.

The dead man appeared to have been somewhat short of stature, slightly built. His most distinguishing feature was the heavy beard that surrounded his face. Holmes dropped to one knee, and whipped out his powerful magnifying lens,

peering through it at the body, as well as at the hilt of the ornamental paperknife that protruded from the cadaver's chest, surrounded by a small brown stain on the man's shirtfront, presumably dried blood.

" An interesting weapon," I remarked, looking at the curiously wrought Oriental workmanship.

" Turkish, according to Miss Holmes," replied Steere.

" She has positively identified it as hers ? " asked Lestrade.

" As positive as anyone could be under the circumstances, sir. We have no formal statement from her as yet."

Holmes appeared to have finished his inspection of the corpse, and was now examining the ground around it. " Has the body been moved ? " he asked.

" No, sir," replied Steere. " We were at great pains to leave everything as it was found ready for the gentlemen from London. The only thing we did was to empty his pockets."

" So I observe from the mess you fellows made with your footprints," Holmes remarked a little testily. " I shall want to see what you found later on. Very good," he added, standing up, " I've seen enough here. Let us now examine the window where this man allegedly showed his face."

" 'Allegedly', sir ? Surely there is no doubt. Her Highness and several of the other girls have testified already to having seen him looking through the window."

" As you will, Inspector. Of what room is this the window, by the way ? "

" This is the principal's study, sir," replied the Sussex inspector.

We marched round to the back of the building, where a constable was standing. " We thought it best to take no chances," said Steere.

SHERLOCK HOLMES & THE ODESSA BUSINESS   29

" There might be something to be learned here, we felt."

" Quite right, Inspector," replied Holmes. " This may make up for your men's blundering around near the body." Once more he dropped to the ground, this time lying full length on the damp soil, heedless of his garments, as he peered at the marks in the flower-bed.

" Ha ! As I thought," he remarked at length, arising from his recumbent position, and stretching himself to peer through the window. He picked something that appeared to be some kind of dark tangled thread from the creeper that covered the wall beside the window, placing it in an envelope with an expression of satisfaction

" You never change, do you, Sherlock ? " came a cultivated feminine voice from behind us. " Always dirtying your clothes, peeking at things that don't belong to you, and keeping your secrets to yourself."

I turned to face the speaker. The family resemblance was obvious at a glance. Miss Evadne Holmes was a true feminine counterpart of her brother, with the same aquiline nose, deep-set eyes and thin compressed lips. Her strong face would have been somewhat unattractive in a woman, had it not been tempered by a flash of obvious humour that was often lacking in her brother's countenance.

" Evadne ! " he exclaimed. The pleasure at meeting his sister seemed unfeigned, and showed a facet of his character hitherto unseen by me. " Excuse me," he apologised to her. " A little of your flower-bed appears to have adhered to my hands. May I clean myself up a little ? And then, Inspector, if we may examine the contents of the dead man's pockets ? "

Holmes allowed himself to be led by his sister, presumably to some hot water and towels, for he emerged some minutes later looking somewhat less like a rural ploughman.

" Yes, indeed, Russian, as you say," he remarked, examining the papers headed by the Romanoff double eagle. " And, as I thought, Lestrade." He held up a scrap of pasteboard. " Here we have the return half of a railway ticket from Victoria Station dated yesterday. He was intending to return last night. It would be singularly useless to begin looking for his lodgings in this area. And this here," sniffing at a small packet. " Yes, Russian tobacco, I have no doubt. Wouldn't you agree, Lestrade ? " holding out the paper for the other's inspection.

" I would have no idea about that," replied the policeman. " I have little experience of these things."

" I would lay pennies to a pound I am correct," my friend answered. " A small penknife, of cheap German manufacture, and this bottle. What does it contain, Inspector ? "

" We have had no time to submit it to analysis, sir," pointed out Steere, somewhat nettled.

" Just so, just so," replied Holmes, conciliatory. " I notice the bottle is sealed, and the seal is unbroken. My guess is that it is some sort of poison."

" We'd observed the unbroken seal, too, sir, and truth to tell, I'd made the same guess as yourself."

" And that appears to be all, doesn't it ? Other than this piece of cardboard printed in Russian, which I cannot read. Our late friend travelled light, it would appear. I would like to speak with the Archduchess in the presence of one of the academic staff, if I may."

" I'm sure that can be arranged, Mr. Holmes," replied Lestrade. " If

I may, sir, under the circumstances, I feel it would be wisest if the member of staff were someone other than your sister ? "

" Naturally," replied Holmes, easily. " I would have suggested the same thing myself if you had not mentioned it."

BOUT ten minutes later, the two police inspectors, Holmes and myself were seated in a small room together with Miss Simpson, who had been introduced to us as the senior history mistress.

" I trust that you will say or do nothing that will alarm the poor child further," she requested, showing a degree of compassion for her charges that was at odds with her stern forbidding appearance.

" I will endeavour to exercise all the tact and restraint of which I am capable," replied Holmes, with the easy good humour for which he was famous.

The girl was shown in, and we all rose. Truly, I think I have hardly ever seen a more beautiful and nobly self-possessed young woman than the Archduchess Anastasia. She was dressed in the drab grey uniform of the school, but she entered as though she had been decked in a ball gown and a diamond tiara. There was something regal in the way she sat, and faced us with a level gaze with calm grey eyes from within a halo of golden hair.

" Your Highness," Holmes began. " I have a few simple questions to ask you, and though I am not of the police and you are therefore under no obligation to answer my questions, it would be in the interests of justice if you would do me the favour of indulging my curiosity." She bowed her graceful head in assent. " Can you tell us the exact time at which you saw the man at the window ? "

" You mean on the second occasion ? Last night ? " Her English had only the faintest trace of a foreign accent. Holmes nodded. " Yes. It was exactly ten o'clock. The stable clock had just begun striking ten, and that is the time when we are required to put out our lights. I was just moving to snuff out my candle when I saw the face at the window."

" Did you recognise the man ? "

" Of course not ! "

" I am sorry. That was not my meaning. What I meant to ask you was whether the man you saw last night was the same as the man whom you saw previously looking through your window."

" I am sure of it. The same bearded face appeared on both occasions. How can you doubt my word on it ? "

" I am not doubting your word, Your Highness. I simply wished to be certain of the matter. I have only one more question for you at present, which may be difficult for you to answer, but I must ask it. Are you aware if you, or any of your family, are the target of any anarchist or nihilist threats ? "

A slight tremor filled her voice as she replied. " Yes, indeed. My father has been the subject of at least two attempts on his life, and it has been feared by the Russian authorities that my sisters and I may also be the target of the anarchists. I am not frightened of them, though." These were brave words, but they failed to carry conviction, to my ears, at least. Holmes, on the other hand, seemed satisfied.

" Thank you, Your Highness. That will be all for the present."

She rose, and we all rose with her as she left the room, escorted by the formidable Miss Simpson.

" I think we have it now, Mr. Holmes, thanks to you," said Lestrade, " though I have no doubt we would have reached the same conclusion without your help."

" Indeed ? " Holmes cocked a sardonic eye. " And pray, what conclusion have you reached ? "

" The dead man was one of these Russian nihilist anarchists that you mentioned just now. He arrived here with the intent of killing the girl, or maybe abducting her. The phial in his pockets no doubt contains poison, as we agreed, or maybe some sort of sleeping draught which he proposed to administer if abduction was his goal. The first night he made his appearance, he realised that he had been seen, and accordingly made his escape. He returned a few nights later, and was seen again, but this time, the hue and cry was more successful than on the previous occasion. He was discovered by your sister, who surprised him as he was creeping away in his attempt to escape. She bravely attacked him with the paperknife, which she had snatched up as she went outside, and he died in the struggle. Naturally, she wishes to deny any such thing, as she is frightened she will be accused of murder. Well, I would like you to tell her, Mr. Holmes, that in this case, we won't be pressing

charges. I can give you my word on that. The death of one of that type is no great loss, I can assure you."

" You would indeed be foolish to press charges," replied Holmes. " I fear you are on completely the wrong scent. It is a beautiful story, Lestrade. It lacks only the virtue of truth."

Lestrade snorted. " And which of your precious theories is it to be this time, Mr. Holmes ? Surely the answer is staring you in the face."

" Some of the answers were staring us in the face, it is true. But other questions remain. I think we need to speak to Monsieur Leboeuf now."

Inspector Steere passed a request to a constable, who left, returning a few minutes later shaking his head. " Beg pardon, sir," he said to Steere, " but they can't find the gentleman anywhere. Seems no-one's set eyes on him since last night when he found the body."

" Confound you ! " said Holmes angrily to the Sussex policeman. " You've let him slip through your fingers."

I noticed that Lestrade seemed a little less cocksure than he had done a few minutes previously. " I am sure that Inspector Steere has done his best," he said.

" I think it is time I talked to my sister," said Holmes. " In private, if you have no objection, gentlemen. Watson, I require you as a witness. Come." He stalked off, and I followed.

E entered Miss Holmes' study, where she received us pleasantly enough, and greeted me by name.

" I have always enjoyed reading your accounts of Sherlock's adventures," she told me. " I must admit that I never thought I would feature as a character in one of them."

" Well, Evadne," said her brother, settling himself into a chair opposite the desk. " There is more to this than the police know and you want to tell them, is there not ? Does Mycroft know what has happened here ? "

" No, he does not, and I do not wish him to be informed by you, Sherlock, or by anyone else. He suffers from a weak heart, as you know, and the shock would be bad for him. The country can hardly afford to lose him at this hour." I pondered briefly on the workings of this strange family, who seemed to hold the fate of the nation in their hands, before my attention returned to their conversation. " It concerns the Russian treaty."

" Ah," said Holmes. " The Odessa business ? " This was completely outside my sphere of knowledge, and I had no conception of what was being discussed.

Miss Holmes nodded. " The very same. I do not know if Mycroft informed you of the details ? "

" The vaguest outlines only."

" I will not bore you with the minutiae, but suffice it to say that if the French government were to learn of what had been agreed..." She shrugged her shoulders and spread her hands in what I took to be a comic parody of a typical Gallic gesture. " The final draft was here in this room."

" Was ? " interjected her brother. " And it vanished at the same time as your paperknife ? "

She sighed. " Why do I bother telling my brothers anything ? They are always telling me that they know it all before I open my mouth," she complained to me, humorously. " No, you cannot be right all the time, Sherlock," returning to seriousness. " It vanished last night. The paperknife vanished two days ago."

" The day after our mysterious Russian was first seen peering in at the window, in fact ? "

" I suppose so. Yes, that is correct."

" And soon after you had had occasion to converse with Monsieur Leboeuf in this room ? Monsieur Leboeuf is a tall man, I take it ? About as tall as me ? And clean-shaven, of course."

" Of course he is, Sherlock. Why do you bother confirming the obvious after your exertions in the flowerbeds outside ? But it was not after I had talked with him that the knife vanished, it was after I had been holding a discussion in this room with the drawing master, Monsieur Delasse."

Sherlock Holmes' eyes positively sparkled. " Better and better ! " he exclaimed. " We have it all now, I think. Watson, you and I will have a word or two with Monsieur Delasse. How long has he been with you, Evadne ? "

" Since the start of this term only," she replied.

" And how long was Monsieur Leboeuf in your employ ? I use the past tense, because I fear you will never see him again. He is now," looking at his watch, " probably stepping off the ferry from Newhaven in Dieppe."

" Two terms. I now see what you mean, Sherlock. Since the Odessa business. What a fool I have been."

" Hardly, Evadne. I am sure

they came with excellent references and were both skilled teachers. You cannot allow yourself to take any blame."

She smiled. " Indeed they were excellent instructors. I will say that much for them. It will be difficult to replace them with others of equal competence." There was a somewhat ironic smile on her face, which reminded me of her brother's occasional moods. Her ability to see such a side to even the worst of prospects made me warm to her.

" Never fear. I am sure something can be arranged for you and your pupils. Where will we find Monsieur Delasse ? " She told us. " Come, Watson."

The drawing master's room was what might be expected of a Frenchman of an artistic persuasion. Pictures of a certain indelicacy hung on the walls, and certain smells that were not of English provenance filled the air. The man himself was a very caricature of a certain type of Frenchman, with waxed upturned moustaches, and a nervous excitable manner.

" But what is it you want ? " he positively squeaked at us.

" I merely heard of your collection of interesting drawings," remarked Holmes, " and I wondered if you would grant us the pleasure of admiring them."

" I heard you were of the police," said Delasse.

" With them, but not of them," replied Holmes. " The distinction will become clear if you are to cooperate with us by showing us your most interesting drawings."

The other shrugged, and I saw the source of Miss Holmes' comical imitation. " If that is what you wish, *messieurs*."

He fetched a portfolio of papers, and spread them out on the table.

" This one here, by Renoir. Observe the fineness and delicacy of the lines."

No matter how fine or delicate the lines might have been, the subject matter was less than delicate, and showed our Gallic cousins' lack of restraint in matters of the heart. Holmes appeared to be unconcerned with the subject of the drawings, however, and waved his hands over the paper.

" No, no. I mean your latest acquisitions. The ones you came by last night."

" What are you talking about ? " His eyes showed his fear, darting from one of us to the other.

Holmes sighed. " I was hoping that you would display the aptitude for logic for which Frenchmen are famous. But since that is not to be..." He turned as if to leave the room, and put a small whistle to his lips, but did not blow it.

" Wait ! I can help you, I think." He hurriedly reached for another portfolio, and extracted a sheaf of handwritten foolscap sheets.

" Thank you," said Holmes, receiving the proffered papers, and tucking them in an inside pocket after glancing through them. " And now, if you tell us the truth, there is a very good chance that you may follow your colleague home on the next boat from Newhaven."

" And if I refuse ? "

" Then there is every certainty that I will call the police and have you arrested."

" I never killed him ! " wailed the Frenchman. " That was of Jacques' doing, I swear before God."

" Throttled, I take it ? But then you and he dragged the body together to Miss Holmes' window and it was you who rifled her study while Monsieur Leboeuf put on his false beard and looked through the girl's window to frighten her. I must give you credit for allowing Leboeuf to ' discover' the body. Who would ever suspect the man who discovered the body to be the very man who committed the murder ? Whose idea was it to use the Russian as a decoy ? "

" Jacques'. Originally, our plan was simply to steal the papers, taking some plate and other valuables to make it appear as a burglary. You understand, *hein* ? But this anarchist appearing was a gift from God. The girl, Anastasia, gave no description of the man except that of a great bushy beard, which she sketched at my request. It was easy to procure a facsimile. Jacques, being taller, was the one to wear it and look in at the window to distract attention from my work at the other side of the building. I had already marked the place where the papers were kept. We waited, he and I, for the Russian to appear—"

" How did you know he would appear that night ? " interjected Holmes.

" We did not. We were prepared to wait every night for a week or longer if needed. In the event, we had only to wait a few nights. He entered through the back entrance of the grounds. We sprang on him, and I held him, while Jacques did his work. He struggled a little, and then—*pouf* ! "

" And the dagger ? "

" I had taken it from the study after my interview with Miss Holmes. I had a feeling that it would be useful in the future."

" The artistic feeling," Holmes sneered. " Why did you not take these," he tapped his pocket, " at the same time ? "

The other gave another of his comic shrugs. " *Alors*, how could I do that ? They were in front of her face, in plain view. The knife, that was different. That I could take without notice."

" And why," I asked, " are the papers still here ? Why are they not with Leboeuf in Dieppe ? "

Holmes shot me a glance, I am proud to say, that seemed to bespeak admiration.

" Because, *monsieur,* there was every chance that he would be stopped by the police. You have missed him by a matter of hours only. Who would think of looking for these papers here, when the bird has flown from the nest ? "

" Indeed," chuckled Holmes. " One last question. How did you discover that the papers were here and the true nature of my sister's work ? "

" Your sister ? You are Sherlock Holmes ? " Holmes nodded, and the other grinned, unexpectedly. " No wonder we were discovered. The famous Sherlock Holmes. We had no chance, did we ? But to answer your question, which is a good one, I can swear to you before God, on my mother's grave, in any form you please, that neither Jacques nor I have any knowledge of this. The orders came from the Quai d'Orsay to come here and do this work. Other than that, I cannot help you. Believe me."

" I believe you," said Holmes simply. " You are free to go. I would advise going now, and not bother packing any of your belongings."

The little man looked stunned. " You mean it ? "

" I gave you my word. Now go."

We turned and went down the stairs, returning to Miss Holmes' room.

As we descended, I could not refrain from asking Holmes why he had allowed a man who was not only an accomplice to murder, but also an enemy of our country, to go free.

" The dead man is no great loss to the world," replied Holmes. " Even Lestrade has the good sense to recognise this fact. As to the other, it is better for all concerned if the matter is kept hidden, and is not exposed to public view, which, in the event of a criminal trial, would undoubtedly be the case. It may be that I am not strictly within the bounds of the law here, but I am certain that I am in the right. I am confident that I can persuade Lestrade, through hints, of the justice of my actions, and my conscience is clear on the matter."

We knocked on the study door, and were bidden to enter.

" We discovered this in Monsieur Delasse's room," said Holmes, handing over to his sister a sheaf of drawings, which I had observed him pick up as we left the drawing master.

Miss Holmes glanced through them, and her cheeks flushed. " Sherlock, you cannot shock me so easily. I may not be a married woman, but I know the ways of the world. This is a bad joke on your part." She raised her hand as if to strike him, but Holmes stepped back.

" Forgive my antic sense of humour, Evadne. Maybe the next page will be more to your liking." She turned the page and came across the foolscap writing. Her eyes lit

up, and her hand, which had been raised to slap my friend across the face, was joined by its partner in an embrace around his neck.

" You dear darling Sherlock ! " she exclaimed. " You have saved me ! "

" And Mycroft, and my own reputation, come to that," said Holmes, who was as close to total embarrassment as I have ever beheld him. I turned away to spare his feelings.

" Of course."

" Now I must go and put Lestrade's mind at rest," said Holmes, " before he starts to go off on one of his flights of fancy and arrests the gardener. A good fellow in his tenacity—like a bulldog, in fact—but sadly lacking in imagination, except when it comes to deciding who is guilty of a crime. I think I can persuade him that Leboeuf is the guilty party—which he is, by the way— and that it would be a waste of Lestrade's time to pursue the matter any further. The fact that Leboeuf has flown the coop should be enough to persuade him of that."

" But you and Dr. Watson will stay to dinner, I hope, before you return to London ? "

" I gratefully accept, on behalf of Sherlock and myself," I replied, wishing to learn more of this intriguing lady, who was at the same time so similar to, but yet so different from my friend. Holmes looked at me reproachfully and shook his head, but said nothing.

T was obvious to me from the first sight of the body, Watson," said Holmes, as we sat in our rooms in Baker-street. " Surely you, as a medical man, must have noticed the blatant

incongruity. A live man stabbed through the heart would surely lose more blood than the trickle we discovered beside the body and staining his clothes."

" I remarked the fact at the

time," I replied, " but could not attach any great significance to it."

" But," continued Holmes, " you must know that a cadaver stabbed in the same way loses much less blood—about the same amount, in fact, as we discovered."

" You mean he was dead when the knife was plunged into his heart ? "

" Pah ! That simple fact was obvious from so many clues. Did you not observe his boots ? They were completely free of any mud and, as you undoubtedly noticed, the ground was soft and heavy. Not only that, but there were obvious signs that the body had been dragged to its resting place from somewhere else. Those ignoramuses of the local police had obscured almost all other footprints, but that much, at the least, was clear."

" But why did they leave the body outside your sister's study ? Surely that would draw attention to the fact that the papers had been stolen ? "

" Hardly that, Watson. Consider. There was an intruder. His body is discovered. The missing papers, should my sister ever have announced the fact of their having being stolen, were not on his body. This was a blind, Watson, a blind to lead Lestrade and the rest of them in the wrong direction. Who would ever suspect there was a thief on the premises, if the suspected thief's body was there, paperless ? "

" And why not leave the body outside the girl's room ? "

" Come, Watson, surely you can answer that one for yourself ? Did you not notice the height of the window ? How I had to stretch myself on the tips of my toes to peer through it ? And I am not a small man."

" And the dead man was indeed a small man ! " I exclaimed, with a flash of insight.

" Bravo, Watson ! Even the Sussex police would have come to that conclusion eventually. Furthermore, I noticed the footprints in the flowerbed that were almost identical in shape to the ones I left after I had strained to peer through the window. From which, I naturally deduced that the man outside the window was about my height. You saw me retrieve a tuft of fibre from the false beard, which had evidently caught on the plant creeping up the wall. Added to which, the soil took an excellent impression, and the marks of the boots showed clear indications of their being of French manufacture. The missing Monsieur Leboeuf was obviously the man who had frightened our little Russian Archduchess so badly on the second occasion. However, there were also marks, though not so distinct, of some sort of box or platform having been placed there in the past few days. We can assume that the Russian had used some sort of seed-box or packing crate as a support the other day when he was spotted through the window."

" And the other ? "

" There were faint traces, though the police had done their best to erase them, of another pair of boots near the body. These were of French manufacture. I guessed it quite likely that there would be a drawing master, or music instructor of some kind on the staff, and so it transpired. When my sister had explained the existence of the draft of the treaty, the rest was obvious, once you understand the workings of the French mind. It would have been easy for the French authorities to insert the agents into the school, and for them to discover my sister's habits with regard to her government work. We may assume that Leboeuf and Delasse are among the foremost practitioners of their kind. Their methods were almost cruder versions of those that I would employ myself, should I ever find myself engaged in such an enterprise."

" It seems so simple when you explain it."

" Quite so," he replied shortly. " Now, I suppose, I may return to that Bach partita. Maybe you, Watson, would be good enough to draft on my behalf a reply to the Duke of Shropshire advising him to order his son to keep a safe distance from Colonel Moran."

Sherlock Holmes in the Case of the Missing Matchbox

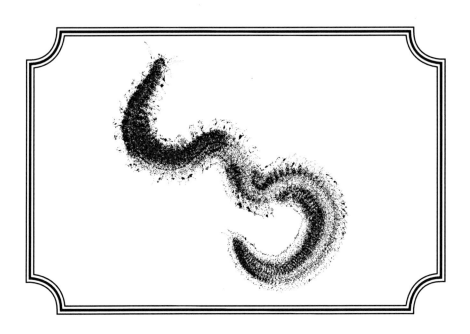

"...THE HIDEOUS PINK FLESHY HEAD OF SOME VILE WORM-
LIKE CREATURE EMERGED. SOME KIND OF GREEN LIQUID DROOLED
FROM WHAT I TOOK TO BE ITS JAWS." (PAGE 53)

EDITOR'S NOTE

In the account of the case entitled Thor Bridge, *Dr. Watson alludes to " A third case worthy of note ... that of Isadora Persano, the well-known journalist and duellist, who was found stark staring mad with a match box in front of him which contained a remarkable worm said to be unknown to science," categorizing this as a " failure, since no final explanation is forthcoming". It is feared that the good doctor's memory was at fault here, since this case, which for some reason remained unpublished by him, possibly in an attempt to protect the name of one of the principals in the case (although Watson used a pseudonym here) was indeed solved by Holmes, at least to the detective's satisfaction. It is here presented to the public for the first time, the line of the unfortunate " Professor Schinkenbein" having died out, meaning that no scandal can now be associated with the late maestro.*

 "I T is one of the pities of our age," my friend Sherlock Holmes remarked to me one day, " that duelling is no longer in fashion."

" On the contrary," I retorted, " I count it as one of the blessings of our civilised world that a man need no longer fear being shot dead or run through with a sword on account of a few careless words he may have uttered. Why do you say otherwise ? "

" I was merely considering the affair of Isadora Persano, as reported in today's *Morning Post*."

" You speak of the opera critic ? "

" The same. It seems that last night while he was dining at his favourite restaurant in Piccadilly, he came into conflict with the composer of operas and other works that have been the subject of recent adverse criticism by Persano for some time now. The composer approached him, and slapped his face with a glove. Persano's Latin blood rose to the insult, and the result was a challenge along the classic lines of a meeting at dawn on Hampstead Heath. Naturally, the other diners in the restaurant overheard the heated exchange, and the police were called, with the result that both men are now in custody."

" And why do you consider it so regrettable that the composer was not permitted to obtain the satisfaction that he imagined he deserved ? "

" Because I attended one of the performances criticised by Persano, and though I generally find myself in agreement with his judgements, in this case I consider his opinion to be sadly mistaken. The work in question was, to my mind, one of the finest musical productions to be encountered in many a year. The worlds of both journalism and music would have been well served, Watson, if Persano had been exposed to the displeasure of Herr Professor Schinkenbein. I very much doubt if the result would have been fatal on either side, despite Persano's reputation in these matters, but a salutary lesson might have been imparted."

I should add here that the world-famous personage I allude to in these pages as " Professor Schinkenbein" bore a different name in reality. To spare his surviving family further embarrassment, I have employed this pseudonym throughout.

Holmes spoke light-heartedly, but yet with some asperity. I happened to know that his work on a recent case had been the subject of some controversy in the columns of the *Morning Post*, where he had drawn the fire of a writer who seemed determined to denigrate his efforts, and I was therefore unsurprised to hear him speak this way of the press.

" Come, Holmes," I expostulated. " Duelling is the practice of an older and more barbaric age, and it is well that we of this country have outgrown the practice. Persano, whatever his origins—"

" He hails from Argentina," Holmes interjected.

" —should learn that we are a civilised country and do not tolerate such practices here."

Holmes cocked a quizzical eye at me. " Then it would surprise you to learn that I have had at least seven such meetings in the past three years ? "

I started from my seat. " Holmes ! " I exclaimed. " I had no idea of these activities of yours. On what grounds have you been engaged in these *affaires d'honneur* ? You must promise me that this practice must cease. Obviously, since you are here and we are conversing

together, you must have come out as the victor on these occasions. I hardly like to ask, but..."

" What happened to my opponents ? " Holmes finished my thoughts. " I am happy to say that they still walk the streets of this fair city, chastened, and sadder, but yet wiser men. I have yet to make a permanent disposition of any of them, but it will be a long time, if ever, before they repeat the follies that led them to meet me under those circumstances."

" These were not personal insults that led you to this course, then ? "

" By no means, Watson. Though I am not without my share of self-regard," (I smiled inwardly to myself at this, for if Sherlock Holmes suffered from a fault, it was one of excessive pride in his admittedly considerable abilities) " I do not regard insults against my person as being worthy of the death of the utterer of the same. These conflicts were, if you will, an attempt to force a course of self-reflection on those individuals who prey on and abuse those who are weaker than themselves, and possess no means of self-defence."

I was pondering the singular morality of this position, when we heard a ring at the front door.

" A client ? " I asked Holmes.

" I am not expecting any such," replied Holmes. In a few minutes, however, there was a knock at the door of our rooms, and Mrs. Hudson ushered in a heavily built elderly gentleman, with a shock of white hair atop a round, somewhat cherubic face. When he removed his hat and overcoat, he revealed, despite the earliness of the hour, formal evening wear, albeit in some disarray. A scarlet cravat at his throat, secured with a gaudy jewelled pin, and a corresponding scarlet patch of lacy cloth that I took to be a hand-kerchief protruding from his breast pocket, added splashes of colour to the otherwise austere black and white of his formal attire. A breath of fresh air somehow seemed to fill the somewhat tobacco-laden atmos-phere of our room.

"Sit down," said Holmes, wav-ing him to an empty chair. "Pray indulge your habit of taking snuff if you wish. I will content myself with my pipe, with your permission. I trust your night in the Bow-street cells was not too uncomfortable?"

I noticed the tell-tale smudges on the sleeve which told of our visitor's habits in the matter of tobacco, but I was at a loss as to how Holmes had arrived at the second conclusion. So, apparently, was our visitor.

"Mr. Holmes," he exclaimed in a heavy German accent. "I had heard of you as a magician, but how do you know of where I spent last night? Why, I have not even told you my name! I regret, by the way, not having being able to present you with my card upon my arrival here."

"My dear Professor Schinkenbe-in, I would be ignorant indeed if I did not recognise one of the great composers of the age. And as to your whereabouts, they are, I fear, a matter of public record," picking up the newspaper, and displaying the relevant article to the astonished musician.

The professor put his head in his hands. "My contract," he wailed. "Now the management of Covent Garden will never ask me to conduct there again. My career in this coun-try is ruined. Maybe in every coun-try in Europe. And all because of that damnable Persano." His voice rose to a shriek. "I should have never challenged him! I should have shot him down on the spot like the dog he is!" His voice cracked,

and I had actually begun to fear for his sanity as he continued to rave in this manner. Indeed, I had risen from my seat, prepared to restrain him, should it become necessary to do so, when Holmes spoke.

"And with what reputation would you have emerged from such an affair?" Holmes' quiet words acted like a glass of water thrown over the seemingly near-hysterical German, who suddenly ceased his ranting.

"You are quite correct, Mr. Holmes," he admitted, in a perfect-ly calm voice. "Of course it would be to no-one's advantage had I acted in such a fashion."

"Nonetheless," replied my friend, "though you acknowledge the truth of what I have just said to you, you still yearn for revenge, do you not?" The German nodded. "And you are wondering if I will be the one to administer the revenge on your behalf?" The musician once again gave his silent assent to Holmes' proposition. "My dear Professor, I have to tell you that, much as I may sympathise with you, and much as I may find myself in agreement with your position, it is neither my pleasure nor my place to go about the streets of Lon-don doling out summary punish-ment on behalf of my clients. Your work, Professor, when you stand on the concert platform in front of an orchestra, is carried out in here." Holmes tapped his head. "And so is mine. I am, as Watson here will tell you, not a man of action, but of thoughts." (Again I smiled inward-ly, given the nature of our previous discussion.) "Should you wish me to solve a mystery for you, or should you ever do me the honour of in-viting my violin and myself to take our place under your baton, I would be delighted to serve you in those regards, but I am not willing to put right your petty jealousies regarding matters which are, after all, a matter of artistic interpretation."

The musician flushed. "Mr. Holmes, I fear I have made a mistake in coming here. I had not expected to find the great detective so averse to a little practical matter."

"I fear I, too, was mistaken," replied Holmes, coolly. "When you came through the door, I was anticipating with pleasure the start of a friendship with a civilised man of culture. I regret that I, too, appear to have misjudged my acquaintance."

The professor flushed an even deeper red, and the veins on his forehead stood out as he rose to his feet. "Sir," he proclaimed in ringing tones. "I demand that you give me satisfaction."

Holmes' reply was a lazy laugh. "Professor, consider your reputation and your contract with Covent Garden," he sneered. "If you are worried that one challenge to a duel could have an adverse effect on your reputation, just consider what two such challenges in as many days would do."

"Pah!" replied the other. "Upon reflection, I withdraw my challenge and wish both you gentlemen a very good day." So saying, he replaced his hat, and marched out of the door, closing it behind him with a definite bang.

"There! That will hardly endear him to Mrs. Hudson," chuckled Holmes. "He did little to endear himself to me, I must confess. Why is it that men of such genius—and I freely admit that the man has the best grasp of any composer now living regarding the development of the theme of an aria—are such children when it comes to other matters?"

"What was his true motive in visiting, do you think?"

"Ah, so you remarked that, too? 'Pon my word, Watson, you are coming on admirably." Such words from Holmes were not an everyday occurrence, and I felt myself well praised. "Your thoughts first, then?"

"It is obvious that he is no physical coward. I noticed the scars of the German school of fencing which they practise at their universities, known as *Mensur*. I have witnessed such duels, and no man who is a coward would take part. I would therefore see no reason for his requesting you to take his place in this affair on that account, at the least."

"Good, Watson, good," he replied, rubbing his hands together. "So far, we are in complete agreement."

"But beyond that, I fear I am puzzled," I confessed.

"Yes?" replied Holmes. "So was I, I admit, until I noticed the direction of his gaze while he was venting his spleen towards the unfortunate critic."

"I failed to notice that. I was more concerned with his words and the state of his mental equilibrium."

"As he intended you to be," commented Holmes. "He was scanning my shelves, and his eyes came to rest on the portion of my bookcase that deals with the effects of poisons. No doubt you observed his spectacles?"

"Gold-rimmed pince-nez," I confirmed.

"Indeed they are. But maybe you failed to remark the thickness of the lenses? With such glasses, it would be easy for him to read the spines of the volumes on the shelf. Schinkenbein needs such in his work to observe the minute subtle details on the stage of the operas he conducts from the orchestra pit. I would venture to suggest that they are especially designed in some way to magnify his vision. Not only that, but Professor Schinkenbein's memory is renowned throughout Europe. He never conducts with a score, but keeps the whole of the opera, the notes and the libretto, in his head. It would be a trivial matter for him to commit to memory the titles and authors of the books there."

" To what end ? "

" Can you not guess ? The professor, as we have both observed, is no stranger to the art of the duello. He feels himself insulted by the unfortunate Persano's criticism, or maybe for some other reason as yet unknown to us, and requires satisfaction in the manner to which he is most accustomed. However, he has come to a country where such practices are frowned upon, and he finds himself in a position of public notoriety as a result of his impulses. I do not believe that this will result in the withdrawal of his contract with Covent Garden—indeed, I venture to predict that there will be no seats available for the next few weeks at least, as the public will want to view this fire-eating maestro with their own eyes. However, he still seeks his revenge, and, having heard of my reputation as possessing some small knowledge of the methods by which criminals achieve their ends, he decides that he will take advantage of my reputed expertise, without, as he fondly imagines, my being aware of his doing so."

" You mean that the critic Persano is now in danger of being poisoned by Professor Schinkenbein ? "

" I mean that Professor Schinkenbein currently believes that he will poison Persano. Whether he will actually attempt the deed or not is a matter for conjecture. In the event that he does so, I would venture to suggest that the attempt will fail. You will remember the Twickenham case last year, where the husband somehow failed to administer what was to have been a fatal dose of strychnine to his wife, missed his mark, and accordingly disposed of the neighbours' cat ? Poison is not the almighty tool that mere dabblers in crime believe it to be."

" But the professor is a man of learning and intelligence," I objected. " Surely it is unlikely that he would fall into the same error as the late Mr. Mallinson, whose wits, you must admit, were not of the sharpest ? "

" That is true," admitted Holmes. " All the same, I do not consider Persano to be in immediate danger from the quarter of the Professor."

" Why," I asked, as the thought occurred to me, " is Professor Schinkenbein currently at liberty, since he was taken into custody last night ? And do you believe that Persano is also now released from the cells ? "

" An excellent question, Watson." He scribbled a few lines on a piece of paper, and rang the bell for Mrs. Hudson. " Take this to the post-office, if you would be so kind, Mrs. Hudson. It should be sent reply-paid. There, that should give us our answer," he said, as the door closed behind our worthy landlady. " That is a telegram to Gregson at the Yard. Even if he is not in charge of the case, he owes me enough favours from the past to assist me."

The answer was received within the half-hour. " It would appear," said Holmes, reading the telegram that Mrs. Hudson presented to him, " that charges against both parties have been dropped. Both claim that words were spoken in the heat of the moment, and the influence of the grape was not absent."

" That hardly corresponds with what we saw just now, or indeed with what you observed," I remarked.

" You are correct there. I begin to fear a little more for Persano's safety. But there is nothing to be done at present about this matter. Indeed, I confess that it seems we are building this particular house upon sand, and there is little of import that we can do at this time."

I T was some two weeks after the conversation described above that we received a visit from an unexpected source. The artistic director of Covent Garden Opera House, Mr. Daniel Tomlinson, sent a message to Holmes requesting him to visit him at his offices.

" You are going ? " I asked Holmes, who appeared to be deep in the throes of some chemical experiment when the note was brought to him.

" Indeed we are going together," he replied. " This analysis is making damnably slow progress." He seized a glass beaker from the table that served as his laboratory bench, and tossed the contents into the fire, which leaped up with a brilliant green flame. " Copper," he observed sourly. " That much I knew before I started. Come, Watson. Bring your medical kit with you. If your Army revolver is to hand, you may also wish to equip yourself with that. I have a premonition that both of these may be of some use to us." I had no idea of his reasoning, but gripping my doctor's bag, in which a loaded revolver now lay incongruously beside a stethoscope, I followed Holmes into a hansom cab.

" Mr. Holmes, I am sorry to ask you here at considerable inconvenience, rather than meeting you at your own premises," apologised Mr. Tomlinson. " There are, to be frank, few times when I can be

spared from my post here that are congenial to those of more conventional working hours." He was a tall slender man, whose thin ginger hair receded from a high forehead.

" I understand perfectly," smiled Holmes. " My own habits are not of the most regular, but I appreciate your consideration."

" To come to the point quickly," went on Tomlinson, " we are without a conductor for this evening's performance of the opera *Cosimo de Medici*."

" By Professor Paul Schinkenbein, who is also acting as the conductor ? " asked Holmes.

The other bowed slightly. " Indeed so. And it is Professor Schinkenbein who is missing at this moment."

" Surely the performance does not start for another two hours at least ? " I objected. " Could he not have been delayed, and he will appear in good time to direct the orchestra ? "

" Ordinarily, that would be the case," replied Tomlinson. " However, the Herr Professor, if I may term him so, is usually punctual to a Teutonic fault." There was a faint air of mockery in his tones, which vanished as he continued. " However, today he was due to be present here two hours ago. He had expressed his dissatisfaction to Signora Cantallevi, the soprano, regarding the phrasing of some of her solo arias, and he had arranged to work with her on these."

" He has forgotten his appointment ? " I suggested. " Or else he has simply overslept ? "

" I am afraid, Doctor, that we are ahead of you there. We have already sent round to the hotel where he is lodging. Not only is he not at the hotel, but it would seem that he never appeared there following last night's performance. The porters do not recall seeing him enter the establishment, and when the maid went to his room this morning, it appeared that the bed had not been slept in."

" The name of the hotel ? " asked Holmes, and made a note of the reply on his shirt-cuff. His eyes glittered as he leaned forward. " Who was the last person to see him here in the theatre, do you know ? "

" That would be myself. I am not responsible for what we term the 'front of house' business—that is, the ticket receipts and so on—so when the stage has been cleared and the scene set for the next night's performance, I make a check of the green rooms and ensure that all the artistes are ready to leave, lest they be accidentally locked in the theatre. I am then myself free to leave. After last night's performance, which, I may tell you in confidence was not of the highest standards, especially the second half, Professor Schinkenbein was the only occupant of the green rooms. I reminded him of the time, and he dressed himself in his coat and hat, and accompanied me to the stage door, where we parted company."

" What time was this ? "

" Sixteen minutes past eleven by the Professor's watch, which is, as you might expect from such a man, accurate to the minute. He

remarked on the time as we closed the stage door."

" Did you notice where he went after that ? " asked Holmes.

" I cannot swear to it, but I seem to have a memory of his summoning a hansom and entering it." He closed his eyes in a seeming aid to concentration. " Yes, indeed, that is what he did."

" He summoned a cab ? " enquired Holmes. " Would it not be more usual for him to make arrangements for a cab to be waiting for him ? "

Tomlinson frowned. " As you say, that was usually the case."

" Was he usually the last to leave ? " asked Holmes.

" By no means. Indeed, it was one of our little jokes among the staff here that it would be impossible for him to take an encore, as he would be in the cab driving home as the applause died away."

" So last night was exceptional ? Did he offer any explanation as to the change ? "

" None. I assumed, I suppose, that he had been working on today's proposed rehearsal with Signora Cantallevi."

" When did he and she agree on the arrangements for this rehearsal ? "

The other chuckled. " Mr. Holmes, I can assure you that 'agree' is hardly the term I would choose to apply to this matter. It was during last night's interval that the Professor stormed into Signora Cantallevi's dressing room and roared at her that she was murdering his music."

" He told you this ? "

" Not at all. Everyone backstage could hear his words. And I must confess, Mr. Holmes, that we theatre folk are somewhat fond of gossip. Everyone was listening intently to what was being said. Not that we could avoid hearing," he added hastily, " as neither the Professor nor the Signora is among the most discreet and unobtrusive of conversationalists."

" I think I understand the situation," said Holmes, with his characteristic half-smile. " So there would be no difficulty in confirming this ? "

" None whatsoever."

" The lady is of Italian extraction, I take it ? "

" As it happens, that is not the case," replied Tomlinson. " She assumed the stage name of Cantallevi some years ago, along with the Italian designation of Signora. She originally hails from South America—Uruguay or Argentina, if I remember correctly. Her true name that appears on the contracts is Maria Muñoz."

" And where is the Signora now ? "

" In her dressing room. She is, if I am any judge at all of her character, extremely angry at being kept waiting. Patience, as well as tact, does not count among her virtues."

" Maybe it would be best if we were to visit the Professor's room first ? " suggested Holmes.

" If you wish. I had rather hoped, though, that you would be able to find the Professor himself."

" It is a capital mistake to theorise without data, as I have remarked to Watson on past occasions. At present, I lack sufficient data, and I wish to acquire such data as may be obtained from a study of the Professor's room. Following that, I may be in a position to help find the man himself."

Somewhat chastened, Tomlinson led the way through a maze of corridors lined with stage properties of all kinds, until we came to a door on which a neatly written card announced that the room was for the use of Herr Professor Paul Schinkenbein.

" Are these doors ever locked ? " asked Holmes, trying the door and pushing it open.

" Very occasionally," replied our host. " Maybe a singer has been given a valuable piece of jewellery from an admirer which she will be expected to wear when she meets the admirer after the performance... Sometimes the tenor or baritone will require, shall we say, a little privacy when visited by his admirers..." His voice tailed off, and he coughed. " I think, as a man of the world, you understand my meaning here ? "

" Of course," said Holmes. " I am aware of such matters in the world of the theatre. Did the Professor ever lock his door ? "

Tomlinson flushed. " Are you implying, sir.. ? "

" I merely enquired whether the Professor ever locked his door," replied Holmes, mildly.

" He commenced the habit some three or four weeks back. Before that, his door was always left unlocked. It was unlocked last night when I was making my final rounds."

" And on those occasions when his door was locked, Signora Cantallevi was not to be seen elsewhere in the theatre, I take it ? No, no, you need not answer that question, as your face has told me everything. Rest assured that you have said nothing to me that can be interpreted as being to the discredit of either party. Let us move on to another subject. When you met the Professor last night, did he tidy away any papers before you and he left the room ? "

" I have no recollection of his doing so."

" And yet you believed he was working on today's projected rehearsal ? "

" My belief only. He never said so outright."

Holmes stooped to the floor and retrieved a scrap of paper. He held it up for us to examine, but I could make little of it. It appeared to be a piece of ordinary brown paper, such as is used to wrap parcels. The letters " INA" were printed in white on the red corner of a postage stamp that adhered to one torn edge.

" Does the Professor smoke ? " asked Holmes. " I know for a fact that he is a snuff-taker."

" I have never observed him smoking."

" Strange, strange..." Holmes muttered to himself, looking at a line of at least twenty matchboxes on the dressing table. " Watson, what do you notice about these ? "

" They are all of different brands. I see no duplicates here."

" Nor I. Furthermore, all these are of subtly different sizes, if you will observe, arranged with German precision from left to right in order of their overall size."

" There is a gap there, towards the right," I remarked.

" Indeed," said Holmes. " I would wager that the Professor has that missing box in his possession at this very moment."

" Mr. Holmes," called the theatre manager. " Look here." He pointed to the waste-paper basket, which was full of live matches.

" At least twenty boxes' worth, I would say," remarked Holmes. " When are these baskets emptied ? "

" Three times weekly. In fact," he pulled out his watch, " probably within the next hour."

" Why on earth would someone go to this trouble to procure an empty matchbox of such precise dimensions ? " I wondered aloud. Holmes said nothing in reply, but raised his eyebrows.

" What other surprises has the Professor left for us ? " he asked, rhetorically, casting about the room.

I noticed what appeared to be some cotton wool with the matches, matted in places with a curious green material, seemingly liquid that had dried, and I called Holmes' attention to it.

" Good, Watson, good. Would you have the goodness to use the forceps from your medical bag to remove it, and place it in this envelope ? Thank you. And I would advise sterilising those forceps before they touch your next patient, Doctor." I remembered the Professor's apparent interest in poisons, and shuddered.

" Now," remarked Holmes, " for our prima donna. I somehow doubt her current willingness to receive visitors."

We had reached the singer's door, and Tomlinson rapped smartly on it.

" Enter," came the imperious command. The singer was standing in the middle of the room. A beauty of the Latin type, her dark eyes flashed angry fire at us as we entered.

Tomlinson introduced Holmes and myself to the singer, who surveyed us with a critical eye. " You, I have heard of," she addressed Holmes. " You are the man who finds things, no ? I tell you, I do not want you to find the pig of a Professor Schinkenbein. I do not care if I never see his ugly face again. Whatever he was to me in the past, he is nothing to me now. Nothing, I tell you, nothing ! "

Holmes started to reply, but was seized by a fit of coughing. " Excuse me," he apologised, as he retrieved a throat pastille from his pocket and unwrapped it, before putting it into his mouth. He indicated the wrapping that he still held in his hand, and the soprano waved a languid arm in the direction of the waste-paper basket in the corner. Holmes walked over and deposited the paper there before returning to the centre of the room. Unseen by any except me, he palmed a few scraps of paper from the basket and placed them unobtrusively in his pocket.

" I fear, Signora," Holmes addressed the diva with grave courtesy, " that we have disturbed you unnecessarily. My apologies." He sketched a bow, and backed out of the room.

" I was under the impression that you wished to talk with her," said Tomlinson.

" I have seen and heard all I needed," replied Holmes. " And besides," shrugging, " she does not seem in the mood for conversation. Come, Watson, I believe we have learned all we can here for the present."

"THINK we now have the threads, Watson," Holmes remarked to me as we sat in the cab transporting us to the hotel where Professor Schinkenbein had been lodging. " I begin to believe that we are now on the trail of a case that may prove to be of more than average interest in the details, however mundane the basic facts."

" I confess that I am still in the dark," I replied. " I have, however, drawn my own conclusions regarding the relations between the Professor and Signora Cantallevi. I find it hard to believe, though, that a man of such gifts as the Professor could behave in such an immoral fashion."

Holmes turned to me with a half-smile on his lips. " Watson, you are the very rock of British respectability itself, but you must learn to make allowances for the artistic temperament. Geniuses such as Schinkenbein are not bound by the mundane trappings of everyday folk. In any event, I had established that there was a lady in the case two weeks ago."

" But that was before we were even aware there was any case to be examined," I objected. " And how could you possibly know such a thing ? "

For answer, Holmes merely gave me an enigmatic smile.

" What was the paper you retrieved from the Signora's dressing room ? " I asked him.

" Ah, you noticed my little sleight of hand, did you ? " he replied. " See for yourself."

The papers consisted of several scraps of a photograph, which had been ripped to shreds. Two of the fragments bore traces of handwriting, which might well have been an autograph.

" My money, were I a betting man, Watson, would be on this having been a photograph of Professor Schinkenbein," he remarked as the cab drew up at the hotel.

" Would it be possible for me to examine the rooms in which Professor Schinkenbein has been staying ? " enquired Holmes of the hotel's manager, who had received us in his office.

" In the usual run of things, I

would be compelled to refuse such a request," replied the other. " Since you have done us so many good turns in the past and saved the good name of the hotel from scandal, I cannot refuse you this, Mr. Holmes."

" I am confident that no breath of scandal can attach itself to the hotel in this case," Holmes assured him. " I merely need to ascertain a few facts. Have the rooms been cleaned since the Professor last entered them ? "

" Almost certainly."

Holmes' face clouded. " No matter," he replied. " Would you have the goodness to have me shown up there ? "

The manager pressed a bell, and one of the porters led us up the stairs to the missing Professor's apartments.

" Ha ! " exclaimed Holmes. " I fear that the hotel staff have been too busy for us to discover anything of value." He peered about the bed-room, lifting the bed-cover and looking under the bed. " Ha ! What is this ? " He reached under the bed, and withdrew a small scrap of brown paper.

" The same kind of paper that we found in his room in Covent Garden ? " I asked.

" I believe so," replied Holmes, withdrawing it from his pocket and laying it side by side with the scrap he had just discovered. " Yes, they match perfectly. And what's this ? " pointing to a few handwritten letters.

I read, neatly printed in black ink, what appeared to be the ends of a few lines of address:

> " ...*uñoz*
> ...*illa de Correro 419*
> ...*ro Central*
> ...*s Aires*
> ...*ENTINA*"

" Clear enough, wouldn't you say, Watson ? "

I thought for a moment. " He received a package from Argentina ? "

" Of course, Watson. And Signora Cantallevi's true name ? "

" Muñoz, of course," I recalled.

" My Spanish is a little less than fluent, but it would seem to me, Watson, that what we have in front of us here is the fragment of the return address written on a package sent to the Professor by a relative of the singer. I would venture to suggest that the second line originally read 'Casilla de Correro 419', the Spanish for *poste restante*, at the central post office, 'Correro', in Buenos Aires. Add this to the fragment of Argentinian stamp that adhered to this scrap of paper that we found in the dressing room, and I think there can be no doubt."

" But what could the Professor possibly want with a package from Argentina ? What could it possibly contain ? "

" Something that would fit inside a certain matchbox," replied Holmes enigmatically. " And I begin to fear the worst."

" I hardly know what you mean by this," I shuddered.

" I hardly know myself," confessed Holmes, " but I fear we are on the trail of some devilment."

Holmes continued to search the bed-room and sitting-room in his typical fashion that appeared almost absent-minded, but in truth missed nothing. At length he turned to me and sighed. " Nothing more. The housekeepers at this hotel carry out their appointed tasks too well," he complained. " Believe me, half the unsolved crimes of London would remain unsolved no longer, if the housekeepers of this world were not so desirous of removing every alien object, and scrubbing and polishing every surface in sight."

We went downstairs and re-entered the manager's office.

" May I talk to the staff who deal with your guests' post ? "

" Of course," replied the manager. " I trust that your inspection of the room was fruitful ? "

" Indeed it was," Holmes assented, " though I suppose that I must compliment you on the efficiency of your staff, who make the work of a detective such as myself more difficult than it need be."

The elderly porter responsible for sorting and delivering the hotel guests' post entered the office.

" Simpson, you have my full permission to answer any questions these gentlemen may see fit to put to you," the manager told him.

" Thank you," said Holmes. " Now, Simpson, my questions are concerned only with those items addressed to Professor Schinkenbein. Did you receive any special instructions from the Professor regarding these ? "

" Why, yes sir, I did. I have never heard of anything like it from any of our other guests, but the Professor told me that if there was to be any letters or packages addressed to him from South America—Argentina, or those parts—I was not to deliver them to his room, but to forward them to another address."

Holmes sat forward in his chair. " Is that address in London ? " he asked.

" Yes, sir, that it is. I have it written down here, sir, in this book of mine," he explained, drawing a tattered notebook from an inside pocket of his uniform.

" Aha ! " exclaimed Holmes, examining the relevant page. " You and I, Watson, must lose no time in visiting number 23, Brixham Gardens."

⁘⟢⊙⟣⁘

RIXHAM Gardens turned out to be a dreary row of red-brick houses in North Hampstead, bounded at the back by the railway, with the small park that gave the street its name at one end of the street.

" I wonder why he chose this area as his little hideaway," Holmes wondered aloud.

" Perhaps it is near to Miss Muñoz' dwelling ? " I suggested.

Holmes clapped his hands together. " There are occasions, Watson, when you positively sparkle. I am sure you have hit on something very close to the truth."

We paid off the cab, and rang the bell of number 23. There was no answer, but we could hear some sort of laughter from within.

" There is someone at home," I remarked, " but they seem unwilling to answer the door."

" Or else they are unable to do so," replied Holmes, enigmatically.

" Let us break down the door and enter, if you fear foul play."

" You underestimate my skills as a housebreaker," Holmes reproached me. So saying, he went to the side of the house, leaving me standing guard outside the front door. I had just raised my hand to ring the bell once more, when the door opened, and Holmes let me into the hall. His face was grave.

" I fear the worst," he said to me in a low tone. The laughter we had heard earlier came from upstairs, and now we could hear it more clearly, sounded disjointed and, if such a word can be used of laughter, irrational.

" Your revolver, Watson," Holmes advised me, as we mounted the stairs. I withdrew it from its unaccustomed resting-place in my medical bag, and gripped it tightly in my right hand.

" Here, I think," whispered Holmes in a low voice, pausing outside a closed door. " On my word, Watson. One... two..."

On " three" he wrenched open the door and flung it wide.

Never in my life have I beheld such a sight. The room was bare of all furniture, save a deal table and two chairs. In one chair sat the body of Professor Schinkenbein, naked from the waist upward, with a hideous rictal sneer on his face. His garments were strewn around the floor. A mere glance was sufficient to tell me that life had fled the body some time before.

" The poor devil," whispered Holmes. " The poor devil," he repeated softly.

Our gaze was torn from the hideous sight of the deceased composer by the other man in the room, whom I recognised as Isadora Persano, the journalist, and erstwhile challenger of the Professor. He was seated at the other chair facing the Professor, and he stared at us, wide-eyed.

" No more, no more, you shut the door, and then no more," he remarked to me, in a conversational tone. " You mount the grade, without my aid, though you're afraid, and won't be stayed."

" What the deuce do you mean by that ? " I asked him. Holmes laid a hand on my sleeve.

" I fear the poor fellow's wits have deserted him," Holmes said.

As if to confirm this, Persano burst into song. " And the little pigs sing, ring-a-ding, ring-a-ding,"

he carolled gaily to us as we approached him.

" No ! As you value your sanity ! " Holmes spoke to me in a hoarse urgent whisper, as I reached out my hand to the half-open matchbox that stood on the table in front of the unfortunate lunatic. " Look from a safe distance, if you must, but do not touch."

I peered at the opening, and the hideous pink fleshy head of some vile worm-like creature emerged. Some kind of green liquid drooled from what I took to be its jaws.

" What is it, Holmes ? " I gasped.

" I know not, and I care not," he replied. If I have ever seen Sherlock Holmes afraid, it was on that occasion. The blood had drained from his face, and his jaw was set. He masked his face with a handkerchief so that only his eyes were visible, and drew on his gloves. " Have the kindness, Doctor, to pass me your longest pair of forceps, and if you have such a thing as a specimen jar for the collection of bodily fluids, I would welcome the loan of that as well."

I passed him the required utensils, and he deftly captured the creature, removing it from the box, and transferred it to the jar. It feebly spat the green fluid in his general direction, but seemed to lack the strength to reach him with its vile spittle.

" I am relieved to see that it lacks an infinite supply of this hellish fluid," remarked Holmes, screwing on the lid of the jar with his gloved hands. The worm writhed inside the jar, still spitting feebly. Now we could see it, it appeared to be about four inches long, as thick as a child's finger, and as pink. The face, if it may be so described, appeared grotesque and almost evil in its aspect.

"And now, if you have morphia or some other such drug in that bag of yours, I would advise that you administer it to this poor fellow here," said Holmes, "while I summon the police and the lunatic asylum."

"I had my suspicions," remarked Holmes, when I discussed the case with him later, "almost from the start. It was when we visited Covent Garden and discovered the Professor's attachment to Miss Muñoz that my vague fears became more concrete. Of course, I knew that the fair sex was involved from the beginning when Schinkenbein first visited us."

"How did you know there was a lady in the case ? " I asked Holmes.

"Elementary. I observed a strong odour of feminine perfume when he entered the room. It was not the kind of scent that I could imagine being used by any man, no matter how artistic his temperament. It was obvious that he had been in recent close, if not actually intimate, contact with a young lady of looser morality than the kind of which you would approve, Watson," he wagged a finger at me, " in the past twenty-four hours."

"I bow to your superior reasoning here," I replied.

"Surely you also observed the oddities in his attire when he visited our rooms ? " Holmes asked me.

"I remember the cravat, the topaz scarf-pin and the scarlet lace handkerchief," I replied.

Holmes laughed out loud. "That, my dear Watson, was no handkerchief. Had you examined it more closely, you would have identified it as a lady's garter."

I confess I blushed. "What sort of blackguard would parade himself in society with such an intimate item so prominently visible ? I suppose we can take it for granted that this was not a sentimental memento of the Professor's wife ? "

"According to my sources, his wife—or should we say his widow—is a somewhat elderly German *Hausfrau*, currently residing at the family home in Berlin, and is hardly the type of lady to wear such garments. No, I am sure that the open display of such an object was intended as some sort of trophy signifying his conquest of the lady in question, of whose identity we are already in no doubt."

"The utter cad ! " I exclaimed. "The world is well rid of him."

"From the viewpoint of today's morality, you may well be correct there," Holmes admitted. "But he is a sad loss to the world of opera."

Once again, I found myself in silent disagreement with my friend's eccentricity in the matter of morals.

"I can guess a little," I replied. "Persano and Muñoz arrived together in this country from Argentina as lovers."

"That much I have ascertained from other quarters," he affirmed.

"And she subsequently transferred her affections to Professor Schinkenbein. This aroused the ire of the slighted Persano, who took his revenge in the form of his criticism of Schinkenbein's music."

"Excellent, Watson. Your intuition and judgement when it comes to affairs of the heart are truly admirable." I flushed a little. "However, when it comes to the truly

rational aspects of these matters..."
He shook his head sadly.

I continued, a little abashed. " I would suggest that the supposed subject of the public quarrel in the restaurant was a pretext for a challenge over Miss Muñoz."

" Something along those lines, I agree. Certainly, all was not as appeared at first sight in that incident, I am sure."

" After that, I am unsure of the course of events."

" I am reasonably certain that the original intention of fighting a duel was a serious one on both sides," said Holmes. " Both had something of a reputation in their own countries as duellists, and neither was lacking in physical courage. Their arrest and subsequent detention must have brought home to them that such a course of action was not practicable in this country."

" And at this point, we had our visit from the Professor ? "

" Indeed. He was probably examining my shelves for methods of poisoning with serious intent, but I feel he may have been laying his murderous plans even before that time. The package containing the worm was dispatched from Argentina by Miss Muñoz' relation—a brother, maybe, but it is unimportant—before the incident of the threatened duel. I am guessing that her former paramour was continuing to importune Miss Muñoz against her wishes, and she, too, wished to see his demise. It would be easy for her to acquire some sort of exotic means of death from her own country that would baffle our English authorities."

" And the worm ? What of that ? "

" The Natural History Museum in South Kensington has been unable to identify it. The green spittle has been analysed, and is confirmed as containing a powerful alkaloid with varying effects on its subjects when absorbed through the skin. For some it causes failure of the respiratory system, but others seem relatively unaffected in that regard. However, it in every case it appears to exercise a powerful effect on that part of the circulatory system that leads to the brain, leading to a loss of mental faculties, as we saw in the case of poor Persano, and most probably the Professor as well before his death."

" I can vaguely understand the reasons why Schinkenbein would want to encompass the death of Persano, given the goads that resulted from the criticism of his work. But how did he meet his own end ? "

" I would have thought you could have deduced that yourself, Watson. When Schinkenbein ventured to criticise the phrasing of the diva's arias, all passion fled. You saw her reaction to his name for yourself, and you also handled the fragments of his inscribed photograph which she had ripped to shreds in her fury."

" And the rejected lover decided to take his own life ? "

" I believe so. We have been fortunate that the authorities have been willing to accept a verdict of accidental death, and his widow will suffer no loss of reputation. My belief is that he first goaded the worm into releasing its foul liquid on himself, and in his last moments of sanity, passed the matchbox to Persano."

" The matchbox still puzzles me, I confess. Why was that matchbox missing from the line, and why were all the other matchboxes in his room in the first instance ? "

Holmes smiled. " I do not know, and I can only make a guess here.

The original intention was to present Persano with a matchbox containing the worm, exchanging it for the box of matches which Persano carried with him to light his cigars. The problem with this plan was that the matchbox had to be of the same brand as Persano's customary matches."

" So that was the meaning of the collection of matchboxes that we discovered ? " I asked.

" Precisely. My surmise here is that Miss Muñoz was unable to recollect Persano's habits precisely, and the different types of match were purchased by Schinkenbein as an aide-memoire. The fact that they were arranged in order of size is a tribute to Schinkenbein's Teutonic sense of neatness and precision, rather than on account of any practical reason. Hence my amusement at the time when you mentioned the size of the matchbox."

" You had obtained the solution at that stage ? "

" I was close to a solution, but lacked the closing evidence. What we subsequently learned at the hotel filled the gaps in my knowledge."

" It sounds plausible, at the very least," I replied.

" I think it is more than plausible; it is probable," he replied. " I have no wish to rake up more scandal by asking questions of Miss Muñoz, and it fits the facts as we know them."

" A sad affair," I remarked.

" Indeed. I must admit, looking on this business, that there may be something to be said for your conventional ideas of morality, Watson, if disregard of the same can bring about such consequences. On the other hand," he added, turning to his violin, " our lives would be less interesting if everyone shared your beliefs."

So saying, he started to saw away at his fiddle in a tune I recognized as one of the arias from the late Professor Paul Schinkenbein's *Cosimo de Medici*.

Sherlock Holmes
& the Case of
the Cormorant

WE STOOD TOGETHER IN SILENCE, GAZING ACROSS THE BAY TO
ST. MAWES AND ST. ANTHONY HEAD, WITH ITS FAMOUS WHITE-
PAINTED LIGHTHOUSE AT THE FOOT. (PAGE 63)

EDITOR'S NOTE

In The Veiled Lodger, *Dr. Watson states:*

"*I deprecate, however, in the strongest way the attempts which have been made lately to get at and to destroy these papers. The source of these outrages is known, and if they are repeated I have Mr. Holmes' authority for saying that the whole story concerning the politician, the lighthouse, and the trained cormorant will be given to the public. There is at least one reader who will understand.*"

This cryptic utterance has baffled students of Holmes' history and cases for many years. The story alluded to was, for a long time, considered to be unwritten, existing only in the memory of Holmes (and possibly Watson), and the facts held in reserve against the possibility of an attack on Watson's records as described above.

It was with great pleasure, therefore, that the following account was discovered in the deed box which had once been the property of John Watson, MD. The MS had been carefully placed in not just one, but three stout manila envelopes, each sealed with the impression of two signet rings, one of which bore the initials "SH" and the other a simple "W". The outermost bore the words, "The Case of the Cormorant", and this is the title by which I now make this available to the world.

M Y friend Sherlock Holmes had been suffering from a surfeit of cases which admitted of no easy solution, and which had at the last caused a seeming debilitation of even his apparently indestructible faculties. As his friend and his medical adviser, I persuaded him that a temporary retreat from the metropolis was in the best interests of his health and he assented with an alacrity which somewhat surprised me.

My suggestions that we spend a week enjoying the pleasures of the Normandy coast at Deauville or some similar watering place did not meet with his approval, however, and he proposed as an alternative that we travel to the westernmost county of our principal island— Cornwall. I was happy to fall in with this idea, and welcomed the prospect of bracing walks along the rugged coastline of that most entrancing, and in many ways one of the most mysterious, of counties.

Accordingly, we reserved rooms, assembled our garments and other accoutrements necessary for a stay in the countryside, and travelled on the express train from Paddington Station to Falmouth. Upon arrival, we enquired as to the whereabouts of the lodgings where we had secured accommodation, and on finding that they were close by, Holmes proposed stretching our legs after the train journey by walking to our destination, and sending our luggage on by trap. The plan seemed to me to be a good one, and we strolled through the streets of the charming old town, taking in the quaintnesses and sights as we did so. By the time we had reached the home of our landlady, Mrs. Buncombe, I for one felt no pangs of regret at the decision to remain in our native land rather than making a journey to foreign parts.

Holmes seemed indifferent to the natural beauties of the surrounding countryside, as he did to the man-made interests of the place, but contented himself with an examination of the plants and vegetation growing along the hedgerows, occasionally referring to a small handbook on such matters that he carried in his pocket.

After our welcome by Mrs. Buncombe, we found ourselves seated in her guest drawing room, where on a polished table before us stood a tea-tray, brought in to us by our smiling landlady. On this in turn stood a steaming teapot, and scones served with the finest Cornish cream and jam which had its origins, so Mrs. Buncombe had assured us, in the wild strawberries growing in the area, Holmes stretched his legs to their fullest extent, and sighed with what appeared to be genuine pleasure.

" I foresee an interesting week here, Watson," he remarked to me.

" By 'interesting', I take it you mean 'relaxing', do you not ? I am delighted to see you taking an interest in some of the glories of nature, rather than the sins of your fellow man, but I feel you should at some time in the coming days lift your eyes somewhat in order to appreciate the beauties of the whole landscape, rather than the individual plants that compose it."

" By no means do I intend to allow myself to become sunk in idleness, Watson, but I will, even so, attempt to avail myself of the opportunities for mental refreshment to which you allude. However, at this juncture, the matter of physical refreshment would appear to be of more importance." So saying, he proffered the plate of scones to me, taking two of them for himself and placing them on his plate. I feared for my friend's continuing health if he continued to refuse to allow himself to unwind, if the process of prolonged mental relaxation may so be described, but determined to hold my peace for the nonce.

 WAS awakened early the next morning by the sound of gunfire from outside the window of the room I was sharing with Holmes. I turned to alert Holmes of the fact, but the other bed was unoccupied. Glancing at my watch and noting the time, as my association with Holmes had trained me to do as a matter of course, I hurriedly pulled on some clothes and made my way downstairs, where I let myself out through the back door of the house, which was unlocked.

On arrival at the small orchard at the rear of the house, I encountered Sherlock Holmes, calmly reloading his revolver with fresh ammunition. A row of bottles which had once contained beer stood on a sawhorse some ten yards away, with the necks of the leftmost six bottles shattered.

" Holmes ! " I expostulated. " This is intolerable ! Revolver practice at the hour of half past five in the morning is not only eccentric in the extreme, but positively inconsiderate of others. I would experience no surprise if Mrs. Buncombe, who is, I would remind you, an elderly widow living alone except for any lodgers, decided to throw us out of the house forthwith and invited us to make our way back to London."

Holmes regarded me, a faint smile on his lips. "Watson, you serve as my guide and conscience in these matters. I do confess that the further implications of this little exercise of mine had slipped my mind. I awoke to the unaccustomed sound of birdsong, and a likewise unfamiliar vista of green leaves, and decided to avail myself of the solitude afforded by the early hour. On encountering these bottles, it occurred to me that this would be a suitable occasion to renew my skills with the revolver. I seem to remember your expressing displeasure at my doing so in our rooms at Baker-street at one time."

"Quite so, Holmes. There is a time and a place for such an exercise, and half-past five in the morning is no time, and the interior of our rooms in London is no place." I spoke with some heat.

"Tush, Watson. I fear you are quite vexed."

"I am indeed. I would suggest that you apologize to Mrs. Buncombe at the earliest possible opportunity, and that you and I work together now to remove and dispose of any broken glass, which will undoubtedly pose a danger to any passers-by."

"Very good. As you say." Holmes pocketed his revolver, after, I was happy to note, first removing the cartridges from the cylinder. "I will indeed extend my apologies to our worthy landlady at the first possible opportunity, and we will dispose of the débris that I have created. Ah—"

Mrs. Buncombe had appeared in the back doorway of the house, and was staring at us across the orchard.

Holmes and I walked to meet her. I was pleased to see Holmes' stride appear a little less confident than usual, and I had hopes that my words might have had some lasting effect on him.

As we approached Mrs. Buncombe, Holmes, who had opened his mouth to speak, was forestalled by the good lady herself.

"Did either of you two gentlemen happen to hear that Jim Pollard shooting at them crows?" she enquired of us. "He ought to be stopped from doing such a thing of an early morning. It's not a fit practice for Christian folk to be out killing the Lord's creatures at that hour. Deaf as I may be, the sound of that dratted gun, if you'll forgive the word, woke me up out of my bed."

Holmes and I exchanged glances. Holmes, I could guess from my past experience of his moods, was struggling to contain his laughter, so I replied in his place.

"Indeed we did, Mrs. Buncombe, but we saw nothing." I spoke loudly and distinctly. As we had discovered the previous day, and as she had admitted to us herself, the good lady's hearing was not of the keenest. Holmes had turned away, seemingly seized with a violent fit of coughing.

"Well, I must thank you two gentlemen for taking the trouble to see what was going on. Since I am alone in the house as a rule, it is a comfort to me to know that you are here," she replied. "And since you are both up and doing, it seems to me that a cup of tea would be welcome."

"Thank you, Mrs. Buncombe," I replied. "You are quite correct in your surmise."

"Then I will just be running along and putting the kettle on. I will call you when your tea is ready, if you want to stay outside a little longer."

As she made her way to her domestic mysteries, I turned to Holmes. " We were lucky that time, Holmes," I said as sternly as I could manage. " We must give thanks to Jim Pollard, whoever he may be, for his unconscious intervention in our affairs."

" Indeed so," said Holmes. " Come, let us carry out your excellent suggestion of clearing away the remnants of my targets."

As we carefully collected the glass fragments and placed them in a wooden seed-tray, he remarked to me, " Do you remark anything strange about these bottles ? "

" Not that I have noticed. I assume that you have done so ? "

He nodded. " There are several noteworthy points. The first is that of their very existence. If you remember at last night's excellent dinner, Mrs. Buncombe, when she presented us with a bottle of claret as an accompaniment to the roast shoulder of lamb, remarked that she was Temperance, and that alcohol never passed her own lips, though she was not averse to her lodgers partaking of the same."

" True, but these bottles could be the leavings of the libations of previous lodgers ? "

" A neat alliteration, Watson," he remarked. " Naturally that possibility had occurred to me. However, many of the bottles retain the familiar aroma of good English beer, which would seem to argue that they were emptied relatively recently. In addition, I think we have both observed that our Mrs. Buncombe is clean and tidy to a fault. If these bottles were the leavings of previous guests, I do not believe she would have left them behind that

tool-shed yonder, and even had she done so, she would certainly have washed them clean before placing them there."

I considered this for a moment. " The solution is simple, Holmes," I replied. " These bottles are the result of her gardener, or some outside servant, refreshing himself in the intervals of his toil."

Holmes shook his head. " I fear you are mistaken. Though that thought also crossed my mind, it is not borne out by the bottles themselves. Observe that there are many different brews represented here. You must have remarked for yourself that when it comes to beer, the English workman is a creature of habit. Take from him his usual tipple, and he will be unhappy with any substitute, even if he cannot tell, blindfolded, the difference between the products of different breweries. In addition, the labels on these bottles indicate that their sources are from a wider geography than I would expect to be represented by the establishments of this town."

Holmes' observation appeared to be correct; on inspection, there hardly seemed to be two bottles the same, with some even having their origin in the neighbouring county of Devon. " Your conclusion, then ? "

" This garden is employed as a meeting-place by a number of individuals, who assemble here from a number of diverse locations, and spend some time here—at any rate, a length of time which allows them to enjoy a companionable drink together. Observe," he remarked, leading me down a slight slope away from the house towards a small cove. The orchard extended nearly to the shore, which consisted at this point of a sandy beach. " From here, we are invisible, except from the sea, and that from only the one angle. The trees on either side of this inlet prevent observation from elsewhere. And, confirming my surmise…" he stooped and picked up the end of a cigar from the ground. " I hardly think that this would be one of Mrs. Buncombe's leavings, nor yet one of her gardener's. This is the remains of a truly noble product of Havana—one which I would expect to be enjoyed only by one of the more well-to-do members of our society." He placed the remnant in one of the envelopes with which he was always provided. " And furthermore," he added, " the gentleman suffers from the defect of a missing right incisor. Such a person should

be easy to identify in this rural spot. There cannot be many such here."

We were interrupted in our conversation by the sound of Mrs. Buncombe's voice coming from the house. " There is something that is not as it should be," said Holmes, as we turned and walked back towards the house with its promise of good cheer in the shape of a cup of tea. " I cannot for the moment ascertain its exact nature, but believe me, I sense its presence lurking."

Such dark thoughts were at odds with the blue skies and verdant landscape, edged by the sea, that surrounded us, and I determined to direct Holmes' thoughts to happier things as soon as possible.

ITH this object in mind, I persuaded Holmes to accompany me on a walk to the famous Pendennis Castle, originally built by our Bluff King Hal to protect the realm from invasion. The view from the headland on which the castle stands is truly magnificent, and we stood together in silence, gazing across the bay to St. Mawes and St. Anthony Head, with its famous white-painted lighthouse at the foot.

Holmes stood, seemingly drinking in the view by my side, but to someone who knew him as well as myself, it was clear that the beauty of his surroundings was far from being the principal object of his thoughts. This was confirmed with his next words to me. " The lighthouse was visible from the point where we discovered the cigar end, was it not ? " This was hardly a question requiring a reply, and I refrained from answering. Holmes continued his musings. " And yet, if I am right, it would

not be visible from the house, nor yet from any other place nearby, as the trees would block the view. We will have to return and investigate—later, Watson, later, not now," as I started to expostulate.

" What is the significance of this ? " I asked him. " Indeed, is it likely that there is any significance at all ? "

" I do not know," he replied. " I find it curious, that is all, that a diverse group of men should assemble from where the one spot where the lighthouse is easily seen, and which is in its turn almost invisible from other points."

" Smugglers ? " I suggested, my imagination having been fired by a history of these men which I had recently been reading.

" This is hardly a time when bales of French lace and the like would make it worthwhile running the gauntlet of Her Majesty's Excisemen," Holmes replied. " In any event, landing any such cargo, be it lace, spirits, or tobacco, would seem to demand that such goods be transported elsewhere. There are no roads leading to that place, and I saw no signs of any heavy loads being moved."

" Perhaps the smugglers arrive by boat and depart using the same method ? " I suggested.

" That strikes me as being quite possible," said Holmes. " If I recall the breweries of the beer originally contained in those bottles, each one of them is located in a coastal town, if not a port. So, Watson, we have a secretive band of men, beer-drinkers from different ports of the West Country, chiefly this county, arriving by boat, converging on one spot from which they can only be seen by that lighthouse over there, and presumably departing the way they have come. What does that say to you ? "

" I can only think of smuggling at present."

" I as well," he confessed. " But it does not ring true to me at all. Why would smugglers choose such a place, rather than meeting some distance from the shore and transferring the goods in mid-ocean, where the rule of the excisemen is less likely to be enforced ? Also, the boats used to transport the goods must be small—the water is shallow near that place, and a large boat would have difficulty in drawing near. It

would hardly appear to be worth a smuggler's while to risk several years of imprisonment for a dinghy's worth of brandy."

" But if the cargo were something relatively small, but yet valuable ? " I ventured.

" Indeed, Watson ! Bravo ! I do believe that you may have something there," he congratulated me. " It is hard to think what such a commodity might be, though ? "

" Pearls ? " I hazarded, my thoughts still running along maritime lines.

Holmes shook his head. " I doubt that to be the case. Pearls are not commonly reckoned to be among the principal products of this county. Likewise, I doubt any kind of jewels, though they would likewise meet the criteria you established. My observations would seem to indicate that such meetings have taken place several times over the past few months, and it is impossible that there would be a steady supply of such articles to supply the number of carriers I deduce to have been present. I am at present unable to consider any alternative, though."

" Let us return for luncheon," I suggested. " Mrs. Buncombe gave us to understand that a grilled mackerel apiece would feature as the main dish, and it is a fish of which I am particularly fond."

 FTER luncheon, which lived up to my expectations, I retired to our room. My early rising, which had been occasioned by Holmes' eccentric revolver practice, followed by the walk and the sea air, had left me a little sleepy, and I resolved to take what our Mediterranean cousins term a *siesta*, a practice

which, incidentally, I had often followed in my service in India.

It was with a slight sense of relief that I removed my boots and laid myself on the bed. It seemed, though, that I had hardly closed my eyes when there was a loud knock at the door.

" Doctor Watson ! " came the voice of Mrs. Buncombe. " If you would be kind enough to help, sir ? "

I got up and opened the door.

" I wouldn't have disturbed you, sir, excepting that it was urgent, but it's young Harry Tregeare. He's come over all queer, and Doctor Pengelly is over at St. Mawes right now."

" Very good, Mrs. Buncombe. Please give me a few minutes to make myself ready and I will be with you." I laced up my boots and splashed cold water from the jug over my face. Happily I had thought to bring along my medical bag, which contained the usual apparatus appropriate to my calling.

" Where is the patient ? " I asked Mrs. Buncombe, who was waiting anxiously at the bottom of the stairs. Holmes was nowhere to be seen.

" He's at the 'Lion'," she told me. " In the public bar. But Jim Stott—he's the landlord there—says it's not the drink. He'd only just touched his beer—Harry Tregeare, that is—when he came over all strange."

She led me along the street to the public house, a quaint old-fashioned building. " The door's there," she pointed. " I'm not going in there. I took my oath I would never enter one of those places, and even for Harry Tregeare, I'm not going to break my word."

I lifted the latch of the barroom door and entered. There were perhaps a dozen customers in there, mostly fisherman from their appearance, and they were clustered around a wooden settle on which lay a young man.

" You are the doctor, then ? " asked a stout man wearing a white apron, presumably the landlord of the establishment.

" I am indeed. And this, I take

it, is my patient ? " indicating the recumbent figure.

The others made space for me as I approached and started my examination of the young man, who appeared to be unconscious. " Do you have a cushion or something similar we can place under his head ? " I asked the landlord. " It is not merely for his comfort, but I have no wish for his respiratory faculties to be temporarily incapacitated." The use of such language, as I had hoped, seemed to inspire some respect among the onlookers, and a cushion was speedily produced and placed under the head of the unfortunate sufferer.

As is usual in such circumstances, one of my first actions was to lift the eyelids of the patient. The eyes were turned upward, as one would expect in such a case, but the pupils were contracted, almost to pinpoints. The breathing was rapid and shallow and the pulse fluttered in a peculiar fashion. " I am correct in assuming that he did not appear in a state of intoxication before his collapse ? " I asked, though it was reasonably certain that his symptoms were not caused by alcohol.

" No, sir," replied one of the fisherman. " I'll take my oath he was stone cold sober when he walked in here."

" Though he looked a little queer, like," added another.

" In what way ? " I asked.

" Well, I'd have to say he looked happy, and cheerful, without there being anything really for him to be happy about. I asked him what was up, and he said 'Nothing', so I left it at that, sir. It's not like he was staggering around or anything like that."

I added " irrational euphoria" to my mental list of the patient's symptoms, and then asked, " What happened next ? "

" Well, sir, he ordered his beer— that's it that you see in front of him on the table right now, and b— me if he didn't just fall down of a heap on the floor. So we picked him up and we put him there, and Davy there was going to call for the doctor. But then Jim Stott," he pointed to the landlord, " reminded us that Doctor Pengelly had made his way over to St. Mawes and probably wouldn't be back until later this afternoon. Then someone remembered that Elsie Buncombe had some gentlemen from London staying with her, with one of them being a doctor, that one being yourself, sir."

" I see. Thank you. Does anyone know what he was doing before he entered this place ? "

Another of the fishermen spoke up. " I saw him earlier this morning, working in the garden at Sir Roderick's."

" That would be who ? " I asked the landlord.

" Sir Roderick Gilbert-Pryor, sir," he replied.

" The Cabinet Minister ? " I asked.

" That's the one, sir. He owns the big house up the way."

" I see. Well, based on my examination of the patient, I would surmise that he is in no immediate danger. However, I think at this moment it would be best if he were not moved from here. I am afraid, landlord, that you will have to accommodate your guest here for a few hours longer. If you have a blanket to throw over him, that would be advisable, and a hot-water bottle for his feet would be a welcome touch." I pulled out my watch. " If he has not returned to consciousness by half-past four, have no hesitation in calling on me again."

" Much obliged, I am sure," said the landlord, passing the word for the blanket and hot-water bottle. " May I recommend a pint of the local ale, sir ? On the house, naturally, in gratitude for your help just now."

" With pleasure," I assured him, and raised the foaming tankard. " Your good health, landlord. And good health to all in this room," raising my glass pointedly towards the prone figure on the settle.

⭒⇒◉⇐⭒

 RETURNED to our lodgings after this little episode to discover Holmes waiting for me in our drawing-room. I gave him an explanation of where I had been, and he questioned me minutely regarding the symptoms of the sufferer.

" I am surprised, Watson," he exclaimed, when I had finished recounting the event, " that you failed to recognize the symptoms of opiate poisoning."

I smote my brow. " Of course ! I do not know how I came to overlook it."

" In the same way that most such occurrences are overlooked," said Holmes calmly.

" Explain yourself." I was still smarting from the rebuke he had administered to my professional ability, and I spoke somewhat curtly.

" It is a mere matter of association. Who, for example, would ever suspect the presence of typhoid fever, a disease linked to dirt and inadequate sanitation, in a palace ? And yet, I assure you, such cases occur. Or, for that matter, gout, which is commonly linked to wealthy port-drinking elderly men, in the young daughter of a farm labourer ? And yet, as you well know, there are such cases. Opium, no doubt, is something you associate with India and China and if you conceive of it in this country, it is in connection with fashionable ladies or poets in the form of laudanum— maybe with our urban poor. But to think of opium in conjunction with these hearty fisher lads is inconceivable, is it not ? "

I nodded mutely, convinced of the justice of his words.

" If I ever achieve any small measure of success in my cases," he went on, " it is because I am prepared to conceive the inconceivable, and to accept it as a possibility. I am convinced that the same truth applies to other fields, such as the one of medicine."

I silently swallowed my pride and agreed with him.

" But never fear, Watson," he added. " You have done me a great service in this way. In any case, from what you have described, the patient was in no real danger, and your reputation as a doctor will suffer no injury."

At that moment, there was a knock on the door. " It's Jim Stott's boy to see you, Doctor."

" Show him in."

The urchin, cap in hand, stood in the doorway. " Father sends his compliments, and says to tell you that Harry's now feeling much better and sitting up and talking and such."

I smiled. " Tell your father to give Harry plenty of water to drink, and tell Harry from me not to be so foolish in the future. Do you understand ? "

" Yes, sir," said the boy. I tossed

him a few coppers, which he caught neatly, and he ran off, closing the door behind him.

" I have done you a great service ? How is that ? " I asked Holmes, baffled by his earlier words.

" Watson, I must confess to you that we are not in this town merely on account of a whim of mine. I had a very definite purpose in mind when I proposed coming here. I admit that the prospect is pleasant, the air refreshing, and Mrs. Buncombe a most congenial landlady, but this was not my principal aim."

" What, then ? "

" Where was your unfortunate patient working before he was stricken, did you say ? "

" In the garden of Sir Roderick Gilbert-Pryor," I replied. " The Cabinet Minister."

" I have had my eye on Sir Roderick for some time," replied Holmes. " He is not, I believe, a rich man. His estates in this part of the world scarcely extend past his immediate neighbourhood. Much was mortgaged and subsequently disposed of by his late father, who seems to have speculated unwisely in railway shares. Sir Roderick holds a few directorships in the City, which presumably bring in a little income, but other than that, he would seem to have little money, and yet he manages to entertain on a lavish scale and maintain his position on a level more than consistent with his Ministerial rank."

" His wife's money ? " I proposed.

" There is none. Lady Jocelyn is the youngest daughter of a country parson. It was a love match, and was certainly not contracted for money on his side. Nor hers, I am sure. Whatever the list of sins that Sir Roderick may have committed, fortune hunting would not appear to be included in it."

" You mean that we came here for the sole purpose of examining the state of Sir Roderick Gilbert-Pryor's finances ? " I asked, somewhat incredulously. " Why could not this have been achieved from London ? "

" I have already done all I could in this regard as far as London is concerned," Holmes answered. " I felt it was time to investigate the matter from here."

" You continue to amaze me, Holmes. May I ask why you are doing this ? "

" It is at the request of the Prime Minister," he replied. " He, too, has noticed the discrepancy between Sir Roderick's income and his expenditure. He fears the possibility of an associated scandal, and he wishes to prevent the occurrence of any such. He has therefore retained me to make such enquiries as are necessary."

I could not refrain from bursting out laughing. " So you and I are here at the orders of the British Government ! " I exclaimed. " And what conclusions have you reached so far ? "

" None that makes any sense," he admitted. " The business I uncovered this morning distracted me a little, I admit, but may well be connected with my original object in coming here, now I come to reflect on the matter. The business you have just attended to makes me believe that there is something more in this place that I can use to provide my explanations to the Prime Minister, however."

I considered what Holmes had just said. " This is mere supposition on my part," I admitted, " but what if the operations of which we discovered the traces this morning, whatever they turn out to be,

are definitely connected with Sir Roderick ? "

" I think this connection to be most likely," remarked Holmes, " but without any further detailed knowledge of these operations, we are no further forward in our enquiries, and it is fruitless to speculate on the matter. By the by, Mrs. Buncombe's expression last night after dinner when I lit my pipe leads me to believe she is no lover of tobacco indoors. I will therefore take my pipe and ponder these matters in the garden."

I was left alone in the room, and decided to study the latest edition of the *Lancet*, which I had brought down from London with me. By a strange coincidence, one of the articles dealt with a new drug, based on opium, and developed in Germany. The drug, diacetylmorphine, was being marketed in Germany for the purpose of suppressing coughs under the name of " Heroin", and was claimed by the makers to eliminate the unfortunate dependency, amounting almost to addiction, to which users of morphine were prone. I marked the article, and determined to show it to Holmes when he arrived from the garden. The rest of the journal was of less immediate interest, but I noted the name of one of my former fellow-students at Barts, who seemed to be making a name for himself in a specialised field of surgery.

When Holmes returned from the garden, I showed the article to him. He read it through, with particular attention to the process described therein for the manufacture of the drug.

" I have heard of this opiate," he told me, " but this is the most detailed and trustworthy information I have come across so far. You are to be congratulated on drawing it to my attention. Would you say that the symptoms you observed earlier today corresponded to the description here of a patient who has inadvertently taken too much of the drug ? "

" Certainly, but they could apply to any of the opiates, as you are yourself aware."

" Nonetheless, Watson," and Holmes turned to me, his eyes glittering, " I believe we are about to discover the mysterious source of Sir Roderick's wealth."

" Sir Roderick is not engaged in the pharmaceutical trade, is he ? " I asked.

" He holds a directorship in one of the smaller pharmaceutical companies," replied my friend, " and his name is not unknown among amateur practitioners of the chemical sciences. The production of this 'Heroin' would not be beyond his powers, nor would the procurement of the necessary apparatus pose any problem."

" But surely," I retorted, " even if he were producing this drug, it would be for the good of mankind."

" Ah, Watson, you know only what you read here," pointing to the *Lancet*. " My sources tell me that far from reducing the dependency which makes morphine so undesirable to many, this drug turns its user into a virtual slave, whose animal craving produces physical and mental horrors beyond all imagination. Furthermore, the effects of the drug when it is first administered are

reportedly of an ecstasy beyond compare. I thank you for assisting me to end my dependence on cocaine, but I confess that the pleasure that I obtained from that drug in my idle hours was indeed as exquisite as the pain it cost me to break the habit. If this 'Heroin' is more powerful in each regard…"

" I know what it cost you to break that habit," I replied, " and I salute your courage in having done so."

" What," Holmes continued, ignoring me, " if some unscrupulous fiend were to dose others with this new drug, knowing that they would become, as it were, hooked on it like fish on a line, and would demand more of it, paying any price to obtain their ration ? "

I shuddered. " That would indeed be inhuman," I agreed. " And you believe Sir Roderick Gilbert-Pryor, a Minister of the Crown, is engaged in such a vile trade ? "

" I now have reason to suspect so," replied my friend gravely. " To-morrow, we will attempt to ascertain the truth. If Sir Roderick turns out to have a missing right incisor, I will know that my suspicions are correct."

" And if they are ? "

My friend shrugged. " That is not for me to decide. I make my report to Downing-street, and the matter is then out of my hands. But come, my nose informs me of a roast fowl, and if Mrs. Buncombe's skills tonight match those of last night, we shall be well fed indeed."

HE next morning arrived, thankfully without revolver practice, and Holmes and I settled down to a breakfast consisting chiefly of a fine *kitchari* which brought

back memories of my service in India.

" Today, we visit Sir Roderick," proclaimed Holmes.

" And if he is not at home ? "

" He will not be in London,

during the Parliamentary recess," Holmes pointed out. " This is his only country place, and I think it more than likely that he will be here. It wants three weeks until the Glorious Twelfth, so he will not be on the grouse moors. It is conceivable, I suppose, that he may be staying with a colleague in Scotland, tormenting salmon with those ridiculous artificial flies, but the odds are against it."

" I have never understood your prejudice against angling, Holmes, but let that pass. Let us assume, then, that Sir Roderick will be at home. On what grounds do you propose to make his acquaintance ? "

" We are already acquainted," replied Holmes. " I believe I mentioned last night that he is an amateur chemist of some considerable ability. I, too, have dabbled in the subject, as you know, and he and I once collaborated on a work dealing with the use of acetone as a universal solvent. We have encountered each other with relative frequency over the past few years at meetings of the Chemical Society and the like. On the last occasion we met, some twelve months ago, he apparently was in possession of all his teeth, as I recall, but one never knows what accidents may have befallen him in that line since that time."

We enquired the way to Sir Roderick's of Mrs. Buncombe, and set off on what she assured us was an easy walk. Along the way, Holmes, to my surprise, purchased a bag of small green apples.

" These look nourishing enough," he remarked, in answer to my questioning glance.

" They hardly appeared to be the most appetising specimens on display," I objected.

" They will serve their purpose," he replied, enigmatically.

On arrival at Sir Roderick's establishment, a fine example of the architecture of the last century, but one which had been allowed to fall into decay, Holmes' conjecture was proved to be correct. A servant took our cards, and returned to inform us that Sir Roderick was at home and would receive us. We were conducted to a handsome room that appeared to serve as both a library and as Sir Roderick's study.

The Minister rose from behind his desk to greet us.

" Holmes," he exclaimed, smiling widely, showing us a perfect row of even white teeth, somewhat, I confess, to my disappointment. " How good to see you here. If you'd let me know before you arrived, I would have been delighted to offer you my hospitality. Your assistance would be invaluable with one or two little problems I am currently encountering in my laboratory. I would be more than happy to have you and your friend here as my guests."

Holmes bowed as he introduced me, and I bowed to the baronet in my turn. " You give my poor efforts far too much praise," remarked Holmes. " We are very comfortably lodged in one of the houses of the town, and we would not dream of imposing on your generous nature."

It may have been my fancy, but it seemed to me that a look of relief seemed to pass over Sir Roderick's face as Holmes declined the invitation. " Very well, as you will," he said, " but I must insist on your dining with me some night. Let me see now," he went on, consulting a notebook, " tonight I am engaged, and the next night as well, but maybe the day after that ? Good. I shall expect you about seven, then. And since we are in the country, I feel there is no need to dress. Pray feel free to make yourself as comfortable as you please in these rural surroundings." He could not have been more affable, but I felt that some of his sociability was a little forced, and this was confirmed in his answer to Holmes' next enquiry, about Lady Jocelyn.

" The poor gal is not in the best of health these days, I am sorry to say. She came down from London three months ago, and has hardly left her room since that time. The local doctor, Dr. Pengelly, is an excellent man, and we have also had specialists from London come to examine her, but their efforts to discover the cause of her indisposition have so far remained fruitless."

I forbore from further enquiry, though my professional interest was naturally piqued, but felt it was hardly my place to interfere, and I doubted my ability to be of any practical value in the case, particularly if the finest doctors in the land had declared themselves baffled.

" I am sorry to hear that," replied Holmes. " Please present my regards to her."

" I will certainly do that," replied Sir Roderick. " What, if I may be so bold as to ask, do you have there, by the way ? I am intrigued." He gestured towards the bag of apples that Holmes still carried in his hand.

" Some local agricultural specimens," replied my friend, " which I purchased on a sudden impulse on my way here. Perhaps you would care for one ? " So saying, he pressed one into my hand before offering the bag to Sir Roderick, who looked at him in some perplexity.

" Well, this is most kind of you," said Sir Roderick, selecting an apple for himself, and polishing it on a handkerchief that he withdrew from his sleeve. He inspected the

apple with a critical eye. " I hope you are not offended, Holmes, but I will reserve this for my dessert following luncheon. My digestion, you know."

" Naturally," Holmes replied. In the meantime, I had taken a bite of the fruit that Holmes had forced on me, and discovered it to be as hard and sour as I had surmised from its appearance. I stealthily placed the remainder into my coat pocket, without, I hoped, either of the others becoming aware of my having done so. Holmes, I noticed, was not partaking of his purchase.

After a little conversation between the other two concerning chemical subjects, which, to be frank, was of no interest to me and beyond my powers of comprehension, and a renewed invitation to and acceptance of dinner on the day after the next, we took our leave of Sir Roderick.

" My dear fellow," I said to Holmes, as we were walking down the drive of Sir Roderick's house, through the spacious gardens. " Why on earth did you give me one of those damnable apples ? "

He ignored my words, but fixed his attention on the flower-beds on each side of the path. " Look here, Watson. What do you see ? "

I answered rather sharply, I am afraid. The memory of the apple was still with me, and I feared I had loosened one of my back teeth when biting it. " Poppies, of course."

" Of course," he said. " You were in Afghanistan, were you not ? "

" You know well that I served there in my Army days. I fail to see the point of the question."

" Afghanistan grows a certain type of poppy, as I am sure you are aware," he remarked, in a conversational tone.

" So it does. The opium poppy."

I stopped and looked more closely

at the flowers beside me. " By Jove, Holmes ! And in plain sight of all ! Whoever would have suspected a Minister of the Crown to be cultivating such a thing ? "

" I remarked to you yesterday on the principles of association and incongruity. Consider this to be another example of the same."

" Remarkable," I said.

" Not so remarkable, I feel." We passed through the gates, and Holmes held out his hand to me, in which lay a few long serrated leaves of some plant, arranged themselves somewhat like the outstretched fingers of a hand. " Do you recognise this ? "

I looked closely. " *Cannabis sativa*," I replied. " Another herb, producing fibres used in the production of rope."

" It is also held to produce some sort of effect on those who eat it or smoke it," added Holmes. " I plucked this from Sir Roderick's garden just now. However, this plant is growing rampant throughout the vicinity. I noticed many such examples as we walked from the station the other day. It appears to be a positive weed in this town. Its use must be quite common here."

I considered the other more usual employment of this plant. " This is a port," I remarked to Holmes, " and the ships and boats require hempen rigging. There is nothing more natural that the boatmen here would have cultivated the plant locally for this purpose before the advent of modern transportation permitted the ropes to be brought from a central manufactory."

" Quite possibly you are correct," replied Holmes. " But it is an indubitable fact that the distinctive aroma of the smoke of this herb was to

be perceived just now while we were talking to Sir Roderick."

" He is under the influence of this drug ? "

" Maybe not he. Maybe his wife, or conceivably one of the servants. His wife's being ill may or may not be another suspicious circumstance. Unless I am aware of the nature of Lady Jocelyn's complaint, I cannot be sure. But there are many little factors here, Watson, none of them of great importance in themselves, but added together—"

I stopped suddenly in my tracks, and gave a small cry.

" What is the matter ? " my companion asked me.

" My tooth," I complained bitterly. " Your damned apple." I clutched the side of my face. " I feel I must seek the service of a dentist immediately."

" Dear, dear," said Holmes in an animated fashion. " How very fortunate."

" ' Fortunate', did you say, Holmes ? I am in some pain, I assure you." I was almost angry with my friend.

" Did I indeed say ' fortunate' ? I meant ' unfortunate', naturally," he replied. For a moment I almost believed I had misheard his previous utterance, such was his sympathetic tone.

We enquired of a passer-by regarding the existence of a dentist in the town, and were informed that there was one such, whose services were highly praised by our informant.

" I will wait in the waiting-room while your tooth is attended to," said Holmes to me as we entered the dental surgery. " I trust that there will not be anything seriously amiss."

The dentist, a Mr. Garland, indeed proved to be splendidly competent. Anointing the afflicted sub-molar with oil of cloves, he advised me to avoid using that side of my mouth for mastication for a few days, and invited me to visit him again should the pain continue after that time.

I emerged from the surgery to the waiting room to discover Holmes lounging there, seemingly engrossed in a copy of the Illustrated London News.

" Nothing serious, I trust ? " he asked with an expression of great concern. There seemed to be, however, a sense of triumph in his voice, the reason for which I was totally at a loss to discover.

" No thanks to you," I grudgingly replied.

" I apologise, Watson," he answered me. " Fully and without reserve. I hereby dispose of the offending articles. They have served their purpose—indeed, better than I expected them to do." So saying, he dropped the apples, still in their bag, into a small stream that flowed beside the road along which we were walking. In a slightly better mood than previously, I retrieved the half-apple from my pocket, and sent it flying to join its fellows.

" Our next port of call is the post-office," went on Holmes. " We must act fast, I fear."

At the post-office, Holmes wrote out a telegram to London, which he dispatched reply-paid.

" And now to Mrs. Buncombe's, to await the reply, which should be with us in an hour or less, if luck is with us."

It proved to be about an hour and a half before Holmes received his reply. " Excellent, Watson ! " was his comment upon reading it. " Now let us have a few words with our worthy hostess."

" Mrs. Buncombe," he enquired of her a few minutes later, " two

friends of mine will be arriving in this town later today. Would it be possible for them to take lodging with you, at the same rates as Dr. Watson and myself for one, possibly two nights, from tonight ? "

" With pleasure, sir, though you must admit it is somewhat short notice," she smiled. " These would be gentlemen, I take it ? "

" Two Chinese gentlemen," replied Holmes. Her face changed slightly as she digested the news. " One of them is a product of Oxford University, and a credit to our civilisation and his. As to the other, I confess I do not know well, but I am fully prepared to take full responsibility for him. Naturally, I will pay you in advance for their lodging," he added, withdrawing his wallet, and presenting her with a Bank of England note. " This will compensate you for any inconvenience, I think ? "

" Well, if these Chinamen are known to you, sir, I suppose there'll be no trouble in putting them up here. In the usual run of things, of course, I wouldn't dream of such a thing. But seeing as you are being so generous about these matters, sir, I have to say I will be happy to fall in with your wishes. I'll put them up in the back. I take it they won't take it amiss if they share a room ? "

" Capital ! " he answered her. " Thank you, Mrs. Buncombe. I will leave all the domestic arrangements to your good sense. Now, Watson," he addressed me, as she left the room, " we have work to do, and only a little time to do it in. Tonight, after dinner, we will make another little expedition to the castle."

" Why tonight ? " I asked.

" Because, my dear fellow, Sir Roderick informed us that tonight and tomorrow night he would be

unable to dine with us. I scarcely think that the social whirl of
this charming little backwater is of
such intensity that he is engaged for
those evenings—at least not in the
conventional sense. Furthermore,
I would draw your attention to the
calendar."

"What of it ? "

"Tonight and tomorrow are
nights of the new moon."

"I begin to perceive your
meaning."

"So let us look out some dark
clothing, in which we may not easily be observed, and do you, Watson,
procure a pair of dark lanterns for
us. I venture to suggest that a stout
walking stick might also be of use in
the coming days."

"And you ? "

"I must go to the harbour,
where I will make arrangements for
tomorrow."

OLMES' two mysteri-
ous Chinamen arrived
by train late in the afternoon. One was a small-
er, slightly corpulent, man of about
the same age as Holmes and myself,
who wore Western clothes in impeccable taste. He extended his hand
to me as Holmes introduced us.

"John Chen. Delighted to meet
the Boswell of the great detective at
last," he announced, in English that
was the equal of any gentleman's of
this land.

The other Chinaman was of a
very different character. He was tall
where the other was short, and slender, almost to the point of emacia-
tion, where the other was plump.
He was dressed in a loose-fitting
dark costume of vaguely Oriental
cut, and carried on his back a large
wicker basket, out of which came
strange cheeping noises, accompanied by a strong smell strongly redo-
lent of fish that was not quite fresh.

"This is Wang Lee," explained
Chen. "He speaks little English,
but he is utterly reliable, I assure
you."

The taller Chinaman turned to
Holmes and myself, and bowed to
us, his hands clasped together and
tucked into his voluminous sleeves.

"Happy to meet you," he said in
heavy accents.

"Let us go," said Holmes. "You
will be sleeping tonight at the house
of our landlady, Mrs. Buncombe,
who will be providing us with food.
I trust that Wang Lee can stomach
our European food ? "

Chen turned to the other, and
spoke to him in their curious sing-
song language, receiving a reply in
the same tongue.

"He says that European food is
not to his taste, but for one or two
days, he can stomach it, given the
fee you will be paying him."

"Good," said Holmes. We had
arrived at our lodgings. "I hardly
think that this will be welcome indoors," he said, indicating Wang
Lee's basket. "There is a tool-shed
at the rear that may be suitable for
it. I do not think we need trouble
asking Mrs. Buncombe's permission to use the facility for one night
only." He led the way, and the basket was placed within the shed.

"You have fish ? " Wang Lee addressed me directly.

"What does he mean ? " I asked
of his compatriot.

"Ah yes, of course." Holmes,
rather than Chen, answered me.
"It is natural to assume that some

fish will be required. Watson, I realise it is an imposition on your good nature, but if you would make your way to the fishing port and purchase some dozen of small fish—pilchards or the like, and as fresh as you can obtain them—I am sure that Mr. Lee and his charge would be more than grateful. While you are gone, I will take the opportunity of outlining the situation to our friends."

I was puzzled, to say the least, but Holmes' mysterious commands often failed to make sense at the time, revealing their purpose only later, so I hastened to carry out this strange errand. I returned some twenty minutes later with a paper package suspended at a safe distance from my hand by a loop of string. In truth, the smell of the fish was nowhere near as strong as I had feared.

I returned, and viewed the three men in conference, still standing outside the tool-shed. I presented the package to Wang Lee, who opened it with obvious signs of satisfaction, and disappeared with it into the shed. Loud squawking sounds and other noises came from the shed, which ceased as Wang Lee emerged again.

" All finish," he beamed happily.

" Excellent," replied Holmes. " Then let us go inside."

Mrs. Buncombe rose to the challenge of her Oriental visitors, and greeted them with what appeared to be unfeigned pleasure. Chen won her heart by praising her collection of Oriental knick-knacks brought from the East by her late husband, and Wang Lee sat impassively silent, doing nothing that might cause any offence.

The meal was very much to my taste, consisting chiefly of a roast of pork loin, and if it was not to Wang Lee's, he disguised his feelings well.

After dinner, the two Chinamen retired to their room, and Holmes and I to ours, where we changed our garments and prepared for the evening to come.

" I have already informed Mrs. Buncombe that we will be out late tonight," Holmes informed me as we left the house, " and she has kindly lent me the latchkey."

" What reason did you assign for our absence ? "

" Why, none. She never enquired, and I did not see fit to tell her."

" Holmes, I must ask you this. What are we looking for tonight, and why are those Chinamen staying with us ? "

" As to the first, I am not as yet certain, and as to the second, I propose that you see with your own eyes tomorrow morning."

After a short walk, we reached the castle, and positioned ourselves where we could enjoy a clear view of the lighthouse.

It was, despite the time of year, a somewhat cool evening, and I was beginning to wish that I had packed my hip-flask, which contained some excellent brandy, when Holmes grasped my arm.

" Look ! " he commanded, pointing towards the lighthouse, which was flashing in its assigned pattern every fifteen seconds.

" I see nothing," I complained.

" There, below the cliff, and above the water. One red light and one green. Do you not see ? "

My eyes followed his pointing finger, and indeed, I could just make out two coloured specks of light in the places indicated. It was, as Holmes had remarked earlier, a night on which there was almost no moon, and I had to strain my eyes to discern the details of any objects surrounding the lights. " I see them, Holmes. Are they the riding lights of fishing boats ? "

He shook his head. " No, they are not moving. These are fixed lights. Here," and he passed me a pair of powerful field-glasses, which showed me that that the lights appeared to come from lanterns affixed to poles in the water, the support of the red lantern being taller than that of the green. " With a little mental agility on our part," went on Holmes, " I think we are able to ascertain their purpose."

" Your meaning ? "

" Imagine yourself in a position so that the lights are in line with each other, the red above the green. Where does that lead ? "

I pondered the conundrum which, as Holmes had remarked, required not a little mental effort. " It leads to the cove behind Mrs. Buncombe's house. And these lights therefore serve as a guide to the visitors who come and leave the beer bottles."

" Indeed so, Watson. And look ! " his finger pointed to a barely discernible shape in the water which I recognised, with the aid of the field-glasses, as being a small sailing vessel, scarcely more than a dinghy. " And another ! "

" We should summon the police," I told Holmes.

He shook his head in reply. " This is no matter for the police. Remember, the whole purpose of my investigation is to prevent a possible scandal, not to cause one," he

reminded me. " I am confident we will have our chance to nip this business in the bud tomorrow night. For now, let us content ourselves with being observers, and tomorrow morning, my plan is to discover still more." He rubbed his hands together in anticipation.

I quite forgot the chill of the evening as we spent the next hour observing about a dozen small boats make their way to the hidden cove. Most appeared to come from the open sea, but there was one notable exception—a pleasure yacht by her appearance, which made its way from the general quarter of the lighthouse, starting out some ten minutes after the last small boat had entered the cove. " I had guessed as much," remarked Holmes, when I pointed out this vessel to him. After this yacht had reached the cove, the two guiding lights were extinguished, and we could see no movement for about another hour. I was once again regretting my lack of foresight in the matter of my hip-flask, and was about to propose to Holmes that we quit the place, when he drew my attention to a procession of small boats leaving the cove. " The evening's entertainment is at an end," he said softly to me. " We may withdraw now, I think."

Confident that my friend had solved at least part of the riddle, I thankfully turned my steps towards Mrs. Buncombe's house, and the warmth of my bed.

<hr />

HE next morning saw Holmes and myself at breakfast. We were joined halfway through our repast by John Chen, who bade us a good morning and tucked into his porridge, followed by bacon and

eggs, like any Englishman. Indeed, were it not for his physiognomy, and basing one's judgement only on his speech and dress, one would have taken him for a native of these shores.

" Wang Lee is upstairs, but will

join us when we are ready," he explained, helping himself to toast and marmalade.

"Watson," remarked Holmes to me as we left Chen finishing the last of his coffee. "We will be spending a day on the water. The field-glasses, and dare I suggest it, your hip-flask, would be of great utility, I think. I would also advise warm clothing."

Soon after, he and I, accompanied by the two Chinamen, with Wang Lee carrying the mysterious basket with which he had arrived, made our way to the harbour, where two small rowing boats awaited us, presumably the results of Holmes' visit the previous day.

Holmes greeted the boatmen standing by, and proceeded to commandeer one of the boats for himself and me, leaving the other to be occupied by the two Orientals. John Chen, dressed in a smart blue duffel-coat, manned the oars, with Wang Lee, now in bright unmistakably Chinese garb, and his mysterious basket occupying the bow. Holmes took the oars of our craft.

"I may require you to provide our propulsive power at some future point in our expedition," he remarked to me, "but at present I will indulge myself in a little exercise." I have mentioned in the past that Holmes, though of what appeared to be a thin sinewy build, was possessed of considerable strength which was in no way hinted at by his appearance. He proved himself to be an oarsman of no mean skill, and we were soon in the middle of the channel separating the port from the lighthouse. "You may care to observe that post that we are about to pass," said Holmes.

The post to which he referred was a wooden pole, protruding from the surface of the water for about ten feet. Affixed to the top of the pole was a hook.

"Undoubtedly," I remarked, "this hook was used to attach one of the lanterns that we saw last night."

"I am convinced of it," replied Holmes. "If you will take the trouble to look in the other direction towards our lodgings on the other side of the channel, you will see the other pole to which the green lantern was attached."

I looked in the direction indicated, and indeed, the two poles pointed straight toward the hidden cove at the bottom of the orchard.

"I think there can be little doubt," added Holmes, "of the purpose of these poles, which are clearly placed here as a support for the lanterns that we observed last night. It is plain that they have been placed as navigation aids to guide visitors to this secret landing place."

We rowed on a little further, taking careful note of the position of the poles and their relationship to the lighthouse.

"I think," Holmes remarked, "we were best if we moved to one side of here," and so saying, pulled us closer to the coast, along the shore from the lighthouse, but in a position from where we were still able to observe it.

"What is our plan?" I asked Holmes.

"We attempt to catch some mackerel," replied, bringing out a couple of hand-lines from under the thwart on which he was sitting, much to my amusement, given his past remarks about anglers. "And while we are doing this, we will watch the reactions of those in there," glancing towards the lighthouse, "to the antics of my friends there," glancing towards the boat containing the two Chinese. "By the by, Watson,

I would advise you to pull that cap of yours a little further forward over your eyes. Your face is too visible for my liking."

" I had no idea my appearance offended you to that extent," I retorted.

Holmes chuckled. " My dear fellow, this concerns the matter of your possible identification by person or persons unknown from there," looking once more towards the lighthouse, " and has little to do with my pleasure or otherwise concerning the sight of your countenance."

" What in the world are they doing ? " I asked, looking at the other boat, as we cast the fishing lines over the side of the boat. Wang Lee had opened the basket, out of which appeared a large black bird with a long neck.

" That, my dear fellow, is probably the only example of its kind in the British Isles. It is a cormorant, as you have probably deduced for yourself, but one which has been trained to catch fish and return them to its master. Wang Lee is probably the sole practitioner of the skill in this country, and we are lucky that he is a friend of John Chen who was able to persuade him to help us in this way."

" How do you come to know Chen ? "

" I would have thought it evident. We were fellow students at University. His father is some kind of nobleman in his own country, and he wished one of his sons to learn more about the Western barbarians, as we appear to that ancient civilisation. Chan and I have maintained contact since our student days, and he has been of invaluable assistance to me whenever I have wished to know more about anything concerning the land of Cathay or its inhabitants."

As I watched, the bird dived off the edge of the boat, and disappeared beneath the waves. Some twenty seconds later, the sleek black head broke the surface of the water, a fish of some six inches in length held in its beak.

" Holmes, I appreciate that this Oriental and his bird possess a certain skill, but what is the purpose here ? "

" It is a bow drawn at a venture, I confess, but one that may well prove to be of great value," replied Holmes. " It is a curious sight to watch, is it not ? " I assented. Indeed, my eyes were fixed on the interplay between man and bird, as the latter continued to dive and retrieve silver fish from the depths. Every few attempts, Wang Lee would reward the creature for its efforts by allowing it to devour one of its catch. " My hope is," went on Holmes, " that the inhabitants of the lighthouse will likewise find this an intriguing sight and will show themselves on this balcony the better to observe these strange goings-on. And here," he said, " is the first of them."

A figure had indeed appeared on the balcony, and was watching the antics of the Chinese and the bird with rapt attention. Holmes took the field-glasses and, as surreptitiously as he could manage, watched the other through them. He shook his head. " Not yet, I fear, but there is still time."

He gave no indication of the meaning of his last words, and started to whistle idly, in defiance of the popular superstition among sailors governing the practice. " Aha ! " he suddenly exclaimed. " This is what I have been waiting for ! "

The man on the balcony had obviously been calling to another within the building, though his words were inaudible to us at our distance. It appeared that his call had been answered and he was joined on the balcony by another figure, seemingly clad in a curious white garment.

" We have him ! " exclaimed Holmes, peering through the field-glasses and handing them to me. " You are my witness to this, Watson. Tell me what you see."

I adjusted the focus. " It is Sir Roderick," I replied. " And he appears to be wearing a laboratory coat."

" Precisely so," replied Holmes. " This is not evidence that can stand up in a court of law, naturally, but it is further evidence for my case, even so."

" Evidence of what, Holmes ? "

" Evidence, naturally, that the lighthouse is being used as a laboratory for the production of this 'Heroin', and that Sir Roderick himself is the principal agent in its production. We have seen enough, Watson. It is now time for us to return. May I trouble you to take the oars this time ? I wish to consider our next move." With that, he relinquished control of the boat to me, and curled up in the bow, the smoke from his pipe making us appear from a distance to be more of a steam-launch than a simple rowing boat.

HAT evening, John Chen and Wang Lee having departed Falmouth, together with the cormorant and a suitable supply of fish, which included several fine mackerel caught by Holmes and myself in the course of our surveillance, we prepared for our nocturnal expedition.

" I do not anticipate immediate violence from the principal in this affair," Holmes said to me. " It would be the height of folly for Sir Roderick to attempt any such moves, particularly as we are both known in the neighbourhood, following your recent medical ministrations in the public house. His minions, on the other hand, may prove a trifle less amenable to reason, and so I am taking my revolver as an additional inducement, should my words prove ineffective in this regard. You could do worse than to equip yourself with that ashplant you purchased yesterday."

His words seemed to me to be practical, and I therefore picked up the stout stick, testing its balance, and hoping that I would not have occasion to use it in the fashion that Holmes had just described.

" Tonight, tempting as it may be, I fear that your hip-flask must be left behind, Watson. We must be silent as the grave."

" I trust that will not prove to be a prophetic simile," I remarked.

" Do not fear," said Holmes. " As I say, I am relatively confident that there will be no physical violence on this occasion, but even so, I feel it will be as well for us both to be prepared against such a possibility. Have you the dark lanterns ? Excellent. Let us sally forth, and prepare to meet the foe. I have already marked out a spot where we can wait undetected until the time is ripe."

Dressed in our dark garments, and with black cloths tied about our faces, we must have been nearly invisible from only a few yards away. On this moonless night, though Holmes was a matter of feet away from me as we moved through the orchard, I nonetheless lost sight of him on more than one occasion, and was only able to track his progress from the faint sounds that he made. I had confidence that, with Holmes having displayed his usual sagacity in the matter of concealment, there was little or no danger of our discovery.

On this occasion, since we had a good expectation in our minds of what was about to transpire, the period of waiting did not seem to be so long, as we strained our eyes for the glimmer of light that would show us that the evening's business was about to begin.

After what I judged to be about an hour, Holmes grasped my arm, " Do you see that, Watson ? " The green light had appeared as a faint glow in the distance toward the lighthouse. " The game is about to commence." Even though Holmes spoke in a low whisper, his obvious excitement at the events about to unfold before us was almost palpable. After a few minutes, the red light also made its appearance. As we had surmised earlier, the two lights were almost in line with the lighthouse from our position at the side of the cove.

It was a matter of a few minutes only before the first boat appeared. " I cannot be certain of this," Holmes whispered to me, " but I would wager that this is a local party from this vicinity. The boats from the other villages round about will be along shortly, I am sure."

He was proved correct in his surmise. Over the next twenty minutes, about ten boats appeared and beached themselves on the sandy shore of the cove. None of these was a large boat, and each was crewed by two, or at the most three, men, who joined together in a group which as yet lacked a focus. Obviously, they were waiting for the yacht

that we had observed last night to come from the lighthouse. As we watched, one of them lit a lantern, and swing it over his head, waving it three times slowly from left to right. From the base of the lighthouse, we saw a similar moving light.

" Those signals and acknowledgement are to let him know they are all waiting, and there is no danger ? " I whispered to Holmes.

" I am certain of it," he hissed in return.

Holmes continued to peer through the field glasses that we had brought with us, and I suddenly felt him quiver with excitement.

" It is he ! I am sure of it ! " he whispered to me. " Now we have him, I am positive."

In a few minutes, even without the aid of the field glasses, I was able to discern the dark shape of the yacht making its way from the lighthouse towards us. A few minutes more, and we heard the sound of the boat's dinghy being launched and the regular splashes of its oars as it was rowed towards us.

Holmes put his lips to my ear. " On my signal," he said in a low voice, " we will rush into the middle with our lanterns fully open. Attempt to hold your lantern in such a way that the light will dazzle the others without yourself being so inconvenienced. Though I have remarked, I do not expect violence, be alert for any mischief that may occur."

The two leading lights had now gone out, and the visitors from the yacht stepped out of the small rowing boat, now beached on the shore. Even in the dim light, it was possible to recognise the tall powerful figure of Sir Roderick. I guessed that Holmes would be experiencing a feeling of inner satisfaction that his deductions of the previous days had now finally proven themselves to be correct.

" Now, Watson, now ! " he hissed at me, and sprang from our hiding place, uttering an unearthly scream of a peculiar calibre, the like of which I had never heard him utter in the past, and which froze the blood in my veins. To me, who knew the source of the sound, it was frightening. To the waiting men, who had no idea of where this uncanny sound was coming, it must have seemed almost supernatural. The effect was to make them freeze and stop in their tracks as if they had been turned to stone by some monster or basilisk.

" Do not move, or I fire ! " he cried, brandishing his revolver, which was clearly visible in the light of the lantern that he carried in his other hand. I followed Holmes, my own lantern held high, with my stout stick in my other hand.

Sir Roderick, for it was indeed he, turned to face Holmes, his face contorted in fury.

" What the devil do you mean by this, Holmes ? " he shouted.

" I might well ask you the same, Sir Roderick," replied Holmes calmly. His quiet tone of voice was in complete contrast to the terrifying bloodcurdling scream that he had uttered just a few seconds before.

The Cabinet Minister drew himself up to his not inconsiderable height. " I think you forget my position, Mr. Holmes," he replied. His voice was now as calm as that of my friend, but with an unmistakeable undertone of menace. " I am in a position to make your existence more than a trifle uncomfortable in the future, and indeed, I could make it certain that you would never be able to exercise your pernicious arts in this country ever again."

" I think not, Sir Roderick," replied Holmes. " You hardly imagine that I am doing this on my own account, do you ? "

" There is only one man in this kingdom who would have the power to engage you in such a matter," sneered Sir Roderick.

" Indeed that is so," replied Holmes, " and it is he who has engaged me to investigate this affair."

While this exchange had been taking place, I had noticed one of the ruffians from Sir Roderick's boat moving stealthily in Holmes's direction. With horror, I observed that he held a knife in his right hand, with which it appeared he was prepared to attack Holmes. I dashed forward, raising my stick high in the air, and brought it down hard on the wretch's forearm as he was in the instant of striking forward with the blade. There was a loud crack as the bone shattered, and a clatter as the knife dropped to the ground.

Holmes turned briefly in the direction of the sounds and took in the situation at a glance. " My sincere thanks to you, Watson," he remarked. " It would seem that despite Sir Roderick's protestations, some of the gentleman here would have matters that they would sooner keep hidden." He turned to Sir Roderick again. " May I suggest that you dismiss your minions, so that we may continue our conversation more privately ? " he invited.

" Then we can keep the money, sir ? " one of the sailors asked Holmes.

For a few seconds, Holmes appeared to be taken aback. " I think that had better be left with me, don't you ? " he invited, after a few moments' consideration. Sir Roderick watched with what appeared to be mounting fury as the visitors to the cove deposited envelopes and packets at Holmes's feet, but he was powerless to resist with the other's revolver held to his temple, which not only prevented him from resisting our efforts, but also acted as a deterrent to any who might feel inclined to attack either Holmes or myself.

When the last of these packets appeared to have been delivered, Holmes turned to the assembled men. " I suggest that you leave now, and never return. Your services in this area are no longer required." As they departed, he turned to Sir Roderick, whose face was now a mask of rage.

" Do you realise what you have done ? " he fairly screamed at Holmes.

" I have an idea," replied my friend, smiling.

" In a few minutes, you have completely destroyed the work of several years."

" For which the world and especially those poor wretches who you have enslaved to your drug will be profoundly grateful, should they ever discover the truth. I regard your recent actions in this area as being totally despicable, and unworthy of an English gentleman, let alone a Minister of the Crown."

Sir Roderick had the grace to appear somewhat abashed. " What do you propose doing ? " he asked Holmes.

" I am bound to make a report to the Prime Minister," replied Holmes. " Following that, the matter is in his hands, not mine. He will, I am sure, recommend some course of action to you, and I would be extremely surprised if it encompassed your remaining in the Cabinet."

" I am ruined, ruined ! Have you any idea what you have just done ? " he asked again.

For answer, Holmes gestured to me to pick up the envelopes and packets that had been deposited by the boatmen.

" I think it is time to examine the boat in which you arrived," he said to Sir Roderick, after I had retrieved the last of these envelopes. Some were of considerable weight and heft.

Some of the baronet's arrogance and bluster returned to him. " You may search as long and as hard as you please, Mr. Busybody Holmes," he retorted. " I can assure you that even you will find nothing."

Holmes regarded his opponent keenly in the light of the lantern that he shone into the other's face. " I see you are telling the truth," he said at last. " I now perceive that we should have made this expedition last night."

" You are clever, Mr. Holmes," sneered Sir Roderick. " A little too clever for your own good, I would say."

Holmes chose to ignore this, and turned to me. " Come, Watson, our work here is done. Let us to the police station where we are expected," he remarked significantly. " I would not advise following us," he added to Sir Roderick. " Though the local police do not know the reason behind the Home Secretary's personal request to them, I am confident that they will do their duty in ensuring that we come to no harm."

" You will still suffer for this ! " fairly screamed Sir Roderick. " I am not without influence in certain areas, and my agents have powers beyond your reckoning."

" I fear that you somewhat underestimate my powers of reckoning," smiled Holmes. " I am well aware of your influence in certain circles, and so, may I add, are various others with whom you and I have mutual acquaintance."

Sir Roderick snarled. There is no other word to describe the animal-like noise that he produced in answer to Holmes's words. " I will see you in hell ! "

" We will see about that," Holmes replied. " I expect at least one of us to take up abode in that region at some time in the future."

The other seemed ready to spring on us, but checked himself as Holmes waved his revolver in a significant manner.

" Adieu, Sir Roderick," Holmes called gaily over his shoulder as we left the orchard.

URELY it was obvious from the time that I discovered the beer bottles, even if some of the details were not readily apparent," Holmes said to me as we sat in our rooms in Baker-street a few days later.

" Not to me," I confessed.

" At the time, I remarked on the significance of those bottles, did I not ? It was obvious that there was a group of men, almost certainly engaged in some clandestine activity, who met in order to exchange some kind of goods of such a value to make it worthwhile their doing so. You yourself suggested several items that might form the subject of such transactions. We rejected the romantic notions of pearls or other jewels, given their relative rarity in that area. Had the location being closer to London or some other major metropolis, I might have given more credence to that theory, but in a remote rustic area it was somewhat inconceivable that this would be the case."

" I follow you so far," I replied. " So much is logical."

" We had already determined, had we not, that the items so exchanged would be small and valuable, ruling out the possibility of their being more conventional contraband. I confess that I was somewhat at a loss to determine the exact nature of these goods until I suddenly recollected Sir Roderick's skill in the field of chemistry. What, I then asked myself, could be the result of Sir Roderick's efforts in that field ? It did not take me long to determine that the answer was probably some kind of narcotic drug. The exact nature of such a drug, until we actually visited Sir Roderick, and you supplied me with the article in your medical journal dealing with the same, escaped me."

" You had already linked this mysterious nocturnal gathering with Sir Roderick, then ? " I asked him.

" I could see no other way in which Sir Roderick could be acquiring his income. I had already examined the relevant records of the Stock Exchange, and the Prime Minister had already given me authority to search through the records of his bankers, in which I discovered nothing untoward. It was obvious that any source of his wealth was being derived through cash transactions, rather than any financial manipulations on paper. This argued that the transactions were being carried out between him and a lower class of person, rather than between him and his peers. The combination of the expensive cigar end and the common beer bottles we discovered in the orchard also supported this theory."

" I do not follow your reasoning here, Holmes," I exclaimed. " You clearly remarked to me on that occasion that the smoker of that cigar was missing a prominent tooth, a right incisor if I recall correctly, and I clearly observed that Sir Roderick was in possession of all his teeth, at least those at the front of his mouth."

Holmes smiled at me. " Your memory is not at fault. Have you never heard of dentures ? "

" Of course," I replied, " but what reason could ever convince you that Sir Roderick's teeth were false ? "

" There were two points on that matter that were convincing. The first was Sir Roderick's refusal to sample the apple that I offered him when we visited his house."

" Ah, those apples," I remarked ruefully. " I remember them well."

" On its own, that would have told me nothing, but it provided additional circumstantial evidence that made me suspect Sir Roderick still further. Wearers of false teeth typically are not that desirous of biting into such fruit. The unfortunate accident to your own tooth, Watson, was actually of considerable value to me. While you were having your tooth attended to, I was in the fortunate position of being able to examine the dental records of the patients, unknown to the dentist, and, as I had suspected, Sir Roderick was among their number. From them I was able to confirm positively that Sir Roderick's right incisor was indeed a prosthesis. In addition, as you no doubt remarked for yourself, the chemical stains on the fingers of his right hand told me plainly that he had been engaging in chemical experiments. All circumstantial evidence only, as I am sure you are about to remark, but an additional nail in the coffin of his innocence."

" I begin to understand a little more. But what about the charade with the two Chinamen and the cormorant ? That seemed to me to display, if I may say so, more than a touch of the theatrical."

Holmes shrugged, as if in apology. " Maybe it was," he confessed. " However, it was the best I could devise on the spur of the moment. I had determined that Sir Roderick was using the lighthouse for his own purposes. That fact has since been confirmed, by the way, by Trinity House, whose authorities have interviewed the lighthouse keeper there and ascertained that for several years he had accepted money from Sir Roderick in return for the use of certain buildings there as laboratories for Sir Roderick's chemical work, including the manufacture of the 'Heroin', though he appears to be innocent of any other involvement in the business. He must, however, have had his suspicions about the nocturnal sailings of Sir Roderick's yacht, somewhat aptly named Morpheus."

" Sir Roderick's rent was presumably of sufficient magnitude as to ensure his silence, I take it ? "

" Most probably. I was almost convinced beyond all doubt of this, but required still more evidence with which to provide the Prime Minister, as well as to satisfy my own standards. My goal was to prove, at least to my own satisfaction, that Sir Roderick was engaged in some business at the lighthouse, a place, you will surely admit, where he had no business to be."

" Surely it would have been possible merely to make your own visit and confirm these matters for yourself ? "

" I would have had no right to

enter the premises, and any attempt to force an entry could have rebounded with most unpleasant consequences to the Government if any publicity were to ensue. No, Watson, I had to use some sort of guile in order to establish this fact for myself."

" Such as producing a spectacle of such a nature that sheer curiosity would divert Sir Roderick from whatever he was doing at the time, in order to watch it ? "

" Indeed, Watson. Although such evidence is once again merely circumstantial, the importance of discovering Sir Roderick at the lighthouse dressed in a laboratory coat, in combination with the other clues I discovered, would be sufficiently damning to Sir Roderick's prospects. The appearance of the exotic Chinese fishermen, and their strange method of obtaining the fish from the sea would be, I was sure, of sufficient novelty to draw out not only the lighthouse keeper, but any other inhabitants of the buildings, including Sir Roderick, to observe this strange phenomenon."

I shook my head. " I can see why you did not wish to involve the police," I said, " since an open scandal was to be avoided, but it does seem to me that the use of a trained cormorant in order to flush out your quarry was somewhat excessive in its quaintness."

Holmes chuckled in reply. " You may well be right there. But the results have been highly satisfactory, it must be admitted. As to the events on the final night, I have to confess I was somewhat mistaken in my first assumption of the events that were to transpire."

" I was expecting Sir Roderick to be distributing the 'Heroin' to his crew, and yet we saw none, did we not ? "

" I, too, was expecting the same, and it puzzled me briefly. When Sir Roderick brazenly invited me to search his boat, and I looked into his eyes, it was clear that there was no point in my doing so—there would be nothing to be found."

" What, then ? "

" For reasons best known to Sir Roderick, and the chain of malefactors responsible for the distribution of this foul substance, my surmise, which I have no doubt has been confirmed by Sir Roderick in his interview with the Prime Minister, is that the drug was distributed on the first night to the boatmen, who then received payment for it from those who push the substance into the market, as it were, and then bring the money to Sir Roderick on the following night, presumably retaining some portion of it as payment for their services."

" I can conceive of no other explanation at present."

" Nor I. It would seem to expose Sir Roderick and his confederates to considerable risk of detection, given that they will be busy on two successive nights, but as I remarked earlier, there are no doubt reasons that are unknown to us at present, and quite possibly likely to remain so, as to why Sir Roderick selected this method of operation."

" What will be the future developments in this case ? " I asked.

" As a result of the report that I presented personally to the Prime Minister yesterday evening, we can expect to see the resignation of Sir Roderick Gilbert-Pryor announced in the press either this evening or tomorrow morning. The Prime Minister was instantly convinced of the urgency of the situation and arranged a meeting with Sir Roderick immediately I left Downing-street. Given the delicate state of relations that currently pertains between this kingdom and the Austro-Hungarian Empire, this is without doubt the wisest course of action, as it is essential that Sir Roderick's successor be appointed as soon as possible."

"It seems you have done a great service to the nation," I replied. "Are you not concerned, though, that Sir Roderick will seek some kind of revenge upon you for the harm you have done to his reputation ? "

"I am certain that such will be the case. He has made the acquaintance of one of the confederates of the late Professor James Moriarty, a certain Dr. Juliusz Sommerfeld of the University of Krakow. It is to be feared that the union of two such extraordinarily talented and yet perverted minds may make it inconvenient to stay in London for the next month or so. I therefore propose that we take a true vacation this time, somewhere far from the attentions that are likely to be visited on me by these true gentlemen. Have you anywhere in mind ? You mentioned Deauville, I seem to recall."

"I must confess, Holmes, that I have long desired to see the Great Pyramids of the Pharaohs in Egypt."

"And why should we not do so ? " enquired Holmes in reply.

"The expense, Holmes, the expense," I objected.

He smiled at me. "The Prime Minister was kind enough to offer me some compensation in return for the small service that I rendered to him. Naturally, I declined the honour of appearing as Sir Sherlock Holmes, but he was kind enough to fall in with my suggestion that I be allowed to retain the proceeds of Sir Roderick's enterprises that we collected the other evening. I am happy to say that the amount is quite considerable, and will be sufficient for us to travel to Egypt in the kind of style to which you and I are unfortunately little accustomed. It will make for a pleasant change of air, and I look forward with pleasure to continuing my research on the hidden meanings of some of the hieroglyphic symbols in the temples there that have so far eluded scholars."

⋄═◉═⋄

The singular nature of this story, where Dr. Watson has in this instance failed to protect the identity of the major protagonist by a pseudonym, would seem to indicate that Holmes and Watson indeed feared an attack by Sir Roderick Gilbert-Foyle, possibly with the assistance alluded to by Holmes, and were reserving this account for possible publication in the event of such an outrage. This, of course, is borne out by Dr. Watson's original statement quoted at the beginning of this story, and is given further support by the following written in a different hand on the final page.

"I, Sherlock Holmes, do hereby declare and attest that the account above written by John Watson MD, is a true and accurate description of my doings and associated events in the town of Falmouth, in the County of Cornwall, in July 1897. I hereby give my hand and seal," and then follows an almost illegible signature, of which the first word can be seen to commence with an S,

and the second with an H. There is a witness, with the name printed as " Mrs. M. Hudson", and the occupation given as " householder", and a signature in blue ink, in an obviously feminine hand, below Holmes' signature. The ˙ is given as September 1897, which we may conclude that Watson used some of his time in Egypt to pen this account of his and Holmes' adventure, making a fair copy on his return.

Sherlock Holmes &
The Case of
Colonel
Warburton's
Madness

" I HAVE HARDLY PLAYED THE GAME SINCE MY RETURN FROM INDIA," I
EXCUSED MYSELF. " I FEAR THAT I WILL PROVE A VERY POOR OPPONENT."
" NO MATTER," HE REPLIED. " I AM SURE SOME OF YOUR FORMER SKILL WILL
RETURN ONCE YOU HOLD A CUE IN YOUR HANDS ONCE AGAIN." (PAGE 101)

EDITOR'S NOTES

In The Engineer's Thumb, Dr. Watson refers to one other case that he introduced to Sherlock Holmes, that of Colonel Warburton's madness. This tale is one of those stored in the deed box, and we can only assume that Watson failed to include it in the published stories out of a sense of modesty. In this tale Watson exhibits many of the traits of the great detective, examining evidence and coming to conclusions independently of Holmes. Indeed, Holmes' opinion of Watson's value as an assistant is unequivocally stated here, and this tale, if no other, should give the lie to the idea that Watson was merely the dull foil to Holmes' rapier-like intelligence.

Y friend, the consulting detective Sherlock Holmes, was typically the recipient of direct requests for advice and help, which he provided according to his whims and fancies, usually dependent upon his opinion of whether the case was of sufficient interest to challenge his abilities. On more than one occasion, however, I was the cause of introducing him to a problem. One of these, an account of which I have already given in " The Case of the Engineer's Thumb", was of considerable interest to the authorities, concerning as it did a group of counterfeiters who were undermining the trust that the public places in the currency of this realm. The other case, though of considerable interest to a detective, was of far less concern to the public interest, and concerned Colonel Warburton, the former commander of the regiment in which I had served in my time in India.

The combination of my practice and my marriage had for some time deprived me of the company of Sherlock Holmes, and it appeared that I was settling into a domestic routine which was far removed from the days when he and I had tracked the malefactors of London and brought them to justice. I was more than content with my marriage to Mary, which indeed had brought me all the happiness that I had foreseen when I made my original proposal to her. My practice too, although routine, nonetheless presented enough interest for me to be content with my lot, and not to hanker after the days of excitement in the past.

Since retiring from Army life, I had lost contact with most of my former comrades, so it was with a sense of surprise that I recognised Philip Purcell, whom I had known in Afghanistan as a young captain, when he walked into my consulting room. His complaint was minor—a chill brought on by the sudden change of climate—and I swiftly prescribed him the appropriate medicines before we fell to chatting of old times.

" I would have thought that you would have stayed in the service," said he. " We all imagined that that old ' Death or Glory' Watson was bound for a destiny greater than that of a mere general practitioner, if you will forgive my saying so."

I was flattered by this reminder of my old Army sobriquet—as who could not fail to be ? —but

explained that the wound I had received from an Afghan bullet had
made it more difficult than I had
at first imagined for me to keep up
with the physical demands of army
life. " In any case," I went on, " it
has been my great good fortune to
encounter, and if I may say so, to
have the friendship of one of the
great men of the age, Mr. Sherlock
Holmes."

" I have heard of the fellow," said
Purcell. " I must say, though, that
the accounts I have read make him
sound like some kind of fraudster
or trickster. Of course, one must
always make allowances for the exaggeration of the journalist wallahs
and the fellows who put about those
stories regarding such people. It
would hardly surprise me to learn
that the stories are for the most
part exaggerations, if not outright
fabrications."

Notwithstanding our old acquaintance, I spoke with some heat.
" You do my friend an injustice," I
exclaimed. " And, if I may be so
bold as to say so, you also do me
an injustice. Were it not for my attempts to chronicle the adventures
in which he has been involved, I
venture to suggest that the name of
Sherlock Holmes would be unknown
to the public. He does not seek notoriety or fame—in many cases, he
has given credit to the police where
by far the greater part of the work
in the case has been his. I can assure you in all sincerity that the accounts you have read of his exploits
are nothing more nor less than the
truth."

Purcell had the good grace to look
somewhat abashed and to stammer
an apology. " I confess that I had
never associated the sawbones whom
I knew out East with the ' John
Watson' who was describing Sherlock Holmes. Believe me, my dear
fellow, I had no wish to cast doubts
on your veracity, or the ability of
your friend. Indeed, if he is as remarkable as your accounts make
him out to be, I might even wish to
consult him on a matter close to me.
The problem is, if I may speak totally frankly to you about this, that
I am short of money right now, and
I am not convinced I could afford
the fees that I am sure he charges
for his services."

I laughed. " You do not know
Sherlock Holmes," I replied, still
smiling. " I will not say that he
displays a complete indifference to
money, but it is of less importance
to him than you might perhaps imagine. I have known many cases on
which he has worked for their own
sake, with no thought of reward,
and some which he has taken on for
prominent clients where he has received remuneration which might be
considered exorbitant, considering
the effort involved. If your case is
of interest to him, you might well
expect him to take it up purely as
presenting a challenge to his deduc-
tive abilities."

My friend appeared relieved.
" That is good to hear. And I take
it that he is discreet in his enquiries, and does not publicise matters
that are best kept hidden ? "

I reassured him on that score.
" If you would care to tell me, in
complete confidence of course, of
the general nature of the problem, it
may be that I can give you some indications as to how Sherlock Holmes
will approach your case. Indeed," I
added, not without a touch of pride,
" it may be that some of the methods that he has imparted to me in
the course of our partnership, if I
may term it so, could be applied by
me in order to assist you."

" The matter concerns Alice

Warburton. Maybe you remember her ? ”

“ Indeed I do. You refer to the daughter of the former Colonel of our regiment, do you not ? ”

“ The same. I love her, Watson,” he exclaimed. “ I love her more than life itself, and if that sounds extravagant, believe me I feel it to be true in my innermost heart.”

“ She cannot be more than a child,” I protested.

“ You have been away from the Army for too long,” he smiled. “ Maybe she was a mere child when you left us, but she is now a young woman, 23 years of age.”

“ She was a remarkably beautiful child, I recall.”

“ She has matured into the most beautiful of women,” he replied. “ Not only beautiful in her appearance, but she has the most pure mind imaginable. I am convinced also that she loves me in return.”

I recognised the symptoms of infatuation, not having been immune to the malady myself in the past. Even so, I forbore from smiling, and proceeded to question him further. “ I do not think from what you have told me so far, that you require the services of Sherlock Holmes merely to ensure the success of the upcoming nuptials. There must be some problem preventing the successful completion of your wooing, or you would not be considering the employment of a consulting detective.”

“ I am sorry to say that you are correct.” He sighed deeply, and his head hung on his breast. “ Now that I come to consider it, it may be that a doctor such as yourself will be more use than your friend.” He paused, and I waited for his next words. “ It may not be not so much that there is a problem with Alice herself, as with her father.”

“ The Colonel ? ”

“ That is so. He has given many signs recently when I visited their house that all is not well up here.” He tapped the side of his head significantly.

I was conscious that I was aping many of the mannerisms of my friend, but I sat back in my chair and placed my fingertips together while half closing my eyes. “ Can you be a little more precise as to the symptoms ? ” I asked Purcell.

“ I have been visiting the house for about a year now,” he replied. “ I go there perhaps once or twice in a month, and I stay for one or two nights each time as a guest of the family. For the most part, Colonel Warburton could not be kinder to me than if I was already married to Alice, and his hospitality leaves me in no doubt that I am an approved suitor for her hand. However, commencing about two months ago, there seemed to be a strange change in the Colonel's behaviour.” He paused briefly, and I encouraged him to go on. “ As it happens, Watson, I feel much less restraint in describing these peculiar happenings to you than I would to anyone else, given that you are both an old acquaintance of mine and a medical man.”

“ You intrigue me,” I replied. “ Pray continue.”

“ You must understand,” my friend said to me, “ that the Colonel's wife, that is to say, Alice's mother, passed away some years ago, just before the Colonel's return from India, and the household is accordingly a small one, consisting of the Colonel himself, Alice and two or three servants who live in. They live very quietly in a secluded villa just outside Guildford. I first observed the onset of the Colonel's strange behaviour one morning at breakfast. Alice was suffering from a headache and had elected to remain in her room, so only the Colonel and myself were partaking of the meal. Imagine my surprise, when in the middle of his conversation, the Colonel suddenly broke off in mid-sentence, seizing the boiled egg that he had just started to eat, opened the window, and flung the egg out of the window into the garden with an expression of fury. I was astounded, the more so because he quietly closed the window and returned to the table all smiles, continuing the conversation as if nothing untoward had occurred."

" Most singular," I observed. " This was about two months ago, you say ? " making a note in my memorandum book.

" That is correct, and since then his behaviour seems to have become more and more extreme. Indeed, I fear for his sanity, and hence for the future sanity of my beloved Alice. Though I adore her, I cannot conceive of marriage to someone whose mental state is potentially so precarious. Tell me, Watson," and he leaned forward and almost whispered the next words in a confidential tone, " in your experience as a medical man, is insanity of this kind hereditary ? "

" I hardly consider myself to be an expert in such matters," I replied. " It does appear, however, that disturbances of this kind are often passed from generation to generation. But you have only described one such instance, which might be a trifling matter attendant on some temporary inconvenience. For example, the egg may not have been boiled to his liking and he was suffering, maybe, from the effects of over-indulgence on the previous evening ? I agree with you, however, that his reaction does seem extreme."

" If that were all," replied my friend, " I would not be so concerned, but events of a similar bizarre nature have continued to occur since then. For example, only three weeks ago while I was staying at the house, an event occurred that almost caused me to quit the spot immediately. Indeed, now that I come to reflect on it, I am amazed that I remained as a guest there."

" Pray continue."

" You should understand that the household retires to bed at an early hour—at about 10 o'clock. This is much earlier than my usual time for bed, and accordingly I usually remain awake in my room for several hours, reading, or otherwise occupying my time until I fall asleep. No doubt you, as a fellow old campaigner, pursue similar habits. In any event, it must have been about midnight, and I was wide awake, when I heard an extraordinary noise outside my bed-room door. It sounded like a kind of irregular shuffling, as if someone were dancing or skipping. Naturally, I opened the door and looked out. Imagine my surprise, not to mention my horror, when I beheld the Colonel in his night attire, positively skipping up and down the corridor with a fixed grin on his face. The smile was not one of pleasure, but appeared to me to be that of a maniac. I confess, Watson, I was completely at a loss as to what to do. I had heard something of the strength possessed by lunatics, among whose number I had now no choice but to regard the Colonel, and since I was the only able-bodied man in the house, it did not seem wise to me to involve myself in a physical struggle with him."

" Was he aware that you were observing him ? " I asked.

" Most certainly he was. His

eyes were actually fixed on mine while he was performing these extraordinary movements. For about a minute, I suppose, I was mesmerised by the sight, and I was unable to move from the spot. Eventually, I was able to tear myself away from the horrid spectacle and returned to my room, where I locked the door. I must admit that I was actually worried for the safety of the others in the house, not to mention my own, and I seriously considered raising the alarm and attempting to apprehend and restrain the Colonel. Again, given that I was the only man in the house, this course of action did not seem a wise one to me. I cast around the room for some object I could use as a weapon in self-defence should the Colonel decide to enter the room and attack me."

" You believed that to be a genuine possibility, then ? "

" At the time I did. I was also, as you can readily imagine, afraid for Alice. I stood by the locked door, poker in hand, listening to the strange shuffling sounds as the Colonel continued his exertions. At length, the sounds ceased, and I unlocked my door and stepped out. The Colonel was walking along the corridor back to his own room, seemingly unaware of my presence. Suddenly he appeared to notice me and he turned.

"'Hallo,' he said to me. 'What on earth are you doing with that in your hand ? ', pointing to the poker that I was gripping. 'Come to that, young man, what are you doing out of bed at this time of night ? ' You may well believe that there was no answer that I could give him, especially considering that his face showed absolutely no trace of the exertion that his actions of only a few minutes before must have caused

him. I stammered out some reply of having heard a noise that I believed might have been burglars, upon which he patted me on the shoulder in the most friendly fashion and wished me a good night."

" Is there more ? "

" I am sorry to say that there is. Though the incident of the egg has yet to be repeated, the nocturnal skipping has occurred, to the best of my knowledge, at least twice more."

" To the best of your knowledge ? You cannot be sure ? "

" I felt after the previous occasion that it would not be wise to confront the Colonel while he was in one of these states of mind. Even so, I can positively assert that I have heard the noise of the skipping twice more—both times at midnight."

I pondered this for a few seconds. " And that is all ? "

He sighed. " I would that it were all that I had to say in this regard, but there is more. Yesterday afternoon, I was staying at the Colonel's house. Alice had gone up to Town on some feminine errand, it was the parlour-maid's afternoon off, and the cook had gone to the local shops to order the provisions for that evening's meal. The Colonel and I were alone in the house, and I proposed to write some letters—I am a deucedly poor correspondent, so I felt that this would be an excellent opportunity for me to make amends. The Colonel, for his part, announced that he would take a nap after luncheon, as is his usual habit. I had finished the first letter and had barely started the second, when I heard a noise from the garden, and the sound somehow reminded me of the parade-ground. I may add that the room I occupy while I am a guest there overlooks their garden. Looking out of the window, I observed the Colonel, carrying a broomstick as though it were a rifle, barking out parade-ground drill commands and executing them himself—with some skill, I have to admit. Naturally, I found this disturbing, particularly given the fatuous smile on his face, which gave him an appearance of crude vacancy, a rather different expression from the one which I had observed during his skipping exercises. This last was more maniacal in nature, while on this occasion, the smile had more of idiocy to it. The parade-ground performance must have lasted for somewhere in the region of ten minutes, when the front doorbell rang. I remembered that the servants were absent, and was prepared to let the door go unanswered, lest the caller discover the Colonel in his present condition, when the Colonel himself appeared to hear the sound, and his whole demeanour changed. The rifle on his shoulder reverted to being a broomstick once more, and the vacancy on his face vanished, to be replaced by the usual alert look of intelligence that I am sure you remember well."

" Extraordinary ! " I exclaimed.

" I watched him hurry into the house, and heard the sound of the front door being opened, and the caller admitted. In a minute or so, I heard the Colonel's voice bidding me descend to meet the caller, Chelmy."

" Why would the Colonel desire you to meet this person ? " I inquired.

" Maybe I should have explained to you earlier that this Guy Chelmy is a friend of the family. He has always, as far as I can judge, lived in the area, and is therefore a neighbour of the Colonel. Some time ago, I gather, he was of assistance to the Colonel in some matters concerning his financial affairs—I do not know the details, and I have never asked

for them—in such a way that he acquired and has retained the friendship of the Colonel, and also of Alice. He is in some ways a pleasant enough fellow, if a little strange at times, but is a frequent visitor to the Warburtons and appears to be always welcome there. He and I generally get along well enough, and often play a frame or two of billiards together, at which I confess I almost always lose. He is a player of considerable skill, whatever else he may be."

" Would you regard him as your rival for Alice's hand ? "

Purcell laughed, somewhat unpleasantly. " Hardly a rival, old man. If you had seen the chap, you would not bother asking that question. He is a little shrimp of a fellow. He must be about fifty years old, and looks every minute of it. Without wishing to boast, Watson, I think that if you were laying odds on the matter, I would be an odds-on favourite, and he would be an outsider."

It pained me a little to hear him talk of the state of holy matrimony as if it were a horse race, but determined to hold my peace on that score.

" But there is more," he continued. " I love Alice, and as I told you, I am sure—nay, I am certain—that she loves me. Yet just two days ago, I asked her to marry me."

" And her response ? "

" She told me that she loves me with all her heart, but that she could not marry me. These were her very words on the subject, 'I cannot marry you'. That, and no more."

" You fear that she likewise doubts the mental stability of her father, and wishes to dissuade you from marriage ? "

" It is the only conclusion open to me," he replied. " There was no hint of unfriendliness towards me at the time or afterwards. Her refusal, I am convinced, is not the result of anything I am or that I have done."

" To summarise what you have told me, then." I said, " you have observed Colonel Warburton behaving oddly on at least one occasion, and you fear this behaviour may be the symptom of some kind of derangement. This derangement you fear to be hereditary, and you therefore have concerns—valid ones, I would say at this stage, judging by your account—about marriage to his daughter. His daughter shares these concerns, and has therefore refused your offer of marriage. Does that form an adequate account of the facts ? "

" It would seem to be so. Do you suppose your friend Mr. Holmes will take the case ? "

" I can but ask him," I replied. " Let me have an address where I can reach you, and I will let you know the answer in a few days."

 URCELL'S visit reminded me that I had not called upon Sherlock Holmes in some weeks, and I determined to remedy this omission. Accordingly, the following day saw me mounting the well-known staircase at 221B Baker-street to the rooms formerly shared by Holmes and myself, and now occupied solely by the detective. Mrs. Hudson had given me to understand that Holmes was in residence, but had added that he was " very busy these days".

I was confident, however, that Holmes would welcome my interruption, and my confidence was not misplaced. Holmes opened the door in answer to my knock, and waved me wordlessly to my accustomed armchair.

" Have the goodness, Watson, not to speak a word for a few minutes while I work out the details of this case," he said, but there was that in his face that bespoke some sort of pleasure at the prospect of my company which belied the seeming coldness of his tone.

I silently took my place. After about ten minutes, Holmes made a request of me to verify a biographical detail in " Who's Who", without even deigning to glance in my direction. From any other person, I would have taken this as the height of rudeness, but in the case of Sherlock Holmes I accepted it as a matter of trust in my ability, and I was glad that he continued to regard my assistance to be of value to him in his work.

At length he ceased making notes in his book, and sat back.

" If you would pass me the Persian slipper upon the mantel, I would be grateful." I reached up and handed him the article in question, which was the accustomed, if decidedly eccentric, receptacle for his tobacco. He thanked me and filled his pipe with the coarse shag that he affected, before regarding me quizzically.

" I am delighted for your sake to see that both your marriage and your practice are flourishing," he remarked on an off-hand manner. " Though I must confess to a selfish side of me that regrets the loss of my Watson as a confidant and aide."

" How do you know these things ? " I asked.

" Come, Watson, these are simple matters. Your hat and boots are immaculately maintained, as are all your garments. They are in much better condition, if I may say so, than when you and I shared these rooms. I am sure you have not yet attained the luxury of a personal valet, hence I conclude your wife is ensuring that you are turned out in such splendid style. This, to me, argues a happy marriage."

" I follow you so far. What of the medical practice ? "

" Though your garments are cared for splendidly, they are not in a condition that suggests you sit and wait idly for custom to present itself to you. They bespeak a man of active habits, and given your profession, that would seem to argue a successful practice. There are, of course, other little pointers, such as the stains of iodine on your fingers where you have no injury, and the tell-tale bulge in your hat where you secrete your stethoscope, as I have remarked previously."

I laughed. " I must agree with you on both points regarding my happiness, and congratulate you once again on your perspicacity."

" Quite so, quite so," he replied, and busied himself in lighting his pipe. " And you are here to consult me on some matter on behalf of a friend ? "

" Since I obviously have no troubles of my own, you mean ? " I laughed. " Naturally, you are correct."

" Naturally," he repeated, with a slight smile.

I explained the position of my friend Purcell. During my recounting of the facts, Holmes said nothing, but gazed out of the window, while puffing at his pipe. To those who did not know him, it would appear that he was uninterested in my account, but I knew from experience that he was often at his most attentive under such circumstances. At

length I concluded the tale of Colonel Warburton.

" An excellent summary, Watson. You have a gift on these occasions for presenting the necessary information in an order that makes it easy for me to examine the facts. Would that you exercised the same restraint when chronicling my cases for the benefit of the public," he sighed. " This Colonel Warburton was also your commanding officer in India ? How would you characterise him ? "

" A fair man, well-liked by those he commanded. He had a gift for keeping the regiment contented."

" Any weaknesses that you observed ? " asked Holmes sharply.

" Other than the fact that he drank to excess at times, which was a fault to which the whole regiment, indeed, the whole of the Army at that time in that place, was prone, there is little, except perhaps a fondness for cards."

" Did he play for high stakes ? "

" I was not in those circles," I replied, a little stiffly. " I never heard so, in any event."

" And the daughter ? " asked Holmes.

" She was a mere girl when I left India. She was extraordinarily beautiful as a child, and the pet of the regiment. Other than that, I really cannot furnish any information."

" And your friend Purcell ? "

" A somewhat impetuous young man when I knew him. He seems to have settled down a little since then, but I confess that he was more than a little disrespectful when it came to the subject of marriage."

" And your opinion of Colonel Warburton's madness, if we may term it thus ? "

" 'Madness' may be too strong a term. It is certainly eccentric, to say the least."

" It is very odd," agreed Holmes. " There are several very queer points about it, to me as a layman in these matters, at least."

" Will you help Purcell ? " I asked.

" I will be delighted to give the matter my attention in a few days," he replied. " At the minute, I am engaged in a rather delicate case which involves the Earl of Lincoln and his gamekeeper. Although the case itself is simple, the matter of keeping it confidential is not. After a few days, I am hopeful that I will be able to turn to something more interesting."

" You consider this interesting, then ? "

" Indeed I do. I am of the opinion that there is much more to this case than either you or your friend believe."

" And as for—"

" Ah, the question of money ? I think your friend need lose no sleep on that score. This promises to be one of those cases that brings its own reward."

I refrained from asking questions.

The problem, which at first sight had appeared to be one that had a solution that could be easily determined, seemed to Holmes to have depths unsuspected by me.

" Can your practice and your wife spare you for a few days ? " he inquired of me.

" I can always hand over my practice to Jackson for two or three days, and Mary is able to take care of herself for the same period. Why do you ask ? "

" I am wondering whether you can manage to renew your acquaintance with Colonel Warburton, and arrange to have yourself invited as a guest for a short period, preferably together with Purcell. Regular reports of your observations, addressed to me here at Baker-street, would be most valuable. If you can start today, so much the better."

" That could probably be arranged without too much difficulty. And what of you ? "

" I will make my own plans, and you will be made aware of them, never fear," he replied.

⋅⊷⇒◉⇐⊷⋅

N leaving Baker-street, I hailed a cab and made my way to the address Purcell had given me—a lodging-house in Bloomsbury. He greeted me in the parlour used by the lodgers, and listened to what I had to say.

" I must thank you for this," he said, when I had explained the outcome of my conversation with Holmes. " I feel we can send a wire to the old chap letting him know you are coming and travel down to Guildford without waiting for an answer. He's a perfectly decent old buffer, when he is not suffering from these queer fits. And I remember once how you pulled him through a bout of dysentery when he'd almost given himself up for lost. He'll be delighted to see you again, Doctor, and you would surely like to renew his acquaintance ? " He spoke with the animation I have observed to be common to those of less ripe years when contemplating the meeting of old colleagues.

" Maybe under slightly strained circumstances," I gently reminded him, " after what you have described to me."

" Quite so, but let us send that telegram, and we can be on our way.

I feel that I can speak for the Colonel when I say that you will be welcome in his house."

Nor, in the event, was Purcell's confidence in Colonel Warburton's hospitality misplaced. Having been forewarned of my arrival by the telegram we had dispatched prior to our departure, his welcome was as warm as one could wish for. As he shook my hand with every evidence of friendship, I scanned his face as unobtrusively as possible for signs of the illness that Purcell had described, but was unable to discern any trace of abnormality in his features. He remained a fine figure of a man, tall and powerfully built, and still carried himself with a military bearing. It was not hard to imagine his past as a successful and popular leader of men.

On entering the drawing-room, we were greeted by Alice Warburton, who was acting as our hostess. As Purcell had told me, she had matured into an extraordinarily beautiful young woman, with china-blue eyes set in a face framed by golden hair. I was hardly surprised that Purcell was so strongly attracted to her, based on her appearance, but her conversation seemed to me to be somewhat lacking in vitality and character. I ascribed this, however, to the fact that I was a stranger to her (remembering that she had been a mere girl when I saw her last in India) and her tongue was therefore somewhat constrained by my presence.

The four of us, that is to say, the two Warburtons, Purcell, and myself, took tea, elegantly presided over by Alice. Colonel Warburton proved to be as genial and hospitable as could be desired, and I could detect no trace of the derangement that Purcell had reported to me. The topics ranged from our time together in India to the life of a general practitioner in London. At my earnest request to Purcell, made as we were travelling down on the train, the name of Sherlock Holmes and my association with him were not mentioned.

As we were finishing our repast, the parlourmaid announced the arrival of Mr. Guy Chelmy. I was interested to see the man, given the account I had received of him from Purcell. His appearance as he entered the room was not impressive. Before I started to examine the man himself, I noted the reactions of the others in the room to his arrival—a trick I had observed Holmes use on past occasions.

" You can often learn more about a man, Watson," he had remarked to me once, " by watching those around him than you can by watching the man himself."

Colonel Warburton, I saw, seemed to find Chelmy's presence somewhat objectionable, and though he disguised his feelings well, it was apparent to me, at least, that there was something of disgust in the way he took Chelmy's hand in greeting. His daughter, on the other hand, seemed relatively at ease, though there was something in the way that she regarded the visitor that made me believe that all was not as it appeared at first sight. Although Purcell had denigrated Chelmy as a rival suitor for Miss Warburton's hand when he had described the man, it was plain he considered him as such. A thinly veiled hostility underlay his every move and word directed towards Chelmy, belying his earlier statements to me about their relations.

As to the man himself, it was difficult to make any definite opinion about him. His dress was, if anything, a shade too immaculate and fashionable to be considered in good taste, though there was no one single item that could be judged to be so. His manners were likewise somewhat too formal and elaborate for comfort, but there was nothing on which one could lay one's finger precisely in order to justify such a judgement.

As I was introduced to him, a flicker of recognition seemed to show in his eyes when my name was mentioned, but he made no comment. I did, however, notice him occasionally glancing in my direction throughout the conversation in what might be taken as being a somewhat suspicious manner.

After some small talk, chiefly about the difficulty of cultivating orchids, a hobby apparently shared by both Chelmy and our host, the Colonel announced that Chelmy would be joining us for dinner, which was to be served in a few hours, and the tea-party broke up. Purcell announced that he would take a turn in the garden, and Alice Warburton proclaimed her intention of joining him. The effect of this announcement on Chelmy was pronounced. For a second or two his face contorted in a look of hideous jealousy, which passed as quickly as it had arrived. Indeed, had I not been watching him closely, I would not have been able to swear that anything had occurred. It was obvious that, whatever Purcell may have believed, he was indeed a suitor for the hand of the lovely Alice.

However, Chelmy was all smiles as he turned to me and proposed a game of billiards.

" I have hardly played the game since my return from India," I excused myself. " I fear that I will prove a very poor opponent."

" No matter," he replied. " I am sure some of your former skill will

return once you hold a cue in your hands once again."

As it happens, I had never been a particularly skilful exponent of the game, though I had spent many hours in the Mess hunched over the green baize, but I assented to his importuning.

As we retrieved the cues from the racks in the well-appointed billiard room, Chelmy suggested a wager.

" Shall we say five guineas a hundred ? " he suggested.

" I fear you somewhat overestimate the income of a general practitioner in medicine," I laughed. " If we are to play for money, I would prefer that we play for somewhat lower stakes."

" Ah," he replied, his eyes twinkling. " I had assumed that the chronicler of so many interesting adventures would have received suitable compensation for his labours. My apologies for that mistaken assumption." So saying, he sketched a sort of half-bow, somewhat un-English in its execution. It was obvious, therefore, that he was aware of my association with Holmes.

We agreed on the terms on which we would play, and the game began. As Chelmy had predicted, some of my original skill with the cue returned, but even had I played with the full dexterity of which I had been capable in my younger days, it was clear that I could never have been a match for my opponent, who was a master of the table. Throughout the game, he persisted in making oblique allusions to my friendship with Sherlock Holmes, but I refused to enlarge on the subject. My feelings were that this strange affair of Colonel Warburton's behaviour was in some way connected with this man, and I had no wish to vouchsafe to him more than was necessary in order to maintain a semblance of politeness.

At the end of the third frame, which ended as disastrously for me as had the previous two, I called a halt to the game.

" No matter," he replied, pocketing the modest winnings that I had handed to him. " I trust that the game was not too painful for you," he said, with a smile that had more of cruelty than humour to it.

" Not at all," I replied. I fear my own answering smile was rather forced, not so much at the financial loss I had just incurred, which I could easily afford, but at the insolence of the man, which had expressed itself in many little ways as we had played our game. It is not often that I take a dislike to a man after so short an acquaintance, but there was something about Chelmy that I found distasteful, but whether it was his heavily pomaded hair, or his patent-leather pumps, or indeed, a combination of these and other factors, I was unable to decide. I found it strange, however, that such a man should apparently be an intimate of the Colonel, who was of quite a different calibre.

We parted, I to dress for dinner, and he to the drawing-room where, I have no doubt, he hoped to encounter Alice alone, since we came across Purcell on his way to his room, on the same errand as myself.

I changed quickly, providing myself with sufficient time to write a few lines to Holmes concerning the events of the afternoon, and my impressions of the protagonists in the piece, which I slipped, together with a florin, to the house-maid as we went into dinner, with the request that she post it as soon as was convenient.

Dinner consisted of a delicious mutton curry, of which the three Indian veterans partook with gusto, recalling similar dishes that had been served in Messes in the past as they did so. I noticed that Miss Warburton appeared not to care for the dish, but that Chelmy ate as heartily as the Colonel, Purcell and myself, notwithstanding his lack of an Indian background.

The atmosphere round the table was charged. Chelmy definitely appeared as the odd man out, not merely on account of the fact that he was the only one never to have lived in the East, but because the other members of the party seemed to be bearing some sort of animosity towards him. On Purcell's part, this could well have been the jealousy I had noticed earlier, and Alice Warburton's mysterious attitude still apparently prevailed. I have already spoken of my own feelings, and Colonel Warburton, though remaining perfectly civil, nonetheless managed to convey a sense of displeasure at sitting at the same table as Chelmy. The man himself behaved as if he were unaware of the others' attitudes towards him, and remained unconcerned, continuing to laugh and tell stories, some of which in my opinion verged on being unsuitable for the ears of young ladies.

Since Miss Warburton was the only lady, and she declared herself to be immune to the effects of cigar smoke, the whole party rose and proceeded to the drawing room, where the male members of the party enjoyed some fine cigars provided by the host while sipping a fine crusted port that the Colonel had decanted in honour of his guests. I noticed that the Colonel limited his intake of this noble liquor to a single glass. Alice Warburton provided us with entertainment in the form of a recital of songs, accompanying herself on the pianoforte. To my mind, the choice of material was somewhat on the sentimental side, but it evidently met with the approval of the rival suitors (for so I felt I must now regard them) as well as that of the fond parent, who beat time with his cigar. I continued to observe him, but could see nothing out of the ordinary that could account for the strange behaviour of which I had been informed.

The music put an effective brake on any conversation, which may have been all to the good, given the potentially stormy atmosphere that had been building up during the meal, and very soon after the last song, Chelmy rose from his seat and with one of his over-courtly bows, announced his intention to quit our company. Wishing him a good night and a safe return to his own house, the Colonel saw him to the door, and then returned to us.

" I must retire to bed, Papa," Miss Warburton said to him. " I am sure that you three Indians have much to talk about. Please do not keep him up too long, Mr. Purcell and Dr. Watson. I know how you men can be when you start on your memories." She smiled a smile that would have melted the heart of a statue, and Purcell wilted visibly under its force. " Good night to you all."

As she had predicted, the talk soon turned to our Indian adventures, and talk of comrades, some still alive, and some, sadly, now gone before. Purcell had been applying himself to the port, which, truth to tell, was of a fine quality, and it was this, I fear, that led him to his next unfortunate observation.

" But of all the acquaintances that we have made over the years, I venture to suggest that the doctor here has the most interesting friendship of any man in this room," he remarked to the Colonel, who said nothing, but merely raised his eyebrows in response.

I looked at Purcell and silently mouthed a command to him to cease, but he appeared blind and deaf to all such hints.

" Yes, our old sawbones is the John Watson who writes about the celebrated bloodhound in human form, his good friend Mr. Sherlock Holmes."

The effect on the older man was dramatic. He turned to me and glared furiously. " Upon my word, sir ! I had no idea that you were some sort of police spy. Were it not for the lateness of the hour, and the comradeship of the Regiment, I would have no hesitation, sir, in turning you out of doors this instant. No hesitation, sir ! " he repeated. There was certainly anger in his face, and I imagined also that I detected more than a trace of fear.

I started to stammer some excuse. " Sir, my friend Sherlock Holmes is far from being a police spy. It is true that he has worked with the police on occasion, but he has never taken money from the police for his services, and far from being a spy, he is one of the most honest and law-abiding persons of my acquaintance." I was obliged to stretch the truth a little in my last utterance, as Holmes and I had been compelled to step outside the strict bounds of the law of the land on a number of occasions, but always in the interests of a higher Law.

" Hmph," was the only answer I received, but it was followed by a long silence, during which the Colonel appeared to be lost in thought. Eventually he came out with, " I know you of old, Watson, and know that you are a good man. If you give me your word that Holmes is no spy, of course I will take your word for it."

" I give you my word that Sherlock Holmes is no spy, but is, on the contrary, one of the greatest and noblest men it has been my privilege of meeting."

" That's good enough for me," replied the old soldier, extending his hand to me in a fraternal gesture. " My apologies for the outburst, but you must admit," he chuckled, " that it is something of a surprise to me to discover such a connection so close at hand. Please forgive any harsh words I may have spoken just now to you."

There was now nothing untoward in his appearance or his manner, and I was reminded of the sudden changes in mood that had been described to me by Purcell. " Think nothing of it, Colonel. Such news is always a surprise, even to those with nothing to hide."

" Indeed so," replied the Colonel, and busied himself with relighting his cigar, which had extinguished itself through being left unattended during the recent exchange.

The incident had nonetheless cast somewhat of a shadow over the previously convivial evening, and soon afterwards, Purcell and I both proposed retiring for the night.

" I will stay up for a while longer," said the Colonel. " At my age, you no longer need the sleep to which you were accustomed when younger."

We bade him good night, and proceeded up the stairs. As I was about to enter my room, Purcell tapped me on the arm and gripped my sleeve fast. " I say, old man," he said to me. The effects of the port on his speech were still obvious. " dreadfully sorry and all that about mentioning your friend. I had no idea it would take the old man that way."

" No lasting harm done, I believe," I replied. " But it is somewhat strange that it should affect him in that fashion."

" Good night, then," he replied, releasing my arm from his grasp.

I wished him a good night and retired to my room. I determined to keep as accurate a record as possible of the events in order to aid Holmes when he arrived. Certainly the sudden flush of anger, together with the fear that I fancied was present at the mention of Holmes' name gave me pause for considerable thought. It was hard to conceive of any reason why my connection with such a well-known defender of justice should provoke such a reaction, other than in an evil-doer, and it was hard for me to cast the Colonel in such a role.

If it had been Chelmy who had exhibited such a reaction, it would have been more comprehensible to me, given what I had seen of the man, but on the contrary, Chelmy had not seemed to shy away from the subject, but had rather appeared anxious to engage me in conversation about Sherlock Holmes.

I changed into my night attire, and threw my dressing gown, a fine garment adorned with bright Oriental dragons and other decorations, a present from my dear wife, around me as I sat at the small table in my room to write my account of the events of the evening, and my impressions of them. It did not appear to me that Colonel Warburton was deranged, despite his earlier flash of anger, but the more I considered matters, the more it appeared to me that there was something strangely unhealthy in the relationship between Chelmy and the Warburton household. As I was pondering the reasons for my suspicions which, if I were honest with myself, were based on little more than my personal dislike of the man, I heard a strange shuffling sound in the passageway outside my room. Almost certainly, I felt, this was the strange skipping that Purcell had described to me.

Unlike Purcell, I felt myself up to the task of confronting the Colonel unarmed, and I accordingly opened my bed-room door and stepped out into the passageway. As my friend had described to me, Colonel Warburton, clad in a maroon silk dressing gown, was positively skipping down the passageway, with his back towards me. I moved to the middle of the passage and waited for him to reach the end and turn round.

However, some five yards before the end of the passage, he whirled round abruptly, a wide and somewhat aimless grin covering his face. As he bent his legs, presumably to resume his exercise, I rushed forward and laid a hand on his shoulder.

" Colonel," I said. " Is it not time that you retired to your bed ? " I spoke in a calm quiet voice, though I was somewhat horrified by what I had just witnessed. However, at the first touch of my hand on his shoulder, he seemed to relax. The tenseness of his muscles visibly departed, and the expression on his face returned to normality.

" Watson, I thank you," he said to me in a perfectly calm voice. " I believe I was having one of my nightmares. They come on me from time to time, and I have found myself in very strange situations, having been sleepwalking while being visited by these nocturnal visions."

" If I were your doctor," I replied, " I would prescribe a mild sedative to be taken before retiring. I am confident you would not suffer in this way if you were to drink chloral or some such before going to bed. May I, as a friend, suggest that you consult your usual physician on the matter at an early opportunity ? "

He smiled at me. " Most thoughtful of you, Doctor. I shall do as you suggest tomorrow morning. A very good night to you and my profound thanks and apologies for having disturbed you in this way."

" And a very good night to you," I replied, returning to my room. I recorded the last events while they were still fresh in my mind, adding them as a postscript to my previous writing. Somehow the Colonel's story of nightmares did not ring altogether true. The look on his face had not been one of a somnambulist, and I had never experienced, or heard described in the literature, such a skipping action performed by a sleepwalker. Nor, despite what had been said to me, could I agree with the diagnosis of mental derangement, tempting as it might be as an explanation of the Colonel's extraordinary conduct. More puzzling still, I could not account for the fact that the Colonel was able to sense my presence while his back was turned to me. I had been wearing soft slippers on a carpet, and I had taken great care to make my movements as silent and unobtrusive as possible. After finishing my report, I extinguished the gas, and composed myself for sleep, but lay awake listening for further sounds. After what was probably about an hour of lying awake I had heard nothing, and eventually entered the land of dreams.

HE next morning saw me awake bright and early. The events of the previous evening now seemed like a nocturnal fancy, but I had my written account to convince me of their reality.

Breakfast was a cheery meal. The Colonel and his daughter were both in high spirits, and Purcell seemed to have been infected by their gaiety. There was no sign by the Colonel that last night's events had in any way affected him, until he reached the end of the meal, and threw down his napkin with a satisfied sigh, declaring to Miss Warburton, " I will be going to Dr. Henderson this morning, my dear, but will return in time for luncheon."

" Is anything wrong, Papa ? " she asked, with a note of tender concern.

" By no means, my dear. It is merely that I have had a little trouble sleeping recently, and it occurs to me that chloral drops might be of benefit to me." He turned to me and winked deliberately, but in such a way that I was the only one to observe the gesture.

" Very good, Papa. I shall go to the kitchen now, and give Cook her orders for luncheon ? "

" Yes, yes, my dear. Please do that."

" Excuse me, gentlemen." And with a charming smile bestowed on all of us, Alice Warburton left the room.

" Doctor," the Colonel addressed me. " It is not my place to tell you what to do with your time while you are visiting, but I would strongly recommend that you walk to the top of the rise and admire the view of the town from there. It is very fine. I am sure that young Purcell will be happy to set you on the right path."

" I will do more than that,"

Purcell readily assented. " I am in the mood for some exercise myself, and I will be happy to walk all the way with you."

" Very good," beamed the Colonel. " Please ensure you return in time for luncheon. I am afraid our cook becomes a trifle autocratic at times, and she tends to exercise her dictatorial nature if we are late for our meals."

About thirty minutes later, Purcell and I were walking through the woods at the back of the house. It was a splendid autumn morning, of the kind only experienced in England. I swung my stick with abandon as I strode along the path, glad to be free of the confines of London for a few days.

Purcell burst upon my peaceful musings with, " I heard the old man again last night."

" So did I. I confronted him, and caused him to return to his bed. He explained that he had been suffering from bad dreams, and was sleepwalking. I advised him to seek the advice of his doctor, and told him that I would prescribe chloral in such a case."

" Hence the visit to the doctor this morning ? " asked Purcell. I nodded in reply. " And do you believe that he is indeed suffering from these bad dreams ? "

" I confess I have my doubts, but this did not appear as derangement or insanity to me."

My companion let out a sigh of relief. " That is good news," he exclaimed. " But there is still the matter of the egg that I described to you, and also of the parade-ground antics."

" I had not forgotten those, and of course, they would hardly be connected with the dreams. As matters stand, I am unable to form any opinion on those incidents."

We walked on a little further, and Purcell asked me abruptly, " I wonder when your friend Holmes is going to arrive ? I rather fear for his reception when he makes himself known."

" He can be a master of tact, never fear."

The view from the top of the rise, when we reached it, was indeed magnificent. Surrey does not contain the most dramatic landscapes of our isles, but it has its own charms. We admired the vista in silence for a few minutes, and then by common accord turned to retrace our steps.

We entered the grounds of Colonel Warburton's house through the back entrance. As we were closing the gate, Purcell gave a cry.

" Hey there ! Who's that ? Stop there, my man ! "

I caught a glimpse of a ragged grey coat disappearing behind a herbaceous border. " Stop ! " I echoed, brandishing my stick.

We caught up with the tramp without over-much exertion. He proved to be a tall man, but put up no resistance as Purcell and I laid hold of him.

" Beggin' your pardon, sirs, but I was told to be here."

" Told ? By whom ? " I asked, relaxing my grip on the rogue's collar.

" By the gardener, sir. I'm just an old soldier workin' my passage, as you might put it, doing odd jobs here and there to earn a few coppers."

" And Colonel Warburton's gardener said you could work here ? "

" That's right, sir. He told me to be weeding this flower-bed here." And indeed, the flower-bed to which he pointed did seem to have been attended to recently, and there was a gardening-basket with weeds in it.

" Very good, my man," said Purcell sternly. " But you may be certain that I will be checking your story with the gardener. If I find that you have not been telling us the truth, be sure that I will come back and have you put in charge."

" I have no fear of that, sir," replied the other, touching his greasy cap. " You may ask all you want, and you'll find that I'm in the clear."

" What a villainous-looking rogue," I exclaimed to Purcell as we made our way in search of the gardener.

" Indeed he is. I'll wager he hasn't seen a bath this year, and criminality is written all over his face. It's not my place to interfere with another man's servants, but I am strongly tempted to question the judgement displayed here. Ah, here we are."

I addressed the gardener. " My good man," I began, " we recently encountered some sort of tramp in the garden who is currently employed in weeding the flower-bed by the walled garden. He told us that you had hired him. Would you care to confirm his story ? "

The countryman smiled at me. " Why, bless you, sir, that's the truth. He came to me this morning and said he was an old soldier willing to do an honest day's work for an honest day's pay, so my back being not as young as it was, and the weeds coming up as they do, I thought it was to both our advantage, if you take my meaning, sir."

" Do you often do this sort of thing ? " asked Purcell.

" Many a time," replied the gardener. " The Colonel's a good master and pays me well enough that I can spare a few coppers now and then. I used to serve under him in India, you know, and he's good to us who used to be in the Regiment.

And when I see these younger fellows like the one over there who'd also taken the Queen's shilling in his time, and can't get no steady work, I says to myself 'Edward Soxworth, that could have been you, if the Colonel hadn't given you this job'. So yes, I helps those who's willing to help themselves like the one over there. How was he getting on ? "

" I'm no expert in these matters," I replied, " but he appeared to be doing an adequate job."

" Well, that's all right then, isn't it, sir ? No harm done, no bones broken. And now, sirs, if you'll excuse me, I have a line of beets to be thinning out." He picked up the handles of his wheelbarrow and moved in the direction of the vegetable garden.

" He may be a poor judge of character," I remarked to Purcell, " but his heart is certainly in the right place."

HE rest of the day passed without incident until about four o'clock, when Purcell and I returned to the house, and joined Miss Warburton for tea in the drawing-room. The Colonel had failed to join us in another walk around the district, though we had enjoyed luncheon together, and he had afterwards told us that he proposed to take a post-prandial nap in his study.

" Maybe I should go and fetch him ? " I suggested.

" If you would be so kind, Doctor," Miss Warburton replied. " In the meantime, I will pour your tea."

I knocked on the study door, but there was no answer. I gingerly opened the door, but the Colonel was nowhere to be seen. An account-book lay on the desk, together with a whisky decanter, a soda syphon, and two glasses, both of which appeared to have been used. A search of the other downstairs rooms failed to discover any trace of the Colonel. I returned to the drawing-room to inform the others of my fruitless quest.

" Maybe you should see if he is in one of the upstairs rooms, Miss Warburton," I suggested. " And in the meantime, maybe Mr. Purcell and I should search the garden. If he is not upstairs, your father has probably fallen asleep in the arbour, and needs to be woken."

Purcell and I left our tea and went outside. As we rounded the yew hedge, we saw the yokel who had been hired by the gardener stooping over the Colonel, who was sitting slumped on the garden-seat in the arbour.

" How the devil did you know he would be here ? " Purcell asked me, as we started forward to the scene.

" It was pure supposition on my part," I replied. " Stop where you are ! " I called to the vagabond. " Do not move, or I fire."

" Do you carry a pistol ? " asked Purcell.

" No," I replied in a low voice, " but it will be better if he believes that I do."

The tramp made no attempt to move away, but stood up, and slowly raised his arms, showing that he was unarmed.

" Do not move," I repeated, " or it will be the worse for you." I moved behind the tramp and jabbed my forefinger into the small of his back. Purcell bent over the supine body of the Colonel.

" There's blood here," he exclaimed, looking at the Colonel's head. " This ruffian has obviously made a murderous assault upon our host and was presumably in the act of looting his pockets when we came upon him. I am going to the house to alert the servants and will return directly."

" Is he dead ? " I asked. " I cannot see from here."

" No, but he is obviously the victim of a vicious assault," replied Purcell. So saying, he started back to the house.

My Hippocratic instincts overcame me. " I am going to attend to the injured man," I told my prisoner. " I would strongly advise you not to escape, or to make any movement." I bent over Colonel Warburton's unconscious body.

" You need have no fear that I will attack you, Watson." Sherlock Holmes' voice came from behind me, and I spun round. The vagabond was standing tall, and I now recognised my friend under the grime and the shabby rags. He smiled broadly.

" Holmes ! How long have you been here ? " Though by this time I should have become accustomed to Holmes' mastery in the art of disguise, it was still a matter of astonishment to me that he could so completely throw off his true character and assume a new one so perfectly as this.

" Since this morning, as I explained to you and your friend earlier when you asked me, not knowing that you were addressing me. I must confess," he chuckled, " the two of you appeared to be adequately menacing in your attitudes towards any ne'er-do-well who crossed your path. I quite feared for my safety until I recalled that your Army revolver was safely lodged with me at Baker-street."

" And what are you doing here ? " I asked, now having somewhat recovered from my surprise in seeing my friend in this unfamiliar garb.

" The same as you, Watson. Investigating the causes of Colonel Warburton's supposed madness. I merely chose a different path to follow."

" Indeed you did," I replied, smiling. " But what of the Colonel ? I find it hard to believe that it was you who attacked him and struck him down in this way."

" Naturally I did nothing of the kind. No-one attacked him. See here." He pointed to a stone by the side of the path with fresh blood staining it. " I call you to witness that this stone is in its original position, and has not been moved recently."

I bent down and examined the stone and the surrounding mould. " I agree with you. But in that case, how—?"

" He was walking and fell, striking his head against the stone. It is as simple as that. I had almost completed my honest labours of the day," he smiled, " and was passing when I observed the accident. My first instinct was to render assistance, and I was just helping the Colonel to a more seemly and comfortable position on the seat, when you and your friend appeared on the scene."

" It appeared to me," I said, " that you were also examining the contents of the Colonel's pockets."

Holmes shrugged in reply. " Maybe that was the case," he admitted. " Today has been an interesting day, and I have learned many things. But maybe you had better attend to your patient ? "

" I had almost forgotten." I bent to the prostrate figure and listened to the breathing and heartbeat. " He is unconscious, and breathing steadily. I anticipate no danger, though he should be moved inside the house. But what am I to do with you, Holmes ? "

" How do you mean ? "

" I was left in charge of a dangerous ruffian who has attempted to murder the master of the house. Purcell will arrive to find me in conversation with my colleague and friend. How am I to explain this ? "

" That is easy. You simply point out the stone and the facts of the matter as I have laid them out to you. That should be sufficient to convince even him of my innocence. I, naturally, will remain mute, as befits one of my class, and I will assist in bearing the patient to his house. Then, having received my wages for my day's toil from the good Soxworth, I will depart and make my way to the inn where I will revert to being the more familiar Sherlock Holmes of old."

" That seems to be the wisest move," I replied. On Purcell's return, I explained matters in the manner that Holmes had suggested, and Purcell accepted this account of events readily, as indeed any rational man was bound to do. Holmes and Purcell carried the unconscious Warburton into the house, where Holmes, touching his forelock in the manner of the yokel whose character he had assumed, left us.

Miss Warburton shrieked a little at the sight of her father, whom we had deposited in an armchair, but I sent her out of the room in search of hot water and bandages.

" A bad business," said Purcell. " Do you think he had a queer turn, perhaps not unconnected with those strange fits of behaviour that have been observed in the past ? "

" He may simply have slipped or tripped," I pointed out. " I noticed that part of the path is a little uneven, and the ground is a little muddy at that particular point."

" I wish your friend Holmes were with us now," exclaimed Purcell. " From your accounts, he would be able to take one look at the scene and tell us at a glance what had happened."

" He is not a magician," I laughed. " But he certainly has an amazing faculty for deducing the truth from the most mundane and commonplace of details."

Alice Warburton re-entered the room, together with one of the maids, bearing a tray on which was a basin of hot water, and some cloths to be employed as bandages. I attended to the Colonel, and was relieved to see that his wound was not at all serious, though it had bled profusely. " Do you have some iodine in the house ? " I asked Miss Warburton. " I was not expecting to be acting in my medical capacity, and I have no supplies to hand."

" He will recover ? " she asked me anxiously.

" I have every confidence he will do so. He has suffered a fall, and has lost consciousness as a result, but his wound, though it has bled freely, as is the nature of such injuries, is superficial." As I spoke, my patient stirred slightly and groaned a little. " See, he is not so badly injured after all," I smiled at her.

" I will help you find the iodine," Purcell offered. " I seem to remember seeing it on a high shelf and I am sure I can reach it easily." They left the room together, and I continued to examine my patient. I was, perhaps, not quite as sanguine as I had appeared in front of Miss

Warburton, being aware that injuries of the type suffered by Colonel Warburton can sometimes result in temporary, or in the worst case, permanent impairment of the patient's mental faculties, but in this case I was reasonably certain that the injury was not so severe as to produce such a result.

In a few minutes, the iodine was brought in by Miss Warburton, and the wound now having been thoroughly cleaned, I applied the iodine and bandaged the Colonel's head.

" I would suggest leaving him on this couch," I suggested, " and moving him as little as possible for the next few hours before transporting him to his bed upstairs."

" I will instruct Mary to make up his bed, in that case, to be ready for him," said Alice Warburton.

I looked at her in some surprise. " Surely the bed has been made up already ? " I asked. " Mine was, at any rate, when I went to my room after lunch."

" For some reason Papa's bed appeared to be unmade, or at least in disarray, when I went upstairs to search for him. Mary is positive that she made all the beds this morning, though."

" He told us that he was going to take a nap after lunch," Purcell reminded us.

" So he did, but he said he would rest in the study," I pointed out. " Did he make a habit of sleeping upstairs in the daytime ? " I asked Miss Warburton.

" No, he never did so," she replied.

I pondered this. After luncheon, the Colonel had obviously enjoyed a somewhat varied afternoon. If the evidence of the glasses on his desk was to be believed, he had also entertained a visitor in his study, as well as sleeping upstairs and walking in the garden. " Were there any visitors to the house this afternoon ? " I asked her.

" I did not hear the doorbell," she answered. " And I was in this room almost the whole afternoon." She looked away as she said this, almost as if she had made a confession, but I was unable to fix any reason of this in my mind.

However, even as she spoke, we heard the sound of the doorbell, almost as if to prove to us that if the bell had indeed rung, Alice Warburton would have heard it clearly.

The parlourmaid entered, and announced, " A Mr. Sherlock Holmes, madam. Will you be at home to him ? " I confess I started to breathe a little easier on learning that my friend's powers of reasoning would be brought to bear on the case.

" Why yes, of course, Mary."

The maid remained in the doorway.

" Well, what are you waiting for ? "

" I was wondering, madam, if you wanted me to show him into this room, what with the master laid out there like that ? "

" Please show him in here." Her face was set, and a red spot appeared on each cheek as she displayed as much animation as I had hereto seen in her.

" Very good, madam." After about half a minute, Sherlock Holmes was ushered in, clad in his usual London attire. At times like this, Holmes displayed the most exquisite manners, and observing him, one would have thought him to be one of the wealthy idlers-about-town that have so recently been prevalent in the fashionable districts of the metropolis. He introduced himself to Alice Warburton as if she were a princess, taking her hand and kissing it in a fashion that I had never seen him display before.

"But what is here?" he asked, pointing to the prostrate figure of Colonel Warburton.

I noticed Purcell eyeing Holmes curiously and shrugging his shoulders in a sort of puzzlement. "I am sure I have seen the fellow somewhere before," he whispered to me out of the side of his mouth, "but I'll be dashed if I can think where it is that I have met him."

I turned away to hide my amusement, and went over to Holmes. "The patient you see there is Colonel Warburton, who seems to have suffered a slight accident in the garden. I have just finished attending to his injury, which thankfully appears to be less serious than we had at first feared."

"Can he be safely left in the care of his daughter and your friend, do you think?" Holmes asked me. "I would value a few minutes of your time."

"Certainly." I provided Purcell and Alice Warburton with instructions to call me should they observe certain symptoms, and followed Holmes through the French windows into the garden.

IRST, I must thank you for the excellent report you prepared last night and arranged to have posted to me. It reached me at Baker-street early this morning, and provided me with my ideas of what to expect." Praise of this kind from Holmes was rare, and as such, always welcome to my ears. "If you will tell me what has happened since then, I can likewise inform you of what I have observed."

I informed Holmes of the previous evening's events, as well as those of the day, as observed by myself. He lounged back on the garden-seat, his unlit pipe in his mouth, occasionally interjecting some question.

"You have done good work, Watson," he remarked at the conclusion of my recital. "Your observations certainly provide me with some more definite information on which I may base my deductions. Now I will tell you of my day. I came down from London on an early train, dressed as you see me now, and immediately reserved a room at the local hostelry, where I changed into the character in which you beheld me earlier. Since Colonel Warburton is an ex-military man, I conjectured that he would employ former soldiers as servants, and I accordingly presented myself in the character of one of these when I applied to the gardener for a few coppers in exchange for my services as a labourer. Nor was I disappointed.

"I observed your return from your morning constitutional, as you may doubt recall—no, my dear fellow, there is no need for an apology, as you were only doing what you considered to be your duty as a guest—and I arranged things so that I had a clear view of the Colonel and his guests during luncheon, during which, as you informed me just now, no untoward incidents occurred.

"After luncheon, I managed to find work in a position from which I could observe the study into which the Colonel had retired, though my view was less than perfect, owing to the reflection of the sun on the window. I was, however, able to observe the reception of his visitor—"

I broke into Holmes' account at this point. " What visitor was this ? Miss Warburton informed us that she had not heard the doorbell all afternoon."

" I am sure she did not," he replied. " I would not dream for an instant of doubting her word. The Colonel's visitor entered by the same back gate that you used this morning, and was let into the house by the Colonel through the French windows. The two men sat talking and drinking—I observed a soda syphon and a decanter—you mentioned whisky, did you not, when you gave your account of the search for the Colonel—and appeared to be examining something together that lay on the desk. This was presumably the account book that you discovered there.

After about ten minutes the visitor left—"

" Holmes," I interrupted. " You keep referring to this man without even having bothered to provide me with any description."

" Forgive me, Watson, it had quite slipped my mind to provide you with his identity. The visitor, judging by the description with which you yourself have furnished me, can be none other than your opponent at billiards, Mr. Guy Chelmy. As I was saying, he let himself out of the house in the same way that he entered, and entered the drawing-room, again from the garden."

" But Miss Warburton was in there. Surely she would have noticed his entrance ? "

" Has she denied his presence ? Think, Watson."

" True, she only admitted to not having heard the doorbell. That is deucedly subtle, Holmes."

" To my mind, the whole affair is deucedly subtle. Chelmy appeared to remain in the drawing-room for about ten minutes. I fancied I heard raised voices, but was in no position to move closer without being observed. After he left the drawing-room via the French windows, Chelmy departed the garden by the route by which he had come. While he was in the drawing-room, I had been observing the Colonel seated at the desk, unmoving, with his head in his hands. At this point, I was unsure of his state of health, and I was on the verge of summoning assistance, when he roused himself, and stood up, and left the room, with a somewhat unsteady gait. Tell me, Watson, did he indulge at luncheon ? "

" Not at all. Water was the only drink served at the meal, and I will swear he was not in liquor at that time. Indeed, he has become markedly more abstemious since I knew him in India."

" Indeed ? Since I saw the Colonel take only the one glass of whisky and soda, we must search elsewhere for the cause of his unsteadiness. After he had left the room, I saw him appear at that window there," pointing, " and shortly afterwards at that one there," pointing to the next window. We will examine the lie of the land up there in a little while, but for now, can you recall the location of those windows ? "

" Yes indeed. The first is of the corridor connecting all the bedrooms on this side of the house, and the other is either Colonel Warburton's bed-room or dressing-room— at least the room forms part of his private apartments."

" He passed out of view for about twenty minutes, and I returned to my work among the lupins, while still keeping a watch on the house as best I could. He appeared at the two upstairs windows again, and passed out of sight until he re-appeared in the study. He bent over the desk, and looked at the account-book (or so I suppose) again. Having done that, he passed a hand over his face, and stepped out into the garden with a look of what appeared to be extreme anguish or sorrow. I followed him as unobtrusively as possible, when I observed him stumble and fall. I rushed to his aid, and was then discovered by you and your friend as I was attempting to dispose him in a more comfortable and decorous attitude."

" You also appeared to be searching his pockets when we came across you. What were you hoping to find ? "

In response, Holmes pulled a small blue glass bottle from his pocket, holding it with his handkerchief.

" Poison ? " I asked, with a thrill of horror.

" Nothing so dramatic," Holmes smiled at me in return. " I had observed this on the desk after the Colonel had made his way upstairs, and it was not there when he came into the garden. The conclusion, therefore, was that he had picked it up on his return to the study, and it was therefore on his person. I felt it might provide a clue."

" And does it ? " Holmes unstoppered the bottle and held it out to me to examine. I sniffed judiciously. " Chloral," I confirmed.

" Exactly," replied my friend. " Just as he told you. See here." He once again held out the bottle for my inspection, and I perceived a label, from which I read the name of Colonel Warburton over the name of a Guildford chemist's, with directions for its use.

" So you feel that the Colonel dosed himself with chloral, and this unaccustomed drug produced a feeling of fatigue, causing him to rest upstairs on his bed, thereby causing the disarray that Miss Warburton discovered. Following this, he felt the need for fresh air, and made his way downstairs, and came out into the garden ? " I asked.

" Excellent, Watson. I suspect you have made only one error in your analysis."

" That being ? "

" That Colonel Warburton did not dose himself with chloral."

" I am puzzled," I admitted.

" And so am I," he replied. " But not about that aspect of the affair. Come, I wish you to show me the spot where you observed the Colonel's eccentric behaviour for yourself last night. Let us enter by the study. That will also provide us with an opportunity to examine the room before some over-officious servant arrives to clear away the débris, and will also allow the young couple to continue their conversation undisturbed."

" I had not thought you such a proponent of romance, Holmes."

He said nothing, but smiled enigmatically in reply, leading the way through the French windows to the study, where his first action was to bend over the two whisky glasses on the table. " Ha ! " he exclaimed. " As I suspected. See—or rather, smell for yourself, Doctor. Have the goodness to avoid touching the glasses."

I bent over. " Yes," I confirmed. " One of these contained chloral, without a doubt."

" And I am certain that the one containing the drug was Colonel Warburton's. Let us confirm this. Be so kind as to assist me in this." He pulled from his pocket a small insufflator containing a fine powder, with which he proceeded to coat the whisky decanter. " Only the Colonel touched this while I was observing the two men, I will swear to the fact. Take it up by the neck using this cloth and hold it to the light, Doctor, while I examine it closely," he commanded. He whipped one of his high-powered jeweller's lenses from his pocket, and screwed it into his eye. " Good, good," he murmured to himself. " Now for the glasses." The process was repeated, Holmes making small sounds of satisfaction as he proceeded. " And now," he said, " for the *pièce de résistance*." He removed the chloral bottle from his pocket with the aid of his handkerchief, and let out a sound of satisfaction as he examined its dusted surface. " We have him, Watson, we have him ! " His eyes shone with the thrill of the chase.

" Let me see if I can follow your reasoning, Holmes. You know that the Colonel was the only one to handle the decanter, so you are sure of the pattern of his fingerprints. You are sure that only one glass contained chloral, and that was the Colonel's, so the fingerprints on the other are those of Chelmy. You have discovered Chelmy's fingerprints on the chloral bottle, as well as those of the Colonel, no doubt, so you have good reason to believe that Chelmy administered the chloral to Warburton."

" You have followed my reasoning on these points perfectly, Watson. Bravo, indeed."

" And hence when I said earlier that Colonel Warburton had dosed himself with chloral, you corrected me. I take your meaning now."

" Tell me," said Holmes. " Chelmy has never been in India, you say ? "

" That is what Purcell told me, and Chelmy never mentioned India at dinner last night when we three

old campaigners were swapping yarns of old times."

" And have you observed the Colonel's taste in tobacco ? "

" A cigar after dinner last night. That is all."

" So he would be unlikely to smoke one of these ? " He held up the end of a cigarette I instantly recognized as a *beedi*, a native Indian form of cigarette.

" Most unlikely," I replied. " And besides, it would be impossible for the Colonel to have smoked this."

" Why ? " enquired Holmes, his eyes fairly twinkling.

I perceived that this was some sort of test, which I was determined to pass. " The Colonel has a full moustache, as you no doubt observed, and Chelmy is clean-shaven. No man with a moustache could have smoked this cigarette down to this length."

" Excellent, Watson, truly excellent ! And added to the fact that no such cigarettes were to found in the Colonel's pockets, and I see none here in this room, we may conclude that the smoker of this peculiarly Indian form of tobacco is the mysterious Chelmy. He relished the Indian food last night, you said, and he smokes Indian cigarettes. Do you think we can ascribe an Indian background to the man ? I think so," answering his own question, " no matter how much he would have us believe otherwise."

" But to what end ? "

" Indeed, Watson. To what end ? Come, let us upstairs." As we left the room, he picked up the account book

I led the way, and at his request, indicated the position where I had first remarked the Colonel in his unusual nocturnal exercise.

" Facing this way ? " he asked, standing on the spot I indicated.

" Just so."

" And you were standing where ? " he enquired. I placed myself outside my bed-room door. " What were you wearing ? " was his next rather unexpected question.

" My dressing gown," I replied. " Maybe you would like me to wear it now ? " I enquired in a spirit of facetiousness. Holmes, however, seemed to take the request seriously.

" If you would be so kind."

Though it seemed to me that I was making a fool of myself, I entered my room and slipped on the gaudy garment. Holmes continued standing with his back to me, however. " Thank you, that answers my question perfectly," he replied without turning. " Now if you will revert to more modest attire, I think the time has come for me to go back to London. I will return here tomorrow. Pray excuse me to our charming hostess, and I would strongly recommend that Chelmy not be admitted to the house before my return."

FTER Holmes had left the house, I made my way to the drawing-room, where Colonel Warburton was beginning to stir a little.

" Where is your friend ? " asked Purcell.

I explained the situation, and repeated Holmes' request that Chelmy not be admitted.

" We cannot do that ! " exclaimed Miss Warburton. " Why, he—" and broke off suddenly, clapping her hand over her mouth as if to prevent any further words from escaping.

" I'll make sure he does not show his face in here tonight, Alice," Purcell said. " You should remain with your father in any case, and will be in no condition to receive visitors."

Miss Warburton grudgingly agreed to this, and Purcell and I together determined to lift Colonel Warburton into his own bed. He was a large man, but between Purcell's youth and strength, and my experience in dealing with the sick, we managed tolerably well, and were able to transport him to his room without overmuch trouble.

Dinner was a sombre affair. Miss Warburton sat upstairs with her father, dining off a tray, and Purcell and I ate our meal in near silence. After dessert, we heard the doorbell ring followed by the raised voice of Chelmy, and that of the parlour-maid. The blood rose to Purcell's face, and he half-rose in his chair, his fists balled, but as he did so, the noise of the altercation ceased, and we heard the front door close.

" I don't want the brute skulking round the house peering in at us, in any event," exclaimed Purcell, standing up and drawing the curtains. " I'll just do the same in the drawing-room," as he slipped out. The next I heard was his raised voice from the next room, presumably shouting at Chelmy, telling him in the crudest terms to remove himself from the premises.

" All done," he said, returning to the table a few minutes later. " By Jove, I would horsewhip that bounder in a trice were it not for the fact that he is a friend to Alice's father."

I held my peace regarding this last observation, and we moved onto coffee and port. By unspoken mutual consent, we retired early, after first knocking on Colonel Warburton's door, and enquiring after him.

" He is much better," replied Alice. " He is speaking and just seems a little weak. But if you would examine him one more time, Doctor Watson, before you go to bed, I would feel easier in my mind."

I entered the sick-room, and inspected the wound, which was in truth much less serious than we had previously feared. The Colonel, though his voice was faint, appeared to be in perfect possession of his faculties, and I saw no cause for alarm, informing his daughter of the fact.

" Though if there is any change in the night," I added, " you must not hesitate to wake me up and call for assistance."

" I thank you, Doctor, and I also thank you for bringing your friend to this house." She smiled at me. It was an expression that showed the beauty of spirit of which Purcell had spoken, and had up to that time remained hidden from me.

The night passed peacefully enough, and I was delighted to see Colonel Warburton seated at the breakfast table when I made my way downstairs.

" You gave us a nasty turn yesterday, sir," I remarked to him. " I am glad to see you so well this morning."

" Thanks to your skill and Alice's nursing, I feel like a new man," he replied. " Dashed silly of me to trip and stumble like that. I remember it, you know, as if it were part of a dream."

I made some comment, and applied myself to buttered eggs and kidneys. I had just poured myself a second cup of coffee, when the maid announced the arrival of Sherlock Holmes.

" Show the fellow in," said the Colonel. " I shall be delighted to make your friend's acquaintance. Ah, sir," rising to meet Holmes, " I am pleased to see the celebrated friend of Doctor Watson. Have you broken your fast ? " waving a hospitable hand at the breakfast table and sideboard.

" I have already eaten, thank you, sir," replied Holmes, " and I would like to congratulate you on your speedy recovery. May I borrow my friend for a while ? It is time, I think, that he and I paid a visit to Mr. Chelmy."

There was a look of puzzlement, and maybe once again a trace of fear, on the Colonel's face, but he voiced no objection. His daughter, on the other hand, briefly flashed that smile that had lit up her face on the previous evening.

" Come, Watson," commanded Holmes. " Your coffee can wait."

I was somewhat perplexed as we made our way through the suburban lanes to Chelmy's house, the whereabouts of which we had ascertained from Colonel Warburton's parlourmaid. From his demeanour, Holmes seemed to have discovered the answers to all the questions which remained, to me at least, as mysteries.

We walked up the pine-lined driveway to a somewhat ugly redbrick house, set about on all sides by thick evergreens.

" Some men's houses are like their souls," remarked Holmes, but he had no time to elaborate on this observation, as the door was opened by a sour-faced servant.

" Sherlock Holmes and Dr. John Watson for Mr. Chelmy," Holmes announced firmly in resonant tones. " I rather fancy that he will see us."

" If you will wait one minute, sir," replied the maid, obviously in awe of Holmes' manner. She returned. " The master was just going out, but he can spare a few minutes. I will take you to his study now."

" I fancy he will spare us a little more time than that when he has heard what I have to say," Holmes remarked to me as we were led through the house. " By the way, Chelmy never spoke of his wife, I take it ? "

" His wife ? " I replied in surprise. " I was under the impression that he was unmarried, and had always been so."

Holmes said nothing, merely raising his eyebrows in response and glancing at a bowl of flowers placed in the hallway.

We were admitted to the study, where Chelmy stood waiting. He extended his hand in greeting, but Holmes kept his hands behind his back, gripping his cane, and pointedly rejecting the courtesy.

" To what," asked Chelmy coldly, obviously more than a little discomfited by Holmes' attitude, " do I owe the pleasure of this visit ? "

" I am calling on behalf of Mrs. Chelmy," called Holmes. " I find your actions nothing short of despicable with regard to her, as I find your actions in so many regards." Holmes had drawn himself up to his full height, and towered over the smaller man.

A sneer spread over the other's face. " You have no proof ! " he exclaimed.

" You think so ? " replied Holmes cooly. " Give me ten minutes, and I can convince any twelve good men and true sitting in judgement on you of your nature and your deeds. My proofs are ready formed and fixed in here." He tapped his forehead.

" And what of the precious Colonel Warburton ? " asked Chelmy. " Would the exposure not ruin him ? "

" I think that is a risk that he would be prepared to take," replied Holmes.

" And his daughter ? "

" She will be well rid of you and your evil ways."

" Evil, you say ? It is you who is evil, Mr. Holmes. Snooping and spying on others, and making wild accusations without proof, and without the force of the law to back you, those accusations are worth nothing ! "

I was completely baffled by this exchange, and watching the thrust and parry of the two adversaries left me more than a little confused. " In God's name, Holmes, what do you mean by all this ? "

" Behold the husband of Alice Warburton, or, to give her her married name, Alice Chelmy, though I fear, Joshua Hook, that a marriage contracted under a false name is no marriage at all."

For the first time, the little man seemed staggered by Holmes' words. He turned pale and gasped. " How..? When did you find this out ? "

" Late last night. It is not so easy to assume a false identity, Hook, even when arriving in England for the first time. There are always the little things. For example..." He pointed to a dagger of Indian design hanging on the wall, with the initials JH embossed on the scabbard.

" That is no proof ! " spat the other.

" To be sure it is not," replied Holmes. " I merely point to it as an example of the trail that a careless man will leave behind him. And if you will permit me to observe, Mr. Hook, you have been very careless indeed. The account at Armitage's Bank and the other at the City and National, for example."

" How the devil did you discover

that ? " replied Chelmy, who had now turned almost completely white.

For answer, Holmes pulled out the account-book that I had seen him remove from Colonel Warburton's desk the previous day.

" Aha ! " exclaimed the other. " That is your proof ? If that book goes, then so does all your proof and so do all your accusations ! " He pulled the dagger just mentioned from the wall and withdrew it from its sheath. " Now, Mr. Holmes, you will give that book to me." He moved towards Holmes, the dagger pointing at my friend. I started forward, but Holmes waved me back.

" I think not," he said, grasping his cane in both hands and pulling his swordstick apart to reveal a shining slender rapier, the point of which now almost touched the other's throat. " I believe that this blade would penetrate your body and the point would emerge on the other side before your dagger even started to scratch me. Do you wish to make the experiment ? " His tone was icy.

Chelmy, or Hook, as I suppose I must now refer to him, dropped the dagger. " What do you want of me ? "

" First, I want you to make a clean confession of all your crimes in writing. I then would like you to use the pistol you keep in the drawer there, and to which your hand keeps straying. To use it, I mean,

in such a manner as is expected of a gentleman in your position. No, naughty ! " he admonished, administering a flick of the rapier to the other's wrist, drawing a little blood and eliciting a howl of fury. " The Doctor and I will wait outside. Come, Watson."

He turned his back and left the room, and after a few seconds, I followed.

" What if he does not do as you suggest ? " I asked, when we had closed the door.

" I have no confidence at all that he will carry out any of my requests. He is no gentleman, after all is said and done. I expect him to make a run for it out of the window. Ah, there he goes," as the sound of a window being opened reached us.

" Are we to do nothing ? " I asked Holmes.

" We will await developments here," said Holmes with a smile.

I was puzzled, but trusted my friend's judgement in the matter. However, in about five minutes' time, there was a knock on the door, followed by the entry of Inspector Tobias Gregson of Scotland Yard and two constables, with Hook handcuffed between them.

" As you prophesied, Mr. Holmes," said Gregson genially. " The thanks of the Yard go to you, sir. And a very good morning to you, sir," addressing me. " Always glad to see you and Mr. Holmes under these circumstances."

OU had deduced, of course, that Chelmy, as he was known, was blackmailing Colonel Warburton ? " We were seated in Holmes' rooms in

Baker-street, having returned from Guildford.

" I had guessed something of the sort, from the reactions of the Colonel and his daughter. What was the Colonel's crime that put him in the other's power ? "

" It was not so much a crime as a deplorable error in judgement. As you saw, Hook, to call him by his proper name, had been in India at the same time as the Colonel, but not during your period of service, and obviously not at the time that your friend Purcell served there, otherwise you would probably have recognised him. You mentioned that the Colonel enjoyed gambling, and you witnessed Hook's skill in billiards for yourself. I have no doubt that he is equally skilful in other recreations, possibly including card-sharping, but in any event, the Colonel found himself in debt to Hook, and unable to repay. Hook proposed a monstrous bargain by which he would accept the hand of the Colonel's daughter in lieu of the money owed, and the Colonel, to his shame, accepted the offer. Hook therefore married Alice Warburton, in his new identity, when he returned to England."

" How did you know this ? And why was Alice Warburton living at her father's house when she was married to the other ? "

" I suspected it when I first met the lady. I noticed, when I kissed her hand, the imprint of a ring on the fourth finger of her left hand—a ring which had been worn with sufficient frequency and recently enough to leave its mark. I also noticed, as we were being led to meet Hook in his study, a lady's parasol and a pair of lady's walking boots in the hallway. Clear indication that a lady had indeed been present in the house, leaving some attire behind. When I then noticed some flowers in a vase, arranged in a fashion that could only have been achieved by one of the fairer sex, and which was placed on a lace mat—hardly the taste of a man like Hook, you will agree—it bespoke a more or less

permanent female presence in the house."

" So Alice Warburton lived as a married woman in that house, except when visitors came to call, when she returned to her father ? "

" I fear so. The Colonel would hardly wish to acknowledge a man such as Hook as a son-in-law, and he would have had to provide some explanation to friends as to why a girl like his daughter had married the wretch. I also feel that although Hook had the Colonel in his power by reason of the shameful marriage, the Colonel likewise had some hold over Hook—the fact of his false name, perhaps, and that allowed his daughter to escape Hook's clutches at regular intervals."

" His servants must have been aware of the anomaly—indeed, I feel they were, as they addressed her as 'madam', when I would have expected them to address her as 'miss'," I added. " At any event, she is well rid of him."

" Well rid indeed. Maybe you failed to note the bruises on her arm that I observed as her sleeve rode up when I raised her hand to kiss it. I have no doubt that they were Hook's doing."

" But," I objected, " surely the Colonel must have known that the marriage under a false name was no marriage at all ? "

Holmes shrugged. " Maybe so, but that would make the arrangement with Hook even more shameful, and provide even more of an inducement for Warburton to keep the matter hidden."

" I agree. And what of the account-book ? "

" The late Mrs. Warburton came of a wealthy family, and the family estate had passed to her as the only heir of her parents. When she died, the money passed to the Colonel, who was thereby able to move to England and live in comfort. Hook, at that time unmarried, pursued the Colonel back here, and forced him to keep the bargain that had been made in India—that of marrying Miss Warburton—under a false name. After that, he continued to extort money from the Colonel at regular intervals. The sordid details are all listed in the account-book."

" And the chloral? Why did Hook administer that ? "

" I fear that was a clumsy attempt to encompass the Colonel's death and make it appear an accident. My guess—remember, I did not see everything clearly—is that the Colonel had the bottle on the desk in front of him while they talked and Hook, while the Colonel's attention was distracted, added a generous dose to the whisky and soda. Remember, the Colonel was not accustomed to the drug, and its effects, especially when taken with whisky, could easily have caused an accident more serious than the one that actually transpired. There are several reasons why the Colonel's death would have been desirable to Hook. First, the whole of his wife's estate would then have devolved upon his daughter, and hence upon Hook. And also, given that the Colonel had some sort of hold over Hook, any possible menace would have been removed. And lastly, Alice Warburton would then have been his, and his alone."

" But what of the Colonel's madness, if we may term it so ? The midnight skipping, the egg through the window, and the farcical parade-ground incident ? "

Holmes laughed. " I had dismissed those almost as soon as you described them. What was the common feature of all of them ? "

" I cannot say."

" But I can tell you. They all occurred when Warburton and Purcell were alone together, or in the last case, when you and Warburton were together, and there were no other witnesses. Not only that, there were was very little possibility of any other person witnessing these actions."

" I see what you mean. But they were so varied in their form."

" And that is another point that occurred to me. The skipping is a form of mania, the egg incident argues a form of persecution, and the parade-ground a form of delusion. Tell me, is it likely that a patient would suffer from all three forms of insanity ? "

" I agree with you that it is unlikely."

" I would go further. I would say that it is impossible. When I further add that no damage was caused to persons or property—the Colonel actually opened the window to dispose of his egg, and carefully closed it afterwards, according to your friend's account—these do not sound like the actions of a lunatic."

" But to what end ? "

" Surely it is obvious."

" Not to me."

" Colonel Warburton was well aware of the affectionate relations between his daughter and Purcell. I have no doubt that in the normal course of events, your friend would have been regarded as an eligible suitor. But since the daughter had supposedly been married secretly, it was obviously impossible for her to have any such claimant for her hand. How to dispose of Purcell without exposing the secret ? The Colonel's method was to feign lunacy, in the hope that this would sufficiently dissuade Purcell from any thoughts of an alliance with the family."

" As it very nearly did, and but

for your intervention, might well have done."

" I am glad to have been able to play Cupid in this instance," smiled Holmes. " I have no doubt, that once Hook has been brought to trial and his full villainy exposed, Alice Warburton and Philip Purcell may be legally joined together in holy matrimony with her father's blessing."

" I believe that to be a very probable event," I replied. " However, given her previous history, and her past attachment to Hook, Purcell was hesitant to pursue his suit with Alice Warburton further. Additionally, the young lady herself believed that marriage to him was out of the question as a result of her past. Although the couple were obviously very much attached to each other, the problem was to reconcile the unseemly past to a happy shared future."

" A task more in your line than mine, I would imagine," suggested Holmes as he refilled his pipe. " How did you accomplish it ? "

" Once I had caused Purcell to understand that Miss Warburton had had no choice in the matter, having been a minor when the marriage was contracted, he began to look on a future alliance in a more favourable light. I also pointed out that the matter had not been noised abroad, and that the so-called marriage to Hook was not only invalid, but was not a matter of public knowledge. This further persuaded him in the direction of matrimony. I advised him to look on the whole sordid affair as if she had contracted an imprudent marriage to a man who had died shortly after the wedding. Although his regard for the Colonel has somewhat diminished, he accepted the force of my arguments. As for the bride, I used similar reasoning to persuade her that she was worthy of Purcell's hand."

" And this was sufficient to bring them together ? "

I smiled broadly. " My dear fellow, you are without doubt the greatest analytical detective that has ever lived, and when it comes to matters of pure reason and deduction, you have no peer. In affairs of the heart, though, you must confess that I am your superior."

" I freely admit it," he chuckled. " Pray tell of the presumably vital part of the story that you consider eludes this cold reasoning machine seated before you."

" The vital part, Holmes, is that these two young people loved each other sincerely and passionately. The point that tipped the scale for both parties was my suggestion that they would never find true happiness with any other partner. On considering this, the two flew—I speak metaphorically, of course—into each other's arms. Both of them expressed their sincere gratitude through me to you for your role in exposing Hook and bringing them together."

" It was a relatively trivial affair, once I had visited the house and seen for myself how things lay." He picked up his newspaper, and commenced scanning the agony column, while I continued to ponder the events of the past few days.

" One last question, Holmes. When I encountered the Colonel skipping down the passage, he turned to meet me, even though his back was turned. How did he accomplish this ? "

Holmes threw back his head and laughed. " That, my dear Watson, is something I am surprised you have not deduced for yourself. Think back to the night in question.

Imagine yourself looking down the corridor at Colonel Warburton's retreating back. What is in front of him and you ? "

" A window, without the curtains drawn."

" Quite so. And what were you wearing ? "

" That bright green Chinese dressing gown I showed you the other day." I smote my brow. " Of course ! He saw my reflection as in a mirror. I should have realised that."

Holmes smiled tolerantly. " Maybe you should have done so, Watson, but do not belabour yourself for it.

I have to confess that without your active cooperation and assistance, this case would have taken longer to solve than it did. Indeed, without the assistance you provided, it is questionable whether it would have been solved at all."

At this, which ranked among the highest praise that Holmes ever bestowed on me, I felt a glow of not unjustifiable pride, which was renewed some months later when I attended the wedding of Philip Purcell and Alice Warburton in the capacity of best man.

Sherlock Holmes &
The Mystery of
The Paradol
Chamber

THE ENTRANCE TO THE CELLAR WAS GUARDED BY A SOLID DOOR, SOME SIX INCHES
IN THICKNESS, AND SECURED BY A COMPLEX COMBINATION LOCK. (PAGE 143)

Editor's Notes

The events described in this case, alluded to elsewhere but not described by Watson, show an interesting interplay between Holmes and the official police in the shape of Inspector Tobias Gregson, one of the more capable Scotland Yard detectives, according to Holmes.

Even given that Holmes' appraisal of members of the official force was largely dependent upon their willingness to listen to him and take his advice, it does appear in this instance that Holmes was correct in his judgement. Gregson shows himself at his best here, but *it is no surprise, given the final result of the case, that Watson suppressed the release of the details of the case (the manuscript in the deed box was contained in a sealed envelope)—they could well have led to an official reprimand or worse for Gregson. Holmes also shows a sympathy and human side to his nature that is not commonly encountered in Watson's accounts, as well as an irritability that so often seemed to infuriate Watson. Here, then, is the Mystery of the Paradol Chamber.*

 Y good friend, the consulting detective Sherlock Holmes, was blessed with an almost perfect memory, which allowed him to collect facts and arrange them in such a way that he was able to recall them almost instantly when the occasion demanded. This had been brought home to me in a number of instances, but I had never fully appreciated the force of his mind until the day that brought the business that I have termed the " Mystery of the Paradol Chamber" to his attention.

It was one of those English June days which are more like a return to the days of March than the season indicated by the calendar. The temperature was unpleasantly cool, the sky was grey, and the rain, blown horizontally by the wind, lashed the almost deserted streets of London.

I was at that time lodging with Holmes, my wife having taken herself to the waters of Baden-Baden. I had been prevented from accompanying her on account of my old war wound, which had flared up painfully a little before the time of her departure, and it was a convenience, as well as a pleasure, for me to accept the hospitality of the great detective, and resume our bachelor existence at 221B Baker-street.

I was idling away the time by examining Holmes' library and beginning a re-ordering of his books, which appeared to be in no particular order, making it impossible to locate any desired volume. He, for his part, was standing by the window, watching the rain, and whatever passers-by were braving the weather.

He turned in my general direction. " Please do not disturb the order of the books, Watson. I may need to consult them at some time in the future, and I have no wish to dissipate my energies in searching in unfamiliar places for my old friends."

" But Holmes," I remonstrated.

" These books are in no rational order. They are arranged neither by subject, nor by author, nor in any fashion that I can discern. There is no possible way that you can know where they are."

" On the contrary," he retorted sharply, " I have a full and complete knowledge of the contents and arrangement of the books on my shelves, as I will now demonstrate to you, needless though it is for me to do so." So saying, he turned his back to me. " Pray supply me with a shelf and the position of a title on it."

" Such as the third shelf down in the left-hand book-case, and the fifth title from the left ? " I suggested.

" Exactly like that," he replied without turning. " Hartupp on Probate. It is a red cloth-bound quarto edition."

" Very good," I replied, not a little astounded. " The fifth shelf down on the right-hand case, and the second volume from the right ? "

" The 1872 edition of Debrett's, in the usual binding."

" It is indeed. And the bottom shelf of the same case, tenth from the left ? "

" Bullock and Turner on Deep-sea Pacific Fishes. Cloth-bound in tan buckram," he replied promptly. Now," turning to face me, " please have the goodness to restore order from the chaos into which you have placed those first volumes you have removed from the shelves. Aha ! " he exclaimed, breaking off from his criticism of my attempts to act as a librarian. " This is a strange sort of client, to be sure." The bell downstairs rang as he spoke, and I could hear the landlady, Mrs. Hudson, admitting a visitor. Shortly afterwards, the door opened to admit

a Romish priest, a class of individual who had not, to my knowledge, previously graced the portals of Holmes' establishment.

" Well, Father Donahue," said Holmes genially, " it is a foul day, to be sure. It must have been a cold walk from Euston. Will you take tea, or something a little stronger ? "

The priest gave a start. " How in the world would you be knowing my name, Mr. Holmes ? And how did you know that I had walked from Euston station and I had not taken a cab or an omnibus, or even the Underground railway ? " These words were delivered with more than a touch of an Irish brogue.

Holmes smiled. " As to the last, I see the stub of a return ticket from Watford protruding from your waistcoat pocket. That gives me Euston station. I know that you did not arrive by cab, because I observed you from this window here. The state of your coat and your umbrella—pray give them and your hat to Watson here—leads me to believe that your method of transport was the old standby of Shanks's mare."

" Very good, Mr. Holmes," replied the priest, divesting himself of his wet things. " But my name ? How do you know that ? "

" Even if it were not stitched into your umbrella, Father, I should be a dullard indeed if I could not remember the name of the incumbent of that fine piece of architecture in the Gothic style, Holy Rood Church in Watford."

The little priest stared at Holmes as if at a ghost. " By the living God, Mr. Holmes, do you keep a knowledge of the names of all the churches and their priests in the land in that head of yours ? "

" No, no," laughed Holmes. " Only of those in the Home

Counties." Father Donahue still appeared staggered by Holmes' coup. " But make yourself comfortable, Father, and name your choice. It is a cold day, and I myself will indulge in a small brandy and soda, despite the hour."

" If there is a drop of whisky in the house ? " the priest suggested. " With maybe a little soda water, if you please."

" Watson, if you would," requested Holmes. I sensed that since I had been cast in the role of servant, being somewhat out of favour as a result of my attempts to re-arrange Holmes' books, but I bit my tongue and said nothing as I prepared the drinks.

" Your very good health, gentlemen," proposed the Irishman as he raised his glass to us. We returned the toast, and the ruddy-faced Catholic priest, clad in the sober black of his calling, sipped his drink.

" You require assistance ? " enquired Holmes.

" You once acted for one of my flock, Mr. Charles Underhill, in a matter of some delicacy, and he spoke most highly of you on that occasion. I remembered this when this business on which I am visiting you became apparent."

" Ah yes, the affair of the missing emerald brooch. The milkman was the guilty party there, I recall. I must warn you, though, that I am more a practitioner of criminal than of canon law, and my theological skills are sadly limited."

The priest smiled. " Mr. Holmes, I have a dark suspicion that your skills in criminal law are what are required here. The theology you may leave to me. Have you ever heard of the Paradol Chamber ? "

Holmes shook his head. " I am aware, of course, of the unfortunate French writer Lucien-Anatole Prévost-Paradol. But that is the extent of my knowledge regarding the name. Please tell your story."

" I am, as you are aware, though the Lord God Himself knows how you manage to keep such things in your head, Patrick Donahue, the priest of Holy Rood Church in Watford. It is a very quiet parish, and my flock is a small, but devout one. Among my parishioners is an elderly gentleman, a Mr. Francis Faulkes. He is descended from one of the great Catholic families of England, and his line has never veered from the True Faith. He is given out to be very wealthy, and his gifts to the church over the years have indeed been extremely generous. In the past he has given me to understand that on his death, his considerable estate will be left to Holy Rood Church for the construction of a Lady Chapel. He has never married, and to the best of my knowledge, he has no close relatives who would make a claim on the estate."

" This would be a considerable sum of money ? " asked Holmes. " Father, your glass is empty. Watson," he half-commanded. I re-filled the cleric's glass, and he continued with his story.

" It would, to be sure. I have not made an exact calculation, but thirty thousand pounds in cash, in addition to the proceeds of the sale of his properties, would not seem to be an unreasonable estimate."

" That is indeed a substantial sum," agreed Holmes. " How old is this Mr. Faulkes, and what is his current state of health ? "

" He is about seventy years old— in fact, seventy-one according to the parish register—and he is in excellent health. I am no physician, but to my eyes, he has many more years to enjoy before he quits this world."

" And this Mr. Faulkes is the root of your problem ? " enquired Holmes.

" I would not go so far as to say that," replied the priest. " His money is almost certainly at the heart of the matter, though. *Radix malorum est cupiditas*."

" ' The love of money is the root of evil'," Holmes translated. " Yes, I think that is one point where you and I would agree, Father," he smiled. " There are others, I take it, who also have an interest in this affair ? "

" This is so. And this is where the group I mentioned earlier, the Paradol Chamber, enters the tale. Just over one month ago, Mr. Faulkes appeared at Confession. As you know, my lips are sealed as to what he confessed as his sins. They were venial ones, to be sure, but I gave him a light penance for his misdemeanours, and pronounced Absolution. Following this, he and I were left alone together in the church, and he asked if he could talk to me on another matter. A priest's ear is open to all in distress, and he informed me of some printed matter in the form of leaflets that he had received from a group calling itself the Paradol Chamber. These leaflets appeared to contain threats to his life."

" Were these direct threats ? " replied Holmes, who had been lounging languidly in his chair at the start of this recital, but now appeared to be galvanised into some sort of interest, and sat forward, all attention. " Pray proceed, and describe these leaflets, if you would."

" Each consisted of a single sheet of paper, printed neatly and precisely. I have, as you can imagine, very little experience of this kind of affair, but my knowledge of these matters," here the priest appeared a little embarrassed, " gained, I grant, only from popular fiction such as is printed in the weekly magazines, would seem to indicate that such communications are usually hand-written. They appeared to be direct threats, to answer your first question just now."

" How did Mr. Faulkes come by these leaflets ? Were they delivered by post ? " asked Holmes.

" Now, Mr. Holmes, you have hit upon one of the wonders of the thing. Mr. Faulkes discovered them in his missal when he attended the Sunday Mass."

" So are we to assume that others in the congregation also encountered these leaflets, or is Mr. Faulkes the only recipient of this mysterious group's attentions ? "

" If they did, none has ever told me of them. Indeed, I have asked several of the more reliable members of my flock, discreetly, you may be sure, whether the name of ' Paradol' meant anything to them. None claimed to have heard the name before."

" Most interesting," replied Holmes. " How many of these have been received so far ? "

" Four, one on each of the previous Sundays up to now."

" All the same ? "

" They all convey the same message in principle, but the wording differs slightly in each case."

" And does Mr. Faulkes always occupy the same place at Mass ? "

" Yes, he does."

" So the leaflets would seem to be placed in advance for him and him alone to discover. I see. Who has access to the church before your service ? "

The priest smiled. " The whole town. The House of God is always open for private prayer."

" Quite so, quite so," Holmes

murmured. " Do you happen to have one of these leaflets with you ? " he asked.

The priest smiled. " I had a premonition that you would ask for that," he replied. " I therefore obtained one of these from Mr. Faulkes on the pretext that I would examine its content in order to determine its content and meaning more exactly. He was somewhat reluctant to pass it to me at first, but in the end he relented."

" Your foresight is commendable," smiled Holmes, taking the envelope that the cleric held out to him, and extracting a half-sheet of printed foolscap. " Watson, let us have your opinions on this first."

I determined to show my abilities in the field, since Holmes appeared to be desirous of exposing me in front of our visitor as some sort of revenge for my previous actions. As it happened, my service in India had provided me with the opportunity of playing an active role in the production of the regimental gazette, and I was therefore familiar with the materials and techniques used by printers. Taking the paper, I caught hold of one of Holmes' lenses from the desk, and proceeded with my examination. " Excellent quality laid paper," I pronounced. " High quality rag paper with a watermark that I do not recognise, but if I had to make a pronouncement, would guess was French." I applied the loupe to the printing. " Letterpress printing rather than lithography, and quite probably a hand-press—there is an unevenness that would not be apparent with a stereotype or a mechanical press. The typeface itself is unfamiliar to me, but I think it is almost certainly Continental." I passed the paper to Holmes.

" The typeface is Bodoni," said

he with a glance. " The paper is, I think, Italian, from what I can make of the watermark. If you will have the goodness, Watson, to pass me the seventh book from the left on the second shelf of the central case," and there was a somewhat malicious twinkle in his eyes, " I can confirm this. As to the rest, I concur fully. Excellent observations, Watson, I must admit."

I passed the volume, which proved to be a directory of European paper manufactories, to Holmes, who flicked through the pages, and sat back, satisfied. " Yes, Italian, from a manufactory near Rome. Antodelli e Fratelli. As to the content," he reapplied himself to an examination, " this is definitely interesting. ' You will have the goodness to return to us what is not yours to hold and retain and what is rightfully ours. If you do not do this thing, it is our advice to you that you make your peace with God, for then you will surely meet Him soon'. Signed, if we may term a printed line of type a signature, ' The Paradol Chamber '." His face took on an expression of seriousness. " The others all contained a similar message, you say ? "

" That is so."

" And there have been four so far ? What place does this particular example occupy in the series ? "

" It is the third, the one before last."

" Has the tone, or the urgency contained in the message, increased, do you feel ? Has the level of threatened danger to Mr. Faulkes increased, in your opinion ? I see no time or final date by which the demands are to be met."

The other knotted his brows in thought. " I apologise for not being able to bring the others, or to have made notes of the exact wording, but I recollect that they were all much the same. Certainly there was no date or time set for the return of the property mentioned in them.”

“ Has he, or have you, contacted the police in this regard ? ”

“ I have not done so, and I am reasonably certain that he has not, or he would not have come to me, I feel. This could, after all, be no more than a prank of some kind, though it would be a poor sort of joke, and it would hardly reflect well on me or Mr. Faulkes if we were to waste the police’s time with some sort of hoax.”

“ True,” replied Holmes. “ However, the threat contained in these missives would appear to be of serious intent. Although, based on my past experiences, the official police would have been unable to discover the origin of these messages, they would nonetheless have been able to provide some kind of protection against attacks to Mr. Faulkes.”

“ You take this matter seriously, Mr. Holmes ? ”

“ Threats of this nature are never to be dismissed lightly, Father. It may be, as you say, a hoax of a particularly repellent kind, or it may have a murderous intent behind it. As for the item or items referred to in the message, you have no idea to what this refers ? He has not mentioned anything of this to you ? ”

The other shrugged. “ I cannot say. He is well-known as a collector of antiquities, but I have never even entered his house, so I cannot say for sure on what basis this is said, or what manner of old things he collects.”

“ If those reports are true and we are to believe this,” replied Holmes, “ then we may consider that he has acquired some kind of antiquity to which others may claim ownership, but whether this acquisition

is legitimate or otherwise, we have no way of knowing.” He regarded the piece of paper once more, and frowned at it. “ Though there are no mistakes of orthography here, somehow this does not appear to me to be written by an Englishman. I would also note that the way the longer words are broken at the end of lines does not follow English printers’ practices, but would seem to argue a Latin touch. We may be relatively certain, Father, that your parishioner is receiving his messages from an Italian—possibly even from Italy or Rome. Has Faulkes travelled abroad a good deal ? ” asked my friend.

“ Why, yes, to be sure he has. He has taken an Italian holiday at least four times in the past ten years since I have been priest at Holy Rood. Possibly even five or six, now I come to recollect matters more clearly. I believe he was once received by the Holy Father himself at the Vatican.”

“ Those trips abroad would argue in favour of the theory of a purloined antiquity or some such, would it not ? ” Holmes examined the printed matter once more. “ As I said, I have never heard of this ‘Paradol Chamber’ that claims to be the author of this document, but I would like to look into the matter a little more. Would it cause you or Mr. Faulkes any inconvenience if I were to retain this paper for a while ?”

“ By no means,” replied the priest. “ I can easily explain to Mr. Faulkes that the document is being scrutinised by an expert, and in truth, I would sooner the devilish thing were as far away from me as possible.” He sat forward in his chair, obviously much agitated, and made the sign of the cross.

“ You believe the origin to be diabolical, then ? ” Holmes replied, obviously amused. " I smell no brimstone, and I see no marks of the Devil's hoof."

" It is no joking matter to me, Mr. Holmes, no matter what you may think. Believe me, I have seen the Devil at work, and I believe these papers to be part of his doing."

Holmes leant forward. His tone was now serious. " Father Donahue, I take your meaning. I too have witnessed evil at work, even if I do not see a personification of evil such as the Devil in those instances. I apologise if I have offended your beliefs. I too believe there is some evil—I will not use your terms here—afoot, and I will gladly aid you in discovering it, and laying it to rest."

" Thank you, Mr. Holmes. You put my spirit somewhat at ease with those words. With your permission, gentlemen, I see that the rain has slackened a little, and I will take my leave of you and wish you both a very good day. Having witnessed your knowledge and memory, Mr. Holmes, I will not leave my card, as I am now certain that you need no such reminder of how to communicate with me." He smiled. " You will no doubt let me know as soon as you have come to any conclusions."

" Indeed I will," smiled Holmes, rising, and seeing our visitor to the door. " Well, Watson, what do you make of this ? " as the door closed behind Father Donahue.

" I know not," I replied. " I can make nothing of it other than what has already been mentioned and what I observed for myself."

" Your observations on the paper and printing, if you will allow me to say so, were of a particularly high order and display a true understanding of the subject. Where,

if I may ask, did you acquire that knowledge ? "

I explained my previous experience in the field. " Although I was not responsible for actually setting the type, or for the operation of the presses, I learned enough to be able to direct the printers in their task," I concluded.

" You never fail to amaze me, Watson. Hidden depths, hidden depths. I congratulate you on your observations, and your analysis, as far as it goes, is excellent. It seems to me, though, that the direction of your thoughts may be the wrong track for us to follow. Fascinating as those details may be, I think that the paper and the peculiar Continental printing are dust thrown in our faces to confuse us. Whoever has prepared this has done his work thoroughly, it must be admitted."

" What do you suspect ? "

" I have to think about the matter and consider it more deeply. The matter may be more complex than the worthy son of Erin who visited us just now believes." He paused. " Would you be averse to dinner at Alberti's tonight, Watson ? Or will Mrs. Hudson's simple English fare be sufficient ? "

" That sounds like an excellent plan to me. As the reverend gentleman remarked, the weather continues to improve, and the walk to Alberti's will do us good and enliven our appetites."

As we took ourselves to the restaurant that evening, Holmes maintained a silence as we strolled through the wet streets. I guessed that he was thinking of the problem that had been presented to us earlier in the evening, but in the restaurant, as we were tackling the soup, he started to discourse on medieval manuscripts, and the methods used by the monks of that era to produce the fantastical decorations that adorned their work. To hear him talk, one would have believed him to be a scholar who had devoted his life to the study of the subject, rather than an amateur who had only recently taken an interest in the matter. From that, he passed to a discourse on the art of violin manufacture in the eighteenth century, and a comparison of the glues used by the various craftsmen of Cremona.

" Holmes," I expostulated at last. " You are, without a doubt, at the same time both the most fascinating and the most infuriating man of my acquaintance. This afternoon we were presented with a problem, on whose solution apparently hangs the life of a man, and you prattle of fiddles."

" It is not wholly without relevance," he admonished me mildly. " A detailed knowledge of antiquarian matters would seem to have some application to this case. In any event, since these messages have been appearing over the past four weeks, I feel there is no need for me to act with any urgency in this matter."

OLMES was not often mistaken in his reasoning, and he usually felt it as a grievous blow when his foretelling of events failed to come to pass. So it was in this case of his predictions regarding the mysterious messages sent to our visitor's parishioner.

The next morning saw the arrival of a telegram, followed shortly after this by the delivery of the morning newspapers.

Holmes ripped open the telegram eagerly, and I observed his face turn pale with rage as he read it. " Damnable fool that I am, Watson ! Arrogant, conceited fool, and worse than that ! " He flung the telegram down on the breakfast table and rose to his feet. " If I ever do such a thing again, have the goodness to stand behind me and whisper 'Holy Rood Church' in my ear. The old Roman emperors celebrating their triumphs had more wisdom and self-knowledge than do I ! " So saying, he stormed out of the room to his bed-room, slamming the door behind him with a bang that rattled the very dishes on the table.

I picked up the telegram and read the ominous words, " Faulkes murdered last night mysterious circumstances. Request you come to Watford soonest. Patrick Donahue."

I understood the reason for Holmes' chagrin—only the previous evening, he had lightly dismissed the idea of any further developments, and now, a matter of hours after that confident assertion, he had been proved wrong, in the most tragic way. I knew from experience that there was little in my power to bring him to a better frame of mind. Only action was capable of restoring his spirits, and that was a course to be chosen by him alone, and which could not be forced upon him by me or by any other.

I therefore scanned the newspapers, looking for reports of the case, discovering that the *Morning Post* gave the fullest account.

" Read it to me, Watson," came Holmes' voice through the bedroom door. It took no great skill on my part to deduce that he had perceived my current actions, aided by his acute hearing, which had picked up the sound of the rustling newspapers . I refrained from further comment and commenced reading.

" This is from the *Morning Post*," I began, by way of introduction. " ' We regret to inform our readers of the tragic death late last night of Mr. Francis Faulkes of Watford, the well-known collector and connoisseur. Mr. Faulkes was seemingly struck down by an unknown hand in his Church Lane house. Mr. Faulkes had apparently locked himself in the vault beneath his house where his collection of artistic artefacts and curios was stored for safe-keeping, and was discovered by Albert Simpkins, his servant, following a summons via the house's internal telephonic system. The door to the vault was unlocked and opened from the outside by Simpkins, who discovered his master in a state of collapse, having sustained a severe injury to the head. A doctor was summoned, but was unable to save the unfortunate victim, who succumbed to his injuries within the hour. The police were also summoned, and based on their findings, which have as yet to be revealed to the Press, foul play is believed to be suspected. The celebrated private detective Mr. Sherlock Holmes is currently reported to be in Watford, assisting Inspector Tobias Gregson of Scotland Yard, who is leading the case.' There is a little more about Faulkes' acts of recent charity, and a little about his collection. Do you wish me to read these to you ? "

" If their information regarding those is of the same standard of accuracy as my supposed whereabouts in Watford, you may forego the pleasure," was the reply from behind the door. " Forgive my vile mood, Watson, if you are able to extend the effort. I am aware that you know me well enough to

ascertain its cause, and hope that in this instance *tout comprendre est tout pardonner*."

" Of course," I replied, and continued to scan the other papers. " There is nothing more of the case in any other of the dailies."

" Gregson's being on the case is a definite positive point. He is far from being the worst member of the Scotland Yard detective force, and he has the almost unique distinction of being willing to learn from others as well as from his own mistakes. If I dare show my face to the Reverend Patrick Donahue in Watford, would you be willing to accompany me ? "

" Why do you bother asking me such a question, Holmes ? " I asked. " And, if you will excuse me mentioning it, conversations such as this are best held otherwise than through closed doors."

" Very good," remarked Holmes, opening the bed-room door and re-entering the room. I examined him closely, fearing that he might have resorted to his former debilitating habit of injecting himself with cocaine, but was relieved to detect no traces of his having succumbed to the temptation. He noticed my observations and smiled ruefully. " This time, Watson, my vice consisted of no more than mental self-flagellation. I am still cursing myself for an arrogant prideful fool. The least we can do to redress the balance is to take the first train to Watford and lend what assistance we can in the matter. Before we depart, please have the goodness to look up this Mr. Faulkes in *Who's Who*."

I retrieved the volume and discovered the entry. " Here we are. Mr. Francis Bosforth Faulkes, eldest son of... born... educated Stoneyhurst... served in Grenadier Guards... What information do you wish me to obtain from here, Holmes ? "

" Is there any clue as to how he may have acquired his wealth ? "

I scanned the page. " He has retained the directorship of several City banks, as well as of a Burmese teak importer, and it would appear that his line, though a cadet branch of the family, has retained possession of a considerable fortune. As the eldest son, he would have stood to inherit most, I would venture."

" Anything out of the ordinary there ? "

" I do not know if it is relevant, but he is listed here as being a member of two Catholic orders of chivalry—the Knights of Malta, and the Order of the Holy Sepulchre."

" Neither of those, to the best of my knowledge, has any connection with the name of Paradol, which is still unknown to me."

" Would it be connected with Freemasonry ? " I asked.

" That, of course, is a possibility, but it has no place in the Grand Lodge of either England or Scotland—I may say this with certainty, given—" Here Holmes gave me details of the involvement of members of his family with Freemasonry at the very highest of levels, after first swearing me to lifelong secrecy as to the details. Suffice it to say that his source was unimpeachable. " There are, of course, other such movements, unknown to me, where the name may have significance. But come, let us to Watford, and brighten Gregson's day." It was clear that the thought of a problem on which to sharpen his wits, no matter how distressing the circumstances which had led up to it, was proving sufficient to lift Holmes' spirits somewhat.

On our arrival at Watford, we had no difficulty in finding the house in Church Street where the tragic event had taken place. On giving his name to the constable standing guard outside the door, we were admitted to the dining-room of the house, where Inspector Tobias Gregson was seated at the table, examining a pile of papers. A large ledger also graced the table in front of him.

" Mr. Holmes," he greeted my friend, with what appeared to be genuine pleasure. " I am glad to see you here. This case is one of the more difficult ones I have seen in some time, and your assistance would be most welcome. And Dr. Watson, too. I fear you will not have much to do in the medical line, Doctor, but it is always good to see you."

" It is always a pleasure to work alongside you, Inspector," replied Holmes courteously.

" What do you know of this case ? " asked Gregson.

" My sole knowledge has been gained from what I learned from Father Patrick Donahue yesterday, together with the report in today's *Morning Post* which, given that it reported me as being having already arrived in Watford, I take with a very large pinch of salt."

" The Catholic reverend ? How did you come to meet hi ? "

Holmes outlined the previous day's meeting, during which the police inspector made notes.

" That's a strange business, to be sure," he commented at the end of Holmes' recital. " So the old man was suffering from some persecution mania ? "

" With some reason," replied Holmes, withdrawing the paper that he had been given by the priest and presenting it to Gregson.

" Well, this is pretty solid," replied Gregson, examining the paper from all angles. " Nothing of imagination about this, is there ? Strange paper, and it appears to be an uncommon type of printing to me."

Holmes informed him of what we had deduced of the paper's origins, finishing with, " I think that the origin of this paper may be closer to home, however."

" Who or what is this Paradol Chamber ? "

" Alas, I have no information there. Maybe, though, since I have given you the few facts I possess regarding the case, you might be induced to return the favour ? "

" That seems like a fair bargain," chuckled Gregson. " I will give you the facts as I have them. Mr. Francis Faulkes appears to have been a wealthy man who invested much of his wealth in artistic objects—statues, paintings and the like, most of which are of a religious nature. I cannot pretend to be any kind of expert on these matters, but I believe that some of these are extremely valuable, and some are in excess of five hundred years old. To house his collection, Faulkes converted the cellar of this house into a species of bank vault, with sophisticated locks and alarms.

" It seems that he was accustomed to spend much of his time there, especially in the evenings, examining and cataloguing his collection, and last night was no exception. At eleven o'clock, his usual time for retiring, he had not emerged from the cellar, and Simpkins, his personal servant, communicated with him by the telephonic apparatus installed in the house."

" Ah yes," replied Holmes. " The newspaper mentioned this, and I fear I failed to thoroughly grasp the full meaning."

" It is unique in my experience," replied Gregson, " at least in a private house such as this. Since the door of the vault is so thick, when it is closed it is impossible to hear any sound from outside once inside the vault, and vice versa. Accordingly, Faulkes had caused a telephonic apparatus to be installed, whereby the servants could communicate with him should a visitor chance to call, or should any other matter requiring his attention arise. On occasion, he had been known to fall asleep while in the vault, and the sound of the telephone bell in there, as activated by one of the servants, was then used to rouse him."

" And in this case, it did not ? " asked Holmes.

" That is correct. According to Simpkins, the bell should have rung for at least a minute, and since Faulkes was apparently a light sleeper, that would ordinarily have been ample time to rouse him. Simpkins therefore descended to the vault and proceeded to open it."

" One moment," interrupted Holmes. " How is the vault secured ? "

" By a combination lock. There is no key. The door can be locked from the inside, and Faulkes commonly did so while he was working on his collection. It was so secured last night, according to Simpkins."

" And Simpkins was in possession of the combination ? "

" So it would appear. He freely admits to the knowledge."

" Do any of the other servants possess the combination ? "

" Besides Simpkins, the household consists of a cook, a kitchen-maid and a house-maid. There is also a gardener, but he is employed by the hour, and does not live on the premises. The resident servants have been questioned, and all deny any knowledge of the combination."

" Well then, Simpkins entered the vault, and next ? "

" He beheld his master lying on the floor, with his head in a pool of blood and a fearful wound that had smashed the right temple like an eggshell. A fallen statue was by the body, with the arm broken off and lying by itself nearby."

" The arm had been used as the weapon, presumably ? " asked Holmes.

" Now, Mr. Holmes, this is one of the matters in this case that has me puzzled. No, the arm was not the weapon. The statue is that of an angel, constructed of some sort of plaster or other material, and with a solid octagonal stone base—granite or some such. To judge by the blood and hair and so on coating it, one corner of the heavy base had been used to strike the blow. But I am running a little ahead of myself in my recital of events. Faulkes was not dead, but he was unconscious. With considerable promptitude and presence of mind, Simpkins roused the two maids, and dispatched one to the doctor, and one to the Catholic priest who visited you yesterday. He and the cook stayed with Faulkes in the vault, not wishing to risk further injury by moving him, but attempted to make him comfortable. The priest and doctor arrived within the half-hour, but Faulkes was sinking fast. Both did what they could, but the end was near, and the Catholic rite of Last Unction was administered, the dying man being unable to form the responses. In the meantime, one of the girls had been sent to summon the local police, who immediately contacted the Yard. Hence my involvement."

" A pretty puzzle," remarked Holmes grimly. " We have a man in a locked room, with the sole method of entry known to himself and only one other, so far as we can determine at present. The man is struck down by an unknown assailant, who lets himself out of the locked room and locks it behind him again. Tell me, does the lock require the combination in order to unlock it from inside the vault or to re-lock it ? "

" That is something we have yet to discover," replied Gregson. " I take your meaning. If the assailant was locked in the vault with Faulkes, could he have let himself out and re-secured the entrance ? An excellent point, Mr. Holmes." He made a note in his notebook.

" Is the body still in the place where it was found ? "

" No, we felt it should be moved, and it is now in the morgue at the hospital. But," Gregson smiled, as Holmes started to raise a warning finger, " I have profited by my association with you. Before the body was moved, I adopted your excellent suggestion of using chalk to outline its position and attitude, as far as could be ascertained. The doctor had moved the arms and so on to compose the body for death, but I questioned him closely and I am satisfied that I have an accurate representation of the body as it was originally."

" I am glad to see that my teaching has not fallen on stony ground." Holmes smiled. " You will go a long way, Inspector. I foresee a bright future for you if you continue in this way. And the statue ? "

" That has remained untouched."

" Excellent. Now to the *Dramatis personæ*. What of this Simpkins ? How long has he been in his present position ? "

" He appears to be utterly reliable in his testimony. He has been with Faulkes for over thirty years now."

" I will want to question him, with your permission," said Holmes.

" If I may see your records of your preliminary questions to him, I will avoid duplication, and we may save some valuable time."

" Naturally," said Gregson, pushing a sheaf of papers towards Holmes, which my friend started to peruse. " I thought, however, that you would prefer to see the scene of the murder before anything else."

" Since you have moved the body already," replied Holmes, " there is little advantage to my examining that area immediately. Little will change, after all. On the other hand, the memories of witnesses fade very fast, and it is important to retrieve all those impressions as soon as possible after the event."

" I understand your reasoning," replied Gregson. He asked the constable standing at the door to call Simpkins for questioning.

The man who entered was an elderly man, apparently sixty years or over in age, but still of an upright and sprightly appearance. He was neatly dressed in servant's black, and I noticed that he had already secured a mourning band around his right sleeve.

" This gentleman here is Mr. Sherlock Holmes," Gregson said to him by way of introduction. " He is here to ask you a few more questions which may not have occurred to me when I talked to you earlier."

The elderly servant addressed my friend. " I have to confess, sir, that it is an honour for me to be conversing with the celebrated Sherlock Holmes, whose exploits I have admired when I have read about them. However, I sincerely wish that this meeting was under happier circumstances than the ones in which I find myself at present."

Holmes smiled benignly. " Thank you, Simpkins. I will try to make the process of questioning as painless as possible for you. My first question is with regard to the locking of the door of the vault. Is it necessary to use the combination to unlock the door from the inside ? "

" Yes, sir, it is."

" And is the combination also needed when the door is to be re-locked, either from the inside or from the outside of the vault ? "

" Yes, sir, from both the inside and the outside."

" Inspector Gregson has informed me that your master vouchsafed the combination to you. Has this combination been in your possession for a long time ? "

" No sir, he only gave me the combination just over one month ago."

" Thank you. To the best of your knowledge, are you the only member of this household other than your master who had knowledge of the combination ? "

" Yes sir, I am certain of it. I had been aware for several years, though, because he had informed me of the fact, that a copy of the combination had been lodged by Mr. Faulkes at his bank, and was to be made available to the executors of his will in the event of his untimely death."

" A very laudable precaution," observed Holmes. " Would you care to give us the combination ? " The other hesitated. " There is little merit in your keeping it a secret now. As you have just told us, the executor of the will has full access, and it would be a simple matter for the Inspector here to obtain a court order to release it from the bank's custody."

" Very good, sir." Simpkins seemed to be speaking with some reluctance. " The combination is 22-07-18-73."

" Thank you," replied Holmes, as

Gregson wrote down these numbers in his notebook. " Inspector Gregson has already informed me of your prompt and meritorious actions following the discovery of your master. Is there anything that you would like to add to those observations ? Did your master have any enemies of whom you are aware ? "

The aged servant shook his head. " No sir, I think that I have provided as full an account as is possible under the circumstances. Please rest assured, sir, that if I recollect anything further that would seem to further the inquiry I will immediately inform the police."

" Thank you for your cooperation, Simpkins," said Gregson. " Do you have any more questions, Mr. Holmes ? "

" Indeed I do. Simpkins, can you recollect any visitors who called on your master frequently ? "

" Other than the Italian gentleman, you mean, sir ? "

Holmes, Gregson, and I exchanged glances. " You never mentioned this Italian gentleman earlier," said Gregson sternly. " Perhaps you should tell us a little more about him."

The other was obviously flustered by this request. " Well, sir, I would hardly describe him as a gentleman, if I were to be completely honest with you. Mr. Faulkes was always at home to him, however, and he and Mr. Faulkes spent many hours together in the museum."

" Which museum is this ? " asked Holmes.

" My apologies, sir," replied Simpkins. " We servants often described the master's collection as 'the museum' in jest. What I meant by my last remark was that Mr. Faulkes and his Italian visitor would often spend time with the collection."

" Do you happen to know if this Italian is connected with the antiquities trade ? " asked Holmes.

" I have no knowledge regarding that, sir," replied the other.

" When was the last time that this Italian personage came to call ? "

" Why, sir, last night."

Gregson started to his feet, his face contorted with anger. " Pardon my language, Mr. Simpkins, but blast you, you never provided us with this information when I asked you about the events of yesterday evening earlier. Why did you omit this from your report ? "

" I was not completely convinced that it was of immediate relevance, sir," replied the servant.

" You will permit me, Simpkins, to decide what is relevant and what is not relevant in this case," retorted Gregson, subsiding into his seat.

The other looked abashed. " I am sorry, sir," he replied at length.

" If I may ? " interjected Holmes. " Simpkins, did you admit this Italian visitor, and did you show him out, and at what times did he arrive and did he depart ? "

" He arrived at the house at eight o'clock precisely," replied Simpkins. " I opened the door to him, and showed him into the drawing-room where Mr. Faulkes was waiting for him."

" He was expected, the ? " Gregson asked.

" Yes, Mr. Faulkes had informed me previously that he was expected. He was a reasonably regular visitor to the house. He started visiting the house about four years ago, making his visits approximately once every month, until about a month ago, when he started to visit on an almost weekly basis."

" And what time did he depart last nigh ? " enquired Holmes.

" Were you the one who showed him to the door ? "

" As far as I could tell, he left the house a little before nine o'clock. I was not the one who showed him to the door, you should understand."

" You are sure that he left the house ? " asked Gregson.

The other replied a little stiffly. " I heard Mr. Faulkes and the visitor walking through the hall towards the front door together, engaged in conversation. I heard them bidding each other a good night. I heard the front door open and close, and I heard a single set of footsteps walking through the hallway, and descending the steps to the cellar. I am therefore as positive as I can be that Mr. Faulkes himself let his visitor out of the house and returned alone to the vault. I heard the sound of the vault door opening and then closing."

" And you never heard the door open again ? "

" No, sir, I did not. The door makes a somewhat distinctive sound when opened, and I am convinced I would have heard it, had it been opened again."

" A most astute set of observations," remarked Holmes. " Did you, by any chance, happen to remark the nature of the conversation that they might have had before bidding each other good nigh ? "

The servant's sallow face took on a faint flush. " I am sorry to say, sir, that I did. Their conversation was in the nature of a disagreement." He paused. " Is it necessary for me to report this to yo ? "

" It is your duty, man," replied Gregson, sternly.

" I do not know the nature of the disagreement. Believe me, I am not concealing anything in this regard. However, I heard my master saying, 'I must do it tonight. I have

no choice.' And the Italian visitor saying, 'It shall not happen tonight, and if I could, I would move heaven and earth to prevent it.'"

" And your master's response to this ? " asked Holmes.

" He replied, 'You cannot frighten me further. In any case, my mind is made up.' Following this, he and Mr. Paravinci went outside the front door. I assume that they bade each other a good night before Mr. Faulkes re-entered the house and closed the front door before going downstairs to the cellar."

" Ha ! The mysterious gentleman's name is Paravinci, the ? " said Gregson. " Does this personage have any other name, and is there any other information you can give us about hi ? "

" I am reasonably certain that his Christian name is Antonio. I heard Mr. Faulkes address him as such on several occasions in the past. He lives in London, at an address in Whitechapel, which I will recall in a minute, if you will permit me." He paused, obviously in thought. " Yes, number 42, Greatorex Street was the address on the letters to him from Mr. Faulkes that I conveyed to the post."

Gregson was scribbling furiously in his notebook. " And his age ? "

" I would guess he is in his late twenties. Maybe a little over thirty years of age, but only a little."

" Can you describe hi ? " Gregson demanded.

" There is no need for that, Inspector," Holmes chided gently. " I am sure we will be speaking to the man himself before too long."

Gregson nodded in agreement, and turned back to Simpkins. " This information should all have been given to us earlier." It was obvious that his anger had only abated slightly. " You are fortunate,

Simpkins, that I have not had you arrested for obstruction of justice."

" Come now, Inspector," soothed Holmes. " Mr. Simpkins is naturally in a state of some confusion following last night's tragic events." He turned to the servant. " What words would you use to describe the tone of voice that you hear ? "

" Although the two were obviously in disagreement, there was no anger on either side. If I were to describe the tone of voice of both parties, I would say it was closer to a form of resignation rather than anger, sir." Simpkins was obviously relieved at not having to face Gregson's wrath further.

" If you had to make a guess as to the meaning of the words you overhear ? " Holmes prompted.

" I would not like to hazard any such conjecture," said the other.

" Very good," said Holmes. " I have no further questions at present. Inspector ? "

" Nothing at present," echoed Gregson. " Well, Simpkins, I hope that if anything further occurs to you, you will have the kindness to inform me or one of my officers, regardless of whether you consider it relevant to the enquiry or not." His tone was heavily sarcastic, and the unfortunate Simpkins shuffled his feet, and muttered some sort of apology, his eyes downcast. " You may leave us," added Gregson.

" Well, Watson," said Holmes to me after the servant had left the room. " You were silent throughout the whole of that conversation, if I may term it such. What are your impression ? "

" He is hiding something."

" By Jove, without a doubt he is hiding something," agreed Gregson, angrily. " And I am willing to lay money that he and this Italian devil Paravinci were blackmailing poor Faulkes over some petty misdemeanour that took place long ago."

" Blackmail seems to be a likely possibility to me," I concurred. " Holmes, what is your opinion ? "

" I agree with you both that Simpkins is concealing something from us. However, I disagree with your conclusion that it is blackmail, though I am at present unable to assign a precise reason for my belief. I am certain that we will never be able to extract the hidden information from Simpkins. He strikes me as being one of the bulldog type who, once in possession of a secret, will never surrender it unless it is dragged out by force. The other servants, what of them ? " he asked Gregson.

" You may see their statements here," replied the Scotland Yard detective. " I have no reason to doubt them, but we may summon them for further questioning if you think this would be of value."

" At this point in the enquiry, I will forbear. I think now would be a suitable time to view the scene downstairs. If we could arrange to speak with Father Donahue," he pulled out his watch and consulted it, " in about ninety minutes' time, I would appreciate this. Do you think you could instruct one of your men to arrange this ? "

" Certainly we can do that. I fail to see what information he will be able to provide, though, since he was not present immediately after the attack on Faulkes. I will also send orders for this Italian Paravinci to be brought in for questioning. Does it not seem a coincidence to you that the papers of which you spoke, and a sample of which you showed me earlier are also from Italy ? "

" No coincidence at all. But beware of the obvious, Inspector.

It can often be deceptive," was Holmes' only comment, as we rose from the table and made our way out of the room towards the cellar.

HE descriptions of the cellar both as a " vault" and as a " museum" certainly had much to commend them. The entrance to the cellar was guarded by a solid door, some six inches in thickness, and secured by a complex combination lock. Once inside the cellar, I was astounded, as was Holmes, insofar as I could judge by his reaction, by the works of art contained therein.

Three of the walls were lined with glass cases, containing small paintings, works of art, illuminated books from a bygone age, and gold and silver ornaments, most of them with a religious origin. A few weapons, mainly jewelled daggers and the like, also graced the cases. Larger paintings of a primitive medieval style hung above the cases, and though I would not pretend to expertise in the field, they seemed to me to be of Italian origin. The fourth wall facing the door had no cases arranged along its length, but was lined by a row of some dozen statues depicting angels playing musical instruments, each about four feet in height. There was a gap in the middle of the line of statues, and I immediately guessed that this space had been filled by the statue responsible for Faulkes' death.

Holmes stopped in the doorway, and looked around him.

" It is quite a sight, is it not, Mr. Holmes ? " said Gregson, smiling.

" Indeed it is," he replied. " I am not surprised at the servants' name for this room. This is an impressive door, is it not ? " He swung the heavy door closed, and as gently as it closed, there was a distinctive thud as it swung ponderously into its frame. " Let us open it again," he said, tugging at the handle. As the door swung open, there was a loud creaking sound from the hinges. " As the good Simpkins remarked, it is a most distinctive sound, and I am reasonably certain that he would have noticed it had the door been opened again after Faulkes had returned here." He walked slowly about the room, examining the display of curios, his hands clasped behind his back. " Has anything been removed, do you know ? "

" I see no obvious gaps in the cases," replied Gregson. " All are locked, and none has been forced. I detect no sign of any object or painting hanging on the wall having being removed."

" You would rule out robbery as a motive, then ? " asked Holmes.

" I cannot be completely certain as yet. The ledger upstairs appears to be a meticulous record of all the objects contained in this room. I will naturally have a check made of the contents of the room and compared to the lists in the ledger. I will be surprised, though, if there is any discrepancy."

" I too," remarked Holmes. " However, I commend your attention to detail in making such a check." He broke off suddenly. " How is this room ventilated ? " he asked Gregson. " I take it that these gas lamps have been burning continuously since the body was discovered, and therefore since yesterday evening ? "

" We have not touched them," confirmed Gregson. " If you will take the trouble to look upwards, you will see a sliding grille in the centre of the ceiling communicating with some sort of vent leading to the outside. It appears that the grille can be opened and closed by this cord here," pointing to a loop of stout sash-cord suspended from the ceiling. " We have not touched this, either. And before you start to go off on one of your theories, Mr. Holmes," he smiled, " the vent is a mere nine inches in diameter. I think it is most unlikely that the murderer could have entered and exited the room by that route. There are also two ventilation grilles above the door, leading to the cellar proper. Those are likewise too small for any entry or exit."

" I agree with your conclusions," Holmes replied, apparently not at all offended by Gregson's gentle chaff. " The ventilation has hardly dispersed the smell of ether, though."

" Ether ? " exclaimed Gregson. " I confess that I am suffering from a slight cold, and had failed to remark any such odour."

" I can also perceive a slight smell of ether," I confirmed. " Undoubtedly it is ether, Inspector. No doubt left behind from the doctor's examination of the body."

" No doubt," answered Holmes, absent-mindedly. By this time, he had arrived at the spot in the centre of the room where a chalk outline marked the position of the body as the police had outlined it in the way Gregson had described. A large dark stain marked the floor at the point where the head had lain. " The injury was to the right temple, you say ? " he asked. Gregson confirmed this. " So the body was lying face uppermost, if the evidence of the bloodstain is to be believed ? " The policeman nodded.

" So we may conclude that the blow was struck with the left hand."

" I had remarked that. Simpkins, by the way, is right-handed, as are all the servants in the house."

" Well done, Inspector. Such an early elimination is always of value. Even though you and I still suspect Simpkins of being somewhat less than straightforward, we do not suspect him of the killing, do we ? Never fear, we will soon discover whatever it is that he feels he must keep secret from us. There is a considerable amount of blood, is there not ? We must assume that a major blood vessel was damaged by the blow. And this," he went on, bending forward, " is the angel of death, if we may term it such."

A shiver went over me as he pronounced this description, and even Gregson, whom I had imagined to be immune to such feelings, appeared to shiver at the words.

" With your permission, Inspector, I would like to remove a sample of the hair and tissue attached to this ? " Gregson signified his assent, and Holmes delicately removed a small sample of the gore that was attached to the base of the statue. I Drew closer and examined the object more closely. Obviously one of the set of statues by the wall, this particular angel had been in the act of holding a trumpet aloft. The arm holding the trumpet had broken away from the body, and now lay some distance from it among the bloodstains. I examined the arm as closely as I could without touching it, and discovered it to be hollow, and apparently composed of some sort of earthenware, somewhat similar to terracotta, which had been decorated with paint, as could be discerned from the chips of material surrounding it. I returned to the main body, and examined the base of the statue which, as we had been informed, was composed of stone, in the shape of an octagon.

" Let us try the weight of one of these," remarked Holmes, standing up and moving to the wall. He grasped one of the statues around the middle and lifted. " The weight is concentrated in the base, as you might expect," he observed. " In fact, the whole thing is somewhat like a large hammer."

" Somewhat clumsy and ill-shaped, though, as far as any practical purpose is concerned," I pointed out. " Why, the merest blow would shatter the 'handle'."

" Indeed it would, Watson." The idea appeared to give him pause for thought and he strode back to the centre of the room where he stood, gazing up at the ventilator, and down at the chalk outline and the statue and its detached arm. Gregson watched with amused puzzlement.

Holmes returned to the line of statues, and examined them closely. " This one has been broken and repaired," he noted. " See here, Watson."

I examined the artwork in question, noting that its arm had become detached in much the same way as the one by the body, and had been repaired by a very unskilled hand. " Why, Holmes," I exclaimed, " it seems that the glue used to piece this together is hardly Dry."

" Indeed," said Holmes. " Without knowing the exact composition of the adhesive, we cannot tell the exact date at which the repair was carried out, but my impression that it was within the last few days at most. I have seen enough here for present. Can you give orders that nothing is to be touched or moved, Inspector ? "

" Certainly."

We returned upstairs to the dining-room to find that Simpkins, maybe to make amends for his earlier reticence, had, without being asked, laid out an excellent luncheon of cold meats and salads. We thanked him, and the previous gory scene notwithstanding, fell to with good appetites.

When we were almost finished, and Simpkins had brought in coffee, there was a ring at the front door.

" Ah, the priest," exclaimed Holmes. " I had almost forgotten about him."

Father Donahue was ushered into the room, and persuaded to take coffee with us.

" A tragic business," he intoned, wagging his head.

" And I owe you an apology, Father, for not acting more promptly," replied Holmes contritely. " If I may borrow the words of your Church, with all due sincerity, I pronounce *mea culpa, mea culpa, mea maxima culpa.*"

" There is nothing for which you can blame yourself, I feel," replied the priest. " There was no way that you could have foreseen this."

" Do you have any idea who might have done the deed ? " asked Holmes.

" I cannot say," replied the cleric.

" I understand," my friend replied, pensively. " To change the subject, Father, you were with the unfortunate man when he died. Did he utter any words to you before he passed away ? "

The other shook his head. " Nothing. He was unconscious when I arrived and was incapable of speech. Thanks be to God, he was at least alive, and I was able to administer Extreme Unction to him. There was no thought of my hearing his confession or his performing Penance or taking the Eucharist. I am certain, though, that he died in a state of grace, and that his soul's stay in Purgatory will be a short one."

Such a discussion of religious matters made me uncomfortable and uneasy, as it would the majority of Englishmen. I noticed that Gregson appeared to share my discomfort, but Holmes appeared to be unaffected by this Romish show of piety.

" And as far as you are aware, the doctor likewise noted no words from Faulkes before he died ? " he asked.

" Not that I am aware of. He said nothing to me, if he did. Not that I would expect him to," added the priest, not without a certain humour. " Dr. Addison, like so many of his profession, saving your presence, Dr. Watson, is a so-called freethinker—in other words, an unbeliever."

" Are you aware," my friend asked suddenly, " of the name Paravinci ? Does it mean anything to you ? "

" I believe I may have encountered the name," said the priest. " I have worked with Italian immigrants in the East End of London, and the name is not an uncommon one."

" Antonio Paravinci ? " pressed Holmes.

Donahue shrugged. " Possibly. Antonio is likewise a common Christian name. I do not have any special recollection of anyone by that name. May I ask why you are enquiring ? "

" You may certainly ask, Father, but I am under no obligation to provide you with an answer. Like you, I have my professional secrets." Holmes smiled at the cleric, and the priest, obviously taken with the conceit, smiled in return.

" If you have no more questions,"

said Donahue, " I must away to my flock. More mundane matters, but ones, I assure you, of equal importance to this affair in the eyes of God." He took his leave and departed.

" A strange fellow, that," remarked Gregson.

" But sharp, for all that," Holmes replied.

" Even though he knows nothing of this matter ? "

" He never said that he knows nothing," countered Holmes.

" Did he not ? I rather fancied that he did," answered the police detective.

" Consider his exact words to us. Be that as it may," replied Holmes, " I would like to view the body at the mortuary, if I may receive your permission to do so."

" Granted without reservation," said Gregson. " Dr. Watson, I take it you will want to be present ? "

" Naturally," I replied.

" Good." Gregson scribbled his signature on a piece of paper from his notebook and handed it to Holmes. " Between you and me, Doctor," turning to me, " the police surgeon here strikes me as somewhat of a fool, and I do not altogether trust his conclusions. Your observations would provide me with a more reliable view of the situation."

At that moment, there was another ring at the door, and a constable was admitted.

" Begging your pardon, sir," he addressed Gregson. " We've just had a wire from Scotland Yard in at the station. They have located the Italian party in question, and can be bringing him here within an hour if you wish, or if you prefer, they will hold him in London to wait for your return."

Gregson turned to Holmes.

" I would strongly recommend

bringing him here," said Holmes. " If nothing else, he can be positively identified by Simpkins, and we can observe their reactions when confronted with each other if it appears desirable to do so."

" That would seem to be good sense," agreed Gregson. " Ask London to send him up here as soon as possible, in the company of a pair of constables. Also ensure that Sergeant Wilkerson comes here at the same time," he said to the local policeman, who acknowledged the order and left us.

" Who is this Sergeant Wilkerson ? " asked Holmes. " The name is unfamiliar to me."

Gregson smiled. " He is a new addition to the strength of Scotland Yard, and something of a rarity in our ranks. He is a graduate of Cambridge University, and acts as the Force's expert when it comes to questions of an artistic nature, such as forgery or theft of paintings and the like. His rank of Sergeant is a somewhat honorary one. He is no-one's idea of a Metropolitan Police officer, to be sure."

" You intrigue me," replied Holmes. " I look forward to the pleasure of his acquaintance."

" He will be with us within the hour, I hope."

" Then, Watson, let us make haste to the mortuary," suggested Holmes. " We will return in about an hour, or a little more, Inspector, and inform you of our findings."

 PON our arrival at the hospital, Holmes seemed relatively uninterested in the body of Francis Faulkes after the first inspection, concentrating his attention on the contents of the deceased's pockets, which had been sorted and labelled by the mortuary staff.

I occupied myself with examining the body, concentrating my attention on the right temple, where the ghastly wound gaped. It was a little lower down and to the front than I had been led to believe, and the bone around the hole formed by the angle of the statue's base was obviously crushed. I was surprised, given the nature of the wound and the obvious force with which the blow had been delivered, that Faulkes had survived and had not been killed outright. I had borrowed one of Holmes' lenses to examine the details more closely, and as I moved the glass over the dead man's face, I noticed some tufts of what appeared to be cotton-wool adhering to the inside rim of the nostrils.

" Have you cleaned or plugged the facial orifices ? " I asked one of the attendants.

" No, sir," he replied. " The body is in exactly the same state as it was when it was brought in to us a few hours ago. No-one has touched it, by police orders."

I Drew Holmes' attention to the detail. " Excellent, Watson. I had somewhat suspected that we would find something of the sort. See here." He displayed to me a number of cotton-wool pads which had been found in the dead man's possession. " Not that these are necessarily significant in themselves," he remarked, " but taken in conjunction with this," holding up a small bottle, " I feel that there may be some answer to the problem before us. Note that this pad, especially, has been soaked in liquid at some point in the recent past—the same liquid, I feel certain, that is contained herein."

" What is it ? " I asked.

" Precisely what I expected to find," he replied, unstoppering the bottle and holding it under my nose.

" Ether ! " I exclaimed. " As we noted in that cellar. But what does it mean ? If we had discovered that cotton-wool on the floor, or elsewhere, I would say that Faulkes' assailant had attempted to anaesthetise him. As it is, would he attempt the same on himself ? "

" Inhaling or even imbibing ether is popular as a recreation among certain classes of society, it is true," admitted Holmes. " It is possible that Faulkes would have indulged in this way, but I have my doubts as to that. I noticed in the dining-room a goodly supply of fine liqueurs, and those who appreciate good wine and brandy are, in my experience, unlikely to resort to ether as a solace. I may, of course, be wrong, but I feel that I am now close to a solution here. I am confident that the mysterious Signor Paravinci will supply a few of the missing pieces, and then I will be in a position to confirm my suspicions when we return to London."

I must confess that I was completely in the dark. Before we left, I made a sketch of the deceased's ear at Holmes' request, but I could make no sense of his wishes, as indeed, of the whole business, which continued to be a mystery to me.

We returned to the Faulkes residence to find Gregson still seated at the dining table. A young man, by his looks and dress a workman of some kind, was sitting in the corner, flanked on either side by a burly constable.

" Your sense of timing continues to be excellent, Mr. Holmes," Gregson greeted us. " Mr. Paravinci has arrived not five minutes ago. Sergeant Wilkerson is downstairs with the catalogue, ensuring that the collection is complete and that there is nothing missing." He turned to address the Italian. " We wish to ask you a few questions. First of all, I wish to know whether you are happy for us to speak in English, or whether you wish an interpreter to be provided for you."

" I am happy to speak in English," replied the other, with a very faint foreign accent. " I anticipate no problem in understanding you, and I trust that you will have no difficulty in understanding my replies to you."

" That is a relief," said Gregson. " I dislike working through an interpreter. I must also warn you that this is an official interview, and anything you say will be taken down in writing, and may be used against you in formal criminal proceedings. Is that clear ? "

" Perfectly clear," replied the other. " Am I under arrest ? "

" No, you are not. You are free to leave at any time, but I have to tell you that this will probably be interpreted as evidence of guilt, and you will then be arrested."

The other shrugged. " I understand."

" Please come here and sit facing us on the other side of the table. I am Inspector Gregson of Scotland Yard, and the gentlemen on my right and left are the private detective Mr. Sherlock Holmes and his colleague Dr. John Watson who are assisting me."

The Italian stood, and it was obvious that he was a strong, powerfully built young man, who would have had no difficulty in wielding the statue identified as the murder weapon. He had none of the swarthiness we usually associate with the Italian race and indeed, could easily have passed for a certain type of Englishman.

" You are Antonio Paravinci ? "

" I am," was the steady reply.

" How long have you lived in England ? "

" A little over four years."

" And you have known Mr. Faulkes all that time ? "

" I have known him since before I arrived in England. Mr. Faulkes has been a friend of my family in Italy for many years."

" How do you earn your living ? "

Here Holmes interrupted. " My dear Inspector, it is superfluous for you to ask that question. It is obvious that Signor Paravinci earns his living in the printing trade, spending most of his time as a compositor, as is evidenced by his thumb, and the ink under his fingernails."

Gregson flushed, and the Italian smiled faintly. " Yes, I work at a small printing shop, owned and operated by a fellow Italian," he acknowledged. " Fallini and Company, in Whitechapel. I have been with them since my arrival in this country."

" Did you visit Mr. Faulkes regularly ? "

" I used to visit him monthly, until just over one month ago, when I started to visit him more frequently."

" Would you explain to us why you changed your habits ? "

" I would prefer not to answer that, if you have no objection."

Gregson raised his eyebrows, but continued his questioning. " We have been told that you visited this house last night."

" That is so."

" We were also informed that you and Mr. Faulkes engaged in a dispute as you were leaving the house."

" It was more in the nature of a

disagreement than a dispute," countered Paravinci.

" And perhaps you would care to tell us of the nature of this disagreement ? " suggested Gregson, laying what I felt was an unnecessary emphasis on the last word.

" May I refuse to tell you ? "

" If you wish to keep silent on the matter, you may do so," replied Gregson. " I have no authority to compel you in this matter—as yet. After your disagreement, you left the house ? "

" I did," the other replied.

" And then ? " Gregson sighed. " I hope that you are aware that you are not being very forthcoming, Mr. Paravinci."

" Very well. I will tell you what I did. I left the house and walked to the station. I caught the 9:32 train to Euston. From there, I walked to Euston Square station and took the railway to the Whitechapel station. From there I walked to my lodgings in Greatorex Street. I arrived home between a quarter before eleven and eleven o'clock, I guess."

" Did anyone see you either on your journey home, or when you arrived at your lodgings ? "

" I am sorry that I am unable to supply you with an alibi," replied the other calmly. " Of course I saw many people on my journey, but none known to me personally. It is possible, I suppose, that the ticket collector at this station or even at Euston or Whitechapel might remember me, but otherwise, I am unable to provide proof of my actions. May I go now ? I have work waiting to be completed."

" I have only a few more questions, and then you will be free to leave. First, what is your relationship with Albert Simpkins, the late Mr. Faulkes' servant ? "

" I hardly know him. He lets me

into the house, he shows me to Mr. Faulkes. He has served me with food and drink sometimes. Sometimes he lets me out of the house, sometimes Mr. Faulkes performs that office himself. I know nothing of him as a person."

Gregson wrote in his notebook. " Do you know Father Patrick Donahue of Holy Rood Church ? "

" I know that he is the priest here, and that Mr. Faulkes sometimes mentioned him in conversation."

" I suppose it is useless to ask you to describe the content of your conversations with Mr. Faulkes ? "

Paravinci smiled. " Not entirely useless, Inspector. As you might imagine, we discussed personal matters that I would sooner not mention here. However, much of our conversation revolved around his collection. My uncles in Rome are art dealers and restorers. It is through his dealings with them that Mr. Faulkes became acquainted with my family and with me. Very often I acted as an intermediary in some business dealings when he wished to purchase some item for his collection."

" Did you handle money in connection with these dealings ? " asked Gregson.

" Yes, he used to entrust me with the money for the purchases on occasion. I was able to remit the money to my uncles through my employer, Fallini, more easily than Mr. Faulkes was able to do himself."

" Did you receive a commission for your services ? "

The other flushed. " I did not seek any reward in this regard, but Mr. Faulkes insisted that I take something for my trouble. This money I did not keep for myself, but gave to St Anne's church in Whitechapel. The priest there can

confirm this. Am I now free to go ? "

Gregson sighed again. " You are free to go, Mr. Paravinci, if Mr. Holmes here has no questions ? " Holmes shook his head. " But I would advise you to cooperate a little more freely when you are questioned next time about this matter."

" You think I will be questioned again ? "

" I am certain of it. I must ask you to wait here for a few minutes only while I complete my account of this conversation, following which I will ask you to sign it."

" Very well," replied the Italian, somewhat sullenly, crossing his legs and folding his arms as he waited.

After a few minutes of writing, Gregson pushed a few sheets of paper towards Paravinci and proffered a pen. " Please read through this, and place your signature at the bottom of each page to show your agreement of this being a true and accurate account of our conversation."

The other took the papers, and scanned them rapidly, affixing his signature at the bottom of each page before rising to his feet, and pushing the papers back towards Gregson. " I may go now ? " he asked once again.

" You may indeed," replied the policeman.

As Paravinci turned to leave, Holmes called to him. " One moment, Signor Paravinci. You may wish to make use of this in the near future." He extended one of his calling cards, engraved with his name and the Baker Street address, on which he had scribbled a few words. " Maybe ten o'clock tomorrow morning would be a convenient time for you to call ? "

The other, obviously slightly mystified by this, nodded. " I know

SHERLOCK HOLMES & THE MYSTERY OF THE PARADOL CHAMBER

something of your name and your reputation. I will endeavour to keep the appointment." He bowed slightly, and left the room.

Gregson regarded Holmes curiously. "The man may be in the cells by ten o'clock tomorrow," he remarked. "You noticed, I am sure that he signed those papers with his left hand ? "

"And the deceased's wound would appear to have been inflicted by another's left hand ? Yes, I did notice that detail."

"We know that he regularly handled money, and for all we know, valuable works of art on behalf of the dead man. He is an Italian and a printer by trade. Surely you have not overlooked the connection with the papers received by Faulkes ? "

"I have not," replied Holmes, evenly,

"We know that he was a regular visitor, and that by his own admission he was here last night. Simpkins identified him as last night's visitor just before you arrived, by the way."

"And did you observe the reaction of both men when they were brought together ? "

"There was little to observe on the part of Paravinci," replied Gregson. "However, I noted an expression that appeared to be almost one of sorrow on Simpkins' face when he was led into the room and confronted the other."

"The case against him does indeed look somewhat strong," commented Holmes.

"I would say it is almost convincing," replied Gregson. "I was close to arresting the man on the spot just now for the murder of Francis Faulkes."

"Then it is a very good thing that you did not," retorted Holmes, "for if you had, you would have

been making a blunder of the first order, which would have dealt your career a losing card."

"Come now," exclaimed Gregson. "You cannot believe that he is innocent of the murder of Francis Faulkes ? "

"I am convinced of his innocence of that crime," said Holmes. "And I would strongly advise you, for the sake of your future, if for no other reason, to stay your hand for the next twenty-four hours, within which time I am positive that I will be able to convince you, too, that whatever other crimes of which he may be guilty—and I am not as yet convinced of the exact facts concerning those—Antonio Paravinci is innocent of murder."

"We know who killed Francis Faulkes, do we not, and he has just left the room," protested Gregson.

"I believe the killer never left the vault," replied Holmes calmly.

Gregson had just opened his mouth to expostulate, but there was a knock on the door, and a middle-aged man entered the room in answer to Gregson's summons, peering through his thick spectacles. He was shabbily dressed in a tweed suit, and his thinning dark hair was combed over his forehead. "Sergeant Wilkerson," announced Gregson, and proceeded to introduce us. As Gregson had mentioned earlier, it was hard to associate the man's appearance with his profession as a police officer. From his looks, he would have been more at home in a University, or maybe as the curator of a museum.

"Inspector Gregson has already spoken of you," remarked Holmes. "I had no idea until then that the Metropolitan Police Force included such a rara avis in its ranks," he smiled.

"I believe I am unique, at least

in this country," replied the other, returning the smile, " though some of the Continental forces employ specialists who perform similar functions to my own. Naturally I have heard of you, Mr. Holmes, and you, Dr. Watson, and it is a pleasure to make your acquaintance." He spoke in a reedy voice, with a little of the academic specialist about it, matching his appearance.

" How do the contents of the room downstairs tally with the catalogue ? " Gregson asked Wilkerson.

" I have been unable to discover any discrepancy. I was able to complete the task speedily, since both the catalogue and the collection are excellently ordered, making the task relatively simple. There is, however, a single point that excited my attention."

" That being ? " asked Holmes.

" The catalogue contains not only a full description of the items forming their collection, but also their provenance—in other words, the history of the item before it entered the collection, so far as it can be ascertained—and the price paid for the item. It is with regard to that last that my attention was drawn."

" In what way ? " asked Holmes.

" Mr. Faulkes has been somewhat rash with regard to the payment for many of the items in the collection, in my opinion. It is impossible to fix the precise value of such items with any degree of exactitude, but by my estimate, some items have been purchased for over twice their true value."

" You say some items ? " asked Holmes. " The others were purchased for a fair price, in your opinion ? "

" I would say that the prices paid for the other items were reasonable, or even under the price I would expect to see asked for them."

" Could this not simply be a matter of chance ? " I enquired. " After all, connoisseurs have been known to be in error regarding these matters, have they not ? "

" I would agree that this would seem a likely possibility," agreed the specialist, " were it not for the fact that all these purchases were made from the same dealer in Rome."

" The name of this dealer ? " asked Holmes. " I fancy I can guess, but I would appreciate confirmation of the matter."

" Is this really of relevance ? " asked Gregson. " I really fail to see how the name of an Italian art dealer can be of interest to us. Well, Wilkerson, indulge Mr. Holmes' curiosity."

" The dealers in question are called Paravinci Fratelli—that is in English, the Paravinci Brothers."

Gregson looked stunned. " You were correct in your surmise, Mr. Holmes. This definitely does seem of relevance." He noticed Wilkerson's bewilderment, and hastened to explain. " The Italian whom we have just been interviewing is named Paravinci, and informed us in the course of our questioning that his uncles are art dealers. You now inform us that the money paid to these Paravincis was over double what it should have been on a number of occasions. This would seem to be of significance."

" This is merely my opinion, Inspector," replied the other. " It might be that other specialists would interpret the pricing of these *objets* somewhat differently from my estimates."

" I hardly think it would be a significant difference," remarked Holmes. " You are, after all, the James Wilkerson who published that definitive monograph on the varnishes used by Cremona violin makers of the seventeenth century, are you not ? "

A faint flush stole to the expert's cheek. " Dear me, I had no idea that my fame had spread so far," he exclaimed. " I suppose you are correct. Others might have opinions that would differ slightly from mine, but I do not think it would be a significant divergence."

" It makes the case against young Paravinci look even more damning, does it not ? " Gregson said to us.

" Possibly," replied Holmes, with an abstracted air. " I think that one important fact has been imparted to us just now, though."

" That being ? " asked Gregson.

" That there is no discrepancy between the entries in the catalogue and the contents of the vault. I suppose," turning to Wilkerson, " that there is no possibility that any pages of that ledger have been removed ? "

" None whatsoever. Mr. Faulkes was a very conscientious recorder of his collection. All pages and entries are numbered in sequence, and the removal of a page would be instantly detectable."

" Do you have any knowledge of the statues, one example of which was found near the body ? " asked Holmes.

" The catalogue marks them as being late thirteenth or early fourteenth century Milanese. They were probably made to stand inside a church or private chapel, given their relatively fragile nature and the type of colouring used on them."

" Were they purchased from the Paravinci brothers ? " asked Gregson.

" As it happens," replied Wilkerson, consulting the ledger, " they were not, and he paid what I would consider to be considerably under the market price for them."

" Thank you, Sergeant, that is all we need from you at the moment, is that not so, Mr. Holmes ? "

" I agree. But it may be that we will require Mr. Wilkerson's talents in the future. For now, I have a few further questions that I would like to ask of Simpkins."

Gregson passed the word for Simpkins to be summoned, and Wilkerson left us. The servant entered a few minutes later.

" I have only a few questions for you," asked Holmes. " Firstly, was Dr. Addison usually consulted by Mr. Faulkes as his medical adviser ? "

" Yes, sir. Dr. Addison has been his physician for over fifteen years now."

" Did he ever consult any other doctors ? "

" About five or six weeks ago, he went up to London, and he told me that he was going to see another doctor in Harley Street."

" Do you know the doctor's name ? " asked Gregson.

" I am sorry, sir. Mr. Faulkes did not see fit to give me that information."

Holmes posed the next question. " Can you describe Mr. Faulkes' moods ? Would you, for example, describe him as being a cheerful man ? "

" Up until about a month ago, I would have said that he was cheerful, sir. He was happy, and often smiled and joked about matters with me. But over the past weeks, he seemed to change and become more serious."

" Can you tell us whether this change took place before or after the visit to London that you mentioned earlier ? "

" As I recall, sir, this was after the visit to London."

" And what of his habits with

regard to eating and drinking ? " asked Holmes.

" Again, he used to enjoy his food and drink. I don't want to give the impression that he drank a lot, sir, but he did enjoy his brandy of an evening, and he dearly loved a good beefsteak. But after that trip to London, he went off his food, I'd have to say, sir."

" Did he appear in any way ill, in your opinion ? "

" I'm no doctor, sir, but I wouldn't have said so. He was an elderly gentleman, and he wasn't getting any younger, if you take my meaning. None of us is, come to that."

" Quite," replied Holmes, shortly. " I think that answers my questions admirably, thank you, Simpkins."

The servant bowed slightly to Holmes and left us.

" I think, Watson, it is time for us to return to London. Inspector, I think you now have all the facts in your possession. It is up to you to work on them and conclude the solution for yourself. If you would care to call on us tomorrow at about eleven o'clock, I think that we will be able to close this case satisfactorily."

Gregson looked at me and shrugged his shoulders as if questioning me. As for myself, I had no more idea than did Gregson as to the solution of the mystery. I therefore shook my head, and followed Holmes out of the room.

HE next morning saw Holmes and myself waiting for Paravinci to show himself at Baker Street. Holmes had been irritatingly silent regarding the events at Watford during our return to London and throughout the previous evening.

As soon as we had finished our breakfast, he slipped out of the house, promising to return before ten o'clock. Sure enough, a little before the appointed hour, he returned, bearing a small portfolio of papers. He regard me with a quizzical expression.

" You are, no doubt, wondering whether Signor Paravinci will grace this room with his presence at ten o'clock ? " he asked me.

" I was indeed wondering that," I replied. " How can you be certain that he will make the journey here ? "

" I think that the message I wrote on the card will be sufficient

inducement to bring him to us." As he spoke, there was a ring at the front door, and I could hear Mrs. Hudson admitting a visitor. A minute later, Antonio Paravinci entered.

" I had to come," he started the conversation. " Please explain the message that you wrote on the card you gave me yesterday. 'If you do not come, you will surely be hanged' is not the kind of invitation that I am accustomed to receive. Is my life really in such danger ? "

" Signor Paravinci, I do not think you quite comprehend the situation in which you currently find yourself. I will lay certain facts before you in order to make my point clear to you. Mr. Faulkes is dead through an act of violence. You visited him on the night he died and you are known to have been with him in the room where his body was found and where we are to assume he met his end. You are known to have had a disagreement with him on that very night. You seem unable to prove that you left his house when you claim to have done. Furthermore, you are known to have been entrusted by him with money, and your uncles' business has received unusually large sums of money from him in the past. The average police detective would have no problem in putting these matters together and assuming your guilt. And Inspector Gregson, although his talents are superior to those of most of the detectives employed by the Metropolitan Police, sees no way at present to resolve the issue other than to assume your guilt."

As Holmes continued his recitation, the wretched Paravinci, forced to nod in agreement at every point made by Holmes, grew more and more pale, until I was moved to rise and pour him a glass of water. He accepted it from my hand and sipped gratefully.

"And as a final conclusion," Holmes added, "I am sorry to tell you that my countrymen who would be likely to form the jury in your trial would not look kindly on you, being, as you are, not a native of this country."

"My God!" replied our visitor. "I had not considered matters in the light you have just presented them to me. What am I to do?" he positively wailed.

"You must listen to me, and tell me the truth. I will start by saying that I am positive you did not kill your father."

The effect of these words on the Italian was dramatic. He gave a gurgling cry and pitched forward, the glass of water falling from his hand, and spilling onto the floor.

"Holmes!" I exclaimed. "The man has fainted." I adjusted our visitor's position, and employed the usual methods to revive someone

in that condition. The act of loosening his collar and the use of sal volatile soon returned the patient to consciousness. He looked about him wildly, and fixed his stare on Holmes, who continued gazing at him coolly.

"How... How did you know that Francis Faulkes is— was my father?" he stammered. "I will not deny it, since you already appear to have the knowledge."

"By the ears," Holmes replied. "You may not be aware, but the shape of the ear, as I have remarked on other occasions, furnishes an excellent medium for confirming degrees of relationship. Your ear, my dear sir, is of a most distinctive shape, particularly the shape of the lower lobe, and the antitragus. I have only observed that particular configuration once or twice in the past, the most recent occasion being when I examined the body of Mr. Francis Faulkes in the morgue. The similarity was too marked to be a coincidence."

The other ruefully rubbed the organ in question. "I had no idea I was so distinctive in that regard," he remarked. "What more do you know?"

"I actually know very little as a positive fact, but I can make some guesses, and you may care to confirm them. Indeed, I would strongly recommend that you do confirm them for me, or correct me if perchance I have failed to draw the correct inference. Watson here will tell you that I am not infallible," he smiled, "and I appreciate others setting me on the right track on those occasions, admittedly rare, when I am mistaken." He settled into his chair and continued. "I had guessed before this morning that you were born on the twenty-second day of July in 1873. I am sure that the official records will confirm this."

" You are a true magician, Mr. Holmes. You are correct. How do you know this ? "

" It took no great skill for me to deduce this fact, given the vault under Mr. Faulkes' house and the door to it. Let me continue. My guess is that Mr. Faulkes had paid a visit to Italy, specifically to Rome, some time late the previous year. Some nine months earlier, in fact." He paused to let the full meaning of the words sink into the other's consciousness.

" I admit that Francis Faulkes is my natural father," cried the other. " He was visiting Italy when he met my mother, and they loved each other. He would have married her in an instant, but her parents— my grandparents—would not hear of her being married to any but an Italian. They drove her out of the house, shamed by her condition, but her elder brothers, who were at that time starting in business as dealers in antiquities, gave her shelter, and cared for her and her new-born child—myself."

" Could your father not have married your mother after your grandparents' death ? " I enquired.

" My mother had been made to swear a solemn oath that she would never contemplate marrying anyone except an Italian man. And my mother is a woman of honour— she would never ever break such a promise. But my father—for I can now acknowledge him as such to you, and I may tell you that it is a blessed relief for me to call him by that name at last —continued to love her, and to look after her and me by sending money from England at regular intervals. He also visited Italy regularly, and let me understand, as soon as I was capable of

such understanding, that I was his son, and he regarded me as such in every way, short of marriage to my mother."

" And I take it that the money he paid for the *objets d'art* that he purchased through your uncles was more than the market value for these things, and that the surplus went to you and your mother ? " asked Holmes.

" That is it exactly, Mr. Holmes. When I was a child, he ensured that I was instructed in the English language, and when I came of age, he made arrangements for me to come to England and work here. My uncles had a friend who was in business here as a printer, and it was with this friend that my father arranged for me to find work. It is a trade that I enjoy, and I consider myself to be skilled at it."

" Indeed you are," smiled Holmes. " I have seen samples of your work."

The other looked puzzled, and Holmes withdrew several sheets from the portfolio he had brought with him earlier. " I took the liberty of visiting your employer, Signor Fallini, earlier this morning, and he presented me with these. Here, for example, is a theatre programme where you set the type, printed on some excellent Italian paper from the manufactory of Antodelli e Fratelli. Another excellently produced example of type here, set in Bodoni, this being a restaurant menu. And here is one other example combining the characteristics of the two previous examples—a note from the Paradol Chamber—a proof sheet that I obtained this morning from the pile of waste sheets at Fallini's. It matches this," pulling out the paper that had been given to us a few days before by our clerical visitor. Our visitor turned pasty white, and I feared he was about to lose consciousness again. However, he recovered himself somewhat, and pointing with a trembling hand to the paper, croaked, " How did you obtain that ? "

" I see no reason to withhold that information from you," replied Holmes. " It was given to me by Father Patrick Donahue of Holy Rood Church, and it was given to him for examination by your father. Rest assured that, to the best of my knowledge, the seal of the confessional has not been broken. Father Donahue was rightly concerned about these notes, and consulted me, bringing this as an example. You are not going to deny that you are responsible for this and the other notes from this supposed source ? "

" No, I cannot and will not deny it. I produced all of these, at my father's request."

" Your father requested you to produce printed notes that threatened his life ? " I began, but Holmes checked my enquiry with a waved hand.

" Yes, he did," replied Paravinci, answering my question.

" I think I know why he did this," said Holmes, " and I believe that the subject may be too painful for you to expound. I will, as before, proceed to lay my conclusions before you, and you should confirm or deny the truth of them." The other nodded his head " A little over a month ago, Mr. Faulkes consulted a Harley Street specialist, and received the worst news possible. He had not long to live, and the disease which was slowly consuming him would be hideously painful in its later stages."

" You are correct."

" He confided in no-one except his son, and the frequency of your visits to him increased, as a result

of your filial devotion to him." He paused, and the other nodded. " Now we come to the most painful part of the story. Mr. Faulkes was reluctant, most understandably, to endure the suffering that accompanies his disease, and accordingly determined to do away with himself. As a good Catholic, though, he knew that this was a sin, but he did not inform his priest directly of his intentions, though he did confide in you. I believe, though, that he may have talked with Father Donahue regarding his fears and his despair."

" You are correct so far."

" I believe that one reason why he did not tell Father Donahue of his suicidal intentions was that he intended to leave at least part of his wealth to the Church. Naturally, I am aware that the Church of Rome regards self-murder as a sin. Had he died by his own hand, the Church would not have found it possible to accept his bequest in good faith. Am I correct there ? "

" I believe that to be the case, though I hardly consider myself to be an expert in such matters."

" It was therefore necessary for him, if he were to carry out his intention, of making his suicide appear to be either accidental or murder. I assume that you or he, or possibly the two of you together, decided on the appearance of murder, as a seeming accidental death might well have resulted in a post-mortem examination of the body, revealing traces of poison, or whatever method he had elected to take his life. A supposed murder would point to an obvious cause of death, and divert attention away from the idea of his having taken his own life."

" That is so. He felt that if the ground was prepared for a supposed murder, by means of hints dropped to others, such as the priest, and

seeming evidence such as the 'Paradol Chamber' notes, his death,
though mysterious in some ways,
would not be wholly unexpected."

" Surely, though, you must have
realised that your involvement in
the scheme would place you in some
jeopardy ? As I said earlier, you
were close—indeed, you still are
close—to being measured for the
hangman's noose."

" I honestly had no idea that the
circumstances would place me under such suspicion. I merely wanted
to assist my father, who throughout
my life had been the best of fathers,
given the strange circumstances. I
felt I could do no less for him."

" Can you remember the nature
of the final disagreement that you
had with him ? Simpkins claims
that he heard you and your father
in disagreement before you left the
house, if you recall. How much of
all of this is known to Simpkins, by
the way ? "

" Simpkins had been informed
by my father of the relationship between him and myself. It was never
mentioned by him to me, or me to
him, though he sometimes gave me
some sign through his eyes or his actions that he recognised the fact. As
to the disagreement, of course I remember it perfectly. It was the last
time I saw my father. He was complaining of the growing pain, which
burned inside him. He said it was
becoming intolerable and he wished
to end it as soon as possible. I attempted to dissuade him from sudden action, but his mind was made
up. I wanted him to remain with
us a few days longer, but I could not
change his mind." Here the young
man began to sob, obviously deeply affected by the recollection of
that evening. Through his tears, he
continued, " We went outside, and
we embraced—for the last time. I

knew it was the last time, and my
eyes filled with tears, as they do
now. How I made my way back to
London, I know not. Excuse me."
He pulled out a large handkerchief,
and mopped his eyes with it.

" There is nothing to excuse,"
said Holmes, in a kindly tone of
voice. " Your display of filial affection is commendable, and I do not
see that you could have done anything other than what you did, under the circumstances. Did you
know the method by which your father planned to make away with
himself ? "

The other nodded. " To my
shame, I confess that it was of my
devising."

" The ventilator cord looped
around the arm of one of the statues
and swung as a pendulum, with the
result that when the stone base hit
a solid object, the arm would break
away and the statue would slip out
of the noose, leaving the impression that the statue had been used
as a weapon by the murderer, and
had broken on impact. I observed
that the statue that actually killed
your father was not the first one
on which he, or you, had made the
experiment."

" How did you deduce all this ? "
I asked, unable to contain myself.

" It was obvious, Watson," replied Holmes, a little testily. " The
arm had detached from the statue. There was no doubt in my
mind that the base of the statue inflicted the wound that led to Faulkes' death. From the bloodstains,
it was obvious that the arm had become detached following the impact
with the body and not before. Forgive the graphic nature of the description, Signor Paravinci, but it
was obvious that blood had immediately spurted from the wound with
some force, and the arm had landed

over some of the blood on the floor. There were only two ways for the arm to have become detached in that way. First, the blow could have been delivered with the arm, but this was obviously not the case. All the signs pointed to the heavy stone base of the statue as being the cause of death. The other way the arm could have been broken off the body would have been if it had been used as the handle of the weapon. You saw me pick up one of those statues. It would have been folly for me to grasp it by the arm. The only logical way to grasp it would have been by the torso."

" I am astounded," said our visitor. " How did you come to the conclusion that you did ? "

" Once I had worked out that the arm had broken following the blow administered to your father, it was a matter of calculating out the relative angles of the arm and the rest of the statue, when compared to those of the body and the ventilator cord. My deduction is that the statue was set swinging as a pendulum and pushed to increase the amplitude of the swing, and hence the force with which the statue would strike. When your father judged that the statue was ready to do its work, he could then determine the position where he should stand to await the fatal blow."

I shuddered. " That must have demanded a high degree of courage." I could see in my mind's eye the dying man standing calmly, willing himself not to flinch as the deadly angel swung inexorably towards his head. I noticed Paravinci making the sign of the Cross, his eyes closed, and his lips moving as if in silent prayer.

" Hence the ether," explained Holmes. " I believe, Signor Paravinci, that your father inhaled some ether from a cotton-wool pad before committing himself to his final course of action. This would act as an anaesthetic and help to deaden any pain, as well as dulling his sensibilities. If it is of any comfort to you, I am sure that he felt little or no pain, and we know that his death followed very soon after he had been struck down, and while he was unconscious. I do not believe he suffered. The position and angle of the wound indicate that your father seemed to deliberately position himself to achieve that effect."

" It is some comfort," replied the other. " Do you believe I committed a sin by aiding him ? It is I, after all, who was responsible for setting up the whole business. We tested the idea using some of the other statues, and I fear we broke some of them in our experiments, as you noticed. I cannot help feeling that I have committed a mortal sin in helping my father escape his torment, and that I must be tormented in my turn after my own death."

" These matters are outside my province, I fear," said Holmes gravely. " You must seek that answer elsewhere. As to whether you have committed a crime, I fear the answer to that is in the affirmative. The exact charge would be a matter for the police, but it would not be murder. As to whether you should be tried and convicted for what you did, I cannot, having heard your story, believe that you should suffer the rigours of the law."

" Thank you, Mr. Holmes," replied the other.

" Do not be too hasty, however," replied my friend. " I am a private citizen—I am not the representative of the law, and I have no power to bind or loose. Inspector Gregson will be here shortly, and I promise you that I will do what I can to

assist you by putting your case before him."

" Why, I thank you, Mr. Holmes,"
replied the other.

" You strike me as a well-mannered and well-meaning young man.
I think your conscience will have
more effect on your future life and
conduct than any legal proceedings
could ever do. I have no wish to see
you imprisoned for what, in many
ways, may be regarded as an act of
mercy. I have one more question before Gregson arrives. What was the
source of the name of the Paradol
Chamber ? Was this your doing ? "

" My father allowed me to choose
the wording and the signatory of
the supposed threatening notes. I
selected the name myself—with
the first part of the name being the
first part of my own name, but also
meaning 'against' or 'preventative',
as in the word 'parasol' and so on.
The second part I concocted myself,
from the Latin for pain or grief or
suffering, 'dolor'. And the Chamber referred to the underground
vault. I felt that there was some
sort of mysterious sound there that
would impress and baffle."

" You were perfectly right," said
Holmes. " And here, on cue, is Inspector Gregson."

The policeman entered the room.
" Antonio Paravinci," he intoned,
on sighting our visitor. " I must ask
you to accompany me to the station
to answer further questions regarding the death of Mr. Francis Faulkes
of Watford."

" Are you arresting my client ? "
Holmes asked.

" At this stage, I am not," replied
Gregson.

" In which case, may I suggest,
my dear Inspector, that you make
yourself comfortable in that chair
there, and listen to the story I have

to tell you. I take it you have some
time to spare ? "

" Since it is you, Mr. Holmes, I
will listen."

" Thank you. A cigar ? " Gregson accepted the proffered article,
and settled back in the chair while
Holmes outlined the facts as he had
deduced them and as they had been
confirmed by Antonio Paravinci.
Occasionally Gregson interjected to
confirm the truth of Holmes' narrative with Paravinci.

At the end of this speech, the police inspector sat in silence, finishing the cigar, and obviously lost in
thought. Neither Holmes nor I
moved a muscle to disturb him, and
Paravinci for his part was on the
edge of his seat, biting his lower lip,
with his body tensed.

After about five minutes of
this, Gregson rose to his feet, and
clapped the flinching Paravinci on
the shoulder. " Look here, my lad,"
he said. " You've not been in trouble with the law before this, I know
that. We've talked to your employers, and they say you're a good
worker. You've been a good son, too,
to both your mother, and in your
way you've been a good son to your
father as well. Mr. Holmes doesn't
make many mistakes, and if he says
this is what has happened, and you
back him up on this, I believe him,
and you. Now listen carefully to
me. There's something very interesting going on at the other side of
the road, and I'm going to look out
of the window at it. It looks so interesting that if you were to slip
downstairs, and catch the next boat
train to take you out of this country as quickly as possible, I probably
wouldn't even notice you leaving.
Do you take my meaning ? " Paravinci nodded silently. Gregson
turned to Holmes and me. " Dr.
Watson, Mr. Holmes, could you

give me your opinions, please ? " He pointed out of the window at some unsuspecting coal-heaver. As Holmes and I rose to our feet to join him, I saw Holmes mouth the words " Go now" to our visitor.

The three of us stood side by side, our backs to the room. Not until a full minute had passed after we had heard the door opening and closing did Gregson turn round.

He let out a deep breath. " It would have gone hard on him had I arrested him. He deserves better," he said simply and without emotion.

" Amen to that," I replied.

" Never fear," chuckled Holmes. " I warrant that Watson will never tell this tale to the public, and that Inspector Tobias Gregson will retain his fearless stony-hearted reputation among London criminals. Another cigar, Inspector, before you return to Scotland Yard and tell the sad tale of how the criminal slipped through the net before your arrival here ? "

SHERLOCK HOLMES &
THE GIANT RAT
OF SUMATRA

" ... A NEW TYPE OF VESSEL, WHICH WE CALL A 'TORPEDO BOAT DESTROYER',
DESIGNED FOR THE PURPOSE OF PROTECTING THE FLEET'S CAPITAL SHIPS
AGAINST THE MENACE OF THE SMALLER TORPEDO BOATS." (PAGE 183)

EDITOR'S NOTES

This tale is another of those that Watson chose to bury in the obscurity of the deed box for reasons of discretion. It appears, furthermore, that he also banished much of it from his memory, as his reference to it in The Sussex Vampire has Holmes reminding him that " Matilda Briggs was not the name of a young woman, Watson ... It was a ship which is associated with the giant rat of Sumatra".

The reference to HMS Daring as the fastest ship afloat places the timing of the story at 1895 or thereabouts. This would coincide with the term of The Earl Spencer as the First Lord of the Admiralty who served in that capacity until 1895, replaced by George Goschen. However, it would be foolish to speculate too closely as to the identity of the character referred to as " Lord Haughton", which is an obvious pseudonym, and it is quite likely that Watson deliberately threw sand in the eyes of the readers of this tale as regards the location of " Haughton"'s ancestral seat, etc. We can only guess at the true identity of the other actors in this drama: Captain Frederick Glover, and Senior Lieutenant Ramsay-Moffat. Though HMS Bellorophon and HMS Colossus were indeed capital ships in the Royal Navy in the periods mentioned, no officers of the names given here are present in the Navy List of that time associated with these ships, and reports of incidents such as those described are to be found in no official records.

HERLOCK Holmes was far from being a modest man, and was proud, with some justification, it must be admitted, of his successes. Even given this, there were several cases where his powerful intellect and energy achieved a solution to a problem that was denied to the official forces, but which he resolutely refused to make known to the public.

In many instances this was the result of what he termed " trivia"—though the case had presented apparently insurmountable problems to our friends at Scotland Yard, Holmes' keen brain had cut through the Gordian knot in an instant, and had presented the police detectives with the answer to the conundrum that had been baffling them, often for weeks. These cases he deemed of insufficient interest to excite readers, though to me these exhibited his extraordinary powers to the fullest.

Other cases demanded discretion as regards their publicity. Several of these have been published, albeit using pseudonyms. Those, for example, who seek the monarch of Bohemia, or even the name of the fair adventuress to whom the King of that fictional realm (fictional, that is, at the time of the events described) was attached, Irene Adler, will seek in vain. I have drawn the veil of decency over the true identity of the European ruler to whom Holmes rendered his services. Nonetheless, the essential facts of the matter are as I have described them, as they are in other such cases.

A third class of case where Holmes desired my reticence concerns those matters relating to the safety and security of the realm. Though he refused any honours such as a knighthood or other rank, Sherlock Holmes was well deserving of such recognition, owing to the numerous occasions on which he served his country, usually for no reward. In a number of these, he worked as a direct agent of the rulers of this nation, and in others, his brother Mycroft acted as the conduit between the detective and those holding high office. It was one of these latter that formed the events that I shall refer to as the case of the " Giant Rat of Sumatra".

Holmes had recently returned from a visit to the Continent, where, he informed me later, he had been assisting the *Sûreté Nationale* of France in their capture of the notorious forger and confidence trickster who had been passing himself off with considerable success as Baron Lemaître. My practice was doing well, and I have to confess that it was with more than a little irritation that I opened a telegram from my friend, which read, " Come at once. Your assistance required urgently."

" I really cannot spare the time," I said to my wife. " Mrs. Anderson's case of shingles is coming to a point where I really fear to leave her unattended, and the whole of the junior portion of the Prout family is suffering from whooping cough."

My dear Mary was completely undeceived by my protestations. " John," she told me. " Your patients are not suffering from serious conditions, I am sure. And I know how much you have missed your friend, however much you may

deny it. It will do you good to go off with him on one of your adventures. Simply make your usual arrangements with Anstruther to take over for a few days."

It was true; although I was more than content with my lot as a happily married general practitioner, there was a part of my life that I had come to expect from my association with Holmes that was now missing. As is so common, a woman's intuition came closer to the truth than it was possible for mere male rational thought to achieve, and I accordingly made the arrangements as Mary had suggested.

An hour later, I was climbing the stairs to my friend's lodgings in Baker-street, having telegraphed my acceptance of Holmes' invitation, and entering the well-known room where I had spent so many hours in the past. I cast my eye about the apartment for evidence of change, but much seemed as it always had done in the past—the jack-knife skewering the unanswered correspondence to the mantle-shelf, the Persian slipper containing the rough shag tobacco with which Holmes was accustomed to fill his pipe, and the wall above the fireplace where Holmes had patriotically delineated the initials of our Sovereign with bullets fired from his revolver.

Holmes himself was standing in the centre of the room, coated and gloved, hat in hand, apparently impatient to leave. " Come, Watson," he said, pulling out his watch. " We must make haste."

" Where are we going ? " I asked as we made our way downstairs and passed into the street.

" The Diogenes Club," replied

" Brother Mycroft ? " I asked, having been previously acquainted with Holmes' elder brother and the strange circles in which he moved.

Holmes nodded. " He wishes us to run around on his behalf, or rather on behalf of the government. As you are aware, Mycroft is by no means the most energetic of individuals and he makes use of my energy where he cannot summon up his own."

" You mean that he wishes you to run around on his behalf ? " I corrected, placing a slight emphasis on the pronoun.

" You do yourself a disservice, Watson," replied my friend. " I made a specific request for you to be included in the invitation and I will require your assistance, I am convinced. Mycroft has already informed me that the case is peculiarly baffling to him, and if he finds it so, we can be sure that it will be taxing. I need my Watson beside me."

I was under few illusions that my intellect and powers of deduction were in any way equal to those of Sherlock Holmes or his brother, but knew from past experience that my participation would be chiefly as a sounding-board for the music of Holmes' thoughts, though he was kind enough to say otherwise much of the time.

On arrival at the Diogenes Club, that singular establishment where conversation between members is not only discouraged, but forbidden on pain of expulsion after the third offence, we were shown by a porter into the Strangers' Room, the only location within the Club where Mycroft could converse with us without incurring the wrath of the governing committee.

Holmes and I settled ourselves into the comfortable chairs that the Diogenes provides for visitors and awaited the arrival of the elder Holmes. After a few minutes, the massive bulk of Mycroft Holmes blocked the door, which he pulled to before sinking into another chair, which obviously by its size, if not for his use alone, was reserved for those of similar build.

" Well, Sherlock," he greeted his younger brother familiarly. " I see from the press that you have been busy. I take it that the wife in the Fromalle affair had no knowledge that the rubies had been substituted."

" Not until I brought the fact to her attention," replied Sherlock. " I fear that the marriage will end up in the Divorce Court, but it is probably for the best. He is somewhat of a brute, and I fear for her continued sanity if they are to remain together as man and wife."

Needless to say, I had no knowledge of the matter being discussed. As always, I was struck by Mycroft Holmes' considerable intellect, which seemed to provide him with the most intimate details of events, despite his extreme indolence. He and Sherlock debated abstruse points regarding a political scandal in a remote German barony, while I sat astounded at the detailed comprehension displayed by both participants.

" You did not bring us here to gossip about the Graf von Metzelburg, though, Mycroft ? " said Homes at length.

" No, the matter on which you and Watson can be of assistance is a good deal closer to home. Dr. Watson," he turned to me. " Apologies for not greeting you earlier. I hope that you will serve as somewhat of a brake on my brother's rather wilder extravagant notions. Your good sense will be of great value here." I felt flattered by these words, but given the extraordinary capabilities of the speaker, and those of his brother, I had serious doubts as to any additional value I was able to bestow.

Mycroft addressed us both. " As you know, there is to be a change in the composition of the Cabinet in the near future. One of the alterations will be in the Admiralty, where a new First Lord is to take office. Sir Watkin Goodall has served with distinction over the past years, but the Prime Minister agrees with my suggestion that new blood is required there. The nation at this time needs a First Lord who is able to see past the pipeclay and brass polish and paint, and consider the strength of the Navy in comparison to those navies of our continental neighbours, not to mention those of the United States of America and even of Japan, and take advantage of the new technical developments that are revolutionising the art of naval warfare."

" I am sure when you made this suggestion to the Prime Minister you had a particular individual in mind," Sherlock Holmes remarked.

" I did indeed. Augustus Wilmott, Lord Haughton, the eldest son of the Earl of Harrogate, was the candidate I recommended for the post. He has served with distinction as an officer in the Mediterranean Fleet, and rose to the rank of Captain through his abilities, rather than by reason of his birth. He has a sound practical knowledge of the workings of the Navy at sea, and on his recent retirement from the Service became a director of the firm of naval architects responsible for the design of the latest class of battleships. He is also, as I am sure you are aware, an active Member of the House of Commons. I can think of no better man in the land to step into the shoes of Sir Watkin."

" But there is a problem ? " suggested Holmes.

" There is indeed. Lord Haughton has not been seen for the past five weeks at the least."

" He is up in Scotland, killing defenceless animals, or tormenting fish with artificial flies," Holmes replied. " You would not expect to see him in London at this time of year, surely ? "

" Sherlock, there are times when I despair of you," retorted his brother. " Do you think that was not the first possibility that suggested itself to me ? I have made discreet enquiries among his friends and relatives. None has seen him, received any communication from him or heard word from him over the period I mentioned."

" It would seem impossible for a man of his fame and distinction simply to vanish from view in this way," I broke in. " Surely he must have travelled overseas ? "

" Our agents have scoured Europe," replied Mycroft, " and have failed to discover any trace of Lord Haughton in any of the resorts he is known to have frequented."

" Perhaps he has suffered a fatal accident in some remote spot in the countryside and is no more ? " I suggested. " This is why he is not to be found anywhere you have searched."

Mycroft Holmes turned his lazy gaze upon me. " For reasons I shall go into later, we believe that this is not the case."

" Do you suspect foul play ? " interjected Sherlock.

" With the information available to us at present, we have no positive evidence one way or the other, but the answer to your question regarding suspicion is in the affirmative. Maybe I should outline the case as we have it so far," suggested his brother.

" Pray do so." Sherlock Holmes and I settled back in our chairs, and I brought out my notebook and proceeded to take notes as Mycroft Holmes explained the matter in his usual logical and incisive fashion.

The facts of the matter as he related them were as follows. Five weeks ago, Lord Haughton had been staying at his father's country residence in Hampshire. He had announced his intention to visit former naval comrades in Portsmouth for a luncheon to be given in his honour, and set off alone for the local station at Shawford from where he would catch the train to Portsmouth. The Shawford station-master, to whom Lord Haughton was well known, had noticed him board the Portsmouth train, and a man answering to his description appeared to have been seen at Portsmouth station. However, in the short journey between the railway station and the battleship HMS *Colossus*, in the wardroom of which he was expected as a guest, he seems to have disappeared.

One of the officers on board the *Colossus* watching through field-glasses claimed to have seen a man whom he took to be Lord Haughton on the quay, boarding a small steam-launch, accompanied by two men whom he did not recognise. It was expected that the steam-launch would then bring him on board the battleship, but instead, it steered towards for a small tramp steamer, passing behind the hull of the latter, and obscuring any view of any passengers disembarking or embarking. The *Colossus'* officer watched the steam-launch return to the quay and dock, but saw no-one resembling Lord Haughton leave the boat, though the two men who had accompanied him on board disembarked and walked together in the general direction of the centre of the town. About ten minutes

after the launch had left the coaster, the latter raised anchor and left the harbour. Though the officer reported the incident to his brother officers after the ship had left harbour, it proved impossible to identify the steamer, and since there had been no positive identification of the mystery passenger, it was impossible to persuade the authorities to follow the ship.

The officer, when questioned further, claimed that he could not be absolutely positive that the person he had seen was indeed Lord Haughton, but since he was well acquainted with him, it was considered that his testimony could be relied upon. As to the ship that had presumably carried the passenger away, he was able to give a reasonably detailed description, but it seemed that she had not called at any British ports. He had noticed, however, that the coaster was flying a Dutch flag.

" That would seem to argue that he is on the Continent, as Watson suggested just now," Sherlock pointed out to Mycroft.

" If he is, then he is in some sort of captivity," replied Mycroft. " But we have good reason to believe that he was in this country for some time, even if he has recently been taken to the Continent."

" Your reasons for believing this ? "

" The Admiralty have received letters from him, postmarked in this country. One each day, with the series coming to an end a few days ago. It is this sudden cessation that has brought me to your door, figuratively speaking."

" The letters prove nothing," remarked my friend. " Letters can be written in one country and posted in another."

" The handwritten letters all

contained references to the newspapers of the morning of the day that the letters were written and posted," remarked his brother, a little testily. " It would not have been possible for those letters to have been written in another country and posted in a British post office box at the time given. All the rules of logic make it certain that he has been in this country up to four days ago. He may still be here."

" From anyone else I would doubt the accuracy of that statement, but from you I will accept that this is in fact the case," said Holmes. " I assume that you have made extensive checks on the authenticity of the handwriting ? "

" There can be no doubt as to that," replied Mycroft. " The finest analysts have examined these letters closely, and compared them with confirmed samples of the missing man's handwriting. They are in unanimous agreement as to the fact that these letters could not have been written by anyone other than Lord Haughton."

" And the content ? "

" This is another puzzle. There is little of import in these letters. They appear to be no more than ramblings about his health or the weather or the scenery. I have had photographic copies made, which I will have delivered to you at Baker-street. The originals must, as you appreciate, remain in Whitehall."

" There is no secret writing or invisible ink ? " asked Holmes.

" Sherlock, I believed you had a higher opinion of my abilities than to ask such a question. And to anticipate the next question I believe you will ask me, no, we have examined the content of these messages for a code or a cypher, but have been unable to find any such."

" Are the police involved in the search ? "

" At this stage, they have been given the description of Lord Haughton, but not his name. If they discover a man who answers to the description, they are to inform London immediately. This is to prevent any possibility of panic. The possible abduction of such a prominent member of society would undoubtedly cause considerable public alarm."

" Undoubtedly," Holmes agreed. " How long has the search been proceeding ? "

" Just over four weeks."

" And all that has been received in this time are these letters ? "

" There was a report last week from the local police that a man resembling Lord Haughton had been seen in Nuneaton. It turned out to be mistaken."

" And I assume you are tending to the conclusion that he has been abducted by agents of a foreign power ? " Mycroft nodded his great head silently in answer to his brother's question. " Are there any good reasons why he should be so abducted that you are at liberty to vouchsafe to us ? "

" He has been a serving naval officer on many of Her Majesty's most advanced warships of the day. He is intimately involved in the design and construction of the most modern and deadly of the Royal Navy's ships, as well as serving on various Parliamentary Committees concerned with naval affairs. You would be pressed to find one man who knows more about the operation and design of the ships, as well as the political matters concerned with the modern Navy. That, of course, is the reason why I passed along the recommendation that he become First Lord."

" You should have consulted me earlier, Mycroft. You have wasted valuable time." Holmes spoke sternly in a tone of voice I had never previously heard him use to his brother.

" I admit it, Sherlock. But I was given to understand that you had other matters requiring your attention."

" True," replied my friend, " but you know well that you can always call on me in an emergency of this kind. If I am to assist you in this matter, I will require the loan of the originals of the letters, together with their envelopes, as well as photographic copies for me to retain. A copy of the statement of Lord Haughton's brother officer who claimed to recognise him would also be invaluable. I trust you can arrange that, together with a suitable laissez-passer, to open doors that might otherwise remain shut to us ? "

" I can certainly have all of that prepared for you."

" Please have them delivered to Baker-street within the morning, together with any likenesses of Lord Haughton that you may have. Watson and I will await these documents, and lay our plans accordingly."

ELL, Watson, a pretty puzzle, is it not ? " remarked Holmes as we drove back to Baker-street. " Such an individual typically does not vanish from view unless he has a good reason to remove himself from the public gaze, or unless another party wishes him to be so out of the limelight. The fact that he was escorted to the strange ship and never returned from there, while his companions did so would seem to argue that he was in some way kidnaped or otherwise abducted."

" There is no definite proof of this, if I understood your brother's account correctly," I pointed out. " The officer who described the incident may well have been mistaken, both in his identification of Lord Haughton, and in his description of the events he described."

" And even given that he may have been correct on both those counts, his listeners, including us, may well have been mistaken in our interpretations of those events," added Holmes. " We will have to investigate the events at Portsmouth and discover more. For now," he commented as we arrived at his Baker-street lodgings, " we should examine what Brother Mycroft will send us."

We waited for the promised materials in Holmes' rooms, using the time by verifying details of Lord Haughton's life as recorded in the various reference works filling Holmes' shelves. As Mycroft had informed us, he appeared to be one of the foremost men of the nation in the field of naval affairs. He had served with distinction in ships around the world, including several incidents in the East Indies where he had been decorated for his gallantry, and had commanded several capital ships before retiring from the Navy. His work with the world-renowned firm of naval architects that bore his name had resulted in a stream of orders from overseas as well as from our own Senior Service, and his speeches and statements in Parliament displayed an uncommon grasp of the practicalities of statecraft as it related to naval affairs. Truly, as Mycroft had said, if there were one man who embodied the British naval tradition, it was Lord Albert Haughton.

Our research activities were broken into by Mrs. Hudson, who attracted our attention with a knock on the door and a call of " Mr. Holmes ! Mr. Holmes ! ".

On my opening the door to enquire the reason for her knock, given that she usually directed his clients directly to Holmes' rooms, the landlady appeared flustered. " Begging your pardon, sir," she exclaimed. " I am now accustomed to the police tramping in and out of the house, but this is something else. I'm sure that everything is in order, but it's not what I'm used to."

" What is it, Mrs. Hudson ? " I enquired. " Is something wrong ? "

" It's these soldiers," replied our worthy landlady. " There are three of them with a big box, and they are demanding to see Mr. Holmes. There's nothing wrong, is there ? " she enquired anxiously.

" Nothing at all," I reassured her. " Please send them up."

The three servicemen, when they appeared at the head of the stairs, turned out to be Royal Marines rather than soldiers; a pardonable mistake from one not well acquainted with military matters. Two Marines carried a stout metal box between them, following their Sergeant, who introduced himself to Holmes.

" Begging your pardon, sir, but our orders were to stay in the room while you examined the originals of these documents we've brought with us. We are then to return them to the Admiralty, leaving you with the copies. Is that clear, sir ? If so, sir, I will require your signature on this," producing a sheet of paper.

" I understand, Sergeant," replied Holmes, signing the paper placed before him. " Brother Mycroft seems to be a touch concerned about this business, would you not agree ? " turning to me.

" It would seem he has more than a little justification for being so, if what we were told earlier is correct," I replied.

The sergeant ceremoniously produced a key from an inside pocket of his tunic, and used it to unlock the box, which he then opened, revealing the promised documents. Holmes scrutinised both the letters and the envelopes in which they had been dispatched, holding them carefully by the edges, and peering at them through a powerful magnifying lens. " Little of interest," he said, with an air of resignation, " at least, as far as the actual paper is concerned. All of these are the same paper and envelope. The writing is likewise consistently from the same hand, and the same pen and ink have been used to write every one of these, including the address. There is one point in common, though, regarding the envelopes. I doubt very much whether Mycroft failed to remark the fact, but he omitted to mention it to us. Look here. These are the envelopes of these epistles, arranged in the order of their posting. Observe the postmarks."

I accepted the glass from Holmes and bent over the papers in question. " These are all ports," I remarked. " And the order would seem to indicate a slow trip from Portsmouth along the south coast towards the east of the country."

" Indeed. And that indicates ? "

" That the writer was on board a ship or a boat travelling to the last port mentioned, Gravesend, from which he might have travelled to the Continent, I guess."

" I concur," replied Holmes. " The ship in question was obviously taking its time. Indeed, if you look here," and he pointed to a group of envelopes in the series, " the ship actually doubled back on its course at this point. Obviously it was in no hurry to reach its destination. However, it should be a simple matter to search the records of the ports along the coast, and discover those ships that entered and left harbour on these dates. I am certain that we can then make a unique identification of the ship in question. The question then arises in my mind as to why Mycroft has not informed us of the results of such an enquiry, assuming that such was carried out."

" Maybe because he did not want to arouse suspicion as the result of an official investigation ? " I suggested.

" That is possible," conceded my friend. " In any event, I feel I have gained all that I can from these original documents, and they can be returned to the Admiralty."

The Marines returned the documents to the box in which they had been transported, and locked it.

" And now," said Holmes, as the box's escorts made their way noisily down the stairs, and found their way to the street, " we travel to Portsmouth."

OLMES was silent during the journey to Portsmouth, and I likewise refrained from making conversation, occupying my time by studying the copies of the documents that had been entrusted to us by Mycroft.

The report of the *Colossus* officer was much as Mycroft Holmes had described, and I could gain nothing fresh from its study. The content of the letters was unremarkable, verging on the trivial. They provided little information, and indeed were almost childish in their composition. Indeed, it was hard to see why they had been written, other than to provide a kind of reassurance as to the writer's very existence. As Mycroft had observed, each letter contained a reference to a topical event, which I assumed had been reported in the national press only on the day when the letter was posted.

The first letter began as follows, " Read this, and know that I am well, though living under strange conditions that I am not at liberty to disclose." It continued in the same vein for a mere two or three sentences, referring to a speech made in the House of Commons late the previous evening, and I turned to the next epistle.

" As I mentioned in my last letter, I am still in good health. I am unaware of my current whereabouts, but may assure you that I continue well." Again, the same trite style, with a reference to recent Parliamentary affairs. I sighed, and turned to the next.

This started, " My health continues to be good, and I am in comfortable surroundings." By this time I had almost given up any hope of making any sense of them, and in the last letter that I troubled myself to read, being the fourth of the series, I read, " Some may question the purpose of these letters, but I assure you that they are simply to provide the world with reassurances of my continued health and existence."

Two or three times I was on the verge of asking Holmes for his opinion on the matter, but when I observed him to be apparently lost in deep contemplation, his eyes seemingly closed, I turned back to the documents without a word.

However, as we left the station and proceeded towards the naval harbour, Holmes turned to me, and remarked, " I believe you are correct, Watson. Those letters would seem to have no purpose except to let the recipients know of the continued existence of Lord Haughton."

" How in the world did you know that was the subject of my puzzlement ? " I asked, as always amazed by Holmes' apparent ability to read my mind.

He smiled. " It was somewhat obvious, Watson, from my study of your face and actions as you perused those letters. And yet I believe there is something more to them than meets the eye. Naturally, we may assume that they were written under a certain level of duress, at the orders of his captors, but even so... I thank you, by the way, for your continued silence throughout the journey. There are few companions to whom such a gift is given. We will, I think, make straight for the *Colossus*."

" Do you know she is in port ? "

" I read in Monday's newspaper that having returned from a patrol in the Bay of Biscay, she had been experiencing boiler trouble and accordingly was expected to be under repair for a week or so."

On attempting to enter the dockyard, a sentry guarding the gates stopped us and demanded to know our business. Upon Holmes producing the document from the Admiralty requesting all whom it might concern to give us all possible assistance, the sentry drew himself up to attention and saluted smartly. I half-started to return the salute before I remembered that I no longer wore the Queen's uniform. Holmes appeared to take the matter in his stride, and demanded of the sentry the route we should follow in order to reach the *Colossus*.

On being directed, we passed through the mass of machinery and supplies needed to maintain the ships defending our nation, losing our way and asking for directions several times as we did so. Eventually we found ourselves at the base of the gangway leading to the *Colossus*, guarded by a Marine sentry, who passed a message to the battleship's Captain when we displayed our Admiralty pass and explained that we wished to interview Sub-Lieutenant Fortescue, who had reported seeing Lord Haughton before his disappearance.

Within a few minutes, we were greeted by a young officer who came down the gangway to meet us.

" The Captain's compliments," he announced, " and he would like to welcome you both on board, gentlemen. Please have the goodness to follow me. Take care as you move around the ship, as some of the spaces are rather low." He led the way through a complex mass of steep ladders and narrow corridors until we reached a stout mahogany door, at which our guide knocked.

We were welcomed into the cabin of Captain Frederick Glover, the very epitome of the bluff weather-beaten English sea-dog, who smiled as he extended a welcoming hand and waved us into chairs by his desk. " The celebrated Sherlock Holmes, upon my life," he greeted my friend. " We have no murders on this ship, you know. I fear your talents will find no outlet here. And Doctor Watson himself. Delighted to make your acquaintance. Now, I was told that you wished to speak with Sub-Lieutenant Fortescue, and you bear important papers from my lords and masters in Whitehall ? "

Holmes passed over the document in question, and Captain Glover scanned it in silence. " May I ask whether this is in connection with the disappearance of Lord Haughton ? " he asked.

Holmes frowned. " I had been given to understand that this was a confidential matter, sir."

" There are few secrets on board ship, Mr. Holmes. I can assure you, though, that outside this ship's wardroom, nothing is known of this matter. It would seem to be a matter of serious concern, then ? "

" Indeed so," said Holmes, but would say no more, despite the obvious wish of Captain Glover to be better informed about the business.

" Very good," replied the officer, after about a minute's silence. " There are obviously wheels within wheels here of which I am not permitted to be aware." His tone was stiff. " I take it you will want to see Lieutenant Fortescue now in private ? "

" If you would be so kind as to arrange that," replied Holmes. " I do apologise for the secrecy, but I am sure you comprehend the delicate nature of the situation."

" To be sure," answered the Captain, but to my eye he appeared unconvinced. " I will order the Sub-Lieutenant here, and I am sure that we can arrange suitable privacy for your interview." His tone was still frosty.

As he went to the door to pass along the order for the officer, I leaned over to Holmes and whispered softly to him. " Holmes, I am aware that you dislike this matter of fame and notoriety, but it would behoove you to take the Captain here under your wing, as it were. He has obviously heard of you and your abilities, and he seems excited to have you on board ship as a guest. I am sure he could be of service to us in our investigation were you to attempt to build up a friendship with the Captain. I strongly advise you to flatter the man, and feed his sense of importance. He is, after all, a senior officer in the Service, and can undoubtedly do us a good turn if he is well-disposed towards us."

" Hah ! " exclaimed Holmes, almost silently. " You may have hit upon something there." He seemed to relax somewhat in his chair as Captain Glover returned to us. " Captain," he addressed the skipper, " you mentioned that of course you have no murders aboard the ship. My profession has taken me to many places, but I confess this is my first time aboard one of Her Majesty's ships. I would be obliged if you could enlighten me regarding the crimes that you actually do encounter about this floating village. I am always anxious to extend my knowledge and experience, and who could be better placed to assist me in these matters than yourself ? " There could be no-one more charming and ingratiating than Sherlock Holmes when he chose to be so, and he was now at his best as regards these qualities.

" With pleasure," remarked the Captain, and Glover launched with gusto into a series of tales of petty theft, drunkenness, and occasional assault. He concluded with, " But these must be nothing compared to what you have experienced in London, Mr. Holmes ? "

I was glad to see my friend accept the proffered bait, and he regaled Captain Glover, to the other's obvious pleasure, with a few details of some of our adventures, when a knock on the cabin door interrupted him.

" Enter ! " bellowed Captain Glover, in a voice that appeared to have been forged in the days of sail, when it was necessary to call to men working the sails high up on the masts of the ships of that day. A young officer entered. " Sub-Lieutenant Fortescue," the Captain said to him, thankfully in a more normal tone of voice, " these gentlemen here are Mr. Sherlock Holmes and Doctor John Watson, and they would like to ask you some questions in private." He turned to us. " I will leave you in this cabin. Please pass the word for me when you are finished, and I hope that you will do me the honour of dining with me and some of my officers later in the day." Obviously Holmes' conversation had worked on him, and softened his mood.

" I hope we will be able to accept your offer," Holmes responded. " Now, Sub-Lieutenant Fortescue," he addressed he officer when the door had closed behind the Captain, " I am making enquiries regarding Lord Haughton. I understand that you believe you saw him, or someone very like him."

" That's true, sir," replied the other, and proceeded to confirm the story that Mycroft Holmes had told us earlier, and the written statement of which we had received.

" You did not recognise the two men who accompanied Lord Haughton to the other boat, and returned without him ? " asked Holmes.

" No, sir, I did not."

" And how sure are you that the man you saw was Lord Haughton ? "

" I am as sure as I can be, sir. The man certainly had his general appearance, and in addition, limped in a somewhat distinctive fashion, similar to the way in which I had observed Lord Haughton walking when he had visited the ship on previous occasions. He suffers from a curious dragging and twisting inwards of the left foot, only apparent when he walks fast. I have never observed anything similar."

" Was he dressed for travelling, did you notice ? Was he carrying any luggage ? "

" No luggage, sir, and he was dressed in a frock coat and wearing a silk hat, as I had observed him wear on previous visits."

" Can you describe the ship to which the three men were carried ? "

" A coaster, a tramp steamer. Single funnel, black with a red band, flying a Dutch flag, sir. Her hull was," and he closed his eyes as if in thought, " black, and the superstructure was yellow."

" You cannot remember her name at all ? " asked Holmes.

" Alas, I was unable to do so, as there was another ship in front of the Dutch ship's bows, blocking the name which would have been painted there."

" I would like you to draw a plan of where you saw this Dutch coaster, if you would," Holmes requested, bringing out his notebook and proffering his pen.

" Let me see," said the other, sketching in a plan of the harbour. " We were at anchor approximately here," marking a point on the map, " and the ship to which he was taken was here," marking another point.

" I see," said my friend, taking the book, and examining the plan.

" And you have no recollection of seeing the other two men before ? "

" None, sir," replied the young officer.

" Did he appear to be accompanying them voluntarily ? " asked Holmes. " Or was there any appearance of coercion ? "

" It would be impossible for me to say, sir, from that distance."

" Do you know who invited him to dine on board ? Captain Glover, perhaps ? "

" That would be Senior Lieutenant Ramsey-Moffat. He had served with Lord Haughton on other ships and is a good personal friend, I believe, and he had invited him as a guest of the wardroom on several previous occasions. He was an excellent mimic, and had a very pleasant voice when he cared to sing." For some reason, the young officer started to laugh quietly to himself, as if remembering some incident. " I apologise, sir," he eventually managed to say. " Rather an amusing incident that took place on one occasion that he was with us. He was ready to sing some popular ditty, when a rat entered the wardroom through one of the ventilators. I have never seen such a reaction from a man in my life. He explained to us, when the rat had been removed by a rating, and he had been persuaded to come down from the table on which he was standing, that he had an irrational fear of mice and rats, which always had a similar effect on him. That notwithstanding, we were always happy when Lieutenant Ramsey-Moffat announced that he would be joining us in the wardroom. Although he had been a Captain in his days of active service, he was always ready to talk with any officer and offer advice and assistance. There was one time when Sub-Lieutenant Urquhart was about

to be sued for breach of promise, and Lord Haughton was of great help in the matter. Why, he—"

" I think, maybe, we should have a brief word with this Senior Lieutenant," remarked Holmes, choking off what promised to be a long and irrelevant excursion. " Is there anything else that pertains to the matter at hand that you would like to add before you leave us ? "

There was nothing of that nature to add, and Holmes dispatched Sub-Lieutenant Fortescue with instructions to pass the word for Senior Lieutenant Ramsey-Moffat to join us. After about ten minutes, the officer in question was admitted to the cabin. He was a florid middle-aged man, somewhat more portly than I would have expected of a naval officer, and was breathing hard as he took his place facing us across the table.

" I am a busy man, Mr. Holmes," were his first words to us.

" So are we all," replied Holmes, evenly. " I will not keep you from your duties for long, I expect. I merely wish to confirm a few facts about Lord Haughton."

" Very well. By the way, I should mention that during the time that Lord Haughton was in the Service, he hardly ever used the courtesy title to which he had the right, and was always addressed by his family name, as Augustus Wilmott."

" May I ask whose invitation was extended to him to dine aboard this ship ? " asked Holmes.

" It was mine, sir. I am the only one on board who has served with him previously, and I had invited him to dine on several previous occasions as a guest of the wardroom. He was a popular guest with the officers."

" You had served on ships with him in the past ? " asked Holmes.

" Yes, indeed. It seemed that we were fated to serve together on various ships, and as a result, we became good friends."

" Understandably. And in his last post at sea, when he commanded the *Iron Duke* ? "

" When he took command of her, I was posted here to the *Colossus*, where I have remained since."

" Very good. I have just been informed that he had suffered from some sort of injury that left him with a limp. Do you know how he came by this ? We were also informed that you have served with him in the past, so I consider this to be a fair question," asked Holmes.

The other's already ruddy face flushed a little more. " Is it necessary for you to know this, sir ? " he asked.

" The most irrelevant-seeming facts may take on importance in the future. You may rely on my confidence," Holmes assured him. " If the information has to be made public, there is no need for your name to be associated with it. You may speak as freely in front of Watson here as you may myself—Watson is the soul of tact and discretion."

The other spoke, but still with some hesitation. " This is the first time that I have ever told the true story, and I cannot believe that I am telling it to anyone, even now."

" I thank you for the trust you are reposing in us," said Holmes. He sat impassively, his fingers steepled, as the other told his tale.

" It was while we were serving together on the old Billy Ruffian—the *Bellorophon*. We were stationed near the Dutch East Indies. We had put into the port at Jakarta, and all of us—the officers, that is—had shore leave, and we took turns, as is usual, in remaining aboard and manning the ship. The natives would swarm round the boat, and try to climb aboard. We needed to keep constant watch in order to prevent them from boarding and thieving from us. One night it was my turn to keep watch in this fashion—all the other officers were ashore—and I heard one of the boats coming back early. When it got closer, I saw that it was not one of our own boats, but one of those operated by the Dutch port officials. There were several of the Dutch police officers in it, and Augustus Wilmott was lying in the boat, unconscious, with his leg bound up in bandages. The police demanded to talk to the Captain, but he was ashore, of course, and they had to make do with me, a mere junior lieutenant at the time, but it seemed I was good enough for them. Naturally, I was worried about Wilmott, and I asked what had happened, and how he had sustained his injury. It seemed that he had been in a house of very ill repute indeed, where some very vicious practices went on—I will not enlarge on the details." Here the good fellow stopped for a while, obviously embarrassed by the tale he was recounting. " Suffice it to say that they are those practices of which mariners are often accused. Loathsome and disgusting vices. In any case," he went on hurriedly, " it appeared that there had been some heated discussion regarding money, and Wilmott had been involved in some sort of affray. The police had been called, and Wilmott had fled, not unnaturally wishing to escape any scandal. He had tripped on some filth and his ankle was twisted, possibly broken. The police identified him as one if the *Bellerophon*'s crew and brought him to the ship. It seemed that they had no interest in arresting him or taking matters any further—in fact, they seemed keen to keep the whole thing very quiet and not to make any further trouble—but they brought him back to the ship."

" I see," said Holmes. " And you were the only officer on board at the time ? "

" I was, and I was therefore able to put about the story that Wilmott had been attacked, and had slipped and broken his ankle—for so later turned out that this was the case— when eluding his pursuers. The event was so written up in the log."

" And I am sure that he was grateful to you for doing this ? "

" Yes, he was." He seemed reluctant to discuss this aspect of the matter further, however.

A thought occurred to me, and without thinking, I asked the question that came to my mind. " You were aware that your fellow officer had such, shall we say, predilections," I burst out, " and yet you continued to be friends with him ? " I noticed Holmes glance at me, and then look back at the naval officer with intense interest.

Ramsey-Moffat turned an even deeper red. " He explained to me, in strict confidence, that the affairs of that evening were an aberration. Or rather, that they were a mistake. He had entered the wrong house, as it were, being mistaken as to the true nature of the residents there. In any case, he told me that this was the first time in his life that such an incident had occurred, and that such would never happen again." He paused a little. " And to the best of my knowledge, that is the case."

" Thank you, Lieutenant Ramsey-Moffat. I hope we will meet at dinner this evening with Captain Glover."

" Unfortunately, that will not be possible. Duty forbids." He pulled

out a large ornate watch and examined it. " And duty calls me now."

" Well, then, I must bid you farewell, it seems, and thank you for your help."

The officer left us, and Holmes turned to me. " I sense trouble here. Deep and dark trouble that bodes ill for the Navy, and even for the safety of the realm."

" Because of one foolish incident some years ago that may have been a ghastly mistake ? "

" Indirectly, that might be said to be the case, I suppose. That officer is a plausible liar, though." He sighed.

" Holmes," I exclaimed, somewhat astounded. " Are you insinuating that an officer of the Royal Navy, holding Her Majesty's commission, has been telling us less than the truth ? "

Holmes smiled. " I will not say that his testimony to us was a tissue of lies from beginning to end, but I fear it was largely untrue."

" On what do you base this accusation, Holmes ? "

" Why, on the man's watch, of course. Or, shall we say, the watch that he pulled out of his pocket. Did you not notice the engraving on it ? "

" I failed to do so."

" The initials A.W. cannot under any circumstances be those of Senior Lieutenant Ramsey-Moffat. They could, however be those of a certain other gentleman."

" I cannot conceive of any conclusions you can draw from this."

" I can conceive of too many, Watson, and none of them is a pleasant one. Let us return the use of the good Captain's cabin to him, and we will spend the day in the town, seeking what information there is to be had here. And I believe we could spend a very profitable evening by accepting Captain Glover's hospitality. What do you say to that ? "

" As long as the bill of fare is something other than bully beef and ship's biscuit," I laughed. " Very good. Let us follow your suggestions."

Before we left the ship, we talked to Captain Glover and accepted the invitation. At my urging, Holmes also told him a little more of the case on which we were engaged, while omitting any mention of the story we had been told by his Senior Lieutenant, and swore him to secrecy. As I had expected, the Captain appeared to be impressed by the confidence reposed in him by Holmes, and promised us every assistance in our work.

OLMES was once again pre-occupied as we walked off the ship into the town.

" Watson," he said to me suddenly. " Why in the world would that officer tell us that story with all the details ? Why could he not have told us the story he recorded in the log ? "

" He wishes to set our minds against the missing man ? To prejudice our thoughts against him ? "

" That is my feeling. And again, I ask myself why ? Does he wish us to continue our enquiries less zealously ? If so, he will be sadly disappointed. To every action there is an equal and opposite reaction, and you know well, Watson, that if I am pushed in one direction against my will, I will push back with an opposite force, which will exceed the force with which I am pushed. No, Lieutenant Ramsey-Moffat," he soliloquised, " you make me more, not less, interested in the disappearance of your friend, if friend he truly be."

We walked on until we reached the harbourmaster's office, where Holmes made enquiries as to the identity of the ship that had been described by Fortescue.

" The *Matilda Briggs*, registered in Rotterdam," said Holmes as we emerged from the office. " We now have a name for the ship. It should be easy enough for the Board of Trade to trace her calls at the ports around the coast, and we can then match those to the letters received by the Admiralty. Let us send a cable to the Board of Trade, and ask them to find out more about this ship and where she has berthed recently. Then we will reserve lodgings for the night, as I think we will partake of the *Colossus'* hospitality this evening, but spend the night on shore."

We sent the telegram, requesting that the reply be sent in care of Captain Glover on board the *Colossus*, and Holmes returned to the docks while I booked our accommodation at the George Inn. It had cost Holmes a number of florins to obtain it, but in the end he had a little more information about both the *Matilda Briggs*, and her visit to Portsmouth, as he told me before the fire in the front parlour of the inn.

" A Dutch skipper, and a dusky crew, possibly from the Indies, by the sound of them," he summarised rubbing his hands together briskly. " With one or two Dutch officers. A cargo of miscellaneous items, including sacks of grain and cheap tinware. I cannot attach any significance to that. It is strange, but no-one had any recollection of any previous visits by the ship. Typically such vessels will follow a fixed pattern, I believe, and it is unusual for them to break their habits in this way."

" What about the men who escorted Lord Haughton to the boat ? Did you discover anything ? "

" I was fortunate," he replied, " in being able to talk with the very boatman who carried the missing man to the *Matilda Briggs*. He was able to give a full description of the two Dutchman who escorted Haughton. The descriptions meant nothing to me, except that he mentioned that both men were heavily tanned, and spoke very little English. Though they arrived at the boat at the same time as Lord Haughton, it seems that they did not form a party. The boatman was first hired by them to take them to the *Matilda Briggs*, and following that, he was given to understand that he was to carry Lord Haughton to the *Colossus*."

" What actually transpired ? "

" According to the boatman, Lord Haughton was forced by his companions to mount the accommodation ladder to the coaster, escorted by them. He was received at the top by two of the native crew, and his two Dutch companions re-joined the smaller boat. They then paid him five pounds to return them straight to the dock, and to say nothing to anyone about the event."

" He told you all," I objected.

Holmes chuckled. " I drew him on a bet. I had gauged him, thanks to the betting slip I observed in his hatband, as a man who was not averse to a wager, and I was right in my assumption. I bet him that he had not carried passengers of more than a dozen nationalities within the past month. I was sure to lose my bet, as I had already counted the flags of fifteen nations on the ships in the harbor. I had to listen to tales of Finns and Swedes and Russians before we came to our Dutchmen, but we arrived there in the end."

" And now ? " I asked.

" Now we return to the *Colossus*. I trust that Captain Glover will forgive us for our sins in not dressing for dinner."

HE telegram from the Board of Trade was waiting for Holmes when we boarded the *Colossus* and entered the Captain's cabin. " As I thought," said Holmes, tearing it open and scanning the contents. " There is a perfect correspondence between the ports of call of the *Matilda Briggs* and the postmarks of the letters received from Lord Haughton. We can therefore conclude that he was being held on board the ship, and maybe still is on board."

" Where is the last port of call recorded ? " I asked.

" Gravesend, a few days ago, which corresponds to the last letter received."

" And you think that she is now in Holland, with Lord Haughton aboard ? "

" I believe that is what we are intended to think."

" May I make a suggestion," Captain Glover broke in. " Forgive me, gentlemen, but since you were good enough to take me into your confidence, I have been considering the matter. If you would care to use the facilities available to us, we could send a coded cable to the Admiralty, and the Admiralty agents in Holland and elsewhere on the Continent could investigate the matter and discover the whereabouts and possibly even the intentions of this mysterious Dutch vessel. I confess that I fear for Lord Haughton. Though I am not personally well acquainted with him, he is of course known to me, and he enjoys a sterling reputation among his brother officers, and to see him in Whitehall would be of great advantage to all of us who serve at sea."

"Then let us adopt your excellent suggestion," Holmes said to the Captain, who appeared highly gratified that his idea had been taken up by the famous detective. "Would you have any idea how soon we could expect an answer?"

"Of course, I cannot be sure," replied Glover, "but it seems to me that this is a question that could be solved within twenty-four hours at the very most. You are probably aware that we have agents in every coastal port on the Continent. During the time we await a reply, I would like to extend the hospitality of the Royal Navy to you both."

"Most kind of you," answered Holmes, "but we have reserved rooms at the George, close by the dock." The other's face fell somewhat, as it seemed to me that he was anticipating the cachet of hosting Sherlock Holmes as a guest of the *Colossus*, but his countenance brightened to some extent when Holmes added, "We would, however, welcome the use of a room such as this as a base for our operations while we are in this town."

"Naturally," Glover assured us, the smile returning to his weather-beaten face. "My cabin is your cabin, as the Spaniards almost have it."

"Your cooperation will not go unremarked, I assure you," said Holmes. "Now let us draft this message."

The message was soon written, and passed to the signalman for encoding and transmission over the Admiralty telegraph system.

"And now dinner," invited Captain Glover.

 FTER the admirable dinner, we returned to the George, despite the Captain's protestations, where we turned in and I, for one, slept soundly.

I was awakened early the next morning by a hammering on my door. On opening my eyes, I perceived that it wanted an hour or more before dawn, and I was somewhat annoyed, if not altogether surprised, by Holmes' voice bidding me to awake and dress myself. I hurriedly prepared myself for the day, omitting my morning shave, there being no hot water, and went downstairs to meet Holmes, who was waiting in the parlour together with a seaman whose cap band read "Colossus".

"I beg your forgiveness for this early call, Watson," Holmes apologised to me. "I was myself awakened some time ago by this messenger from the *Colossus*. Captain Glover has received a reply from Whitehall, and requests us to meet him at the dock. It would appear that the game is afoot." Even in the dim morning half-light, I could see that his eyes were positively shining with excitement.

"We are not to meet him on board the *Colossus*?"

"It would appear not."

We hurried through the darkened streets, following our guide, to a part of the dock which we had not visited the previous day. Captain Glover was waiting for us, a broad smile creasing his face.

" I would advise you to don these," he remarked, pointing to two sets of oilskin waterproof clothing, similar to what I now noticed he himself was wearing. " Our vessel today provides less protection against the elements than does the *Colossus*." He gestured to the water below, where a sleek vessel rode the waves. A curiously low and rounded hull gave her the appearance of some sinister sea creature. " Behold Her Majesty's Ship *Daring*, which has been described in the press as 'the fastest ship ever'. She made twenty-eight knots on her trials, approximately thirty-two miles per hour."

" I am puzzled," I said. I admit to having been still somewhat irritated at having been pulled from my warm bed to stand on a cold dockside where a light rain was unmistakably starting to fall, and my tone was somewhat sharp.

" We are on the trail of your quarry," Glover explained. " I received a cable from the Admiralty that the *Matilda Briggs* had departed Cherbourg last night, giving Southampton as her next port of call. I have therefore commandeered the use of the *Daring* to lie in wait for her and to board her if necessary. The 12-pounder gun should prove a sufficient means of persuasion."

" What manner of ship is this ? " I asked, looking down. " She seems to be very long compared to her beam."

" She is a new type of vessel, which we call a 'torpedo boat destroyer', designed for the purpose of protecting the Fleet's capital ships against the menace of the smaller torpedo boats that are now being deployed by navies around the world."

" On this occasion, we do not wish to destroy," remarked Holmes. " But a fast ship of this type will allow us to make an easy rendezvous with a slow steamer such as the *Matilda Briggs*, it is true."

" I have acquainted the *Daring*'s skipper, Lieutenant Fanshawe, with the broad outline of our mission, but no more than that," replied Glover.

" I take it that you will be accompanying us, then ? " I asked Captain Glover.

" Naturally," he smiled. " If the life of a fellow officer is at stake, I have no alternative but to assist. In any event, I would not miss such an adventure for the world." I could not help feeling admiration for such a man, who was willing to expose himself to possible danger (for we had no knowledge of the disposition of the crew of the *Matilda Briggs*) in defence of his fellows. Truly, I felt, the safety of the nation was assured if it was in the hands of such as Captain Glover.

We descended to the deck of the *Daring* where we were greeted by the young Lieutenant Fanshawe, whose manner reminded me of some of the younger officers in my Army days whose pleasure seemed to be chiefly derived from exposing themselves to danger, engaging in tiger hunts, pig-sticking, or steeple-chases. It was clear to me that dash and élan of this type would be a positive advantage to the commander of such a speedy and glamorous craft, and though I experienced a little anxiety at the thought of a trip in the *Daring*, I also felt a sense of exhilaration. Holmes appeared to suffer from no such qualms, but boarded the deck of this strange new vessel as if he had been a seaman all his life. Not for the first time I admired his adaptability to strange circumstances.

" I apologize, sir, for the lack of ceremonial in not piping you aboard," the Lieutenant said to Glover, saluting smartly. " I took it, though, that on an occasion like this it would be somewhat superfluous."

" Quite correct, Mr. Fanshawe," replied Glover. " This is a slightly irregular proceeding, and I do not feel we should be standing on that kind of ceremony here." He then introduced Holmes and myself to the Lieutenant.

" I am sure that you will have more than enough to do once we are underway, Lieutenant," Holmes said to him, " and we will try to keep ourselves from being underfoot, if you will show us where we can stow ourselves."

" I am sure there is room on the deck," replied the Lieutenant. " Please follow me."

It was a tight fit for the three visitors on the small part of the deck that was unoccupied by machinery, despite the vessel's size. Almost as soon as we had taken our places, the engines started, and we could feel the vibration of the reciprocating engines and the three propellers. We rapidly moved away from the dock, and slipped into the Solent, where we picked up speed. The spray whipped off the wave crests, and I began to appreciate Captain Glover's forethought in the matter of the oilskin waterproof clothing.

Sherlock Holmes stood slightly forward of the Captain and myself, standing on a low platform, his long neck craned forward as he strained his eyes towards the horizon, for all the world like some beast of prey on the track of its quarry.

" When did the *Matilda Briggs* leave Cherbourg, Captain ? " Holmes shouted into the wind without turning his head to look round.

" At about ten o'clock last night. We can assume an average speed of no more than nine knots from her, so with a distance of around ninety nautical miles of sailing between the ports, we can expect her to enter the Solent at around eight o'clock— maybe a little before that, should she prove to be faster than our estimate. We have another two hours or so before then."

" That should prove ample in a ship this fast," replied Holmes.

" What," I asked, " if the ship is not going to Southampton after all, but makes for another port ? "

" All watchers along the French, Belgian and Dutch coasts, as well as those on the German and Danish ports on this side of the Skagerrak are on the alert," replied Glover, " as well as a close watch now being kept by all harbourmasters in the United Kingdom."

" I must congratulate you, Captain," Holmes called back to us. " You appear to have sealed every possible exit. I believe you would succeed in my profession were you ever to quit the sea."

The seafarer laughed. " I hardly think so, Mr. Holmes. In this case, it was simply a matter of elementary naval tactics." However, I noted that Captain Glover appeared to appreciate these words of praise from Holmes.

" Hard a-port ! Hold on to the ship ! " the Lieutenant shouted from in front of us, as the ship heeled sharply to port. We were almost flying through the water by this time, and the wind whistled past our ears. Truly, this remarkable vessel deserved the title that it had been awarded by the Press.

Captain Glover pulled his watch out of his pocket and scrutinised it. " We are almost an hour ahead of the timetable we can expect the *Matilda Briggs* to follow," he observed. " We can afford a little time for relaxation, I would think."

As if on cue, the rumble of the engines lessened, and our speed in the water dropped to something more closely resembling my conception of a normal ship's speed.

" Breakfast ? " shouted Lieutenant Fanshawe from the steering position. I wondered about the composition of such a meal on board such a ship, but my curiosity was soon assuaged when a bluejacket appeared bearing three steaming mugs of sweetened cocoa and some hard ship's biscuit.

" I recommend softening it in the cocoa first," Captain Glover smiled to me, following his own advice as I gingerly approached the second item on the menu. Though I have broken my fast more luxuriously on many occasions, that simple food and drink taken as we watched the sun rise over the Solent remains as one of the more memorable meals of my life. Holmes devoured his repast while continuing to scan the horizon.

Captain Glover leaned towards me and spoke in a low voice. " Is it your opinion that your friend has a solution to the mystery ? "

" I believe he does," I answered in the same quiet tone. " But I have no idea what the solution might be, or how he might have arrived at it."

We continued on our way, with the inlet to Southampton harbour clearly visible. Our ship was, so Captain Glover assured me, in a perfect position to observe all the comings and goings of the port, and indeed we saw many different kinds of craft, from the largest ocean liners setting sail for distant parts of the Empire, to smaller fishing and pleasure craft. Several times we spotted approaching steamers that appeared to match the description with which we had been provided, but none of them proved to be the vessel we sought.

At length, Fanshawe called excitedly, " We have her ! " and raced along the deck to join us, passing his binoculars to Captain Glover, who passed them in his turn to Holmes.

" Well done, Mr. Fanshawe," exclaimed Glover. " Intercept her course as you think best. I shall stay well out of your way in this matter."

" Aye, aye. Thank you, sir," replied the Lieutenant, and we heard a series of nautical orders being issued, most of them totally incomprehensible to my ears.

It was not long, though, before it was obvious that we were on a course where we would cross the path of the *Matilda Briggs* in a relatively short time.

" Man the gun, Mr. Fanshawe," bellowed Captain Glover. " We may need to fire a shot across her bow."

" Aye, aye, sir," and a group of sailors took their position by the 12-pounder. My heart was racing as this marine chase drew to a close, and Holmes, I noticed, was white-lipped and tense while we closed in on the coaster. We were now close enough to see the name written on the bow without the aid of a telescope or binoculars.

" Make the signal 'I D', Mr. Fanshawe."

" Aye, aye, sir." Two flags went up the mast and fluttered at the head.

" What is the meaning of that signal, Captain ? " I asked.

" 'Heave to or I will fire into you'," he replied.

Holmes heard this exchange and

whirled around to face us. "We must not fire into her!" he exclaimed. We cannot risk injury to the passenger we believe may be on board."

"Have no fear, Mr. Holmes," answered Glover. "We will do no such thing."

The *Matilda Briggs* showed no sign of stopping or even of slowing. "Damn their eyes!" shouted Glover, angrily. "One over the bow, if you please, Mr. Fanshawe."

The sailors manning the bow gun went through complex well-drilled motions, culminating in a deafening explosion that made my ears ring, with a bright flash and a cloud of smoke issuing from the muzzle of the gun. A few seconds later, a column of water arose some fifty yards ahead of the *Matilda Briggs*.

"Good shooting," commented Glover. The shell appeared to have the desired effect, and the froth of water at the stern of the other ship died away and the *Matilda Briggs* visibly slowed in the water.

"Bring us alongside, Mr. Fanshawe," ordered Captain Glover, and within a few minutes, we were beside the rusty plates of the other's hull.

"We will board her," announced Glover.

"Very good, sir," replied Fanshawe. "I will assemble a boarding party."

"You will do no such thing," retorted the Captain. "By 'we', I mean Mr. Holmes, Dr. Watson and myself only. There are to be no others. However, if we have not returned or otherwise indicated our safety to you within fifteen minutes of boarding, you may lead a boarding party at your discretion. I have my pistol. Are you two gentlemen armed?" turning to Holmes and myself. "I feel it would be a wise precaution here."

"We are not," replied Holmes. "I would prefer not to carry a weapon, but if you feel it would be necessary, I will abide by your decision."

"Mr. Fanshawe, you will provide these gentlemen with pistols," Glover ordered *Daring*'s skipper.

We were duly provided with heavy Navy revolvers, and Fanshawe hailed the *Matilda Briggs*, expressing the intention of boarding. A ladder was dropped from her deck, and we scrambled up it, Captain Glover leading, Holmes following, and myself bringing up the rear.

◦═◉═◦

NCE on board, I looked around. As had been reported, the crew were Asiatics of some description—I assumed from the Dutch East Indies. A savage-looking people, they regarded their visitors with sullen stares. Though none seemed armed, there are enough potential weapons on board a ship of the type of the *Matilda Briggs*, such as marlinspikes and other nautical implements, to give me pause for thought.

"Where is your Captain?"

roared Glover at the closest native, who seemed to be in charge of the others. His only answer was a blank stare, in which incomprehension and hostility appeared to be mixed.

"*Waar is uw kapitein?*" he asked. This brought a response from the crewman, who passed an order to one of the others, using a language that was totally unfamiliar to me.

After a minute or so, a tall European, about fifty years old by his appearance, and with a skin that had, to my experienced eye, seen many a tropic day, emerged from the bridge and joined us on deck.

" Gerard Waalfort, master of the *Matilda Briggs*," he introduced himself in English that was hardly accented. " Is there any way I can assist you gentlemen ? I hope you are aware that your shell has disturbed my crew, and I trust you have a good reason for your actions."

" Indeed we have," replied Holmes, stepping forward. " We are looking for Lord Haughton, whom we have reason to believe is aboard this vessel."

" An English lord ? " scoffed the other. " Does this rusting bundle of steel plates look like a luxury passenger liner to you ? The kind of vessel on which an English lord would travel ? " He threw back his head and laughed.

" Maybe you know your passenger better as Augustus Wilmott ? " s1uggested Holmes quietly.

The laughter choked off abruptly. " He is a lord ? " asked Waalfort. " You are not joking ? " Holmes shook his head. " *Mijn God* ! " exclaimed the Dutchman.

" Ramsay-Moffat did not inform you ? " asked Holmes, smiling gently. By my side, Captain Glover stiffened at Holmes' mention of the name of his subordinate, and seemed about to speak, but I plucked him by the sleeve, and motioned to him to hold his peace. To his credit, he did so, though I could see he was more than anxious to ask questions of Holmes.

" He said nothing," replied the Dutch skipper, before realising what he had admitted. " *Mijn God* ! " he repeated. " Are you some kind of wizard to know these things ? "

" I think you had better lead us to Lord Haughton," Holmes said in reply.

" Very good, Mr. Wizard," was the answer. He led the way down a companionway to a dark and noxious hold in the bowels of the ship. " Here," gesturing towards one corner.

A pitiful sight met our eyes. A gaunt ragged figure, clad in rags and lying on the deck of the hold, stared up at us, and a flicker of recognition dawned in his eyes.

" My God, it's Glover ! " croaked the scarecrow.

" In the name of all that's damnable," said the Captain, seemingly aghast. " Lord Haughton ! "

" Come no closer," replied the other. " I am dying. Come closer to me, and it is your death, too."

" I am a doctor," I informed him. " I can assist you."

" No, do not come near ! " he answered me. " It is certain death for you to approach. I know not what it is that ails me, but suspect the worst, and I am convinced it is deadly."

Despite myself, I shrank a little, but moved to fulfil the duties of my profession. Sadly, it took less than a minute for me to make my diagnosis. " It is the plague, the Black Death," I announced to the others. Holmes and Captain Glover instinctively moved back several paces, but I held my ground.

The dying man looked at me with the calm eyes of those who know their fate, and are resigned to it. " I am sorry, Doctor, to have placed you in such danger."

" I am not afraid," I said. In truth, I was naturally more than a little concerned, but less so than others would be under the circumstances, as a result of my previous exposure to the foul disease during an epidemic that had broken out in my time in India. This experience afforded me, I fervently hoped, some immunity. " Some clean water," I ordered the Dutchman. " And blankets."

I bent over the sick man, and discovered that, in my opinion, based on my previous Indian experience, he had not exaggerated his condition. He had, in my estimation, only a few hours, possibly even less, before his death. The water arrived, Waalfort passed it at arm's length to me, and I held it to the dying man's lips. He drank of it thirstily, and fell to coughing.

" I must inform *Daring* that we are safe—for the moment," said Glover. He left us, escorted back to the deck by Waalfort, and Holmes and I were left alone with the sick man.

" How did you contract the disease ? " I asked him. " Are some of the crew of this ship suffering ? "

For answer, he waved his hand feebly towards another corner of the hold. Holmes moved to see what it was to which he had gesticulated, and I heard his cry of surprise.

" What is it, Holmes ? " I called to him.

" Some animals," he replied. " They resemble rats, but they are larger than any I have hitherto encountered. Hideous creatures the size of terriers."

" They are indeed rats," gasped Haughton. " The giant rat of Sumatra, brought from the East Indies, and a known carrier of disease. There are many of them on this boat. When I was brought on board, I was placed next to the filthy animals, and..." He fell to coughing, vomiting up a sticky mess, and for several minutes was unable to speak, while I mopped his brow with a wet cloth, and provided such comfort as I was able. " I am going," were his next words, as I raised the water to his mouth once more. " I thank

you for your kindness, and—" his words ceased.

I examined him as closely as I dared. " He is dead, Holmes."

" So quickly ? "

" It is a malady that strikes quickly and without notice, and the final stages are mercifully swift," I told him. " May he rest in peace," I added as I closed his eyes, " whatever wrongs he may have done in his life."

We mounted to the upper deck, thankful to be out of the foul air of the hold, and informed Captain Glover of the situation.

" This ship must not land under any circumstances," said Glover. " The danger of the plague spreading to England is too great. Hoist 'V B'—'sickness is contagious' as soon as possible," he ordered Waalfort, who hastened to obey. The crew, for their part, seemed demoralised, and their previous sullen, almost aggressive, nature seemed to have turned to a silent resentment.

Glover then demanded a megaphone and called to the waiting skipper of *Daring*, " The crew of this ship must enter quarantine immediately. Order a suitable ship to bring them off, and then return here. Make sure you have live torpedoes on board and an adequate supply of shells for the gun."

" You cannot sink my ship ! " exclaimed the Dutchman, aghast as he perceived Glover's intentions.

" I can and I will. Your ship is a danger to my country," replied the Englishman imperturbably. " Mynheer Waalfort, I want to point out that you yourself are in grave danger, together with all your crew, of spending the rest of your life in an English prison. If you prefer, I can arrange for your ship to be sunk with all of you on board, and you can take your chances in the water ?

No ? Then I suggest that you accept the course of action I suggest."

" We are many and you are but three," pointed out the other, snarling.

" I feared it might come to this," Holmes interrupted. " Before you start considering that kind of action, you might wish to take one or two other points into consideration."

" Such as ? "

" First, the fact that it is known we are on board this ship. Were we to be missing when the *Daring* returns, I would venture to suggest that you would not even reach jail, but you and your crew would not even reach dry land."

" That may well be true, but I am prepared to take that chance. Anything else ? "

" The most persuasive argument I can make," said Holmes, " is the revolver that Watson here has pointed at your head."

While the last conversation had been taking place, I had crept to one side and pulled the Navy pistol from my pocket, cocking the hammer, and aiming it, unseen by my target, at the skipper. He turned and blanched.

" A convincing argument, I admit."

" And if you wish to consider two further arguments, I am holding one," producing his own revolver, " and Captain Glover has another." The coaster's skipper nodded silently.

" Now order your men to the rail, to sit facing the ocean, with their legs over the side of the ship," said Holmes. When that had been done, he asked, " We have twelve men here. How many are below ? "

" Five stokers and engineers. And there are two officers off-watch."

" I will bring them up here," volunteered Captain Glover. He ducked into the companionway, and returned a few minutes later driving five more Asiatics before him at the point of his pistol. " And now for the officers." This time he entered the superstructure below the bridge, and almost immediately, we heard the cracks of two pistol shots. After a short while, a white man, clad in pyjamas, came on deck, his hands in the air, followed by our brave Captain.

" Where is Jan, the mate ? " asked Waalfort.

" He tried to kill me," replied Glover, laconically. " He failed to do so, as you can see. I am here, and he is not."

The Dutch officer was forced to the side of the ship, where he sat alongside the crew, his legs dangling over the side.

" Can we count on your good behaviour now ? " Holmes asked Waalfort. " Or do we ask you to join the crew ? "

" I will stay here," replied the other, truculently.

" Dr. Watson, keep your eye on him," ordered Glover. " Have no hesitation in firing should he attempt any tricks." The Dutchman stood motionless, his arms folded in front of him.

" What is that about Ramsay-Moffat ? " asked Captain Glover to Holmes, in a low voice.

Holmes briefly outlined the story he had heard from the two *Colossus* officers, as Glover listened in mounting disbelief.

" You suspect my First Lieutenant of some sort of involvement in this affair ? " he burst out at length.

" Waalfort here has already said as much."

" I confess that I have never regarded him highly as an officer on board my ship, and he held his position as First Lieutenant by reason of his seniority rather than his abilities," said Glover. " But for him to be involved in this kind of business... Words fail me." He bit his lips and stood brooding silently until the *Daring* returned.

N an hour's time, we were re-joined by the torpedo boat destroyer.

" Stand to windward," called out Glover. " Let us reduce the risk of infection if we can," he added to us.

" Are you and your crew not afraid of the disease you are carrying ? " Holmes asked Waalfort, curiously.

" Not at all," he answered. " Or, to be more accurate, only a little. All of us have suffered from the *plaag*—the plague—in the past and lived to tell the tale. We are hardened to its effects, as I informed Captain Ramsay-Moffat when we discovered that the rats were carrying it."

" Excuse me," said Captain Glover. " Did I hear you say *Captain* Ramsay-Moffat ? " His tone was quiet, but carried an air of menace about it.

" Why, yes. He is a Captain in the British Royal Navy, is he not ? "

" He is no such damned thing, and never will be, if I have anything to do with it ! " Captain Glover was fairly dancing with rage, and his face had turned an alarming shade of dark red.

" Calm yourself, Captain," urged Holmes. " There will be time enough for this later." He turned back to Waalfort. " Why were you carrying Lord Haughton on your ship ? Was money your motive there ? "

" We were told by Captain Ramsay—" He checked himself, observing a possible further

explosion from Glover, and continued, " Ramsay-Moffat told us that we could expect money from this trip, yes, but this was done largely to protect myself. Years ago in Jakarta while I was serving in the Colonial Police, I committed an indiscretion—it was not a serious indiscretion, and I am by no means the only one to have committed such—but if it were brought to the attention of the authorities, even today, I would lose my pension, and I might even face prison, if proof could be brought against me. I believed that no such proof existed. Ramsay-Moffat, with whom I had been in contact since the days of Jakarta when he was stationed there told me that the man whom I had known in Jakarta as Augustus Wilmott was likely to be made a very important man in the government, and that even without proof, his word would count against mine, no matter what proofs of innocence I produced." He shrugged his shoulders. " And as I confess to you now, I am guilty of those past crimes. I could produce no such proofs."

" Much as I had surmised," said Holmes. " And the idea was to keep your prisoner on board until he agreed not to threaten you and Ramsay-Moffat in the future ? " The other nodded. " And the rats ? Did you know they carried the plague with them ? "

" That, I swear, was not our intention. Ramsay-Moffat had told us that Wilmott had a fear of these rodents and that if we kept him below next to the cage in which they were confined, he would soon agree to our terms. But even when I cabled to Ramsay-Moffat that we suspected we had the plague on board, he would not listen to any change in our plans."

"And so, instead of agreeing to your demands, your prisoner contracted this foul disease, from which he has now died," pointed out Holmes. "I do not know how this is going to sit with an English jury."

"I do not know how Ramsay-Moffat is going to sit with me when I have finished with him," growled Captain Glover.

"Control yourself, Captain," Holmes implored him. "I am sure your feelings do you credit, but let us await the outcome of this episode before we do much else. But, mark!"

A white ship, a red cross pained on her side, was approaching the *Matilda Briggs*. "Your transport to shore, skipper," Holmes announced to Waalfort.

"Hah!" replied the Dutchman, and thrust his hands deep into his trouser pockets.

The hospital ship, the *Nightingale*, came alongside, and the crew of the *Matilda Briggs* were transferred to her, Captain Waalfort leaving his ship last in the traditional fashion.

"To the prison hospital with them," Captain Glover shouted to the *Nightingale*. "They must be closely guarded and kept away from others." He turned to us. "And what do we do? We are possibly infected, and I do not wish to be the cause of spreading the plague throughout the Fleet by contact with *Daring*'s crew."

"May I suggest that *Daring* lower her boat, and the three of us board her and move away from this vessel while *Daring* destroys her. We can then be towed back to Portsmouth,

and the medical authorities can take whatever steps they see fit," I put forward.

"I concur," agreed Glover, after a short pause for thought. "What do we do with the body of poor Lord Haughton, though?"

"Let it be said that he went down with the ship," replied Holmes. "None of this business must reach the public's ears, as I am sure you understand."

"It is a Viking's funeral, I suppose. From all I hear of the man, it is an ending that he would have wished for himself."

The boat was lowered, and Glover and I rowed the boat away from the *Matilda Briggs*. "Ahoy!" he shouted to the *Daring* when he we were at a distance he estimated would be safe. "Fire at will, Mr. Fanshawe," he called through the megaphone we had brought with us.

There was a muffled thumping sound, and a long cylinder seemed to leap from the bow of the *Daring*. "A Whitehead torpedo," explained Glover. "Two hundred pounds of guncotton should put paid to that hell-ship."

We watched the torpedo's trail, easily visible as a consequence of the escaping compressed air by which it was propelled, speeding towards its target. After less than a minute, the sea erupted at the waterline of the *Matilda Briggs*, and the sound of the explosion reached us a few seconds later. Almost immediately, the coaster heeled over, and in a matter of minutes, nothing remained on the surface other than a few wooden fragments, and an oily scum.

"Excellent work by Fanshawe," commented Glover, as we were towed back to port by *Daring* at the end of a long rope.

On arrival at the port, I explained our situation to the doctors who had charge of the *Matilda Briggs'* crew. Based on my report of the nature and length of our exposure, they recommended salt baths for the three of us, together with some unpleasant-tasting prophylactic medicines. Whether it was due to these precautions, or whether it was a matter of luck, I do not know, but we escaped infection.

"N many ways, one of the simplest cases I have encountered," Sherlock Holmes told Mycroft as we sat together in Baker-street. " I fail to see how you missed all the clues."

Mycroft had been persuaded by his brother to leave his familiar circuit of his lodgings, Whitehall and the Diogenes Club on account of the sensitive nature of the information that Holmes was about to impart to us. On arrival at Baker-street, he had sniffed superciliously at Holmes' eccentric domestic arrangements, but had at length allowed himself to be settled in an armchair with a brandy and soda by his side. Sherlock Holmes was now recounting the story to him and to me. On our return from Portsmouth, I had returned to my practice, and I had not seen Holmes for two days while he clarified the answers to a few final problems regarding the case. Earlier that day, I had received a telegram from him, requesting my presence. I was keen to know the details, and I gladly accepted.

I was anxious to know of the fate that had befallen the players in this affair, and I asked Holmes if he had received any news thereon.

" I received a dispatch from the good Captain Glover yesterday," Holmes replied. " He managed to maintain control of his feelings sufficiently to confront Ramsay-Moffat without recourse to physical violence, and presented him with the evidence of his crimes. Given the choice between a court-martial, which might have passed a capital sentence and would undoubtedly have ruined him on the one hand, and the gentleman's recourse in these circumstances on the other, Ramsay-Moffat selected the latter. His body was discovered floating in Portsmouth harbour the same evening, a bullet-hole through the right side of the head. A letter addressed to Captain Glover was discovered in his cabin."

" A most unpleasant business, even for a blackmailer, would you not say ? "

" Most unpleasant," repeated Sherlock Holmes, " in that we had two blackmailers, blackmailing each other. Haughton and Ramsay-Moffat were linked by a cord of mutual distrust and hatred."

" One would have assumed that the two would cancel each other out," I said. " Where both are blackmailers, surely there is nothing to expose."

" Nothing and everything," replied Holmes. " For Lord Haughton, the exposure of his escapade in Jakarta all those years ago would almost certainly lead to the complete collapse of his career. On the other hand, we now know, thanks to the confession he left behind, that Ramsey-Moffat's own promotions were largely due to an admixture of the influence wielded at his behest by his victim, Haughton, and by his destruction of the careers of other officers through bullying and blackmail over minor peccadilloes, as well as outright forgery of orders and documents in a number of cases. Naturally, Haughton was aware of all this, and had it in his power to wreck Ramsay-Moffat in his turn. He was, strange though it may seem, in a stronger position than the other. If he were to expose Ramsay-Moffat, the latter would have nothing on which to fall back, while Haughton, of course, would have his estates and eventually his father's title. The two were like fencers with their foils at each other's throats, neither daring to move forward for fear of the damage they might inflict on themselves."

" How did you come to know that Ramsay-Moffat was involved, Sherlock ? " asked his brother, speaking for the first time.

" From the letters written by Haughton," replied Holmes, bringing out the copies that had been supplied by Mycroft.

" I examined these letters and could make nothing of them," exclaimed Mycroft. " Perhaps you would be good enough to explain yourself here."

" It was not until after we had been introduced to Ramsey-Moffat that the meaning became clear," explained Holmes. Read the first letters of each epistle."

" 'Read'—R." Mycroft turned to the next sheet. " 'As'—A, and the next starts 'My'—M, and the next is 'Some'—S. R A M S... I see it now. Ingenious."

" Too ingenious," replied my friend. " You missed it entirely, and it was too late for me to act on it when I had discovered its meaning. However, it was obvious to me that there was more to these letters than met the eye. The letters were written at Waalfort's orders, I am sure, in order to allay any fears that Haughton was dead, and the captive developed a plan, too subtle for its own good, to communicate with the outside world. The whole message, by the way, read 'R A M S A Y M O F F A T A S K H I M W H E R E I A M'. Following Lord Haughton's contracting the plague, the communications naturally ceased. My suspicions regarding Ramsay-Moffat were aroused, you will remember, Watson, when he told us the whole of the story regarding the past incident in Jakarta—you do not need to know the details, Mycroft. It was a sordid little tale that reflects well on no-one and is best forgotten, but it was indicative of some kind of devilment on Ramsay-Moffat's part. Following his tale to us, I re-examined the letters."

" And that was enough to put you on the track of the *Matilda Briggs* ? "

" The connection was obvious. My enquiries at the docks confirmed that there was a link with the East Indies in the shape of the crew and the officers. We knew that both Haughton and Ramsey-Moffat had served in that part of the world, and it therefore seemed more than likely that Ramsey-Moffat had retained connections there. Waalfort turns out to have been one of the police officials who brought Haughton back to the *Bellorophon* that fateful night. He admitted to us that he had committed misdeeds—maybe he accepted bribes, or worse—and somehow Haughton had discovered this. I have no doubt that Ramsay-Moffat also had this knowledge, and used it to further his own ends.

" After that, it was plain that there was some form of blackmail afoot. Ramsay-Moffat had been using his knowledge of Haughton's past to further his own career, but dared not push too hard, for fear he himself would be exposed. It has transpired that many documents in his Service file are not authentic, and he would most certainly have suffered had their authenticity been questioned."

" What caused him to adopt these desperate measures at the last ? " asked Mycroft.

" I believe it was exactly as we were told by Waalfort," replied Holmes. " Haughton was believed to be on his way to greater things— even if your championing of him as First Lord of the Admiralty was not common knowledge, Mycroft, it seems that he was highly regarded by many. His word would have carried much more weight than previously, and any attempt by Ramsey-Moffat to use his knowledge against his superior would be dismissed as the ravings of a failed rival."

" You appear to have saved the country from two plagues, Sherlock. Not only a physical disease, but also a moral plague that could have infected our political system. Your bravery in confronting this threat is commendable."

" You should rather be commending Watson for his bravery," commented my friend. " To approach and give comfort to a man you know is dying of such a vile disease argues a degree of courage that few possess. I frankly confess, Watson, I am humbled by your actions."

I was embarrassed, and muttered something about its only having been my duty.

" Nonetheless," said Mycroft, " I concur with Sherlock in his opinion."

ATURALLY, none of the above was ever made public, nor do I intend it to be so, given the high positions held by some of the principals of the case, and the importance of them to the Crown. Lord Haughton was given out as having been lost at sea in a boating accident, and the capsized wreck of his yacht was adduced as proof of this.

Captain Glover, I am pleased to say, remained firm friends with Holmes and myself for many years to come, and largely as a result of Mycroft Holmes' invisible influence, rose to the rank of Rear-Admiral, a promotion, in my opinion, well deserved. Waalfort and his crew were held in quarantine, after which time a request was made to the Dutch government, and they were returned to Holland on a Dutch naval vessel. I never discovered their ultimate fate.

Holmes, as was his wont, refused all honours and glory connected with the business, and I followed his lead on this matter, though I have sometimes wondered how my and Mary's lives would have been changed had I yielded to the momentary impulse, and we had henceforth been addressed as Sir John and Lady Watson.

SHERLOCK HOLMES &
THE CONK-SINGLETON
FORGERY CASE

I MADE MY WAY TO BOW-STREET MAGISTRATES' COURT, AN INSTITUTION WITH WHICH
I WAS HAPPILY UNFAMILIAR .... ON ARRIVAL, I TOOK A SEAT NEAR THE BACK OF THE
ALMOST EMPTY ROOM, COMMANDING A VIEW OF THE WHOLE AREA. (PAGE 216)

EDITOR'S NOTE

At the end of The Adventure of the Six Napoleons*, Holmes asks Watson to "get out the papers of the Conk-Singleton forgery case". We may assume that the investigative portion of the case had been completed at the time of the adventure of the Napoleons, and the "papers" to which Holmes referred were notes from which he was to present evidence as a witness in the trials resulting from his investigations, and from which John Watson faithfully chronicled the exploits of his illustrious friend.*

Few readers of the accounts of Sherlock Holmes *as originally presented by Dr. Watson will be aware of the fact that the great detective actually spent a night in the cells as a guest of Her Majesty while under arrest. This may well be the reason why the account of this case was not originally published, and remained locked in the deed box. Despite his seeming fall from grace, Holmes shines in this case, and it is good to see that his past assistance to the Metropolitan Police here bears fruit in the form of Inspector Gregson's goodwill and cooperation.*

 HAD been married for some years when this singular adventure occurred, which involved a series of extraordinary events in connection with the City of London and with the world of finance, far from Holmes' usual area of activity.

For myself, I had some personal interest in the area of stocks and shares and investments. My Army pension, though not in any way an excessive amount of money, nonetheless provided me, when combined with the income from my growing practice, with enough money for my dear wife and myself to live comfortably.

Indeed, there was more than enough for our immediate requirements, and I had invested in the City, using some of the surplus that we been able to save. As I had no reason to flatter myself with regard to my expertise in these matters, and there was no cause for any observer to single me out as a shrewd investor, I had availed myself of the services of a broker in whose hands I had placed myself. I had visited his offices close to Leadenhall Market, when I found myself passing Baker-street on my return to my home, and determined to call upon Sherlock Holmes.

It had been some time since I had paid a visit to my old haunts, but Mrs. Hudson welcomed me as an old friend, and after enquiring after my wife, informed me that Holmes was in residence, and would, she assured me, be glad of my visit.

"He's been busy these past days," she told me, "going in and out at all hours, but he seems to have stayed indoors all day today."

I mounted the stairs and knocked on the well-remembered door.

"Enter," came the familiar voice from within, and I opened the door, to discover my friend lying on his back at full length on the hearth-rug, with his feet propped on the seat of a dining chair. His eyes, which had apparently been closed, opened slowly, and his head turned to face me.

"Well, Watson," he remarked, removing his feet from the chair and slowly returning to a more normal upright posture, "you have been quite a stranger these past weeks. I trust that the demands of managing a portfolio of investments in addition to those of your practice are not proving to be too onerous for you. By the by, I do not recommend moving out of Imperial & Colonial and into Baxter's Patent Bicycles, no matter how the former may have fallen in the past few days. But do not let these merely financial matters depress you. Take a seat, fill your pipe, and make yourself at home."

"You never fail to amaze me," I replied. "I have indeed been to visit my broker, and my holdings of Imperial & Colonial have suffered losses recently. And he was recommending Baxter's as an alternative, advising me to clear out of my I&C, as he refers to them, and to re-invest. But how do you come to know all this about me, and about the Exchange? I had not figured you for an expert in business and financial matters of this kind."

"Nor am I, in the usual way of things," Holmes answered. "In answer to your first question, when I see you with the pink of the *Financial Times* emerging from your pocket, which was never your everyday reading fare when you lodged here, I must conclude that you have taken an interest in the world of the City. I see that you are carrying that parcel containing a small cheese, a Wensleydale, if the shape, size and odour do not lead me astray. Such a cheese is one of the specialities of Crompton's, the cheesemonger in Leadenhall Market, so I deduce

you have visited the City, on a professional financial matter which you combined with the pleasure of indulging in a little luxury. I do remember your telling me once that you had invested in Imperial & Colonial, and when I see the prospectus of Baxter's Patent Bicycle Co. protruding from within the folds of the Financial Times, I must therefore infer, given the precipitous fall of Imperial & Colonial, that you are considering transferring your financial affections elsewhere."

"All this is absolutely true. My wife and I are both extremely partial to Wensleydale cheese, and as you say, Crompton's carries the best in London. Though how you can identify it as such, given the smell of tobacco in here, is beyond my understanding." Indeed, the atmosphere in the room was close, and reeked of the strong shag tobacco that Holmes affected. "And, naturally, you are correct in your financial deductions."

"Naturally," he smiled, refilling his pipe. "And your next question to me will be how I come to know about these things?" I nodded. "I have been engaged in work for one of the financial houses in the City. There seems to be a conspiracy, if that is not too strong a word, to manipulate the Exchange in such a way as to benefit one party alone."

"Surely that is the usual way of such things?" I retorted. "Such manipulations of the market are hardly a novelty, I feel. They hardly call for the services of a specialist in criminal investigation, such as yourself."

"In this case, Watson, it would appear that there is a definite criminal element involved. Many of the shares offered for sale recently on the exchange have been forgeries. For example, the fall of Imperial &

Colonial stock we have been discussing is largely due to this very fact. The majority of bearer certificates, if not all of them, as you no doubt are aware, are unregistered and the transactions of these securities remain unrecorded. Many such have been exchanged recently, with the purchasers being unaware of the fact that they have given good money for worthless paper. That in itself is not surprising, perhaps, but the sellers also seem to be genuinely ignorant of the fact that their shares are valueless."

" I have heard nothing of this," I protested. " I take it that this is not common knowledge."

" It is certainly not bruited abroad," confirmed my friend. " Imagine the panic that would spread throughout the City—nay, throughout the whole nation—were it to be generally known that shares being bought and sold in the heart of London ran the risk of being discovered to be fraudulent and quite literally, not worth the paper on which they are printed."

" Indeed, I shudder to think of the results. It could lead to a run on the banks, and to many other undesirable consequences. Is this the diabolical scheme of an overseas power attempting to subvert the commerce of the realm ? " I asked.

Holmes shook his head. " It would be tempting to imagine that to be the case," he replied. " It seems from my investigations so far, such as they are, that we have here a villain of the native variety, and we are denied the luxury of a foreign plot. Simple greed, rather than politics, would appear to be the driving force here."

" And who is this person ? " I asked. " Have your researches revealed his identity ? "

" As yet that is not the case, I

fear. I am expecting the manager of one of the larger City houses to visit me shortly, who will be expecting greater things from me than I am presently unable to provide." He sighed.

" In which case, I should leave you," I said, rising to my feet.

" Stay here, Watson," he protested. " Surely you and I have worked together in the past often enough for you to know that you are always welcome as my partner and colleague in these little adventures, no matter what the current circumstances may be." There was, it seemed to me, more than a hint of subtle malice in the allusion to my marriage, but I was determined not to let that stand in the way of my regard and friendship towards Holmes. " And indeed, I fancy I hear the good Mrs. Hudson admitting our visitor now."

About a minute later, there was a knock at the door, and Holmes rose to answer it, admitting a grossly corpulent gentleman, who was breathing heavily, seemingly from the exertion of climbing the stairs. He was closely followed by another, who presented an almost comical contrast in terms of his figure and overall appearance, which was of one who appeared to have seen better days, if his attire and the general cleanliness of his person were to be taken as a clue as to his status. The larger man was expensively and well-dressed, though I could not help but remark that some dead leaves seemed to have adhered to the soles of his boots.

He noticed me almost immediately upon entering the room. " Who is this ? " he asked, almost accusingly, looking at me with eyes that seemingly twinkled, but at the same time had an air of suspicion about them.

" This is my friend and colleague,

Doctor Watson," replied Holmes. "Anything you say to me may also be safely said before him. And my visitor," indicating the large man to me, " is Mr. Charles Conk-Singleton, the senior partner of Knight and Conk-Singleton, the well-known City brokers. I have not as yet had the pleasure of being introduced to... ? "

" Edward Masters," replied the other, withdrawing a business card and presenting it to Holmes, who read it and raised his eyebrows.

" It would appear, Mr. Masters, that you and I are in the same line of business," he remarked, returning the courtesy and handing one of his own cards to the man who, now I was able to observe him more closely, appeared to have a shifty look about him, seemingly avoiding Holmes' eye.

" I would say so," replied the other. " I am regularly employed by Knight and Conk-Singleton in the event that there is any business that smacks of illegality."

" I understand," said Holmes reflectively. " Pray take a seat, both of you. Mr. Conk-Singleton, when you came to me a few days ago to request my services, was Mr. Masters already engaged by you in regard to this matter ? " The large man nodded silently, smiling. His air of geniality seemed unchanged. " I am accustomed to being the only hound on the trail," continued Holmes, " unless it is a matter of cooperation with the official police force. Meaning no disrespect to you, Mr. Masters, but I cannot proceed further with the case unless I am to pursue it alone."

" I understand your meaning," said the large man. " You place me in a difficult position, however, given that my partner, Gerald Knight, has already engaged Mr. Masters to

investigate this matter on behalf of the firm." He mopped his brow with a large handkerchief drawn from an inside pocket. Though the room was not excessively warm, he was perspiring heavily, while breathing hard, and his face was flushed. Whether these symptoms were the result of embarrassment, exertion, or were due to some other cause, it was impossible for me to determine with any degree of certainty, but they seemed to indicate some constitutional dysfunction.

" If you are referring to the deposit that you advanced me for my expenses, then you need not worry yourself over the matter," replied Holmes. " I will return the cheque for the full amount—two hundred guineas, was it not ? —in full." He opened a drawer in his bureau and extended an envelope to the other. I noticed Masters' eyes grow wide as Holmes mentioned the sum of money.

A little to my surprise, Conk-Singleton waved the money away. " That was not the object to which I was referring," he said. " The meaning I intended to impart is the fact that Mr. Masters here has been of great service to our firm on a number of occasions and we are accustomed to working with him. We would like to maintain this arrangement as far as possible, and would therefore suggest that he would lead the investigation, and you would act as his junior, if I may use an analogy from the law-courts."

" That would be totally unacceptable," replied Holmes resolutely. " If you wish to retain my services, then you must dispense with those of Mr. Masters here. Who knows what damage he may do to my investigations by pursuing an independent line of enquiry completely antithetical to my methods ? No, sir. You must make a decision as to which of the two of us you will employ on this case. For my part, I am indifferent as to whatever decision you make. I have other clients who will no doubt wish to engage my services in the near future."

" Really," exclaimed the broker, " this is all extremely embarrassing for me. If I had known this situation would ever arise... There is no compromise possible ? "

" For my part, there is none," answered Holmes.

All this time, I had been watching the face of the other detective, which had assumed an expression of increasing hostility during the exchange.

At length, the big man sighed, and turned to his companion. " I am sorry, Masters, but I have determined to engage Mr. Holmes in this matter. I will speak to Mr. Knight about the issue and all will be settled in good order. You may rest assured that Knight and Conk-Singleton will certainly be retaining your services in the future with regard to other business, and all expenses you have incurred so far in this affair will naturally be repaid to you on the presentation of your account."

" I see," was the other's response, delivered in a cold unemotional tone. " So it is to be Mr. Sherlock Holmes who will receive the fees promised to me, as well as the fame and publicity ? Yes, Mr. Conk-Singleton, be sure that my account will be forthcoming to you. A good day to you. And to you and you," he added to Holmes and myself. He let himself out of the door, closing it behind him.

" I am sorry about this," our visitor said to Holmes. " I had no idea that he would take it in this way."

Nor did I expect you to wish to take sole credit."

" I must admit that I am not entirely surprised by his reaction. As to my taking sole credit—" He paused and cocked his ear. " Mr. Conk-Singleton, I fear I am neglecting my duties as a host. Would you care for tea ? "

" Why, indeed—" replied the other, but Holmes had stepped swiftly and noiselessly to the door and flung it open, to reveal Masters, who had obviously been standing with his ear pressed to the keyhole, as evidenced by his falling into the room before recovering his balance, and looking about him with an amazed expression on his face.

" Off with you ! " ordered Holmes. " I will refrain from comment on your actions, and leave Mr. Conk-Singleton to draw his own conclusions." Conk-Singleton, for his part, wore an expression of almost comical surprise on his face as Masters turned away and started to descend the stairs. Holmes reclosed the door, and crossed to the window, where he remained for a few minutes. " He has truly departed now," he remarked, turning back to face us. " I mentioned tea," he added, ringing the bell for Mrs. Hudson as if there had been no interruption of any kind. " Now, Mr. Conk-Singleton," he continued, " please understand that it is not a matter of vanity or cupidity on my part that caused my request. I apologise for having placed you in an awkward position just now, but I think this last development may in a way provide some justification."

The other nodded. " Indeed it may. I am surprised at him stooping to such a trick."

" It is not the morality of listening at keyholes," continued Holmes, " as this, after all, is one of the stocks in trade of detectives of a lower level of ability than myself, such as Masters would appear to be. However, the noise of his breathing as he stooped to listen, and the sound of his hat falling on the floor—you failed to remark those sounds, Watson ? ah, well—provided sufficient evidence to my mind that my decision not to work with such a bungler was the correct one. Mrs. Hudson," he broke off as our landlady appeared in answer to the bell. " Tea for Mr. Conk-Singleton, Doctor Watson and myself, if you would be so kind, Mrs. Hudson, and if there is anything left of that delicious seed-cake that you baked yesterday, it would be most welcome." She departed on her errand.

" There is another aspect to the matter," Holmes went on. " This is obviously not something that I wished to bring up in front of him, but when I last saw that man, he was using a name other than that of Edward Masters."

" You have met him before ? " asked Conk-Singleton. " In a professional capacity ? " Holmes nodded his assent. " In which case, would it not be natural for him to employ an alias to avoid recognition by those villains on whose trail he was set ? I can hardly see that in itself as a reason to cease an association with him."

" There would certainly be some truth in that assumption," agreed Holmes, but knowing him and his moods as I did, I felt that his words lacked a certain conviction, and I determined to ask him more after our visitor had departed.

" But to return to our business," went on Conk-Singleton. " Have you advanced any further since our last meeting ? "

" If you are asking whether I have any more definite suspicions as to the identity of the culprit, I fear my answer must be in the negative," Holmes answered him. " Ah, the tea and the seed-cake. Excellent, Mrs. Hudson, thank you." The business of distributing the refreshments fell to my lot, as Holmes continued. " As to the counterfeits themselves, it would appear that these are presently restricted to the stock issue of three companies alone. These are the Imperial & Colonial Preferred A certificates, of which you are already aware, of course, as well as the shares of the Eastern Union Railway, and those of the Cobden Alkali Manufactory."

" Bless me ! " exclaimed Conk-Singleton. " These are all shares in which our firm has dealt extensively over the past few months." The broker took out his handkerchief once more and fanned himself with it.

" Not your firm alone," remarked Holmes. " Watson, I believe your broker has also dealt in the I & C Preferred A stocks ? "

" Indeed he has done so on my behalf."

" The name of your broker ? " enquired Conk-Singleton. On my informing him, he smiled broadly. " An excellent firm," he announced. " I would rate them almost as highly as our own, but if you ever decided you were in need of a change, Doctor, be assured that you will find a warm welcome at Knight and Conk-Singleton in the event of your crossing our threshold and putting your business our way."

" Furthermore," Holmes went on, " it is obvious to me that these counterfeit certificates are being produced in this country, and are not, as you assumed in our earlier meeting, originating from overseas. Whether the perpetrator does or does not share our nationality I have, of course, no way of knowing, but you may regard it as an established fact that the actual operation is being carried out in this country. There are too many clues as regards the paper and other physical properties of the counterfeits for it to be otherwise."

"And to what end is all this taking place?" I could not restrain myself from asking.

"That, Watson, is a question best answered by Mr. Conk-Singleton, since he spends his days dealing with these things." He turned to our visitor, who seemed a little embarrassed by the attention.

"It is perhaps difficult to explain to a layman," Conk-Singleton said to me. "Believe me, this is a complex and delicate business in which we are engaged, and there are, perhaps, too many ways in which an unscrupulous rogue could profit from this sort of business. But when I come to consider it some more, maybe there is no definite profit that could be made from these actions. The mere disruption of the markets caused by the lack of trust is sufficient reason for us to engage Mr. Holmes' services. There is no more to report?" he turned back to Holmes.

"I have nothing on which I wish to make an announcement at present," he replied. "I expect results from my enquiries in the near future, though."

The other appeared disappointed. "I had expected, from your reputation, and also from the fee I have already remitted to you, that you would have some opinions on the matter by this time. Believe me, this is more than a mere abstract puzzle to my partners and me. This is a matter of more than slight concern to us, and I was convinced that you would have some more information to offer me by this time." His heavy jowls shook as he wagged his head. "Do remember that there will be an additional reward should you discover the perpetrator of these deeds."

"I prefer," said Holmes, obviously a little irritated by this reaction, "to have all my facts in front of me before expressing an opinion. Detection is more of a precise science than some of the business activities carried out in the City, I believe."

Conk-Singleton took the hit without flinching. "Very good, Mr. Holmes. I shall expect a report in a few days, mark you." He rose from his seat. "My thanks to your housekeeper for her cake, which, as you claimed, was excellent. I trust that your future findings and opinions will prove to be of equal excellence." So saying, he let himself out of our door, and we heard the sound of his heavy footsteps descending the stairs.

<hr />

 ELL, Watson," said Holmes to me, following the departure of our visitor, "And what would you make of that, pray?"

"What a rogue!" I exclaimed.

"To which of our visitors do you refer?" asked Holmes, laughing.

"I mean the detective Masters, who sets himself up as your competitor."

"Maybe you have hit upon the correct term for him," agreed Holmes. "I believe that possibly he failed to recognise me, but I certainly remember him well. We have indeed met professionally, as I mentioned, but we were then on opposite sides of the law. His true name, as I am sure you surmised, is not Edward Masters. I was once of assistance to Inspector Bradstreet in assuring his arrest and conviction when he was using the name of Edgar Madingley. I find it a little strange that he should have wanted to renew my acquaintance by coming here, though. My name is hardly unknown to the criminal classes of this country, and I would have assumed that he would recognise it on Conk-Singleton's proposal that he pay a visit to me."

" On what charges was he convicted ? " I asked. " It is interesting that the poacher should have turned gamekeeper, so to speak."

" I fear that the poacher is still a poacher," was my friend's reply. " The world of detection in this country is a small one, and I am aware of all the competent practitioners of the science currently in London. And Mr. Masters or Madingley, or whatever he chooses to call himself at this time, is not among their number. He was convicted, under a third name, that of Eric Morden, which I believe to be his real name, on charges of uttering fraudulent cheques and sentenced to eighteen months' imprisonment. That was nearly three years ago, and he has had time since then to re-establish himself in some way, since he is now obviously in the good graces of Mr. Charles Conk-Singleton and Mr. Gerald Knight. I wonder though, Watson,. Birds of a feather, would you guess ? "

" I cannot be certain. I am, however, unsure exactly why I say this," I replied, " but I have no intention of moving my investments into the hands of Knight and Conk-Singleton. Something about Mr. Conk-Singleton has failed to fill me with trust, despite his seeming friendliness and good nature."

" Your instincts are often in perfect working order, fear not, Watson. Apart from any other consideration, recall the response he gave to your question regarding the possible use of the counterfeit certificates."

I racked my brains to recall the answer I had been given. " I cannot recall that he gave any definite information."

" In a sense, you are correct," said Holmes. " But if we are to be strictly accurate, he provided you with three answers—each one of which contradicted the other two. First he told us that it was too complex for those of us not engaged in his trade to understand. Then he told us that there were too many ways in which the counterfeits could be used. Lastly he changed his tale yet again to tell us that the counterfeits were of no possible use to a criminal. Would you say that these were the responses of an honest man ? "

" I would say there was something very strange about them, now that you mention it."

" Indeed. And furthermore, maybe you noted his boots ? "

" I did. They were speckled with mud and leaves. One of which, I perceive, he has left here on the carpet." I bent to pick up the object, and was about to toss it on the fire when Holmes stayed my arm.

" I wish to examine that," he informed me, taking the leaf from my hand, and placing it on the table by the window where he proceeded to examine it with a high-powered lens. " As I thought. Do you recognise this leaf, Watson ? "

" I confess that botany is hardly one of my special interests," I replied. " I take it that this is somewhat out of the ordinary ? "

" That it is," replied Holmes. " This would appear to be the leaf of a eucalyptus tree, which is not a native of this country. The climate of the City of London would hardly appear to be one conducive to its flourishing. And the soil from his boots, if you will have the goodness to place that small deposit by the hearthrug on a sheet of paper, Watson ? " I collected the sample as requested, whereupon Holmes subjected it to the same intense scrutiny as he had earlier given to the leaf. " The provenance of this grey clay is slightly more difficult to ascertain, but I think we can be certain that this did not come from the City any more than did the leaf."

" And the conclusions you draw from this ? "

" As with the counterfeit share certificate, there is nothing of a definite nature to be learned as yet. I would merely remark that it is strange that a senior partner in a brokerage such as Knight and Conk-Singleton would be roaming the suburbs—for I can recall no location in the centre of this city where a tree such as this grows—on a business day such as this."

T was a bright clear afternoon on the day following these events that one of the most extraordinary incidents to take place in the course of my friendship with Sherlock Holmes occurred. I had once again called on Holmes, and he and I were walking in the park, enjoying the fresh air, and the song of the birds. Holmes, as was his wont on such occasions, appeared to be noticing everything going on around him, while apparently merely strolling idly. As we turned towards the Serpentine, I had occasion to remark a strange occurrence.

" Holmes," I remarked to my companion. " Do not look now, but it appears to me that we are being followed by the man in the dark overcoat wearing a bowler hat."

Without turning his head, Holmes answered me. " Have you only just remarked him, Watson ? He has been following us since we left Baker-street, and he, or one of his companions, has been standing outside my window since this morning."

" Who is he then ? " I asked. " Is this not a matter of some concern to you ? "

" I believe he is one of Gregson's or Lestrade's minions," answered Holmes, " and I freely confess to you that I am unsure as to his reasons for following me."

As it turned out, we were not long in doubt. We had stopped to view the wildfowl congregating on the surface of the water, when our follower caught up with us and addressed himself to my friend. " I take it that you are Mr. Sherlock Holmes ? " he enquired.

" Yes" replied Holmes.

" In which case, sir, I am sorry to inform you that I have a warrant for your arrest," displaying a piece of paper bearing an official heading.

" But this is outrageous ! " I exclaimed angrily. " On what charge ? "

" Assault and battery occasioning grievous bodily harm," replied the plain-clothes man. " The offence was committed last night upon the person of a certain Michael Frignall."

" Absurd ! " I exclaimed.   " Do you know the person whom you are arresting ? "

" I do indeed, sir, and it gives me no pleasure to be carrying out my duty, I can assure you. You, I take it," and he actually tipped his hat to me, " are Doctor Watson, I assume ? "

" I am indeed.   May I be permitted to accompany you and Mr. Holmes to the station ? "

" In the normal way of things, I would have to refuse, but given your reputation and that of Mr. Holmes, I will allow it this time."

Holmes had remained silent and impassive throughout this exchange, and showed no emotion on his face.   " Shall we go, then, McKenzie ? " he asked the detective.

" You know me, Mr. Holmes ? " The policeman was taken aback.

" Of course," replied Holmes genially. " You were assisting Inspector Gregson in one of the cases where I offered a little assistance.   The Drebber murder, if you recall." This case is one of which I have recorded the details elsewhere, under the title of *A Study in Scarlet*.

The detective flushed.   " Fancy you remembering me, sir ! I'd only just started out in the Force then, and it was a real treat to watch you at work. That's what makes it such a blooming shame that we have to bring you in today, sir." His regret seemed unfeigned.

" Who is this Michael Frignall who is supposed to have been assaulted ? " I asked. " What manner of man is he ? "

" I am afraid I cannot answer that, sir.   He's just a name on the charge-sheet to me. You and I will take a cab to the Yard, Mr. Holmes. If you don't mind, Dr. Watson, you will have to follow in a separate vehicle. I'll let them know you are arriving, and there'll be no problem with your coming in." So saying, he hailed a passing hansom, which he and Holmes entered before clattering off in the general direction of Scotland Yard. A minute or so later, I hailed a cab of my own, and was soon trotting after them.

WAS admitted without any difficulty, and was shown to the room where Holmes was seated at a table facing Inspector Gregson.

" Ah, Doctor Watson," the Inspector greeted me. " I am sorry to see you under these circumstances."

" Maybe you can tell us more about this offence of which I am accused," suggested Holmes. " I fear the good McKenzie has not been taken into your full confidence regarding this matter."

" That last is true," admitted Gregson. " Well, Mr. Holmes, it is a strange business, as I am sure you need no telling. About ten o'clock last night, a man who gave his name as Michael Frignall presented himself at the Pentonville police station, complaining that he had been violently assaulted. He was suffering from a broken nose, and there were severe contusions to the upper body. His story was that he had just left a public house in the area when a tall figure stepped from the alleyway beside the hostelry, and fell upon him, causing the injuries that he had sustained."

" Was any weapon involved, according to this man ? " asked Holmes.

" No.   The assault was carried

out using fists alone, according to the victim."

" And what links me to this assault ? " Holmes' tone was relaxed, even amused, but there was an undercurrent of seriousness beneath his words.

" Apparently the assailant muttered something along the lines of 'That will teach you to meddle with Sherlock Holmes' as he left his victim, and dropped this at his feet." He pointed to a small pasteboard square lying on the table—one of Holmes' calling cards. " This is one of your cards, I believe, Mr. Holmes ? " asked Gregson. " I have seen them often enough."

" I cannot deny that it is my card," replied Sherlock Holmes. " Though I deny being in that area at that time last night, and it would hence have been impossible for me to have committed the offence complained of."

" So you say," replied Gregson. " I assume you have an alibi ? "

" Alas," replied Holmes. " I spent the evening in my rooms in Baker-street, bringing my records up to date. I saw no-one."

" Doctor Watson was not with you, then ? " asked Gregson. His voice betrayed some worry.

" I saw no-one after seven o'clock in the evening, when Mrs. Hudson brought in my dinner," repeated Holmes, " until seven o'clock this morning when she came to clear away the remains of that meal— by my request, I had asked her not to disturb me after dinner—and to bring in my breakfast."

" How very unfortunate," said Gregson. " I suppose that there is no possibility that she could vouch for your not having left the house during the course of the evening ? "

" Inspector, I appreciate the effort you are making to establish my innocence, but I cannot in all honesty assist you further by providing an alibi. I would remind you that this is not the first time that my name has been misappropriated by the criminal classes, many of whom, as I am sure you are aware, would like nothing better than to see me removed from the streets of London."

" I am aware of that," replied Gregson, " and believe me, we are taking this into account. There are two other points that I have to take into consideration, however. The first is your undoubted skill in pugilism. It would appear that the assailant was likewise some sort of boxer, as evidenced that the assault was carried out with fists alone. The other is that the victim gave a description of his attacker that is a remarkably good description of you, Mr. Holmes. Perhaps you would care to read the statement taken at Pentonville police station last night." He passed another piece of paper to Holmes, who perused it.

" Indeed, it is a very detailed description," he commented, raising his eyebrows, " even if a little flattering to my personal vanity in places."

" Who is this Michael Frignall, anyway ? " I asked Gregson.

" No-one of importance," replied the policeman. " He works as a clerk in some firm in the City— Knight and Conk-Singleton, stockbrokers, I believe."

Holmes and I exchanged glances. " You are sure of his employers ? " asked Holmes.

" They are given at the top of the statement you hold in your hands," said Gregson. " Is the matter of any significance ? "

" Quite possibly, Inspector. Forgive me if I prefer to play my cards close to my chest at present, though."

Gregson chuckled. " I know you too well, Mr. Holmes, than to pry into matters where you have no wish to have me pry. But," and his voice became serious once more, " you are under arrest at present, and though I can offer you the best cell on the premises as accommodation, it will still be a cell while you await trial at the Bailey, unless the magistrate will grant bail at tomorrow's hearing. Believe me, I will do what I can to make your stay with us as comfortable as possible, but I warn you that unless you can come up with some alibi, I fear the worst."

I was struck with a certain horror. The penalty that would be levied upon Holmes was not likely to be a light one. Worse, perhaps, would be the damage to his reputation. It would be hard for Holmes to advertise his services as a bringer of miscreants to justice were he to be punished for a common crime such as this. Despite Gregson's obvious goodwill towards my friend, my heart sank somewhat at the thought of what lay in store for Sherlock Holmes.

" I have a request, Inspector," said Holmes, looking the policeman in the eye. " It may be that you would exceed your powers a little in granting it, but for old times' sake, eh ? "

" Tell me what it is that you want of me, and I will give you an answer to the best of my ability."

" I wish your permission for me to visit the scene of the alleged crime tonight at the hour when you were told it occurred last night. Naturally, I would expect you and some of your men to accompany me. Escape is the last matter on my mind at present, I can assure you."

" It would be most irregular," replied Gregson, " but I am in a position to grant your request. If we depart at a quarter past nine, that should allow us to reach Pentonville about a quarter before ten, which was when Michael Frignall was assaulted."

" Shall we say 'claims to have been assaulted' ? " said Holmes, quizzically. " By the by, I assume there is no problem with Watson's joining us on our little trip ? Assuming, that is, Doctor, that you wish to accompany us on our excursion."

" How can you doubt my intentions on the matter ? " I responded, more than a little nettled by his words.

" I should never have doubted my Watson. I apologise," replied Sherlock Holmes.

" By no means do I have any objection," said Gregson. " I will make arrangements to have you admitted to the Yard and shown to my office at around nine this evening, Doctor."

I thanked Gregson, and bade farewell to him and my friend, who seemed to be remarkably unconcerned about his sojourn in the jaws of justice, and the possible consequences that might ensue.

 S Gregson had promised, my way was prepared for me when I came to Scotland Yard that evening. He greeted me heartily. " Mr. Holmes is in his cell. Would you like to visit him there, or will you wait until he is brought to us ? "

" I would prefer to wait," I answered. Truth to tell, I would have been embarrassed to see my friend in those circumstances, and I am certain that he, too, would have suffered from a crisis of humiliation had I seen him there. " How is he behaving ? What is he doing ? " I asked.

Gregson chuckled. " He is behaving as if he were at his rooms in Baker-street," he replied. " He has called for pens and paper, with which I have supplied him, and he has sent out for some tobacco for his pipe. When I visited his cell two hours ago, he was stretched at full length on his bed, with his eyes closed, but he was not asleep, for he greeted me by name, without even opening his eyes."

" No doubt he recognised your step," I remarked.

" No doubt. Tell me, Doctor, in strict confidence, do you believe he is guilty ? "

I was torn. All the evidence, such as the calling card, and the minutely detailed description, coupled with the inability of Sherlock Holmes to provide an alibi, pointed in the direction of his guilt. But my loyalty to my friend, not to mention my knowledge of his upright and honest nature that would not allow him to deny such a thing, led me to believe in his innocence. I explained this to the Inspector, who listened to me thoughtfully.

" Your thoughts and mine, Doctor, run along similar lines. As a policeman, I cannot ignore the evidence in front of my own eyes. As a sometime colleague and, I hope it is not presumptuous of me to say so, a friend of Sherlock Holmes, I am somewhat at a loss, since I cannot believe him to have committed such a crime. If he had performed these actions, I am sure that he would have had an excellent reason for doing so."

" And he would have told us those reasons, I am sure," I replied.

At that moment, there was a knock on the door, and Sherlock Holmes entered, escorted by two uniformed policemen.

" Excellent," said Gregson, pulling out and examining his watch. " We have a growler waiting, I believe, which should let us arrive at the time you requested, Mr. Holmes."

The journey to Pentonville was a silent one. The uniformed policemen sat like unmoving wooden statues on either side of the prisoner, who sat wrapped in his own thoughts, which neither Gregson nor I would have dreamed for a minute of interrupting.

" We are here," announced Gregson, as the carriage drew to a halt. " The public house from which Frignall made his way is over there," gesturing with his stick. " The alleyway from which his attacker emerged is here," pointing to a dark entrance on the other side of the road, " and this spot here," striding to a spot midway between two streetlights, " is where the attack took place, according to Frignall."

" As I thought," said Holmes, whose voice had taken on a strong resonance, which I recognised as a sign that one of his theories had just been vindicated. " Tell me, Inspector, how tall is the man who was attacked ? "

" Smaller than you or I, Mr. Holmes. He would just about come up to your chin, I guess."

" So he was about this height ? " replied my friend, pointing to one of the constables. " Excellent. Now, the attack took place here, you say ? " standing at the spot previously indicated by Gregson.

" Precisely so."

" Now, Constable," went on

Holmes, addressing the policeman whose height had been established as that of the victim. " I want you to tell me the colour of my eyes."

The constable looked puzzled. " I don't know that. I never noticed."

" Then come closer, man, and look for yourself."

The perplexed policeman stepped closer to Holmes. " I can't see in this light," he complained.

" Then perhaps I am facing in the wrong direction," said Holmes. He slowly revolved through a full circle, the policeman presenting a comical spectacle as he followed Holmes' face, peering closely.

" It's no good. I couldn't tell you whether they're blue or green or brown or what," he announced at length.

" Very good, constable," replied Holmes. " And now, if you would, name the stone that decorates my scarf-pin."

" Same again. Not enough light for me to say," replied the puzzled officer.

" Let me revolve once again. Maybe the light shining from another angle will be able to help you discern it more clearly." Once again, Holmes spun slowly round, the constable fixing his eyes on the scarf-pin in question.

" I wouldn't swear to it, but I think that's one of those orange stones—a topaz, I think they call these things."

" Excellent ! " replied Holmes, obviously in high spirits. " Thank you for your invaluable assistance, Constable."

Gregson appeared to be completely baffled by these actions, but I was beginning to have some ideas of my own regarding my friend's motives.

" We may return," Holmes said to Gregson, using the same tone of voice to the police officer as if he were the captor and not the captive. Holmes and the policemen, including Gregson, made their way to Scotland Yard in the carriage that had brought them, and once again I was permitted to share the vehicle with them.

" I know it is late, Inspector," said Holmes, " but I would impose on your kindness for perhaps twenty minutes more."

" Very well," replied Gregson. " This whole business brings me no pleasure, I am sure you are aware, and I am happy to lend you what assistance I am able. I am still somewhat in the dark, I confess."

" Then let me be the bearer of light," smiled Holmes. " Be so good as to read the description of the attacker that Mr. Frignall provided."

" Six feet and two inches in height, dark hair, long aquiline nose, grey eyes... " Gregson's voice trailed off. " Now I begin to understand what you were doing back there. There is no way that he could know the colour of your eyes, given the light at that time and that place."

" Precisely. Especially since he was supposedly being attacked by me at the time." Holmes smiled a thin smile. " Pray continue."

" Wearing a dark topcoat, silk hat, and white scarf fastened at the throat with an amethyst pin. I see. It was impossible for Robinson, who, by the by, is one of our more observant constables, to determine the type of stone in your pin."

Holmes' smile was still in place. " I think you see my point now, Inspector ? "

" I do indeed."

" Maybe I can add one more item to the list ? You have my card that was discovered at the scene of the attack ? " Gregson opened the file on the desk, and retrieved it. " No, no, do not give it to me. I would ask you to examine the right edge of the card. Do you discern any dents or nicks in it ? "

" Indeed so," replied Gregson, after a close examination of the article in question. " There are marks as if a thumbnail had scored marks in the pasteboard."

" It was indeed a thumbnail," replied Holmes. " The nail of my right thumb, to be precise. I have developed the habit, when passing out one of my cards, of marking it in this way to show the date on which I presented it. It is simple to do, takes very little effort on my part, and is a practice that has proved of value in the past, as I have no doubt it will in this instance. Count the marks, if you would, Inspector."

Gregson bent over the card again. " There are two here, then a gap, and then ... seven together."

" Precisely. And today's date ? "

" The twenty-eighth."

" Correct. Two and eight."

The policeman considered this for a few seconds. " So that would indicate that you presented the card yesterday ? "

" Correct, my dear Gregson. In this way, should one of my cards be misused, as this one has been, I have only to refer to my records to discover those to whom I have been introduced recently, or at any rate, on the twenty-seventh day of a month at some time in the past. In that way, I am able to establish the identity of the culprit in a very short space of time."

I was struck by the simplicity, as well as by the ingenuity of Holmes' device, the existence of which came as a complete surprise to me, even after all the time that I had known him.

" So, Mr. Holmes, to whom did you pass out cards yesterday ? " asked Gregson.

" There was only one, to the man who appeared with Charles Conk-Singleton at my rooms in Baker-street yesterday. The man who now calls himself Edward Masters, but is known to Inspector Bradstreet here at Scotland Yard as Edgar Madingley, or alternatively as Eric Morden."

Gregson frowned. " I have some recollection of that name. The confidence trickster and forger ? Bradstreet took the case, with some assistance from you ? " Holmes nodded. " And what was he doing visiting you ? "

Holmes, confident of the other's attention, proceeded to relate the circumstances that had led to the visit. Gregson frowned, and tapped his teeth with the end of his pencil.

" It seems obvious to me that this was an attempt to blacken your name by this man Morden," he remarked.

" I think there is something more to it than this, though," replied Holmes. " I would be greatly obliged, Doctor, if you could send word to your wife that you will be absent from home tonight, and if you could return to Baker-street and keep watch there, that would be highly appreciated. Gregson, if you could spare a couple of your plain-clothes men to remain in the vicinity, ready to assist Watson should he whistle for help, I would expect some interesting results. I myself, having been subject to arrest, will have to remain here, out of sight of those who are no doubt watching Baker-street in my absence."

" What do you mean, Holmes ? " I asked, curious as to what he had in mind.

" I am sure that Inspector Gregson is correct as far as one of the motives for this little comedy is concerned. My reputation would no doubt have suffered were I to be convicted and sentenced—"

" An outcome which I can promise you will not take place, since the police will withdraw charges in the magistrate's court tomorrow," broke in Gregson. " You have proved to my satisfaction that the charges against you are demonstrably false."

" Thank you." Holmes inclined his head. " There is a secondary purpose to all this, though, I am sure, and that is to keep me away from Baker-street while Morden, or Masters as I suppose we must call him now, or those close to him, enter and search for any evidence I may have uncovered with regard to this business."

" I had already informed my wife before I came here this evening that I might very well be absent for the whole night," I told Holmes. " I will be happy to act as the watchdog of your interests in this regard."

" That shows an excellent sense of foresight," he replied. " I knew I could rely on you. Good old Watson." This simple phrase, delivered in a tone of the utmost sincerity, showed the human side of Holmes' nature that he typically kept hidden, and indeed, few suspected its very existence.

" And I will be happy to help in any way within my power," added Gregson. " It has been a long day, but I dare say I could provide assistance if there is to be a chance of setting this business straight."

" Excellent ! " said Holmes. He leaned forward, his elbows on the table, and his eyes shone. " Do you, Watson, stay in the unlit room. Leave the front door and the door to my rooms unlocked. I have no wish to cause Mrs. Hudson unnecessary trouble as a result of the

thieves having to break down any barriers. You will find my revolver in the middle drawer of the bureau, and cartridges in the drawer below that, but I do not think you will require their use. The lead-weighted riding crop should prove a sufficient deterrent should you need one. On the entry of our visitor—which I expect to take place around two or three o'clock in the morning—give three sharp blasts on your whistle. Gregson, that will be the signal for you and your men to apprehend the villains." He yawned. " And now, if I may, I will avail myself of the hospitality of the Metropolitan Police, and return to my cell."

Gregson pulled at a bell-rope that hung behind his desk, and a uniformed constable knocked at the door and was admitted. " Take the prisoner to his cell," he commanded. It was hard for us to realise that Holmes was indeed a prisoner in the eyes of the law, and when he had departed, after bidding us a good night, Gregson and I looked at each other and burst out laughing.

" He is a rare one, to be sure," said Gregson. " It is as if he were in a hotel, the way he behaves, demanding to be taken to his cell in that way, and ordering us about as if we were his servants." There was no malice in his words, and his face creased in a broad smile beneath his moustache. " Do you believe that he is correct in his guess ? "

" I have no way of knowing the answer with any certainty, of course, but in my experience, when Sherlock Holmes makes guesses of this nature, they are usually correct."

" We must be off, then. You to Baker-street, and I to procure the services of two of our plain-clothes men. You have a whistle ? Mr. Holmes seemed to assume that you had such a thing in your possession."

" I do indeed. I will bid you farewell—a temporary farewell, I hope, since we expect to see each other in a matter of a few hours."

" I hope so," replied Gregson, pleasantly.

 RETURNED to Baker-street to find all lights extinguished, Mrs. Hudson having retired. Mindful of Holmes' instructions, I left the front door unlocked, and mounted the stairs to Holmes' rooms, which I unlocked using the key with which Holmes had permanently entrusted me, and quietly closed the door after me. I refrained from turning on the gas lights, but made my way to the bureau, relying on the light from the window, whose curtains remained open. I was in two minds as to whether to take the revolver, but eventually decided to leave it in its resting place, but had no hesitation in taking the riding crop to which Holmes had alluded. It was a more formidable weapon than its appearance would suggest, with the hollow handle being filled with lead, allowing it to be reversed and used as a life-preserver.

Nonetheless, I had no desire to be placed in a situation where I would be forced to use it. I settled myself in an armchair from which I could observe the door of the room, but where I would initially be hidden by the door itself from the view of anyone entering the room.

It was a long wait, and a cold one. The fire had not been lit, or even laid, it appeared, and the absence of any light combined with the events of the day conspired to produce a sense of fatigue. More than once I found myself awaking with a start as a cab or some tradesman's wagon clattered along the otherwise deserted street. On the last of these occasions I started awake, but could hear nothing outside the window. I listened more carefully, and was rewarded by the sound of at least one pair of feet climbing the stairs outside the door slowly and carefully. My nerves on edge, I watched the handle of the door turning in the moonlight streaming through the window, and the door slowly opening.

I strained my ears to catch a faint whisper. " This door's open as well," I heard. " This is too blooming easy, George."

" Just be thankful there's no Sherlock Holmes about tonight, then," came another voice.

I reached for the riding crop, and fingered the whistle that hung from a lanyard around my neck. Two dark shapes entered the room.

" Where do you think it would be ? " came the whisper.

" Search me, Bill. There's too many papers for my liking."

" We can start with the desk. Open the lantern. Carefully, mark you." I had already smelled the hot metal that informed me a dark-lantern was being carried by the housebreakers, but before they could fully open the slide, I had blown three sharp blasts on my whistle. The effect was instant—the two criminals froze in their tracks, illuminated by the half-open lantern, while a thunder of boots up the stairs told me that Gregson and his men were arriving on the scene, as previously arranged.

I was informed by the flash of light through the doorway that the police had arrived, with Gregson at their head.

" We're nabbed, Bill," said one of the burglars, seemingly resigned to his fate. " Seems like you was expecting us, sir," he nodded to me, having observed my presence with the aid of the police lanterns. " I take it you're Mr. Sherlock Holmes himself ? "

" I am not," I replied. " But it is Sherlock Holmes who is responsible for your arrest, even though he is not present in this room. Who sent you here ? " I asked him.

" I'll make my statement at the station, if you don't mind," was the reply, delivered with a certain degree of dignity.

" You'll be there soon enough, my lad," Gregson said to him good-humouredly. " You'll be joining us, Doctor ? " he said to me.

" I will come along as soon as I have finished calming Mrs. Hudson, whom I fear we have woken," I replied. I went downstairs, and called through the door leading to Mrs. Hudson's apartments, reassuring her that no damage had been occasioned, and that she was in no danger. She seemed reassured by my words, and I returned to the now empty room and locked the door, remembering the old proverb about stable doors and bolting horses, before leaving the house and locking that door as well. The police four-wheeler was waiting for me in the street outside, and we were soon on our way to Scotland Yard.

<hr />

N arrival at Scotland Yard, the two criminals were led to a room for questioning by the plain-clothes men who had arrested them, and Gregson and I entered his office to confer.

" I think," said Gregson, smiling, " that we will not disturb Mr. Holmes' sleep. I intend to bring these two into court tomorrow, to face the music before Holmes appears and we drop the charges. If what Sherlock Holmes suspects is true, there may be some friends of theirs in court to see him, and it will be interesting to observe their faces when these men appear."

" That would seem to be an excellent plan," I said, " and I concur with your idea of leaving it as a surprise."

" And now," he added, yawning widely, " I suggest that we attempt to sleep. I have a camp-bed in the next room which I use on such occasions. You are welcome to it, should you wish. Alternatively, we could offer you a cell for the night."

" I am an old campaigner," I assured him. " I would have no difficulty sleeping on the floor, if that were all that were available. However, I will not deprive you of your cot. A cell will provide me with the shelter I need for the night. I trust you will be able to provide me with hot water and a razor in the morning ? "

" Of course." There was a knock on the door, and one of the plain-clothes men who had been questioning the burglars entered.

" We found out that our precious pair, whom we've seen several times before in court, were employed by a Mr. Edward Masters to search for any documents belonging to Mr. Holmes relating to the City brokers Knight and Conk-Singleton."

Gregson and I exchanged glances. " Our friend Morden makes another entrance," commented Gregson

drily. " Very good, Saunders. Ensure that they appear at Bow-street
tomorrow immediately before Mr.
Holmes makes his appearance."

The officer left us, and Gregson
rose to his feet. " I will show you
to your cell, Doctor. Believe me,
our cells are less inhospitable than
you might imagine from the name
alone."

As he said, the bed, although
hard, was clean. Truth to tell, I was
sufficiently fatigued to have passed
the night comfortably on a bed of
nails, such as those used by Indian
faqirs to demonstrate their supposed
spiritual powers.

I was awakened by a uniformed
constable bearing a mug of hot water, some soap and a razor, along
with a towel. " Inspector Gregson's compliments," he smilingly
informed me as he handed me the
shaving tackle, " and he would like
to invite you to share his breakfast
when you are ready."

" Thank you. Please inform the
Inspector that I shall be ready in a
few minutes." I discovered a small
hand-mirror wrapped in the towel, and I made a hasty toilet before
meeting Gregson.

" Ah, Doctor," he greeted me. " I
trust your night was not too uncomfortable ? " I reassured him on that
score, and he hospitably waved me
towards a steaming pot of coffee, accompanied by porridge and kippers.

" I have taken the liberty of sending portions to Mr. Holmes in his
cell. Hardly standard fare under
the circumstances, but I feel I can
do no less."

" He has suffered worse in his
time, I can assure you," I told him,
and fell to with a good appetite.

" The hearing of the two beauties
we bagged last night should begin at
9:15. Mr. Holmes appears immediately following their hearing," he

informed me. Gregson looked me
up and down. " I have a clean collar
here, should you feel in need."

I accepted gratefully. Although
I do not consider myself to be overly concerned with my appearance, I
feel that it is somewhat incumbent
upon me to set some sort of example, especially in official business of
such a nature as was to be transact-
ed in a few hours.

On finishing our repast, I accepted the proffered collar, and we went
to see Holmes.

" I have a surprise for you this
morning," remarked Gregson to
Holmes, his eyes twinkling. " I will
not tell you about it, but I think it
will amuse you. As regards your
own trial, of course, you need have
no fears. Speaking on behalf of
the police, I will drop all charges
against you. Will you be laying any
counter-charge against your accuser
for laying false information against
you ? "

" I think that will probably be
unnecessary. I am almost certain
that I can procure evidence that will
allow you to arrest him on a somewhat more serious charge."

" As you wish," replied Gregson.
" Do you wish to shave and make
yourself look a little more presentable prior to your appearance before the magistrates ? " he enquired
solicitously.

" I will do so, though I do realise that my chances of conviction or
otherwise are not dependent upon
my appearance. Thank you."

" Doctor," Gregson said to me,
as Holmes left the room. " You can
be of great assistance to us by going to the court early, and keeping
your eyes open for familiar faces, especially for Eric Morden. My guess
is that he will be there in order to
observe the fruits of his labours—
that is, he will wish to see Holmes

remanded until the next Assize sessions. If you see Morden, I would like you to observe him as closely as you can during today's proceedings, and note his reactions to today's events. It is likely that he suspects that his hired guns have misfired, to use a metaphor, but I am almost certain he will not expect to see them in the dock today."

" I will be happy to do this," I replied. " The more so, as I believe it will add to the evidence that Holmes needs to solve this case involving the City."

" Good man," said the policeman. " Let us meet after Holmes' case has been dismissed, and you can report to us then."

I made my way to Bow-street Magistrates' Court, an institution with which I was happily unfamiliar, and ascertained from one of the porters there which courtroom would be used for Holmes' hearing, and hence that of Morden' two accomplices. On arrival, I took a seat near the back of the almost empty room, commanding a view of the whole area. I had not long to wait before a man whom I recognised as Morden entered, and took his seat two rows directly in front of me. I had my hat pulled well down, and my coat collar turned up in order to avoid his recognising me, but in any case, he appeared not to be interested in me or any others in the courtroom, but sat back in his seat, almost with the air of a theatre-goer awaiting the rise of the curtain on a favourite drama.

The other spectators of the day's proceedings appeared to be members of the legal profession, mixed with some younger men whom I took to be law students, and some seeming indigents, whose interest was almost certainly not of a forensic nature, but was due to the fact that the courtroom was well-heated, and formed a shelter from the light rain that had started to fall outside. At the front of the court, in the area reserved for witnesses, was a pale young man, whose face, including his nose, was swathed in bandages. He turned, his eyes searching the room, until they alighted on Morden, to whom he gave a signal of recognition which was returned, as far as I could judge from the back of his head. It took little effort on my part to judge that this was the victim of the attack supposedly carried out by Holmes.

At length the magistrate and clerks entered, and we all rose. There were two cases to be heard before the usher called for William and George Stoker. The visitors of last night entered the courtroom, flanked by two policemen, and I noticed Morden give a visible start as he recognised the names and faces of the men whom we believed he had hired to steal Holmes' papers. Now that I could see the pair in broad daylight, it was obvious that they were related; almost certainly brothers, if their physiognomy was any guide.

The evidence given by the plain-clothes man was uncompromising. Gregson had obviously given instructions that my name not be mentioned as part of the proceedings leading up to the arrest, and indeed, even the name of Sherlock Holmes was not pronounced in court—only the address of 221B Baker-street being given. Likewise, the information concerning Morden that had been obtained through the confessions of the two men remained hidden from the court, with solely the mere facts concerning the breaking and entering being put forth. In a matter of minutes the magistrate had determined that the two should be remanded in custody pending the next Assize Sessions, and they were led away back to the cells. I seemed to notice a sense of relief on the part of Morden, as the whole of the hearing passed without his name being mentioned.

" The next case," announced the usher, " is that of Sherlock Holmes, charged with assault upon the person of one Michael Frignall, occasioning grievous bodily harm."

Holmes was led to the dock, and a stir of excitement ran through the spectators, as they saw in the flesh, more than likely for the first time, the figure whose name had become a byword in parts of the popular press.

Inspector Gregson stepped forward, asking and receiving permission to address the Bench.

" Your Worship, the Metropolitan Police would like to request that this case not be prosecuted further, owing to severe doubts concerning the reliability of the testimony provided by Michael Frignall, and would further request that all charges pending against the prisoner be dropped."

" You are sure of this, Inspector ? " asked the presiding magistrate.

" Quite certain, Your Worship."

" Very good. So be it. Mr. Sherlock Holmes, you are a free man. There is no charge pending against you."

The effect of this on Morden was dramatic. With a loud cry of " No ! ", followed by an obscenity that I refuse to repeat here, and which brought the court ushers hurrying towards him, he sprang from his seat and made for the door, passing close by me. His face had turned almost black with rage, and was tortured into a scowl that was terrifying to see. It was clear

that the double shock of seeing his henchmen in the dock, and his opponent set free in this way had affected his nerves. I waited a minute or two and followed him out of the courtroom. Gregson and Holmes were already waiting for me there.

" Congratulations," I said to Holmes, shaking him warmly by the hand. " I am delighted to see you a free man."

" Perhaps not as delighted as I," he replied with a chuckle. " I saw friend Morden just now as I was entering this vestibule. He failed to notice me. I take it that the dismissal of the charges against me was not to his liking ? "

" He was livid, Holmes. I have rarely seen a man in a state of such extreme fury."

" Excellent. Men in that state of mind are likely to make mistakes. And now," turning to me, " to work. May I ask you, Watson, to trouble yourself to visit the offices of Knight and Conk-Singleton, and make enquiries as to the possibility of your putting some business that way ? "

" I have no intention of doing any such thing ! " I retorted. " Do you think I would seek favours from one who has wronged you so monstrously ? "

" Calm yourself. I have no intention that you should ever actually place your financial affairs in their hands. I merely require you to engage our friend Conk-Singleton in conversation for the space of at least one hour. It is essential that you talk to Conk-Singleton and no other. Can you contrive to discuss these matters for that length of time ? "

" When do you want me to do this ? "

" As soon as is convenient. Do not waste time by going home to change," he added, as I scanned my appearance. " You are a doctor, after all, and it is common for your profession to be awake at all hours, tending to the sick. I am sure that Conk-Singleton will excuse any irregularity in your attire."

I somewhat reluctantly agreed to his proposal, and set off for the City, enquiring of a policeman where the office was to be found. I was directed to an old-fashioned office on the second floor of a commercial building, where I enquired of the clerk if I might speak with Mr. Conk-Singleton. The clerk appeared to be on the point of denying me entrance, when Conk-Singleton himself appeared in the doorway of one of the back offices. He started as he caught sight of me, appearing embarrassed by my presence. Nonetheless, he greeted me affably enough, though appearing more startled by my presence in his offices than might reasonably be expected.

" Halloa ! Doctor Watson. I was hardly expecting to see you here so soon. Are you here to put your business affairs in our hands, as we discussed the other day ? " He spoke jocularly, but I replied with all seriousness.

" I wish to explore this possibility, at the very least."

" Good, good. Excellent, in fact. Perhaps you could wait for five minutes ? " he invited me. His manner now appeared brusque, almost to the point of nervousness. " Perhaps Huston will show you into our waiting-room ? " he added meaningfully as he retreated into the office whence he had appeared, closing the door behind him.

The clerk took the offered hint, and opened the door to a small, sparsely furnished room, which was apparently the room that the firm of Knight and Conk-Singleton used to accommodate those visitors who had come without appointments, or who were otherwise forced to wait. He was courteous enough, but it appeared to me that he closed the door behind him in a somewhat meaningful manner.

There was one window in the room which faced towards the river, away from the street, and for want of any other entertainment, I amused myself by attempting to recognise as many landmarks of the City as possible. Two masterpieces of Sir Christopher Wren's genius, the Church of St Mary Woolnoth and the Monument to the Great Fire, were both visible, as were various other churches to which I was unable to put a name. While thus engaged, I heard a door open and close, and the sounds of footsteps descending the staircase. I had previously remarked that the front door made a very distinctive sound when opened and closed, and that the porter greeted each entering visitor in a loud voice, and bade them farewell as they left, as I had passed one man leaving the building as I entered it. Even so, I heard no such sounds signalling the departure of the visitor. To my surprise, I noticed that the man who had presumably just descended the stairs had exited through the rear of the building, and was crossing the yard directly below my window. Though I could not be certain, the figure appeared to be that of Eric Morden. As I bent forward to gain a better view, the door behind me opened, and the clerk coughed discreetly.

" Mr. Conk-Singleton can see you now," he announced.

I thanked the clerk, and made my way to the office from which Conk-Singleton had appeared earlier.

His earlier nervousness seemed to have vanished entirely, and he greeted me in the most affable and courteous manner.

As requested by Holmes, I managed to protract my interview with him for approximately an hour, without committing myself to any course of action concerning my finances. I learned, though, that Conk-Singleton appeared to have intimate knowledge of the workings of many large commercial houses in the City, and he was well-connected, by his account at least, with some of the major figures in the world of national finance.

During our conversation, which was pleasant and cordial enough, I had heard the door of what appeared to be the room adjacent to that where we were holding our discussion opening and closing to admit a visitor, at which Conk-Singleton raised his eyebrows, but offered no comment. About ten minutes after the door had opened and closed, I heard the door open and close again, and the sound of two men speaking in low tones. It was impossible for me to distinguish the words, but I fancied that I could distinguish the tones of Sherlock Holmes. Conk-Singleton likewise seemed somewhat distracted by the muffled sound of the conversation, but made no comment. At the end of our discussion as he rose to let me out, he suddenly asked me, " Have you heard anything recently from your friend Mr. Holmes about the matter about which he is acting on my behalf ? "

" Why, no," I answered. " I have not heard anything from him on that score."

" But he is working on the case ? " he persisted.

" As far as I am aware, he is still doing so."

" Ah, good. I had feared he might have been detained." There was a subtle emphasis on the last word, which, coupled with the glimpse of Morden apparently leaving the building by the rear, led me to believe that Conk-Singleton had at least some awareness of the events that had recently befallen Holmes.

Naturally, I was going to give no information to him on that score, any more than I had the intention of providing him with my custom with regard to my meagre portfolio of investments. As I stepped out of his office, I observed that the door of the office next to Conk-Singleton's was open, and I saw, seated at the desk therein, a thin cadaverous-looking man, whose face with its sunken cheeks and dark deep-set eyes, exhibited all the hallmarks of villainy, in my view.

The porter escorted me courteously to the front door of the building, and I enquired about the identity of the thin man I had seen through the door.

" That's Mr. Knight, sir, the senior partner," he explained to me. " A very exacting gentleman, sir, in his standards." He refrained from making a direct comparison, but the unspoken contrast with another was implicit in his tone. I thanked him, and stepped out onto the street, where I hailed a cab for Baker-street.

HEN I reached Holmes' rooms, I discovered him already there, lounging in a chair, his legs thrown over one arm of the chair, smoking his pipe and gazing fixedly at the ceiling.

He waved a hand languidly in my direction as I entered, and I took the unspoken hint, settling myself in a chair, and lighting my own pipe. After about five minutes of companionable silence, Holmes spoke.

" Thank you for your efforts with Conk-Singleton," he commented. " Keeping in his office in that way was invaluable. I had a most interesting conversation with Mr. Gerald Knight while you were engaged in the next room."

" I fancied I heard you," I replied, " and so, too, I believe, did Conk-Singleton."

Holmes cocked his head quizzically. " Indeed ? I am not overly concerned by that, though."

" And what did you learn from the senior partner ? I caught sight of him as I was leaving, and I must say that I have seldom seen a more villainous-looking man of business."

Holmes chuckled. " He is hardly an invitation to trust, is he ? I admit that I was somewhat taken aback when I entered. However, it seems to me that this is one instance where appearances may be deceptive. I have some faith in Mr. Knight's inner honesty and goodwill, despite his outward demeanour and looks."

" And not in Conk-Singleton's ? "

Holmes nodded in confirmation. " My conversation with Knight was primarily conducted in order to ascertain who it was who had engaged Morden. And, as I had suspected, it was not Knight, despite Conk-Singleton's claims, who had done so. That business was done without the knowledge of Knight, who was only informed of this engagement after the fact. And furthermore, it was Knight who had suggested that I be retained on the case, after he discovered that Morden's services had been secured, and he had instructed Conk-Singleton to dispense with Morden, and replace him with me. He was somewhat surprised, shall we say, when I informed him of Conk-Singleton's visit with Morden the other day."

" And I have something to add to this," I burst out, and told Holmes of what I had seen from the waiting-room window before I had been admitted to see Conk-Singleton.

" Good, Watson, very good," he remarked. " I think that our friend suspects that we are on his trail, do you not agree ? Otherwise there is no call for him to use the back entrance. Another interesting point that I discovered concerns the clerk of the firm who was assaulted the other night. Michael Frignall was taken on only a matter of a few weeks ago, at the behest of Conk-Singleton. Knight has hardly set eyes on him since he joined. Apparently Conk-Singleton was constantly sending him on errands about the City, and he spent the majority of his time with the firm out of the office, it seems."

" You use the past tense ? "

" Yes. Frignall has been absent from his post for the past week, which period, I hardly need remind you, includes the time of the alleged assault."

" He is Conk-Singleton's creature, then ? "

" We must assume so. I instructed Knight to say nothing to Conk-Singleton of the conversation that he and I had held, or even to mention my visit. I am still unsure as to Knight's complete honesty, though I am more than inclined to give him the benefit of the doubt and to see him as the honest half of the partnership. His manner struck me as being essentially frank and open, compared to that of his partner. Of course, appearances may be deceptive, but I have no reason at present to believe otherwise."

" So have you come to any conclusions regarding the matter ? "

" Still none that I would regard as being definite as yet, but I am convinced that Conk-Singleton is in some way involved with the counterfeit certificates, even if he turns out not to be the prime mover behind the scheme, and that Morden is the arm used to execute many of the operations in connection with it."

" And to what end ? "

" There are many ways of manipulating the Exchange in such a way that the unscrupulous may profit," replied Holmes. " For example, the price of a particular stock may be depressed artificially in order to take advantage of a contracted purchase at a lower price in the future. For men such as Conk-Singleton and Knight, there could be many ways in which they could profit by such a manipulation. There are one or two other matters to investigate before I am certain of all my facts," Holmes added. " Let us make our way to Ealing as soon as is practicable."

" To Ealing ? " I enquired. " It hardly seems to me to be a centre of financial activity."

" You might be surprised by what we can discover there," my friend answered, smiling. He passed me a slip of pasteboard, on which were printed the words " Edward Masters" and an address in Ealing. " This is the card that Morden presented when he visted here. Ealing certainly has some connection with our investigations, you may be sure."

" You propose to beard the lion in his den, then ? " I asked him.

" I would hardly dignify Eric Morden with the title of 'lion', but the answer to your question is in the negative, at least as a first step. Come, Watson. Time is a-wasting, and we should be off."

N our arrival at Ealing, Holmes made straight for a street, the name of which I recognised from the card that Morden had presented in his role as Masters, the private detective.

" Aha ! " exclaimed Holmes. " As I had surmised." The building which was listed as the office address of Holmes' rival was furnished with a number of brass plates outside the front door, indicating that the premises were in use by a number of different trades and businesses. The name of Edward Masters was among them. " Do you notice anything about these ? " he asked me, gesturing with his stick towards the brass plates.

" It appears to be a representative selection of various types of business and profession, such as I would expect to see here," I replied.

" Indeed so," he answered. " I was, however, referring to the plates themselves, rather than to the legends upon them."

" None of these seems to show any signs of wear, such as would be occasioned by cleaning, though all seem to be polished recently. I would guess that all these businesses have either been established recently, or have lately moved to this building."

" Very good, Watson. You continue to show improvement," said Holmes, speaking in a matter-of-fact tone with no hint of condescension. " We may also guess that this was a private residence until recently. It is not common for so many different enterprises to make their way to premises like this simultaneously. We must find out more," pointing to a notice at the front of the building announcing a vacancy regarding one of the sets of offices within. So saying, he led the way to the offices of an agent specialising in commercial property.

" I was considering renting an office in the South Ealing Road," he told the clerk, naming the street which we had just quitted. " There appeared to be a vacancy at number 17."

The clerk shook his head. " I regret that we do not deal with that property, sir. However, if I may interest you in this one... ? "

Holmes waved aside the proffered details. " I had taken a fancy to the location of that building," he informed the clerk. " I suppose you cannot inform me as to which agent I should apply regarding rental of premises there ? "

" I do not know for certain," replied the other, " but you might try Duckworth and Draper at the other end of the High Street."

" Much obliged," replied Holmes, putting on his hat and leaving the agency.

At Duckworth and Draper, our enquiries met with some more success. " Yes, sir," Holmes was informed. " There is a small set of rooms to let at the rear of the building with shared facilities. The rent would be very reasonable."

" Indeed so," agreed Holmes,

scanning the papers that had been passed to him. " May I enquire on whose behalf you are handling this business ? In other words, who is the landlord who is letting these premises ? "

" The landlord of this building is a Mr. Charles Conk-Singleton, who has a business in the City, I believe, and has recently purchased the building, which used to be a family residence. May I show you the offices now ? " asked the clerk.

" Maybe later today," replied my friend vaguely. " I have some other business to transact." He appeared to be on the point of leaving, and suddenly halted in his tracks. " This may seem a trifle irregular," he remarked to the clerk, " but if I might borrow the key, I could inspect the premises for myself, and save you the trouble of having to show me around."

" I am sure that would be in order, sir," answered the other. " However, please understand that I must consult my superior on the matter."

" Of course."

In a few minutes, the clerk returned. " There will be no difficulty, Mr. Draper tells me, if you will provide me with your name and address." He passed a memorandum book to Holmes, who scribbled some words within it. " Thank you, Mr. Gregson." I refrained from outright comment at this style of address, but determined to discover the truth of the matter later. " Here you are, sir. One key for the front door of the building, and one for the office at the back on the second floor. You will recognise it easily, I think, as there will be no plate on the door. At what time may I expect you to return the keys ? "

" In an hour or two at the most," replied Holmes.

As we left the estate agency, I

could not help but ask Holmes about the name by which he had been addressed.

" I could not risk giving my own name, nor yours," he replied. " It would undoubtedly raise the suspicions of Charles Conk-Singleton were he to learn that I had taken an interest in the premises. I am sure that Inspector Gregson will have no objection to my borrowing his name once we apprehend the villains responsible for these counterfeits." We walked a little further.

" Holmes," I exclaimed. " This is not the way to the South Ealing Road. Are you not going to inspect the premises ? "

" Not at present," he chuckled. So saying, he withdrew from his pocket two small tins that had once contained tobacco, and made impressions of both keys in the clay that now filled them. " We will inspect the premises at our leisure, I think. However, I think that we will pay our call there outside the usual hours of business, and quite conceivably in company with Inspector Gregson. So you see, Watson, my furnishing of Gregson's name to the agent is not perhaps as inappropriate as you might have at first imagined."

" You had suspected that Conk-Singleton owned the building ? " I asked.

" To be frank, that was a twist that had not occurred to me," Holmes replied. " I had guessed that Conk-Singleton had helped Morden to set up his business, such as it is, but I had not suspected such direct involvement."

" Where are we going now ? " I enquired.

" Before we return the keys to the agent, we shall pay a call on Messrs Bilton and Sons, who are printers here in Ealing."

" Would they by any chance be printers of items such as share certificates ? " I drew this bow at a venture, and was gratified to see Holmes' reaction.

" Indeed they are. Well done, indeed, Watson."

We arrived at the printing works, and Holmes asked to see Mr. Bilton, whereupon we were shown into the presence of an elderly gentleman who received us with a grave old-fashioned courtesy. His lined face and workman-like hands told us of a life spent hard at work in his chosen trade, and his general attire and prosperous appearance displayed the fact that his labours had received their deserved reward.

After a few minutes' conversation in which Sherlock Holmes briefly introduced himself, he came to the point.

" I understand that your firm carries out engraving and printing of valuable items such as share certificates ? " he asked.

" We do not actually do the engraving here," explained Mr. Bilton. " The preparation of the plates is carried out by specialist engravers, who then send the engraved plates to us."

" I see," said Holmes. " And then, after the certificates have been printed, what happens to the plates ? "

" That depends," was the answer. " In many cases, the plates are defaced and then destroyed, but occasionally they are retained in case of another issue at some time in the future. In such cases, the engraver will often simply re-engrave the date of the issue, using the old plate. Of course, we keep all plates which may be re-used safely under lock and key in the safe. After all, it would never do if someone were to start printing new share certificates. Why, it would almost be like printing money, would it not ? " He said this last with great earnestness and sincerity, and it was impossible to believe that this venerable tradesman could in any way be connected to the counterfeiting which was threatening the world of the City.

" I understand," said Holmes. " It would indeed be a terrible thing. May I ask what became of the plate for the Imperial & Colonial issue of three years back in March ? "

" Dear me," replied the old man. " I would have to refer to my books. What an extraordinary question, though. May I ask why you are making this enquiry ? " Obviously the name of Sherlock Holmes that was printed on the card that Holmes had passed to him earlier meant little to him.

" I have reason to believe that someone is counterfeiting Imperial & Colonial stock certificates," replied my friend. " I merely wish to reassure myself that the source of these forgeries is some place other than this."

" I can assure you, sir, that it would not be from here that such forgeries would be issued." He was almost comical in his vehement denial of the possibility. " But just to put your mind at rest, I will show you the ledger entry, where all our work is entered." He reached behind him, and pulled down a large leather-bound volume. " In the month of March three years ago, you say ? " he asked, as he scanned the pages. " Ah, here we are. This is one case where we retained the plate, and according to the ledger, we have not used it again for a re-issue."

" Also the Eastern Union Railway issue which I believe to be of approximately the same date, and the Cobden Alkali manufactory. I confess, I do not know that these certificates were of your manufacture, but I have good reason to think this to be the case."

After further reference to the ledger, Bilton reported that these last-named securities had indeed been printed by his company, and that the plates had been retained and not destroyed.

" May we see the plates ? " Holmes requested.

" Bless my soul ! You really are inquisitive, are you not ? " chuckled Bilton.

" It is my trade," replied Holmes equably.

" Each to his own, I suppose. Still, there is no harm in your seeing the plates, if this will put your mind at rest." He noted the numbers from the ledger on a piece of paper, felt in his pocket and pulled out a large bunch of keys. " This way, gentlemen, if you please."

He led the way into the next room, where a large safe door, the size of a house front door, graced one wall. " As you can guess," he explained, " some of the printed items that we produce are valuable, and we must store them securely before they are delivered to our customers."

" A very wise precaution," commented Holmes. " And who holds the keys to this safe, besides yourself ? "

" My sons, Geoffrey and Colin. There are times when I am not available at the end of the day when the work is to be secured, and I would trust none of my workers with such a responsibility. Now," he went on, inserting his key into the lock, " we will find the first plate for you, which is numbered as 1332 in the ledger. Please wait outside the safe, gentleman. I will be with you in a matter of a minute or two." Having opened the door of the safe, which opened smoothly and almost silently, being counterweighted, he stepped inside, and snapped an electrical switch. " All the latest inventions, you see, Mr. Holmes," he explained with some pride, as an electrical lamp flooded the interior of the safe with light. " Now let me see..." His voice tailed off. " There must be some mistake here. And here. And here. Bless my soul ! " His voice, from inside the safe, held a note of anxiety. " Mr. Holmes and Dr. Watson, may I ask you to step inside and join me ? " We did so, and he gestured to racks lining one wall of the giant safe. " These, you see, are where we store the plates. They are all in order, as you can observe, but there is a gap between number 1331 and number 1333. That, Mr. Holmes, is the first of the plates about which you were enquiring. And see here, and here. Two more gaps in the sequence, and the plates are not here. Dear me." The little man appeared to be quite overcome, and mopped his brow with a large silk handkerchief. " What must you think of us, Mr. Holmes ? "

" I suppose there is no chance that these plates have slipped out of the rack or have been placed in the wrong location ? " I suggested.

" It is a possibility," he admitted. " Would you gentlemen care to assist me ? My back not being as young as it once was makes it more difficult for me to bend and search underneath the racks and so on."

Holmes and I joined in the search, but the missing plates were nowhere to be seen.

" I confess to you, Mr. Holmes," said Bilton, when we had exhausted the scant possibilities for concealment offered by the safe, which he had closed and re-secured before returning to his office, " that I believed we had a perfect system to keep track of such things. The fact that the plates are missing is bad enough, but what makes it worse is that if they have been removed, this can only have been done by one of two people. One of my sons." He sat there, obviously shaken by this turn of events, but looking Holmes in the eye. " I am sorry that this has happened, and that such a scandal should affect this firm. It is really quite inconceivable that he should ever betray my trust in this way."

" That who should betray your trust, Mr. Bilton ? Believe me, sir, no scandal need necessarily appear."

" My elder son, Geoffrey, is the one whom I would suspect. He has fallen in with a bad set."

" Cards ? Horses ? " I suggested.

The old man shook his head. " I know that he has been engaged in speculation on 'Change," he answered. " He is secretive about his finances, and I do not seek to pry, but I believe that he has encountered serious reverses in the field."

" Do you know the name of his brokers ? "

" I heard the name, but took little note of it, and it has slipped my mind. I would probably remember the name were it mentioned to me."

" Knight and Conk-Singleton ? " suggested Holmes.

" That name is definitely familiar to me," said the unhappy Bilton. " Yes, I seem to remember his mentioning that he was using that firm some time ago. Perhaps six months before now."

" And when would the presence of the plates last have been noted ? " asked Holmes.

" We carry out an annual check of our inventory. It would have been in place then. About six months ago..." He broke off. " You feel there may be some connection ? "

" I am positive of it," replied Holmes. " But no blame can attach to you, of that I am sure. Would it be possible to see your son ? "

" I would be delighted if you would speak to him on this matter."

Bilton senior rang for a senior workman, and requested that " Mr. Geoffrey" be sent to him.

" Do you wish to interview him in private ? " he asked Holmes.

" He may speak more freely in your absence," replied Holmes, reflectively. " On the other hand, your presence would remove any suspicion of coercion. I leave the question of whether you stay or leave to your discretion."

" In which case, I will stay," answered the old man. " I wish to hear with my own ears what my ne'er-do-well son has to say for himself. I am sorry to say that his behaviour since the death of his mother some ten years ago has not always been of the most praiseworthy, and I have been too concerned with my business to be the father I should have been."

" Do not blame yourself," Holmes told him kindly. " We cannot all be responsible for others' weaknesses."

At that point, the door opened, and Geoffrey Bilton entered. He was a fine figure of a man, though his appearance was chiefly remarkable for a somewhat saturnine countenance, which turned to a scowl of displeasure as he registered the presence of Holmes and myself. There were distinct signs that he was not altogether comfortable at being summoned.

" You wished to speak to me, Pater ? " he drawled, in a tone of voice that struck my ears as being somewhat insolent.

" It is not I who wishes to speak to you—at present," answered his father. " Mr. Sherlock Holmes here wishes to ask you a few questions."

The effect of my friend's name on the young man was remarkable. He turned pale, and clutched for support at the table in front of him.

" I see my name is familiar to you," remarked Holmes, with a smile.

" You know all ? " stammered Geoffrey Bilton. All his former arrogance and bluster appeared to have left him.

" No," replied Sherlock Holmes, still smiling. " It would be somewhat of an exaggeration to say that I know all, but I have strong suspicions, and I would like your help in confirming them."

The other seemed to relax a little. " I will help you if I can. If it will only rid me of the man who is poisoning my life."

" You refer to Edward Masters ? " asked Holmes.

" Yes, d—— him ! " cried the other. " And Charles Conk-Singleton with him ! " Following this outburst, he seemed to slump, almost in a gesture of defeat, and Holmes waved him to a vacant chair, into which he sank.

" Perhaps you can provide us with a history of what has happened," invited Holmes.

" I will be happy to do so. I am ruined in any case. You should know, Pater, that my passage to America is booked on a steamer leaving Liverpool next week. I intended to leave a full account of my doings behind me. Mr. Holmes here has only brought matters forward."

I was touched, as who could not fail to be, by the evident distress now apparent in the young man's voice. " Let me explain how this whole wretched business came to be," he continued. " Games of chance and gambling had never attracted me, but I reckoned than a man of above average intellect, such as I know myself to be, could make investments that would secure a good return on his money. Accordingly, I started to make my investments, and things went well at first."

"When was this ? " asked Holmes, whose pencil was poised above his notebook.

"Some two years ago. I had heard that Imperial & Colonial was a 'coming thing', as they say in the City, and accordingly determined to invest in them. This was about nine months ago. The rumours about the firm were true, and my small holdings doubled in value in a very short space of time. But the very appreciation of their value meant that I was unable to purchase more of the same—they had risen beyond the reach of my purse. And then it was that I remembered that our firm had had the printing of the original bearer certificates. What, I asked myself, if I were to avail myself of the plates, and run off additional certificates ? Naturally, I have skill in setting up and operating the presses, and it was easy for me to do this work late in the evening, when the workmen had all gone home. Of course, I cleaned everything after my labours, and replaced the plate in the safe."

"You young dog ! " exclaimed his father. " To think that I trusted you in everything regarding the business, and had planned for you to take my place at its head."

His son accepted the reproof without protest. " I am not defending my actions, Pater, other than to state that I am ashamed of them. I am simply giving an account of what has transpired."

"I am curious," enquired Holmes. " I assume that these bearer certificates were signed by the officers of the company, and that they were numbered. How did you achieve your ends with regard to these features ? "

"As to the signature, I confess to having a minor talent for forgery, which I swear I had not employed for unlawful business before this. At school I achieved a certain notoriety for my ability to imitate any boy's hand. As regards the numbering, it was there that I made my mistake that led to the situation in which I now find myself. The numbers were hand-written by the company officers after delivery. I had some idea of the system employed for the numbering, since I already held some legitimate bearer stock, but I was forced to use conjecture as to the actual numbers of the certificates. It was also necessary, if I were to realise any gain from the sale of these certificates, to deal with another broker than the one whose services I had hitherto employed. I chose the house of Knight and Conk-Singleton almost at random."

"And this would be about six months ago ? " asked Holmes.

"Closer to seven," corrected Bilton. " I took my forged certificates with me on my first appointment to see Conk-Singleton, confident that my use of the original plates and paper made them undetectable as counterfeits. I presented the certificates to Conk-Singleton, explaining that they had been left to me as part of a legacy, and he promised to dispose of them on my behalf, and asked me to visit the offices to collect the proceeds of the sale the next week." Here the young man paused, and mopped his brow. " When I entered Conk-Singleton's office, his manner was markedly less affable than it had been on the previous occasion.

" ' What the deuce do you mean,' he fairly roared at me, 'by offering me forgeries for sale ? '

" I confess that I was so dumb-founded by his words that I had no thought of denying the charge. ' How do you know they are forger-ies ? ' I asked him.

" He leaned back in his chair and smiled, with the lazy ease of a tiger that has scented its prey. ' My dear Mr. Bilton,' he said to me. ' Your skill as a printer does credit to your father's firm and to his teaching of his trade to you. However, you should know that bearer certificates with the same numbers as the ones you presented to me recently passed through our hands.'

" I was, as you can imagine, com-pletely taken aback. 'What do you propose doing ? ' I asked him.

" ' Why, nothing at present. The question you should be asking, my dear Mr. Bilton, is what you should be doing to ensure that I contin-ue to do nothing.' He smiled, Mr. Holmes, and it was such a smile as I never wish to see again.

" To cut a long story short, he agreed to keep the forgeries a secret from the police, and even to dispose of them on the market at the market price, and to hand over the proceeds to me."

" But there were conditions ? " asked Holmes.

" Of course, and I think you have already guessed what they are. He made detailed enquiries as to the operation of the business, and re-quested me to deliver the plates of the Imperial & Colonial certificates to him through an intermediary, immediately following the annual check of the contents of the safe."

" Did he say why you should not carry out the printing yourself as you had before ? "

" He explained to me that it there was less risk of discovery if he were to arrange for the printing to be car-ried out away from the works. He also told me that the plate would be returned to me for replacement in the safe before the next check, so there would be no risk of the decep-tion being uncovered. I also had to procure some of the paper that is used for the certificates, but since it is of a common type, used for many purposes other than the production of bearer shares, it was a relatively easy matter for me to remove a good number of sheets without attracting any notice."

" And what of the other plates ? "

" Conk-Singleton requested those plates about a month after I had delivered the Imperial & Coloni-al plate to him. Somehow, he was aware that Bilton and Sons had been responsible for the prepara-tion and printing of these bearer certificates."

" Have you any idea where and how the plates are being used for the production of the counterfeits ? "

" I am certain that Masters, whom Conk-Singleton later desig-nated as his intermediary in this matter is involved in the produc-tion," replied Geoffrey Bilton, " but I am unable to tell you where the work is being done. We have met by pre-arrangement in a public house, where I have handed over such ma-terials—plates or paper—as had pre-viously been requested in letters from Conk-Singleton."

" You do not know that Masters has taken premises here in Eal-ing ? " asked Holmes. " And that those premises are in fact owned by Charles Conk-Singleton, who lets them out to him."

The surprise on the other's face

was unfeigned. " Believe me, I had no idea of this," he exclaimed. " Why, if I had known these things, I would have exposed him to the police and taken my own chances with the law."

" Which is probably why he never informed you of the fact," commented Holmes drily. " Well, Mr. Bilton," turning to the father, " it is not my place to tell a father how to treat his sons, but I can tell you that if your son were to turn Queen's Evidence, it would go a long way towards mitigating any sentence that might be passed on him in a future trial, if indeed there were to be a trial. In such an event, I would be inclined to extend an olive branch of forgiveness. I have to tell you," addressing the son, " that you have informed us of your decision to leave the country, and it would be my duty to inform the authorities of that fact, advising them to keep a watch at the ports. I would strongly advise you to assist the police to the utmost of your abilities, rather than running away. If you take the former course, be sure that I will use whatever influence I have with the police on your behalf."

" Believe me, Mr. Holmes, and believe me, Pater, you cannot begin to understand what I am feeling at this time at having betrayed your trust in this way." Tears started to his eyes as he spoke these words, and I could see his father visibly relax his stiff posture as he beheld his son's remorse. " I will not fly," he continued. " I will stand and help the rogues receive the punishment they so richly merit, even if it means my accepting penalties myself."

" I am proud of your decision, my son," replied his father, with a catch in his voice. " With the aid of Mr. Holmes here, I am sure we can restore the good name of our firm.

Rest assured that you have my full support in this."

It was touching to see the old man and his son apparently so reconciled, but Holmes was not given admiration to of such displays of emotion, and he broke in upon the pair.

" Have you ever seen any of the counterfeits produced from the plates ? " he asked the younger Bilton.

" Never," replied the other.

" I have brought one with me," replied Holmes, who extracted a sheet of paper from a tube that he had been carrying with him since we left Baker-street, much to my puzzlement.

Spreading it out on the table, father and son examined it together, both bringing printer's loupes to bear.

" Almost perfect," commented the father, " other than the smudging at the lower left corner. We would never have let such a slip leave our works."

" You are obviously a man who loves perfection in small details," smiled Holmes. " A man after my own heart. What I would like you to do," turning back to the son, " is to send a message to Conk-Singleton, informing him that you have somehow caught sight of one of these certificates, which you immediately recognised as being one of the counterfeit shares, due to the flaw that your father has just pointed out. Suggest to him that you are introduced to the printer of the counterfeits and you can point out what is needed to improve the quality of the work."

" And then ? " enquired the young man.

" I will be waiting, together with the police. We will be able to have the whole gang behind bars if you can bring them together."

" That would include me ? " asked Bilton.

" Sadly, yes," replied Holmes. " You can hardly expect to escape scot-free from the consequences of your folly. On the other hand, as I mentioned, your cooperation will certainly be taken into account at the time of your trial."

" I will help you, all the same," replied the other.

" How did you usually communicate with Conk-Singleton ? " asked my friend.

" Usually I received messages from him, asking me to meet Masters at a designated time, in a place chosen by Conk-Singleton. However, he did leave an emergency address to which I could direct telegrams in the event of any urgent communication being required. Is it your opinion that I should use that means in this instance ? "

" Indeed so. I leave it to your discretion to suggest the meeting place, but ensure that it is not the premises used by Masters. What I ask of you, though, is that you ensure that you, Conk-Singleton, and Masters,

together with any others involved in this business, be at Masters' office in the South Ealing Road at some time shortly after your initial meeting. I have every reason to believe that the counterfeiting is being carried out from there, but in the event it is not, I leave it to your ingenuity to move the party to those premises."

" I understand. Let me compose the message, and I will show it to you before I send it to London."

He wrote on a piece of paper, and showed it to Holmes, who nodded approvingly. " Excellent," he commented. " If you will provide me with the address, I will send this off together with one or two telegrams of my own."

This being done, Holmes pocketed the paper. " We will take our leave of you. And I expect to see you later on, Mr. Bilton," looking fixedly at the younger man, " in company with your erstwhile colleagues. And to you, sir," addressed to the senior Bilton, " I extend my sincere thanks for your cooperation in this matter. I trust we will all meet again soon."

E left the printing works, and returned the office keys to the agents, Holmes making some noncommittal remarks regarding the possible future lease of the premises. We then made our way to the post-office where, together with Geoffrey Bilton's telegram to Conk-Singleton, Holmes sent one of his own to Gregson, requesting the police detective to come to Ealing, and specifying the location within the building where we were to meet him. After leaving the post-office,

we entered a locksmith's, where Holmes had requested that keys be made from the impressions he had made earlier.

The locksmith initially demurred, but Holmes persuaded him to carry out the work, after establishing his identity to the tradesman.

After he had obtained these duplicate keys, we took ourselves to a public house, the windows of whose saloon bar overlooked the premises occupied by Masters. We ordered a rude meal of ham and eggs, all the while watching the comings and goings at the house. We had not long to wait before a telegraph messenger appeared, and rang one of the bells at the front door. After about a minute, the door was opened to him, and we saw a man whom we recognised as Edward Masters receive a telegram from the messenger.

" That will be the summons from Conk-Singleton, I am positive," said Holmes. " Excellent," he added some ten minutes later, as we watched Masters leave the premises, and lock the front door carefully behind him. From the lack of lights in the other windows, we guessed that there was no other occupant currently in residence.

" Come," Holmes said to me, as we watched our quarry disappear down the street. " Let us make our way inside." We left the inn, and in the gathering dusk, made our way to the front door of the building from which Masters had emerged. " I could, naturally, have used my picklocks, had I brought them with me," Holmes muttered as he fitted the recently crafted key into the lock, " but in lieu of them, it will be expedient to use these keys. Their use will likely provide us with the additional advantages of speed and stealth. As it turns out, we could possibly have arranged to retain the originals, but it suited my purposes to have these duplicates to hand, in case of any delays or hitches."

While I kept a careful watch for any passers-by, Holmes opened the door, and we slipped inside, locking the door after us. The building had originally served, as Holmes had surmised, as a family residence, and the hall passage led from the front of the house to a back door, which Holmes unbolted.

" Gregson and his men should have no problem in entering," he remarked, as he led the way

silently up the stairs. " And here is our office, I think," pointing to a door with no nameplate. " Perfectly located." I noticed that the office next to the room bore the nameplate of Edward Masters. " A back room would be a necessity for him, if he has to do most of the printing at night. A light displayed at the front of the house on the side of the street would undoubtedly attract unwanted attention. And now," closing the door and leaving it unlocked, " to let Gregson know where we are." He removed three candles from his pocket and arranged them on the windowsill, equally spaced. " It is now eight fifty-five. The message that young Bilton wrote suggested a meeting at Ealing station at nine fifteen, and I expect them to arrive here at some time after nine thirty. Gregson should arrive on the previous train at five before nine, that is to say now. It is time." So saying, he lit the candles. " There, that should serve as a signal to Gregson. I have already informed him of the address in my wire to him, but it is sometimes less than easy to locate a building from the wrong side like this, especially in the dark."

I reached for my pipe and filled it, but as I retrieved my matches from my pocket, Holmes placed a hand on my arm, staying my action. " The smell of the tobacco would alert the friends for whom we are waiting to our presence," he murmured softly. " Believe me, I feel the need as much as I believe you to do. Snuff, maybe ? " he offered, extending a tin to me. " Take care not to sneeze, though," he cautioned me.

I was about to avail myself of his offer, when a sharp rattle sounded at the window.

" Aha ! Gregson warning us that he will be with us soon. I asked him to throw a couple of pebbles at the window which contained three candles. It is a pleasure to be working with a man who follows instructions." Even as he finished speaking, I could hear the stealthy tread of several men moving up the stairs, followed by a knock at the door. Holmes moved to the door and allowed Gregson, accompanied by three burly constables, to enter.

" Well done, Mr. Holmes," Gregson congratulated Holmes, in a soft voice. " You expect your stratagem to succeed ? "

" I do," replied Holmes. " I have every reason to believe that once we enter the room next door, we will discover the materials and the machinery that have been responsible for producing the counterfeits, together with some of the counterfeits themselves, and most importantly, the players in the drama. And I am confident that the bait is strong enough to entrap all of them. Hark ! " he suddenly exclaimed, holding up a hand. " They are here before I expected." Sure enough, Holmes' sharp ears had detected the sound of the front door being unlocked and opened, followed by the sound of at least three pairs of footsteps ascending the staircase.

By the time the new arrivals had reached the top of the stairs, Holmes had snuffed the candles on the windowsill, ensuring that no light would spill from the cracks in the doorway. We stood in silence, and could hear heavy breathing from outside the room, presumably from Conk-Singleton, as the key turned in the lock of the next door. After a short while, there was a " pop" as the gas was lit, and the sound of low voices emanated from Masters' office.

" Let us move," Holmes breathed to Gregson. Stealthily, the six of us moved out of the room, and assembled outside the next door.

" On my mark," commanded Holmes, a police whistle ready to raise to his lips. " One... two..." and blew a blast on the whistle. Gregson and his men rushed through the door, with Gregson crying in a loud voice that the occupants of the room were to stay where they were, and not to move. Holmes followed them, almost sauntering in a leisurely fashion, forming a contrast to the activity of the official force, and I brought up the rear.

The first thing that I noticed in the room was a large copperplate press, taking up almost one half of the space, with a stack of paper by the side of it. On the other side was a small pile of printed sheets, which I took to be counterfeit certificates.

Conk-Singleton was obviously shaken to the core by the entrance of Gregson and the constables, and started visibly, but that was nothing compared to his reaction when he recognised Holmes and myself. His mouth dropped open, and the colour drained from his face, turning it an ashen colour. He clutched at his chest, and as a doctor, I had genuine concerns that he was about to suffer some sort of seizure. Indeed, I was about to rush forward, and offer him my professional aid which, as a matter of my Oath, I was bound to give, when he appeared to recover a little. I remained watchful for further signs of weakness, however, as events proceeded.

As for Morden, he gazed wildly about him, like a rat caught in a trap, nervously seeking some escape, or possibly considering some excuse he could use for his being in the same room as the counterfeit certificates and the means of their production. His eyes blazed fury at Holmes, and he was muttering vile epithets semi-audibly as Gregson advanced towards him. Geoffrey Bilton, for his part, stood calmly to one side, obviously resigned to his fate, with a manly demeanour that excited my admiration, despite his actions in the past.

" Charles Conk-Singleton, Geoffrey Bilton, and Eric Morden, I have warrants for your arrest," announced Gregson in ringing tones. " I must warn you now that anything you say will be recorded and may be used in evidence against you at your trial."

" On what charges ? " spluttered Conk-Singleton, who appeared to have recovered a little of his poise.

" Conspiracy to defraud would be one of the least of the charges, I believe," Holmes informed him. " There are various other matters concerned with forgery, and the receiving of stolen property, to wit, the plates used to create the counterfeit securities."

Conk-Singleton reeled visibly as Holmes listed these possible charges. " I assume that you have proof ? " he stammered. For answer, Holmes nodded silently. Conk-Singleton turned to Morden, his face creased in fury. " This is your doing, you incompetent fool ! " he fairly roared at his confederate. " It was your idea to bring Sherlock Holmes into this affair in order to divert attention. Instead of which, the whole business has come crashing down on our heads. I will make sure you receive the maximum sentence when we stand in the dock together."

" And I you," retorted Morden. " If you had not approached me with this scheme, I would be a free man."

Conk-Singleton retorted with an insult that does not bear repeating here, and Morden riposted with a foul oath. In their rage against Holmes and against each other, they appeared to have forgotten Geoffrey Bilton, who had been led away quietly by one of the constables, following a sign from Gregson. Holmes was standing by, observing the quarrel, a sardonic smile on his lips.

" Honour among thieves, would you say, Gregson ? " he observed mildly.

" You may be right at that, Mr. Holmes," replied the policeman, smiling broadly. " But this little comedy must come to an end. You handle Morden, Jenkins and Douglas," he said to the constables, " and you come along with me," to Conk-Singleton.

As Conk-Singleton was led away, he turned to Holmes. " You treacherous fiend," he hissed. " Believe me, I will seek your ruin."

" You may seek it," replied Holmes equably. " I doubt if you will ever realise it. Farewell. I expect to see you at the Bailey," he added, as Conk-Singleton disappeared down the stairs, preceded by the handcuffed Morden and his escorts, and followed by the solid form of Inspector Gregson.

" A good night's work, would you not agree, Watson ? " said Holmes. " There is time, I think," consulting his watch, " for us to return to Town for a late supper at Alberti's, if the notion is agreeable to you ? "

" Indeed it is. An excellent suggestion."

We collected our hats and coats, and, passing and hailing the police officers whom Gregson had left to guard the premises, made our way to the station.

VER the excellent meal and the bottle of Lacrima Christi that accompanied it, I questioned Holmes on further details of the case.

" I fail to understand why Conk-Singleton engaged your services in the first place," I said to Holmes, who chuckled in reply.

" It was almost c1ertain that I would be called in, either by the police, or by a rival broker, to assist with the case. As Conk-Singleton himself admitted, if you recall, Morden suggested that I be called in to assist with the discovery of the counterfeit certificates. What better way of keeping track of my movements and learning of my discoveries than by engaging me, and thereby diverting suspicion from himself ? Who would ever suspect a criminal of hiring a detective in order to catch himself ? In addition, by requesting me to serve under the direction of Morden, he could be sure that my energies would be directed by Morden towards dead ends, and I would be unable to solve the case."

" But you refused to be directed by Morden ? "

" Naturally I refused. And this provided something of a crimp to his plans. He had to fall back on the rather crude expedient of having me arrested and charged with a crime I did not commit. The unfortunate clerk who suffered the injuries alleged to have been inflicted by me was, I am sure, handsomely rewarded for his pains. Gregson will almost certainly discover who actually broke the nose and bruised the body of Michael Frignall, but my opinion is that it was Morden himself. Happily, Conk-Singleton and Morden are such bunglers that it was easy for me to disprove their lies. Frignall's description of his alleged attacker was obviously based on Morden's recollection of the way I was dressed when he met me earlier in the day and repeated by the victim with no regard to the circumstances under which he was allegedly attacked. The false charge also served, as we discovered, to remove me from my rooms while an attempt was made to remove whatever evidence I might have accumulated on the case."

" Gregson's dropping of the charges certainly came as a great surprise to Morden when I observed him in court," I said.

Holmes laughed outright. " Good old Gregson ! I was extremely fortunate to have him assigned to my case. He is, as I have remarked to you before, one of the more competent of the Scotland Yard force, and remarkably quick on the uptake of new theories and ideas. I am certainly in his debt."

" And he in yours," I reminded Holmes. " Without your aid, he would never have been credited with the detection and capture of Conk-Singleton and Morden."

" True," mused Holmes. " Maybe we can consider honours to be even in this instance."

" But how did you come to hit upon Ealing as the location for all these events ? I know that Morden's card gave Ealing as his address, but I fail to see how you then came to discover that the printing was being carried out in this town."

" Tut, Watson. You failed to remark the state of Morden's hands when he visited us, then ? Printer's ink firmly embedded under the nails and in the pores of the skin. I am amazed that you could overlook that. Added to which, of course I was aware of his past history as a forger. There were two additional points that linked Conk-Singleton to Ealing, and hence to Morden.

You remember the eucalyptus leaf that he carried into my rooms on his boots ? Ealing is one of the few locations in London where such a tree is to be found. When I spotted that peculiar light grey clay on his boots, as well as on those of Morden, it confirmed my suspicions that the two of them had been together in Ealing. To what end ? I asked myself. Since Conk-Singleton was employing Morden's services, it would have seemed only natural for Morden to have visited his employer, rather than the other way around. There was obviously a good reason for Conk-Singleton to make the trip from the City, which involved some activity of Morden's—and that was printing, judging by the state of his hands."

" So you knew almost from the start that Conk-Singleton was involved in the matter ? "

" I suspected, Watson, I did not know. There is a big difference. I required proof, and I also needed to know the mechanism by which this all took place. Geoffrey Bilton has been instrumental in providing these details, which will make a strong watertight case when Conk-Singleton and Morden stand in the dock." Unexpectedly, Holmes started to laugh softly.

" It is not like you, Holmes, to make light of others' misfortunes in this way, even when they are wrongdoers," I remonstrated.

" I apologise, Watson, for my seeming heartlessness. A somewhat ironically amusing sidenote has just struck me."

" That being ? "

" That Charles Conk-Singleton paid me by cheque, did he not, in order to investigate the case ? Since he no longer currently retains control over his funds, I am free to cash the cheque that he paid me. He has therefore himself defrayed the costs of the investigation that has resulted in his arrest. There is a certain sweet irony in that, do you not agree ? "

I was reluctantly forced to agree with Holmes' views on the matter.

" There was also," he added, " the matter of a handsome reward he offered me, though the exact amount was never specified by him, to be paid on the conviction of those responsible for the forgeries. My personal opinion is that I will never be paid that reward, and I must therefore content myself with the two hundred guineas that he has paid me as a fee." So saying, Holmes divided the last of the wine between our two glasses, and sat back, a half-smile of contentment on his face.

Sherlock Holmes
&
the Enfield Rope

"I CONFESS THAT I ARRANGED THE CARDS LAST NIGHT SO THAT I WAS TO PARTNER YOU,
SIR, AND WE WERE TO PLAY AGAINST LADY ENFIELD AND VON GRÜNING." (PAGE 264)

Editor's Note

When searching in the deed box, I came across this adventure, sealed in three stout envelopes, all bearing the now familiar " SH" and " W" seals, but otherwise unmarked. On opening the envelopes and reading the story, it was obvious to me why this account of Holmes' doings had never been published.

Though Watson sometimes made oblique references to Sherlock Holmes' work for the British Royal Family in some cases, he would naturally be reluctant to present the Prince of Wales (later King Edward VII) as he is exhibited here. Later generations, of course, are aware of the all too human traits associated with " Bertie", as the Prince was known to his intimates, and are less likely to be shocked by them than would be Watson's contemporaries. The political implications described here are also less important than they would have been at the time, of course, but the Prince's gloomy prediction regarding his nephew was to be sadly fulfilled in August 1914, some 17 years after the events described here.

Quite apart from the Royal connection, the case is interesting to Holmes scholars for the way in which Watson has to impersonate Holmes at one point, and suffer as a result of the deception.

 WAS constantly reminded, during the course of my association with the celebrated detective Sherlock Holmes, of his indifference to many of the matters that we normally associate with civilisation. While it is true that his manners at times could grace a Court occasion, there were other moments when his general behaviour smacked of bohemianism, if not downright eccentricity.

I encountered him in one of these latter moods when I walked in on him one day, following a morning spent attending my cases, and beheld him wrapped in his dressing gown, unshaven, and seated cross-legged in front of the fender, filling the atmosphere with the blue fumes from his pipe, and adding to the noxious atmosphere by holding a smoking kipper, transfixed by a toasting fork, in front of the flames.

" Holmes," I remonstrated. " It is half-past three in the afternoon. I am at a loss as to why you are still in a state of undress at this hour, and why you are performing this operation with a kipper. The smell, if I may speak frankly, is intolerable. I shall open the window, unless you particularly wish me not to do so."

" I have good reasons for keeping the window closed," he replied, a little testily. " Indulge me a little, if you would. As to the first charge you bring against me, I was awake all night, and have only just arisen from a belated slumber. As to the second, it is connected with the first."

" On what business were you engaged that required you to be awake all night ? And if you require something with which to break your fast, I am sure that Mrs. Hudson would oblige, though she might think it eccentric to be providing kippers at this time of the day."

To my relief, Holmes laid down the fish, where it smouldered gently on the fender. " I am assisting Lestrade with the Henley case," he commented. The name meant nothing to me, and I raised my eyebrows. " It is a crime of a singularly obnoxious nature," he explained, " and one that is not capable of a simple explanation. Much of the solution will depend on the speed with which a vile odour, such as the one of burnt kipper, will dissipate in a closed room."

" I would recommend," I suggested, " that this particular room remain closed for a very short time and that you open the windows as soon as possible. I seem to remember your telling me yesterday that Lady Enfield was due to call on you in less than an hour's time today. You particularly wished me to be present, as I recall."

Holmes smote his brow. " You are perfectly correct, Watson. My apologies for my inattention. The interest presented by the puzzles at the Henley boathouse had driven the proposed visit from my mind. May I ask you to open the window while I make myself somewhat more presentable for the benefit of our distinguished guest." I hastened to carry out this command, disposing of the blackened kipper as I did so, while Holmes took himself to the bedroom, from which his voice presently emanated. " Watson, if you would be kind enough to summarise any information about the lady in question from the reference works on the shelves, I would appreciate your doing so."

I collected the information from *Burke's* and *Who's Who*, informing Holmes, " She appears to be the second wife of Lord Enfield. Born in America, *née* McDougall, daughter of a Chicago flour and wheat magnate, but has lived in this country since the age of fifteen and is now aged thirty-seven. Little more of interest, I fear, unless you are interested in the hunts with which she rides to hounds, or the charities of which she is patron ? "

" Those are of little interest at present," commented Holmes, emerging from the bedroom and now clad in conventional attire, appearing considerably more presentable than when I had first entered the room. " My thanks to you for your disposal of the fish." He sniffed the air. " It is no longer as apparent as it was, I feel." Seizing a pen, he wrote a few words on a piece of paper, and rang the bell for Mrs. Hudson, to whom he presented the sheet, instructing her to send it as a telegram. " There, that should put Lestrade on the right trail." He strode to the window and started to close it, the odour of kipper having, as he had remarked earlier, significantly weakened. " I fancy I see the lady in question arriving now, though I might have expected her to use a private carriage rather than a hansom cab."

We heard the sound of the bell downstairs, and a visitor being admitted. Presently there was a knock on the door, which I opened to a handsome lady in early middle age. She was undeniably one of the most beautiful and fashionable ladies to have graced Holmes' rooms, but there was an air of concern that lined her face, and gave her the appearance of a woman a little older than I knew her to be from my previous researches.

Holmes rose to meet her and shook her hand before ushering her to an armchair.

As she sat, she sniffed the air.

" Am I mistaken, Mr. Holmes, or is there a smell of fish in this room ? "

I was forced to turn my face away at this question, and developed a cough to cover my amusement, hardly hearing Holmes' reply to the effect that it was the result of an experiment that he had been conducting.

" No matter," she said. " I had already heard from other sources that your methods and personality were, shall we say, eccentric. I am pleased to note that at least some of the rumours surrounding you are true."

Holmes raised his eyebrows. " Indeed ? And what are the other rumours, if I may ask ? " he asked, in high good humour.

Our visitor replied in a similar vein. " Why," she replied, " they say that you are never wrong and never beaten by the problems presented by a case."

" Then they are in the wrong," declared Sherlock Holmes bluntly. " Dr. Watson here will tell you that I have not always solved my cases, and that I make mistakes in my reasoning—not often, it is true, but enough to acquit me of any charges of infallibility that may be brought against me."

Lady Enfield laughed. It was not the timid repressed giggle of a Society lady, but that of a full-blooded woman who was capable of appreciating life in all its richness. " All the better. Had you been in agreement with those two assessments, I would be forced to concur with the opinion formed of you by one of your detractors." Holmes cocked his head on one side expectantly. " My acquaintance—I will not dignify him with the name of friend— informed me that you were the most insufferably arrogant man on earth, to his knowledge, at any rate."

Instead of Holmes becoming angry at this slur on his character, he in his turn threw back his head and laughed. " I would assume that acquaintance to be Lord Witherfield," he commented.

" How the heck— I mean, how in the world would you know that, Mr. Holmes ? " she asked, her British manner of speech slipping for a moment, revealing her American upbringing.

" Oh, Watson will inform you that I have my methods," he replied airily. " But may I enquire what brings you here in such a hurry, without the knowledge of your husband, or indeed, without your servants being aware of your visit ? "

Our fair visitor started. " Maybe some of the tales they say about you are true, Mr. Holmes. How... ? "

" Simplicity itself. You did not arrive in a private vehicle, but a hansom cab. This, I assume, was to avoid the notice and attention that would have been apparent, and would eventually have come to the attention of your husband, had you used a private carriage and employed your grooms and coachmen. I observed you conversing with the cab driver as you approached this building, and it was obvious to me that you were unfamiliar with the exact location of my lodgings, the whereabouts of which you could easily have ascertained from your servants before leaving home. If additional proof were needed, I need only remark on the state of your shoes. I am sure your maid would never permit you to leave the house with your shoes in that condition, if I may be permitted to say so."

" Well, Mr. Holmes, you have indeed hit the nail on the head. I am here without the knowledge of my husband, or indeed, as you rightly say, without the knowledge of the servants. It concerns a very delicate matter indeed. You may be relieved to know, Mr. Holmes," she smiled, " that the man who told me you were never wrong also informed me that you were among the most discreet of men, and never betrayed a confidence."

" I can confidently assert that to be the case, at any rate," replied Holmes, " and the same goes for Dr. Watson here, naturally."

" In that case, I will speak freely," replied Lady Enfield. " You may know that I married young, to a man who is considerably my senior."

" I had heard that," replied Holmes. " It is not, after, all, altogether uncommon for our noble families to ally themselves with American capital in this way."

" Do not mistake my meaning here," replied our visitor. " Albert—that is to say, my husband—is the kindest and most loving of men. I really have nothing to complain of in regard to his treatment of me. He is, however, a little older than myself, and this can create a certain—shall we say 'tension' ? in our marital relations." The last phrases were delivered in a mumble, during which she gazed at the floor. Holmes said nothing in reply, and waited motionless, his fingers steepled. After a pause of a few minutes, Lady Enfield regained her composure and continued.

" As you may know from your reading of the Society pages in the newspapers, it is common for me to attend functions without my husband. It was at a ball that I met and deepened my acquaintance with—" Here, our fair visitor seemed to be overcome with embarrassment once more, and words seemed to fail her. Wordlessly, Holmes poured a glass of water from the carafe standing beside him and handed it to her. She

accepted it with a word of thanks, and after a few sips, continued her story. " Forgive me if I do not speak his name out loud. I am under an obligation to him not to do so, and yet..." Her voice tailed off.

" Maybe I can be of some assistance here ? " suggested Holmes. " At whose ball or party did this occur ? "

" It was a soirée held by the Duchess of Essex. A small affair, attended by twenty people at the most."

" Aha ! " exclaimed Holmes. " In that case, I am able to make a guess as to the identity of the gentleman in question." He scribbled in his notebook, and tore out the leaf before handing it to our guest.

She glanced at the paper and nodded. " Yes, it was he," she confirmed, handing the paper back to Holmes, who tossed it into the fire. " I ask you, Mr. Holmes, could you have resisted such an appeal ? "

" In my particular case," replied Holmes, with a wry smile, " I feel I am unlikely to be exposed to such temptation. But your point is well made, nonetheless."

" Do not think badly of me because of this," she went on. " He turned my head. Even though at my relatively advanced age I should be immune to flattery, he said to me such things as I have not heard said to me before." She ceased, seemingly sunk in reverie.

" But there is a problem ? " Holmes suggested, after a pause of a minute or so.

" Yes, there is. The Prin— I mean to say, the gentleman in question, is fond of gaming, particularly the game of whist, baccarat no longer being played by him since the scandal of a few years ago. He has been known to lose—and sometimes to win—several tens of thousands of pounds in one night."

"And no doubt on average he loses more than he wins ? " asked Holmes.

She confirmed this with a nod. "Now we come to the reason for my consulting you. His pockets, though deep, are not bottomless. You have heard of the Enfield Rope ? " she asked suddenly.

"Naturally," replied my friend. "A necklace of the finest South Sea pearls of incomparable lustre and colour, beautifully matched in size and all perfectly formed, which has been in the possession of your husband's family for nearly one hundred years. It is said to be priceless."

Lady Enfield gave a bitter smile. "Would it were priceless, or at any event, that no value could be set upon it ! " she exclaimed. "The gentleman under discussion, finding himself embarrassed following a particularly heavy loss at the tables, and knowing of the existence of the Enfield Rope, requested that I lend it to him. A request from that quarter is equivalent to a command from anyone else, and I had no choice but to comply."

"I assume he wished to use it as security for a loan ? " Holmes asked.

"That is so. He explained that it was to be returned to me as soon as his monthly allowance was paid to him on the 25th of the month. And indeed, on the 26th of last month, he returned... this." She reached into the bag she had brought with her and extracted a double rope of the finest pearls I have ever beheld.

"I fail to perceive the problem," Holmes frowned at her.

"The problem is," she replied firmly, extending the jewels to Holmes, "that this is not the Enfield Rope. These are fake, Mr. Holmes. As fake as a three-dollar bill." Her American origins showed themselves once more in her agitation.

Holmes took the necklace from her hand, and examined the pearls. Suddenly, he placed the jewels to his mouth and appeared to be biting them. "I agree," he replied after a few seconds, handing the necklace back to her. "These are some sort of counterfeit, composed of resin of some type, if I might hazard a guess. Have you made any conjectures as to the fate of the genuine pearls ? "

"I have my suspicions. My chief fear, though I personally think it unlikely, is that he has retained the original gems, and continues to use them as security for loans. That is, if he has not sold them outright, but I do not believe that to be the case."

"And you would wish me to... ? " Holmes leaned forward in his chair, and fixed our visitor with a steady gaze.

"Mr. Holmes, I cannot lie to you. Quite apart from the matter of these pearls, I feel that I have been badly used by him, though in my heart I still feel a good deal of affection for him. I confess that I had heard rumours before our friendship, but perhaps foolishly, I felt that they would not apply to me, and that I could introduce some stability, as we might put it, into his life."

"And that was not the case, obviously ? "

"No. He has taken up with at least two others since we parted less than two months ago, though I would like to believe that these are trifling affairs, and not on the same level as the friendship that exists between him and me. But even leaving this out of consideration, I have done a foolish thing as regards the pearls, and I do not know how I will ever face my husband should he ever discover the truth. As I told you, he is a kind and generous man, and has treated me well—perhaps better than I deserve. It would be repaying him poorly were he to suffer the loss of the pearls. The other may come to his ears, as it has come to the ears of many husbands who have also been betrayed in this way. That last is a matter between him and me alone, though."

" Where is your husband now ? "

" He is abroad in Baden-Baden, and returns in two weeks' time. Almost certainly he will want to see me wearing the Rope on social occasions, as it is one of the family treasures."

" Will he notice the substitution, do you think ? "

" Almost without question. He is knowledgeable in these matters, and observant with regard to them."

" Then you wish me to retrieve the pearls within that period ? " She nodded. " And, forgive the question, but there may be some expenses involved in their recovery. How do you propose to meet them ? "

For almost the first time since she had entered, I detected what appeared to be a look of relief on our visitor's face. " That, Mr. Holmes, is one of the least of my worries. I am independently wealthy, and can pay almost any amount within reason without my husband's being aware of the fact."

" Up to the full value of the necklace ? " enquired Holmes.

" Yes. It would be a strain on my resources, but it could be managed. I am confident that with your abilities, such an eventuality would not arise. I need hardly add that the fee for your services, in the event of your success, would be considerable."

" I understand," replied my friend. " Do you happen to know the value of the loan that he secured ? "

" I understood it from a mutual friend to be in the region of five thousand guineas. The pearls are worth many times more than that, of course."

" Of course," agreed Holmes, noting these details in his notebook. " There are several other matters on hand at the moment that exhibit a somewhat more interesting aspect— from the purely technical point of view, you understand," he added hastily, as our visitor appeared to be taking umbrage at his words. " However, your case, regardless of the eventual size of my fee, presents many fascinating aspects from the social side. You may rest assured that I will assign your case the highest priority, and hope to have an answer for you within a few days. I take it I may send you telegrams at your London address without their being read by the servants ? "

Lady Enfield nodded. " My thanks to you for your understanding," she murmured to Holmes as she left the room. " I look forward to hearing from you soon."

" Well, Watson," said Holmes to me, turning away from the window from which he had watched Lady Enfield hail a cab. " And what do you make of all this ? "

" The old adage ' Hell hath no fury like a woman scorn'd' would seem to apply in this case."

" I fancy you are right. But there is a good deal riding on this case, Watson, more than she told us. Possibly more than she is aware."

" How do you reach that conclusion ? "

" I watched her departure just now. Though she had told us that no-one in her household had been informed of her business with me, I noticed a suspicious figure, badly disguised as an idler, watching this house from the street opposite. His garments and attire were those of a working man, but his general posture and attitude were those of the upper classes. Always look at the man, Watson, not the clothes in which he is temporarily clad. As soon as Lady Enfield hired her cab, the rascal commandeered another which had been waiting, and set off after her."

" There is only one person who could have an interest in preventing the pearls' recovery," I ventured.

" I would disagree with that analysis," Holmes corrected me. " Whatever his other faults, I do not believe Lady Enfield's former paramour could sink to that level where he would deceive a lady in that fashion. The substitution of the genuine pearls is almost certainly not his work, but that of others, maybe even someone in his household or immediate entourage who became aware of the business."

" It is possible," I suggested, " that the counterfeits were introduced by the person from whom he obtained the loan while the pearls were being held as security ? "

" That strikes me as being more likely, in fact. But we must also consider the other—that the substitution was made by one of his retinue. The question now arises as to in how much personal danger we now find ourselves."

" My dear Holmes ! " I exclaimed. " Are you suggesting that there might be an attempt to silence you ? "

Holmes nodded gravely. " This is a matter of some delicacy, and the interests of the counterfeiters would in no way be served by my laying the facts of the matter before the public. I fear you would also be included in these plans, Watson. You may dismiss yourself as being of no importance to these people, but you have obtained a reputation—justly deserved, I may add—as my assistant. Mark you, the attempt to prevent my recovery of the pearls and the exposure of the substitution may not take the form of an assault, at least, not initially. Given what I know of this type of person, I am confident that I will be offered some sort of financial inducement to abandon my efforts."

" You astonish me," I cried. " Though I had heard rumours of wild goings-on at Marlborough House and other places, I had no idea that things had sunk so low with him."

" As I say, do not blame him, but blame those around him who hope to find some glory when the Widow of Windsor finally opens his path. Or, as you suggest, those who loaned the money may be the guilty parties. In either event, I would strongly recommend that you maintain a state of vigilance similar to that which you exercised when you served in the Hindu Kush."

As the reader may imagine, Holmes' words made a strong impression on me. I was forced to attend a patient residing at some distance from Baker-street, and I was beset by constant imaginings that the passers-by in the street were conspiring against me. I began to understand more completely the state of mind to which doctors of the nervous system have given the name " persecution mania", and my fears were increased by the knowledge that, should any blow be struck against Holmes or myself, strong pressure would be placed on the police to treat the incident as an accident, and to avoid further investigation.

Holmes noticed my agitation when I returned to Baker-street, but assured me that there would be no danger that evening. I did, however, place my Army revolver within easy reach before retiring, and slept fitfully.

⋆⟫◦⟪⋆

 HE next morning saw me awake early, but Holmes was up before me, eating his breakfast, when I emerged from my bedroom. He greeted me nonchalantly.

" It has come already," he informed me, pointing to an envelope lying on the table.

" What does it say ? " I asked.

" As I expected. I am offered two thousand guineas to inform Lady Enfield that my attempt to reacquire the pearls has been unsuccessful. A princely sum, is it not ? " He laughed, though without any real humour, at his own play on words. " However, the sender is discreet enough not to mention his name. I am to indicate my acceptance of the offer through the agony column of the *Times*."

" And you will not accept the offer, of course ? "

" Naturally I will refuse it," he replied. " Quite apart from any other considerations, my services are not to be bought and sold to the highest bidder. There is something particularly repulsive, Watson, about the kind of person by whom the principal in this affair is surrounded, if they stoop to these depths. By Jove, it is almost enough to make one sympathise with the Republican Radicals."

I knew Holmes' present words against the Monarchy to be no more than the expression of his feelings of the moment against those now seemingly ranged against us, but in some respects, I could not but agree with his sentiments.

" How will you word your refusal ? "

" I will not reply for at least a few days, if at all. That will buy us a little time in which to pursue our investigations. In addition, it may help to sow a little confusion in their ranks."

" After which time, you expect violent means to be used against you—against us, rather, I should say."

" You are afraid, Watson ? " There was no mockery in his tone, but a sincere concern. " My egoism should not lead you into this kind of position. You are, naturally, free to dissociate yourself from this business at any time."

" I confess that I am concerned. I would hardly be human were I not. But I have confidence in your abilities, as well as my own, to ensure our well-being, and that alone, if not our friendship, would be sufficient to keep me by your side."

He clapped me on the shoulder. " Capital, Watson ! Forgive my doubting you in this matter. Let us to work, then. To start, let us assume that Lady Enfield's former paramour raised the money himself, rather than deputing one of his friends to do so. I hardly consider that he would willingly allow his intimates to know that he was in possession of the jewels for such a purpose. Where, in your opinion, would he turn ? "

" I think we may dismiss the

possibility of his visiting a common pawnbroker's," I smiled. " It would be far more likely, to my mind, that he would seek the loan from one of his friends who owns some sort of bank or business than from one of his aristocratic friends, who, as you say, might be shocked by the idea of his action in borrowing the pearls. From the little I know of these levels of society, the nobility are typically more impoverished than the bankers and tradesmen in his circle. I would therefore suggest that these last are the most likely sources of his loan."

" I would concur with your conclusions. That group, I feel, should form the starting point for our enquiries. Let us examine the Society pages of the newspapers over the past few weeks, distasteful as the task may be, and make a list of those reported there as members of his circle who fall into the category we have delineated."

Seated opposite each other at the large table, Holmes and I combed through the journals of the previous weeks, adding names to a list on a sheet of paper that lay between us. The work was soon finished, and Holmes regarded the list with satisfaction.

" You and I, Watson, must make a few calls. However, it is not advisable that the gentleman who has been watching this house since this morning should be aware of our activities. We should make use of the rear door of the building. It is doubtful whether our friends will have sealed that exit. Let us call on those we have listed in the order of the alphabet, making our first visit to Mr. David Abrahams."

 BRAHAMS received us in the office of his private bank. His appearance was that of a polished and well-mannered gentleman, with little to betray his Levantine origins.

Holmes placed his query delicately, asking merely whether money had ever been advanced to the leader of the social circle.

" Indeed yes," replied Abrahams. " His tastes are somewhat extravagant, and he is most generous to his friends, especially his ' special friends' of the fair sex." He shrugged. " It must be said, though, that this generosity is often made through the good offices of other friends, myself included."

" And on what security do you make these loans ? " enquired my friend.

" I do not regard these as loans, but as investments," replied the banker. " Speaking in the assurance that this will go no further, I typically have no confidence that many of them will ever be repaid. I know of your reputation, Mr. Holmes, and I know that this will go no further." Holmes inclined his head. " As I say, these sums of money may go under the name of ' loans', but I doubt that I will ever see many of them again." He shrugged once more. " I am a wealthy man, and I can afford this. I therefore do not ask for any security regarding these transactions."

" But why do you do it ? " I burst out. Holmes smiled indulgently at me, but it was Abrahams who answered.

" First," he said, smiling, " one does not refuse a request from one in that position. Even if no benefit were to accrue to me from these matters, I would have no option but to comply. To be fair, he typically makes such requests only of those who can bear the burdens he places on them. Hardly ever have I heard of any other cases. But for me—I am not considered to be English, though I was born here and have lived in this country for my entire life. Even so, there are those who consider me to be some kind of dirty foreigner. Our friend, to his credit, takes little or no notice of such trifles. Through his friendship, which I believe to be genuine, I have gained entry into those parts of society that would otherwise remain closed to me. I may tell you, in confidence, that one day I expect to be Sir David Abrahams. No promises have been made, but heavy hints have been dropped. And through such acceptance, I am brought into contact with those circles where I may do business of a more profitable nature. Does that answer your question, Doctor ? "

" Thank you," I replied. " That is most interesting."

" You mentioned," Holmes said, " that requests of this type are made to a limited circle. Perhaps you could examine this list and confirm for us that those here are indeed recipients of such demands ? " He passed over the sheet on which he and I had worked earlier.

" My name is at the top, I see," remarked Abrahams with a smile.

" If you look, you will see that these are in alphabetical order."

" Ah, of course." He pored over the paper. " Not him," he said, pointing to a name on the list. " Nor him. Otherwise, I think that list is accurate. Congratulations, Mr. Holmes. Your reputation appears well-deserved. Wait, though. There is one name missing. You should add Mr. Oliver Blunt to your list."

" The Blunt of Blunt's Sauces ? " asked Holmes.

" The very man. He has made a small fortune from these condiments that are to be found on almost every table in the land, and he has recently made an entry into society, and been welcomed at Marlborough House on many occasions. However, he has made somewhat of an enemy of the Press—I am not sure of the details, but I believe a libel suit was involved. For that reason, his name often fails to appear in reports of social occasions."

" What manner of man is he ? " enquired Holmes.

" If it does not sound presumptuous, coming from my lips," replied Abrahams, " I would have to describe him as a parvenu. His manners are sometimes not of the standard expected by those around him, and he has what may be described as a forceful manner." He smiled ruefully. " He seems to believe that money in itself is the solution to most problems, and if such an approach fails, I regret to say that he has little hesitation in using violence to achieve his ends."

" Violence ? "   asked   Holmes. " Can you be more specific ? "

" I can give you an example. There was an occasion only last month when he and Sir Percy Bassett-Stringer disputed some relatively trivial matter—I believe it concerned some technicality to do with fox-hunting—a pastime that holds little interest for me. The argument became somewhat heated, and ended with Blunt stripping off his jacket and challenging Sir Percy to a bout of fisticuffs. This, mark you, in the middle of a supper-party given by one of London's most fashionable hostesses. Luckily, this all took place in the smoking-room, with no ladies present, but the affair ended without bloodshed, I am happy to say. It is perhaps fair for me to add that both of the principals had imbibed rather freely, but even so, it was a most regrettable incident."

" Most regrettable indeed," replied Holmes. " I am indebted to you for your candour."

" And I, for my part, am most impressed by your perspicacity in drawing up the list. Should I ever have occasion to require some sort of detective in my affairs, I will have no hesitation in retaining your services."

" I look forward to that time," replied Holmes courteously.

ND now," said Holmes, as we left Abrahams' offices, " we seek Mr. Oliver Blunt, I fancy."

" Where is he to be found ? " I asked.

" Like every good tradesman, I expect him to be seated behind his desk at his place of business. We will make our way to the manufactory of Blunt's Sauces, at least at first. We will require a train from Liverpool-street station. Should our quarry prove not to be in residence there, at least we can be informed as to his whereabouts."

We were soon seated in the train that took us to the small town in Essex in which the famous Blunt's Sauces were prepared and from which they were distributed around the country. I sniffed the air as we alighted from the train. " Somewhat familiar," I remarked, smiling, " and infinitely preferable to the odour of over-cooked kipper."

" I concur," agreed Holmes. " Come, let us follow our noses."

A few minutes' walk soon brought us to the gates of the manufactory, where we were asked our business. For answer, Holmes presented his card, which was accepted, and we were bidden to wait while the clerk conveyed our request to see Oliver Blunt.

After a few minutes he returned.

" Mr. Blunt will see you now. He tells me to inform you that he can give you ten minutes of his time."

" I expect more from him than that," Holmes said to me in an aside as we followed the clerk. " And I am not referring only to the time he can spare us."

We were ushered into the private office, a spacious apartment whose windows commanded a view of the works. Blunt himself was a short man, with a tendency, in my professional opinion, towards elevated blood pressure. His short ginger hair, extending into luxuriant side-whiskers, framed a round brick-red face from which small eyes peered suspiciously at us.

" Which of you is Holmes ? " he snapped at us. " I have little time to waste with persons of your rank, and I only admitted you out of curiosity."

" Dear me," exclaimed Holmes. " May I introduce my friend, the celebrated detective Sherlock Holmes," indicating me, " and I am John Watson. I sometimes have the honour of recording the exploits of Mr. Holmes in the press. Perhaps you have seen some of them ? "

" I have, and I confess that they provide me with some entertainment. Well, Holmes," turning to me, " what have you come to ask of me ? "

I was somewhat angry with

Holmes for putting me on the spot in this way, but once the cards had been dealt, there was no alternative but for me to play the hand. " Mr. Blunt," I began, " I understand you to be a member of a group frequenting Marlborough House."

" So ? " he answered. " I take it that is not to be held against me ? It is, after all, the residence of the foremost gentleman of the land."

" This particular gentleman, I understand, is occasionally financially embarrassed, and requires assistance in these matters from time to time."

" That is so. Make your point, if you would."

" Are you one of those who relieve that embarrassment ? "

" I am, and I am not ashamed to admit it."

I glanced at Holmes, but he appeared to be unconcerned with the conversation that was taking place, gazing about him almost abstractedly. I therefore felt I had no alternative but to proceed with the questioning. " When you carry out such transactions, is it customary for you to demand some sort of security ? "

Blunt looked at me angrily. " Well, and if I do, what business is it of yours, Mr. Holmes ? I am not a patient man, and I will terminate this interview forthwith if you do not soon come to the point."

" In that event, Mr. Blunt, I would be obliged if you would confirm that you made a loan some two months ago against the guarantee of a rope of valuable pearls ? "

" I did. What of it ? "

" And you returned those pearls on the repayment of the loan ? "

" Naturally. What do you take me for ? "

" And those pearls never left your possession during the term of the loan ? "

Up to now, Blunt's demeanour had been one of belligerent bluster. Now he appeared to lose much of his confidence. " I cannot honestly say that was the case," he replied.

" Pray continue."

" The sum requested was beyond my immediate abilities," he explained, now in a markedly more subdued tone. " I was forced to borrow a substantial portion of the total myself. Indeed, I found it expedient at that time to borrow the full amount, and was asked to provide my own security, which I provided in the form of the pearls that had been passed to me in that capacity. When the loan that I had extended was repaid, I was able to repay my own loan, and I received the pearls in return. I passed them straight back to— to the gentleman to whom I had extended the loan."

" For how much was the loan in total ? "

" I really do not see that this is any of your business."

" I insist on knowing," I told him, in as firm a tone as I could manage.

" Very well. The loan was for five thousand guineas," he replied, truculently.

" Did you examine the pearls before passing them back ? " I asked.

" No, I did not. They were still in the same sealed package in which I had loaned them."

" Were you aware that the pearls were not the property of the gentleman to whom you extended the loan ? "

" I had guessed it, but felt it impolitic to make enquiries. I can make a shrewd guess as to their origin." His smile accompanying these words was singularly unpleasant.

" But you examined the pearls

when they were returned following your repayment of the loan made to you ? "

" What is all this about ? " His choler seemed to have returned. " Will you not inform me why you are asking these questions ? "

" I am merely attempting to ascertain the time at which the false pearls were substituted for the real ones," I answered.

The change in Blunt's countenance was dramatic. From the deep ruddy complexion that had marked him when we first entered, his face had now changed to a ghastly pasty white colour. He seemed to gasp for breath audibly as he sank back into his chair and closed his eyes. At first I believed he had fainted, but it appeared to be simply a strong reaction to the news. " My God ! " he exclaimed at length, opening his eyes. " Do you mean to tell me that I returned false gems to— ? " He fanned his face with a large red hand. " Am I suspected of having made the substitution ? "

" At present, the enquiries are in a very preliminary stage, and I am unable to answer that question," I replied. " It would be in your interests, however, to inform me of the identity of the person who lent the money to you."

" It would not be in my interests at all, if you will permit me to correct you on that score, Mr. Holmes. The person from whom the money was borrowed has the power to squash you and me as we would crush a beetle, and would do so with as little thought. You must believe me in this." He was shaking as he spoke, as if in the grip of a fever. " That knowledge has placed me in an intolerable position. You as well, I fear, Mr. Holmes. I would beware the danger that awaits you, sir." He paused for a moment, and then spoke with a renewed vigour. " Be gone from here ! If you value your life, you should depart this place. The danger is not from me, understand that. Be gone ! Be gone ! " His voice rose in a crescendo at these last words, and I feared for his sanity as his eyes bulged in terror.

Holmes gently grasped my arm. " Come, Holmes, let us away," he remarked to me. We departed, leaving the shaken Blunt a mere shadow of the hectoring bully whom we had first encountered.

" ELL, Watson, and what do you make of that ? " asked Holmes, as we made our way back to the station.

" For my part, I consider that you played me a foul trick in making the exchange of roles in that way with no warning." I was angry with Holmes as a result of the position in which he had placed me, and the emotion showed itself in my voice.

" I apologise," replied my friend. " The notion came to me so rapidly that I had no time to explain it. I have my reasons."

" I shall be glad to hear them," I replied, somewhat coldly. The memory of having been thrust into the role of Sherlock Holmes without prior notice still rankled, and the subsequent exchange with Blunt and the man's arrogant manner had failed to improve my temper.

" I felt it would be advisable, given my original assumption that Blunt was the source of the danger that appears to be surrounding us, that he remained unaware of my identity. I confess, though, that you disappointed me."

" I can hardly be blamed for that," I retorted, stung by Holmes' words, and strode on briskly ahead of Homes, careless of whether he chose to follow or not.

" You misunderstand me completely," he answered. " Listen, and then judge. It was, I confess, my aim in presenting you as myself, to somewhat lessen the opinion that he might have of my abilities. The scheme failed miserably, due to your skill in questioning him, which followed exactly the lines I would myself have taken. When I said that you disappointed me, I should rather have said that I disappointed myself by underestimating your abilities."

I digested these words in silence for a minute or more as we continued our journey towards the station. " I do not know," I replied at length, " whether the implication that I would be incompetent in my impersonation of you is adequately compensated by the praise you have now bestowed on me."

" I apologise for my recent actions. They were unwarranted, and I must ask your forgiveness. You are naturally free to depart and to cease your association with me," Holmes remarked, " though I have to say that I would be lost without your support. I can assure you of that fact, and can also state with perfect sincerity that your presence and companionship would be sorely missed, should you decide that you no longer considered me as a friend."

Despite myself, I was touched by Holmes' speech. An apology of this sort from him was a relatively rare event, and I swallowed my pride and accepted him at his word. " There is no question of my deserting you,"

I declared. " I will accept your apology for this latest incident, on condition that you give me your word that you will never attempt such a thing again."

" I agree to that," Holmes replied, " though I fear that you and I are now in some increased danger. I now perceive that I was mistaken in my original assumption. The danger does not come from the source that I originally assumed, that is to say, Blunt, but from another quarter entirely."

" From where, then, if not his friends ? "

" From across the North Sea, and not from the Prince's friends, but from a relative. A nephew, to be precise."

" You mean the German Kaiser ? "

" None other. The rivalry between him and his uncle, the Prince, is well known. The enmity—there is no other word for it—he expresses in his yachting at Cowes every year—is but one facet of the jealousy he bears. Your conversation with Blunt just now served a purpose in addition to the one I just outlined. While you engaged him in conversation—and I say again that you carried out that role admirably—I was able to look around the room for clues that could aid us in connection with our quest."

" With what success ? "

" I first remarked some envelopes with German postage stamps. These appeared, from what I could make out, to be from business concerns. The science of industrial chemistry is somewhat more advanced in that country than this, and it is more than likely that Blunt does business with such enterprises in order to procure some of the ingredients that go to make up his famous sauces. That gave me the first inkling of the German connection. There was, however, much more."

" That being ? "

" When you informed Blunt of the substitution of the pearls, and he sank into his fit, I was able to glance at the photographs on his desk. Among them was one of the German Emperor, signed, with a personal dedication to Blunt. The socially ambitious Blunt obviously enjoys acquaintanceship with at least two of the royal families of Europe."

" Do you believe Blunt's reaction to the news of the substitution to be genuine ? "

" Perfectly genuine. Imagine the reaction of Marlborough House if it were to be discovered that Blunt had substituted counterfeits and returned them to the Prince. I almost begin to feel sorry for his predicament, ground between two powerful jaws, one on each side of the North Sea."

" For what purpose has this substitution been carried out by the Germans, do you feel ? " I asked.

" The humiliation of the heir to the British throne," replied Holmes. " If it were generally known that the Prince is in the habit of borrowing money secured by collateral that he later appropriates for his own use, the prestige of the British royalty in general, and that of the Prince in particular, would be sadly diminished. Whatever our personal feelings as to the morality of the Prince's actions, it is incumbent on us to prevent such a scandal."

" But who would believe such a story ? "

" Many would be happy to do so, and even if they were not completely convinced of its veracity, would be only too happy to lend an ear to the tale. There are many who do not wish him well. We must act quickly, Watson, as Blunt is now aware that we know of the substitution. If he imparts this knowledge to those who extended the loan to him, it will force the hand of the perpetrators. We must prevent this, if possible, and at all events, expose these people for what they are." He spoke resolutely, with his jaw set, and his eyes blazing. Despite myself, I found myself pitying the German Emperor who had dared to set his wits against the greatest detective of the age.

On the train back to London, Holmes was preoccupied with his own thoughts, and I did not dare disturb them as he sat curled in a corner of the compartment, his pipe gripped firmly between his teeth. On our arrival at Liverpool-street station, Holmes turned to me. " I think we will go and visit the estimable Mr. Abrahams once more," he said. " He seems to be well-informed about the doings of the Marlborough House set, and I have no doubt whatsoever as to his ability to keep these matters confidential."

On arrival at Abrahams' bank, we found the doors being shut and locked at the close of the day's business, but after a few words, Holmes persuaded the doorman that we wished to see Abrahams on a private matter, unconnected with the bank.

Abrahams himself welcomed us to his office with a wide smile. " I had not expected to see you gentlemen again so soon," he said. " I trust this does not mean that I am now a prime suspect."

" Far from it," replied Holmes. " I am afraid that we require your assistance once more, however."

" If you feel I can be of use, I am prepared to assist you," replied Abrahams. " I enjoy observing a master of his trade at his work, no matter what his trade may be."

"What I particularly wish to know on this occasion are the names of any members of the German legation who are regular members of the Marlborough House set."

Abrahams appeared lost in thought for a moment. "There were several—but there are none now— one of the Military Attachés, a Graf Grüning, used to visit. He was particularly friendly with Blunt, but there was some unpleasantness regarding an allegation he made about Lord Abernethy a week or so back. Though nothing was said directly to him, the word was discreetly passed to him that he would no longer be welcome, at least for a short while."

"You would not happen to know if he is still at the Embassy?" asked Holmes.

"I have certain knowledge that he was there just over a month ago. I had occasion to lend some money to him a few weeks before, and he repaid me then when I visited him at the Embassy. I imagine that he would still be at his post there."

"The amount of the loan?" demanded Holmes, leaning forward urgently.

"It was quite large. Over five thousand pounds," replied Abrahams. "Indeed, it was exactly five thousand guineas."

"And what security did you demand?"

"In his case, none," replied Abrahams. "He is well aware of my acquaintances in high places in the British government and in society—in some cases, I may even be privileged to call them friends—who would be prepared to expose him at the highest level should he fail to repay the loan. It would, as you can imagine, be the cause of a relatively major diplomatic incident were he to default."

"Did you ask the purpose of the loan?"

Abrahams shook his head. "That is not my way, Mr. Holmes. My clients, like yours, no doubt, are entitled to their secrets."

"Even so, that is most helpful, Mr. Abrahams. I think, Watson," turning to me, "we have an excellent view of events now, do we not?"

"I confess I am still somewhat in the dark as to the precise details," I admitted, "but I am certain that you have uncovered the general scheme of things."

"Let us away. Again, my sincere thanks to you, Mr. Abrahams, and I sincerely look forward to our next meeting."

We walked along the street, Holmes singing softly to himself, a habit which I had not heretofore noticed. I listened carefully, and realised that he was singing the verse of our National Anthem containing the words, "Confound their politics, Frustrate their knavish tricks", and smiled to myself.

⁕⁝◎⊜⁝⁕

N reaching Baker-street, Holmes plunged into activity, surrounding himself with directories and other books, together with the scrapbook in which he maintained records of all that attracted his interest and attention.

"Watson," he commanded me, imperious as any general commanding an army, "You will go to Lady Enfield's house, and ask her for the loan of the counterfeit pearls she showed us the other day. For myself, I must consider a course of action that will not only restore the pearls to her, but will also restore honour to those to whom it is due, even if in some cases they are not wholly deserving of it. May I suggest that you take with you the Gladstone bag equipped with the strong lock. The riding-crop may also prove a useful item, I suggest." The riding-crop to which Holmes alluded had a handle filled with lead, and had the potential to act as a potent life-preserver when reversed. The idea that I might require its use filled me with a sense of anxiety, amounting almost to fear, when I realised the pass to which matters had now come.

I left Baker-street on my errand, and had almost reached the Park, when I felt a heavy hand on my shoulder.

"Mr. Sherlock Holmes," a rough voice with a distinctly foreign accent came from behind me. "It is the opinion of those who are over you that your meddling must cease." At this, my right arm was seized above the elbow, and I was held from behind in a grip from which, try as I would, it seemed impossible for me to break free.

"You will come with me," said my as yet still unseen assailant. A four-wheeler drew up beside us, and I was propelled inside. My attacker followed me into the carriage, and I saw him for the first time. A large brute of a man, strongly built, with close-cropped hair and a bristling moustache, he held himself like a Guardsman, sitting bolt upright while maintaining his painful grip on my arm. I guessed him, from what little I knew of the breed, to be a Prussian Junker.

As we moved off, I became aware of another man in the carriage. Dressed in a somewhat opulent fashion, with an astrakhan coat, and a gaudy silk scarf at his throat,

his somewhat soft and feminine face was framed by a light wispy beard.

"May I trouble you, Mr. Holmes, to open that bag?" he asked me in a soft voice, almost without a trace of an accent.

"With pleasure," I replied, forcing a smile. As he peered into the empty bag, I observed a look of anger flash across his face. "Where are you going now?" he demanded of me in a furious tone.

"That is my business," I replied. "I do not see how this could possibly concern you." While I was talking, my left arm was seeking the riding-crop in my coat pocket, and as I finished speaking, I withdrew it, and used it to slash my captor across the face. He gave a loud cry, and clapped his hands to his cheek, seemingly overcome by the stinging pain. Reversing the weapon, I brought the heavy lead-weighted handle down on the hand of the other man, still gripping my right arm, as hard as I could manage. He howled with pain, and immediately withdrew his grasp, nursing the stricken hand with the other. I struck again, this time at his head, and he slumped away from me, stunned.

I seized the bag, opened the door of the carriage, and though the carriage was still moving, tumbled out into the roadway. By great good fortune, I immediately recognised the place where I had fallen as being close to Lady Enfield's residence, and I raced towards the house, attracting no little attention from the bystanders as I ran.

I was admitted immediately, much to my relief, and I explained my errand to Lady Enfield without, however, acquainting her of my recent adventure.

"Do you think that Sherlock Holmes will recover the genuine

pearls ? " she asked me as she handed the counterfeits to me and I placed them in the bag.

" I have every confidence that he will do so," I replied. " I can tell you now that we are already following the trail. I will say no more at present, but I am sure that all will be revealed by him in the fullness of time. May I ask you for a favour, though, Lady Enfield ? "

She smiled winningly and nodded her assent.

" I wish to leave the house unremarked," I continued. " There are those who are following me, and whom I have no wish to meet. Would it be possible for me to be loaned a footman's livery, and make my way from your house through the servants' entrance ? I will send later for my present garments to be carried to Baker-street."

" What a strange man you are, Doctor, I must say," she replied, smiling, and looking me up and down. " Yes, I think there will be a suit of livery that will fit you, if that is what you wish." She rang a bell and gave instructions to the maid.

About fifteen minutes later, dressed in the Enfield livery, I left the house by the tradesmen's entrance. I noticed my erstwhile captors waiting near the front door, the one nursing an arm in an impromptu sling, seemingly constructed from a handkerchief, and the other's face decorated by a livid welt stretching from one ear to his nose. Though both noticed me, neither paid recognised me or paid me any attention as I strolled along the street in my character as a servant.

On my return to Baker-street, Holmes seemed astounded at my appearance.

" What in the world has been happening, Watson ? Have you the

pearls ? And why are you in a servant's livery ? "

I explained the events of my journey to him, and his face clouded. " My apologies once again, Watson, for having placed you in this position. However, the fact that they mistook you for me points clearly to one thing."

" That being ? " I replied.

" That Blunt is in communication with the Germans, and has informed them of my interest, and has described the appearance of the man he believes to be Sherlock Holmes. There is no other way that you could be mistaken for me, and addressed by my name in that fashion. I do not know the identity of the larger of the men, but I am certain from your description that the other is Graf Grüning, whose photograph has appeared with relative frequency in the illustrated papers. Von Grüning arrived here about three months ago from Berlin, where he was apparently one of those close to the Kaiser."

" So you believe Blunt is involved in this ? "

Holmes shook his head. " I believe that he has acted as the dupe of the Kaiser, but little more than that. However, following our visit to him, he has doubtless informed the Germans of the interest we are showing in the affair. Unhappily for you, he was mistaken in his identification, but it has at least tipped his hand and let us know where we stand. And now," opening the bag and withdrawing the rope of pearls, " we have these little beauties."

" What do you propose doing with them ? " I asked.

Holmes replied, his eyes twinkling, " I have plans for them, Watson, never fear. Your account of the assault on you earlier makes the anticipation of my solution all the more pleasurable. And now, I am sure you wish to divest yourself of the servant's garb in which you currently find yourself. My congratulations to you on your ingenuity, by the way. It is obvious that you are developing a certain facility in these matters of subterfuge. And I, too, wish to exchange my raiment."

We departed the sitting-room for our respective bedrooms, and when I returned, clad in attire that was more suited to my temperament and station, I beheld Sherlock Holmes, whom I did not at first recognise, dressed as he was in a frock coat and accompanying garments of a distinctly un-English appearance. On my asking him the meaning of this disguise, he replied in a distinctly American tone of voice, " You see before you Tobias K. Mellinthorpe, a citizen of the fair city of Cincinnati, in the state of Ohio."

" That is as may be," I replied. " And what is Mr. Mellinthorpe's role in this comedy to be ? "

" Why, he is a collector," replied Holmes in his usual tones. " He collects pearls and other valuable items. While you were out obtaining the counterfeits from Lady Enfield, I caused enquiries to be made in certain circles. The word is out that there is a rope of fine pearls to be disposed of—discreetly, you understand. This is not an item that is to appear on the open market, and the clientele for this is a small and select one, if not altogether illustrious."

" They are already selling the pearls ? " I asked. " For what purpose ? "

" They can hardly expect to retain them," he answered. " They are too distinctive to permit of that. In any event, the cash would be welcome. However, they have made a mistake in offering the pearls for sale in this country, even through the third party they are employing for the purpose. Our criminals would never dream of purchasing something so distinctive. Had they moved the pearls to the Continent, I have no doubt that some enterprising receiver would have taken them off the Germans' hands in one country, and offered them for sale in another. I therefore propose to make an offer for them in my new character as Tobias Mellinthorpe."

" But do you have the cash to purchase them ? "

" I have no intention of purchasing them," he replied enigmatically, as he made his way to the door, and taking up the bag containing the counterfeit jewellery. " I will be two or three hours away. Do not admit anyone," he warned me. " I will give the same instruction to Mrs. Hudson."

 OLMES returned in high good humour within the appointed time. " Tobias Mellinthorpe is no more," he declared, stripping off the white wig he had been wearing, flinging it onto the hat-stand, and depositing the bag on the table. " He has served his purpose. And now to the next stage of the plan.

Let us together to Mr. Abrahams once more. I do not think your assailants will dare attack the two of us." As it transpired, there was no sign of the Germans as we left Baker-street, and though both Holmes and I were on the alert, we did not see them during the whole of the journey.

Abrahams received us with his

usual courtesy and warmth. " Dear me, Mr. Holmes, you seem to be becoming quite a fixture here," he joked. " Maybe I can offer you permanent employment ? "

" Hardly that," replied Holmes. " However, I come to beg a great favour of you—one which would undoubtedly raise you considerably in the eyes of the society in which you move."

Holmes had baited his hook skilfully.

" What can I do ? " asked Abrahams. His tone was casual, but his eyes betrayed his interest.

" I wish you to give a soirée or some similar social event tomorrow evening," replied Holmes. " It is essential that at least the Prince, Lady Enfield, Mr. Oliver Blunt, and Graf Grüning attend, but the more the merrier, as the saying goes. The exact time and place I leave to your discretion, and the nature of the event likewise, but it is essential that those I have mentioned are together in as public a place as possible as soon as is convenient."

Abrahams spread his hands in a gesture of helplessness. " Do you consider me a magician ? " he asked, rolling his eyes.

" I consider you to be an extremely capable man," replied Holmes. " If I did not do so, I would not be wasting my time talking with you. Of course, I forgot to mention that any expenses you incur will be recompensed."

" It is not the money," protested Abrahams. " As I told you on another occasion, I am a rich man by most standards, and the expenses would not affect my well-being. What concerns me is the time needed to write the invitations and to make all the arrangements to ensure all those you mention will attend. But," meeting Holmes' steady gaze,

" I am sure it will be possible. I take it you and Dr. Watson will be present ? "

" Naturally, but we may decide to arrive a little earlier than the other guests. Please be sure to let us know when and where the event will take place and we will make our plans accordingly."

" Very good. Note that I do not ask the motives for your request, Mr. Holmes. I am sure that you have your reasons."

" I do indeed, Mr. Abrahams. Once again I am grateful to you for your cooperation."

" A capital man, that Mr. Abrahams," he said to me as we left the bank. " Would there were more like him."

" Where to now ? " I asked, as he hailed a hansom.

" Lady Enfield's residence," he answered, giving the directions to the cabbie.

Lady Enfield met us in the drawing-room, and offered us tea, which was brought to us by a maid.

" Your clothes, Doctor Watson, are waiting to be sent to you. I trust there is no hurry there ? "

" None at all," I assured her. " I will return the livery when my garments are sent to Baker-street."

" And what brings you here ? " asked Lady Enfield to Holmes. " Have you retrieved the pearls ? "

" I have come to return these to you," replied Holmes, opening the bag in which I had previously carried the counterfeit jewels and which Holmes, in his character of Mellinthorpe, had also transported them. " You may rest assured, though, that whatever harm your friend may have caused you, he is not the cause of the substitution of the pearls."

Lady Enfield sighed. " I suppose it was too much to hope for that you could retrieve them and discover the perpetrator of the fraud. I am merely thankful that my trust in my friend was not misplaced, at any event," she said to Holmes. " I thank you for your efforts, all the same, and I am grateful. You will send me the bill for your trouble soon, I expect."

" I certainly will not be sending you any account until after tomorrow evening. After then, I may do so, or I may not, depending on the results of a little experiment I am carrying out. May I make a request ? "

" Naturally, but I cannot promise I will grant it. What do you wish ? "

" Mr. David Abrahams will be giving a party of some kind tomorrow night to which you, as well as the Prince—" I observed Lady Enfield give a delicate shudder at the title, but Holmes continued, " as well as Helmut von Grüning and Oliver Blunt are invited. You should wear the pearls I have just given to you. No, I beg you," he pressed, as she opened her mouth to protest.

" You have hardly named a group in whose company I could feel less comfortable," she protested. " I hope that you have an excellent reason for this ? "

" I do, and I think that when the reason is unveiled, you will approve it," answered Holmes. " In any case, I am sure that Abrahams will invite others, more to your taste. If you would care to list a few names, I am sure that he will abide by your suggestions."

HE next morning's post brought an invitation for Holmes and myself to attend a gathering that was to be held that evening at Dorchester House, the London residence of Sir George Holford. I remarked on the venue to Holmes.

" Sir George does not use the house a great deal for entertaining," he answered me, " and as an intimate of the Royal Family in his role as Equerry, he is almost certainly acquainted with Abrahams and is happy to lend his residence for the purpose. Abrahams is obviously a man of considerable resource, Watson, and not a man to be underestimated."

" At what hour is the entertainment to start ? "

" It is given as half-past nine for ten. I think that we may well wish to be there well before the start of the entertainment."

Arrayed in formal evening wear, we made our way to Dorchester House a little before the time stated.

" I am lucky to have such friends," answered Abrahams, when I made some remark about the house. " I help them at times, and they help me with such matters in return. That's what friends are for, eh ? "

" I am sincerely grateful," Holmes told him, " for your hard work in arranging all of this. How many people will be appearing ? "

" I have invited some forty guests, of whom I expect most to be present. I have had to invite several more members of the German Embassy staff in order to soothe their ruffled feelings, since Graf Grüning was invited, but they were not. Lady Enfield also sent me a list of some friends with whom she told me that she would feel more at ease."

" Admirable," replied Holmes.

" Believe me, you have done a great service."

As we were speaking, the footman announced the arrival of the party from the German Embassy. I recognised the occupant of the carriage on the previous day, his face still bearing the red mark I had inflicted with the riding-crop. The others I did not know, but Holmes pointed out to me the German Ambassador and the Political Attaché. " It is good that they have arrived," said Holmes. " I anticipate some amusement later in the evening."

I noticed von Grüning looking in our direction. Eventually he started to make his way, seemingly reluctantly, in our direction.

" I was not aware, Mr. Holmes, that you were an intimate of these circles," he addressed me, clicking his heels and bowing.

It was Sherlock Holmes who replied. " I fear you are addressing the wrong person," he smiled. " I am Sherlock Holmes. May I present my friend and colleague, Dr. John Watson."

The look on von Grüning's face was instant and dramatic. " I believed that you were Watson," he stammered to Holmes. " My apologies for the mistake." He bowed once more.

" Perhaps you were misinformed," Holmes offered, not without a touch of malice to his words.

" Maybe so," agreed von Grüning, and turned his back on us, making his way over to Oliver Blunt, who was conversing with another group in the opposite corner of the room. Holmes and I observed with some amusement as the German detached Blunt from his friends, and was obviously remonstrating with him in a low but urgent tone, gesticulating at Holmes and myself from time to time.

All conversation suddenly ceased as the Prince of Wales entered the room. It was the first time I had been in close proximity to him, and I was struck by his carriage and the air of dignity with which he bore himself. To my surprise, Abrahams, in his capacity as host, guided him first to Holmes and myself, introducing us to the Prince.

" Ha ! So you are the celebrated Sherlock Holmes of whom I have read so much ? " he greeted my friend. " I take it you are not on duty, as it were, tonight ? "

" As it happens, your Royal Highness," replied Holmes, " I am very much on duty. I hope that I will be able to provide some entertainment for you and at least some of the guests here tonight as a result of my work."

" Excellent, excellent," replied the Prince vaguely, smiling through his beard. " And this is Dr. Watson, I take it ? " turning to me. " Ready as ever to record the exploits of your friend, what ? Enjoyed your pieces in the *Strand* magazine."

I bowed and mumbled some inanity, and the Prince moved on.

" That has annoyed the Germans," remarked Holmes, amused. " Abrahams committed a grave breach of etiquette by introducing us before the Ambassador, but the worst is yet to come for them."

The evening proceeded, with the guests moving freely between the reception rooms of the great house, and after supper, the party split into tables for whist. Holmes drew the Prince as a partner, and found himself playing against Lady Enfield and Graf Grüning.

For my part, I found myself partnering an amiable Countess, and playing against our host, who was partnered by a senior member of the Foreign Office. I am a wretched whist player at the best of times, but luck was on our side that evening, and we were able to hold our own against the superior play of our opponents.

As we played, one of the sudden hushes fell which sometimes overtake such gatherings. In the silence, von Grüning's voice could be heard at the table next to ours, asking Lady Enfield why she was wearing false pearls instead of the genuine gems of the Enfield Rope.

If anything, the silence became more intense, as every face turned to the Prince's table.

" I do not know what you mean," stammered Lady Enfield, obviously uncomfortably aware of the eyes of the whole room upon her. " These are genuine pearls. How can you make such an accusation ? "

" I happen to know that you are wearing counterfeit pearls," replied von Grüning, standing up. " If you will have the goodness to remove your necklace, and pass it to me, I can easily verify this."

" Are you mad ? " barked the Prince, obviously embarrassed at this breach of manners. " Sit down, Herr Grüning."

Von Grüning flushed, obviously feeling the insult occasioned by the Prince's omission of his title and the 'von' of his name. " With all due respect, Sir, I wish to prove the truth of my words."

The Prince flushed a deep red, but grunted his assent, and Lady Enfield unclasped the necklace, and handed it to von Grüning.

" Now, you see," he sneered triumphantly, rubbing the pearls against his teeth. For the second time that evening, his face changed. " But this pearl appears to be genuine ! " he exclaimed. He repeated the process with a pearl at the other

end of the rope, and his expression became even more stricken.

" Perhaps a loupe would be of assistance ? " offered Holmes, smilingly drawing a lens from his pocket and offering it to the German, who snatched at it.

Von Grüning held the necklace closer to the gasolier above, and peered through the lens at the pearls. " This is the Enfield Rope ! " he cried. " This is the genuine article ! "

" And pray, what did you expect it to be ? " The Prince's tone was icy.

" I think, Sir, he expected this," replied Holmes, withdrawing what appeared to be the twin of the necklace from the tail pocket of his coat.

At the sight of the other gems, von Grüning dropped the necklace and loupe and stood as if stupefied, unmoving and open-mouthed. Holmes moved swiftly to retrieve the fallen articles, and handed the necklace back to Lady Enfield, who replaced it around her neck.

The Prince stood, and confronted the German Ambassador, who shamefacedly rose to his feet and stood, head bowed. " Your Excellency," said the Prince, in a voice that was no less chilling for being soft. " One of your staff has offered an unthinkable insult to one of my friends by doubting her word and her honesty. I demand that he apologise forthwith for this intolerable breach of manners."

Following a barked command from the Ambassador, the wretched von Grüning stammered out some sort of apology to Lady Enfield and to the company at large.

" Furthermore," the Prince continued, " I fail to see why this man should remain as a member of the German Legation. I expect confirmation that he has left for Berlin by midday tomorrow at the very latest. Do I make myself understood ? "

The Ambassador bowed. " Perfectly clear, your Royal Highness. May I have your leave for myself and my staff to withdraw from this gathering ? "

" I would be delighted, as I think all in this room would be, if you were to do so forthwith," replied the Prince coldly. There was a stir as the Germans departed, bowing deeply as they did so. I noticed Blunt, whose face had turned a deathly white, and who appeared stricken at this turn of events.

" I think, Mr. Holmes, you owe us an explanation," said the Prince to my friend, lighting a cigar.

" With your permission, Sir, I would prefer to give this explanation in private to you, Lady Enfield, and our host Mr. Abrahams alone. The story is not one that should be noised abroad too widely. Maybe we can meet at Marlborough House tomorrow ? "

" So be it," answered the Prince. " Tomorrow at ten. I shall expect you and Doctor Watson together with Lady Enfield and Abrahams."

The evening progressed, and though I was eaten up with curiosity, as I believe were all the other guests, Holmes preserved a discreet silence.

As we made our way to Baker-street, I ventured to ask him for some more details of what had transpired, but he replied with a smile that I was not to put myself before princes in this regard.

E were admitted to Marlborough House the next morning, and shown to a comfortable room, luxuriously furnished, in which the Prince was already seated, smoking one of his inevitable cigars.

" I have been racking my brains," he said to Holmes, " and I have no idea what has been going on. I confess I am as anxious as a schoolboy to know the truth of this story. Abrahams and Lady Enfield should be with us soon." Even as he spoke, the two in question were admitted to the room. At a word from the Prince, they took their seats in chairs between him and myself, facing Holmes, who stood to address us.

" First, your Royal Highness, I must confess that I am in possession of the facts regarding the loan of the Enfield Rope to you by Lady Enfield as security for a loan. I would request that you do not ask me how I came to know this, as I regard my source here as being privileged." The Prince nodded in agreement, though I fancied I could perceive some reluctance in his acquiescence. " The loan was made to you, Sir, was it not, by Mr. Oliver Blunt ? " Without waiting for an answer, he continued, " As it transpired, Blunt was not in possession of the sum you demanded—"

" I would prefer that you use the word 'requested' with reference to that business," interrupted the Heir coldly. " I do not issue demands, I make requests."

" Your pardon, Sir," replied Holmes. " The sum requested, as I say, was not immediately forthcoming, and Blunt was forced to borrow the money himself from Graf Grüning, handing over the pearls as security. We have Mr. Abrahams to thank for his assistance in determining this."

" Good Lord ! " exclaimed the

Prince. " I would never have placed the man Blunt in such a deuced awkward position had I known that he would have had to borrow the money himself. Go on, Mr. Holmes."

" Your Highness may not be aware of the fact that Blunt has strong commercial links with Germany, and appears, from a photograph on his desk, to have personal ties to your nephew, Kaiser Wilhelm." The Prince snorted at this news. " The irony is that von Grüning himself could not raise the capital, and was forced to borrow the money from Mr. Abrahams here."

Abrahams looked stunned at this news. " I had no knowledge of the purpose or the destination of the loan," he explained to the Prince. " I knew von Grüning to be a gambler, and I assumed that the loan was for that purpose."

" I hardly feel that any blame can attach to you," said Holmes. " You made the loan in good faith, without questions and without security, as you explained to me earlier. May I add, Sir," turning back to the Prince, " that without Mr. Abraham's help, the pearls in question would in all probability be making their way to Berlin."

" So far, you have explained how the pearls came to be in the possession of von Grüning, but you have yet to provide a reason for their substitution by counterfeits," complained the Prince.

" That, Sir, was to be my next point. I am sorry to say that you were the target of a plot to destroy your reputation. The idea, hatched in Potsdam by your nephew, was that Lady Enfield's pearls would be substituted and subsequently revealed as counterfeit in a public event, and in the ensuing explanation, the whole business of the loan and your borrowing the pearls would be made public."

" How can you be sure that the plot came from Potsdam, and was not the initiative of von Grüning ? "

" I took the trouble to look into his past. He was an intimate of your nephew, Sir, and was undoubtedly sent here specifically to cause trouble and to embarrass you."

The Prince shook his head. " Little Willy," he muttered to himself. " One of these days you will do an unbelievable *Dummheit*, and the whole of Europe will suffer." He looked at Holmes. " Continue."

" It is obvious that the pearls had been studied previously in order to make a counterfeit." Holmes looked at Lady Enfield, who spoke in a soft voice.

" In the past, the Enfield Rope has been on public display on loan to the Museum. It is well described, and the descriptions could, I imagine, be easily obtained by anyone who wished to discover more about the pearls."

" I assume that the counterfeit was created some time ago in Germany, awaiting a time when it could be used, being brought over to this country by von Grüning," added my friend.

" And what in the world would they expect to do with the real pearls ? " asked the Prince. " Surely not even my nephew would contemplate destroying such a perfect example of the jeweller's art ? "

" They attempted to sell them through illicit channels," replied Holmes. " Naturally, our English criminals have more sense than to purchase something so distinctive. My guess is that the Germans would have attempted to transfer them to the Continent and dispose of them there."

" But Mr. Holmes," interrupted

Lady Enfield. " There is one piece of the puzzle missing—the most important piece. How did I come to be wearing the real pearls yesterday evening, and how were you in possession of the fakes ? "

" Come to that," added the Prince, " I am at a loss to understand why the real pearls had not already left the country."

" Let me explain," smiled Holmes. " Yesterday I visited the dealer acting for the Germans. He is a past master at disposing of stolen property, and he is, in the circles he frequents, a famous man in his trade. I visited him in the character of an American collector, and after examining the pearls, I promised to call back later with the cash to purchase them. While his attention was distracted during our converse, I managed to exchange the pearls for the substitutes, thereby gaining possession of the real thing."

" Excellent," chuckled the Prince. " So the receiver of stolen goods was left with the counterfeits ? "

" He was not even left with those by the time I had finished with him," smiled Holmes. " I left him, carrying the real pearls, and deposited them, in a locked bag, at the Left Luggage office at Waterloo station. I then returned to our friend, still in the character of the American collector, and requested another examination of the pearls, which I duly pronounced to be counterfeit. He was forced to agree with my appraisal, and thereupon began to utter comprehensive curses at the German nation in general and von Grüning in particular. His belief was that he had previously been shown and evaluated the genuine pearls, which had been exchanged for the counterfeits by the Germans after the deal had been struck."

" And then ? " asked the Prince, sitting forward in his chair.

" Given his reputation and the risks that he ran of arrest and imprisonment, it was a reasonably easy matter to persuade him that it would be in his best interests to make over the counterfeits to me, and to inform the Germans that the sale to Tobias K. Mellinthorpe was progressing smoothly. I now had both sets of pearls in my possession. The real ones I gave to Lady Enfield, and I hope your Ladyship will forgive my little deception in letting you believe I had not recovered the pearls."

" My dear man," laughed Lady Enfield. " I was not deceived for a minute. As soon as you had left me, I examined the pearls, and discovered you had returned the originals. I knew that there would be some good reason for your not having mentioned this to me, so I decided to play along with your game, whatever it might turn out to be."

Sherlock Holmes appeared a little nonplussed by this revelation, but continued. " My little comedy was to be played out with the help of Mr. Abrahams here, who exerted himself mightily to set the stage. I confess that I arranged the cards last night so that I was to partner you, Sir, and we were to play against Lady Enfield and von Grüning."

" You... you..." spluttered the Prince.

" Never fear, Sir. In our game of whist, I played as honestly as any man, and did not use whatever skills of sleight of hand I might possess."

" Still..." The Prince subsided somewhat.

" It was a relatively easy matter to provoke von Grüning into making his accusation. You may recall some of my remarks, Sir, that led up to his declaration."

"Now I see," replied the Prince. "I had at first marked it down as deliberate rudeness, but I now perceive your objective. Congratulations, Mr. Holmes. The look on von Grüning's face when you revealed the duplicates was priceless."

"The credit goes to Mr. Abrahams and also to Watson here, who was actually attacked by von Grüning a couple of days back, in the belief that he was myself."

"The swine!" exclaimed the Prince. "Believe me, Willy will know about this, and he will be most unwelcome at Cowes this year. I trust, Doctor, that there are no adverse results as a result of your ill-treatment?"

"None, Sir," I replied.

He nodded. "Mr. Holmes, you have my gratitude. Tell me, what can I do to show my appreciation for your work?"

"I incurred some trifling expenses in connection with the case," replied Holmes. "Other than that, the solution was its own reward."

"Send your account to my secretary," replied the Prince. "And, my friend," he said to Abrahams, "some sort of future honour has been mentioned in the past, has it not? I think we may be able to advance the date of this. Perhaps at

the New Year? And as for you, Lily," turning to Lady Enfield, "as you know, I find it difficult to apologise, but—" There was real tenderness in his tone.

"Bertie, there is nothing to forgive," replied Lady Enfield, gazing at the Prince with frank adoration.

"My dear, there is a good deal I must say to you—" began the Prince, seemingly oblivious of our continued presence.

"We have your Highness's leave to withdraw?" asked Holmes, signalling to Abrahams and myself to rise.

"Oh, to be sure," replied the Prince, vaguely, his eyes still locked on those of Lady Enfield.

The three of us quietly made our way from the room, leaving the two alone together.

"I admire your exquisite sense of tact," remarked Abrahams to Holmes as we left Marlborough House.

"I see no reason," replied he, "why a Prince, no matter what his faults, should be denied the same privileges as those enjoyed by the poorest of our citizens. I refer to the right to be left alone with one whom he loves and who loves him. Come," he said to Abrahams and me, "it may be early in the day, but I think some small celebration is called for. Do you drink champagne, Mr. Abrahams?"

Sherlock Holmes & The Strange Case of James Phillimore

"*Canetons à la mode russe*, that is to say, young ducks in the Russian manner, roasted, and served in a nest of *pommes duchesse*, with a special sauce containing a preponderance of beetroot, the whole garnished with red and black caviar." (page 270)

Editor's Note

The reason why this case was never laid before the public in Watson's or Holmes' lifetime is probably the unfavourable light it sheds on Holmes' relations with the official police. From his dealings with Inspector Lanner as described here, it is obvious that the links between Holmes and the Metropolitan Police could be tenuous at best, and stormy at worst. Almost certainly, Watson would not want this animosity with the authorities to sully the reputation of his friend.

The case itself is referenced by Watson in Thor Bridge *as that of "Mr. James Phillimore, who, stepping back into his own house to get his umbrella, was never more seen in this world". Curiously, he describes this as an "unfinished tale" and implies that Holmes never solved the mystery. It is hard to understand why he should have done this—Watson's categorisation of the case in this way is a mystery in its own right, worthy of the attention of Holmes himself. There is no scandal to be hidden, no person of importance to be shielded, and no obvious reason at all why it should be ignored in this way.*

The only explanation I can offer here is that Watson was so overcome by the horror of the charnel-house scene he briefly describes here that, following the catharsis of writing this report (which was scribbled hurriedly, with almost no corrections or crossings-out, though the final section appears to have been added later), he expunged the details from his memory, remembering only the most superficial facts of the case.

HE case I describe here started almost as a comedy, which swiftly transformed itself into a tragedy, ultimately involving the loss of three lives, while presenting Holmes and myself with a scene of the utmost horror, the likes of which I hope never to encounter again.

A little time after the events I have previously described under the title of *A Study in Scarlet*, Holmes and I were seated in our rooms in Baker-street. I was perusing the pages of a popular novel, and Holmes was examining the agony columns of the day's newspapers.

" It is a dull day for me," he complained, " when even the agony columns refuse to provide entertainment. You may find it hard to believe, Watson, but there are days when I regret having taken up this profession, and long for the sedate life of a Norwich solicitor, which I believe is one my late father would have wished for me."

" Your talents would be wasted in such a backwater," I remonstrated. " You have proved, at least to my satisfaction, that your powers of reasoning are unique, and you are putting them at the service of society by choosing your present occupation."

There was a knock at the door, and Mrs. Hudson, our landlady, entered.

" Excuse me, sir," she said to

Holmes, " but there's a foreign gentleman downstairs who says he needs to see you now."

" Send him up, Mrs. Hudson. Well, Watson, maybe this day will present some sort of novelty, after all."

The door opened again, and we beheld a striking figure. Tall and sturdily built, his most distinctive feature was a large white moustache that reminded me irresistibly of a bicycle's handlebars, sweeping in graceful curves nearly to his ears. The nose above was large and deeply veined, probably signifying a liking for the bottle, and the eyes were lively and humorous. The hair, once he removed his somewhat battered and shabby bowler, was sparse, and what remained was the same colour as the moustache.

" Will you take a seat ? " invited Holmes. " You are... ? "

" My name is François Lefevre," replied the other, in a marked French accent. " You, I take it, are Monsieur Holmes, and this must be the good Doctor Watson. *Enchanté.*" He bowed slightly from the waist as he sat down.

" You have a problem ? " enquired my friend.

" But yes. Of a surety I have a problem. My work is stolen from me ! " His accent thickened as his excitement rose.

" This sounds most serious," replied Holmes. " Maybe you can tell us something of your work, and the details of the theft."

" First, I must explain who I am and my position. Maybe you have not heard my name, but I am able to assure you that I am at the head of my profession here in London. I hold the position of *chef de cuisine* in one of London's top clubs,"— here he named the institution, which I do not judge it proper to reveal here—" and I have acquired an international reputation for my work."

" I have eaten there myself as a guest on several occasions," said Holmes, " and I must compliment you on your skill in managing the kitchen."

Our visitor bowed slightly in acknowledgement of the compliment, and continued. " Of a necessity, I must visit the other establishments in London from time to time and sample their offerings. Maybe there is something new that even I can learn from them. Naturally, my counterparts also come to visit me and partake of my creations. We know each other well, and make each other welcome. It is a friendly rivalry such as may obtain between true connoisseurs and virtuosos." He paused, and Holmes motioned for him to continue. " Imagine my surprise when I visited the G— Hotel, where a friend of mine heads the kitchens, the other night—last night, in fact—and I saw listed on the menu *canetons à la mode russe,* that is to say, young ducks in the Russian manner, roasted, and served in a nest of *pommes duchesse,* with a special sauce containing a preponderance of beetroot, the whole garnished with red and black caviar."

" It sounds an appetising dish," I interjected.

" It is more than appetising," replied Lefevre. " It is of a divinity beyond compare." He made the typical French gesture of kissing his fingertips. " I devised this masterpiece for the banquet given by the Worshipful Company of Glovers to the Czar and Czarina when they visited London some years ago, and it has formed a part of the menu offered to guests at the Club since then." His French accent was now barely distinguishable.

" So you were not expecting to see this on the menu of the G— Hotel ? " asked Holmes.

" There is no way I would have expected to see it there. I ordered the dish, and it was close to perfection, I am sorry to say." In answer to Holmes' unspoken question, he answered, " I say that I am sorry, because there was almost no difference between what was set before me that evening, and the masterpiece that issues from my own kitchens."

" You are claiming that someone stole your unique creation ? Would it not have been possible to reconstruct the recipe following the consumption of the dish prepared under your direction at your place of work ? "

The other shook his head. " In theory, that might appear possible to those who are unaware of the subtleties of my trade. However, each *chef* has his own little secrets that are unique to him and his kitchen alone. In this case, it is to do with the use of the zest of a lemon and egg white in a certain combination, and I flatter myself that though it would be impossible for even a master of the trade to detect their presence to the point where they could be identified with certainty, their absence would change the character completely, and I would know immediately were they absent. In this event, I knew that the dish I was eating was indeed my own original creation, transferred to another kitchen without my knowledge."

" Is it not possible," Holmes asked, " that one of your staff might have copied the recipe and sold it to the *chef* at the G— Hotel ? Or even that one of your staff may have left your employ and gone to work there and presented the recipe to him ? "

" It is possible, I suppose, but unlikely. M. Gérard and I are friendly, as I mentioned, and I regard him as the very soul of honour. I cannot believe that he would ever countenance such an act by a former member of my staff, any more than I would allow one of his staff to bring me the method of preparing one of his creations. We are artists, Mr. Holmes, and we have an artist's pride. My recipes are mine and mine alone, and details of the final stages of preparation are not readily available. I take a personal interest in the dishes that leave my kitchen, and in this particular case, I am careful to finish the dish myself."

" Excuse me," enquired Holmes, a queer smile on his lips, " but are you from the North or the South of France ? "

" I am from the South, but I do not see that it makes any difference to the matter in hand."

" Not, perhaps, from the West, from the region of Bristol ? " suggested Holmes.

Our visitor looked astounded. " How could you tell ? " he exclaimed, all trace of the French accent now gone.

" There are certain tricks of the English language that seem almost impossible for Frenchmen to pick up—the aspiration of the letter ' h ', for example. One other is the ' th' sound that you pronounce so perfectly. Certain of your vowels taught me of your possible link to the West Country. And when I see you with one of the latest English novels in your coat pocket, a title, moreover, that depends on the subtle play of words for much of its effect, I am forced to consider the possibility that your English language ability is much stronger than your original speech would suggest."

Our visitor laughed out loud. " You have me to rights, Mr. Holmes. But I assure you that in many ways I am indeed French. I have lived many years in the country and I speak the language almost as well as I do English. My story is a simple one. Long ago, I served in the British Army as a cook, and I was sent to the Crimea to ply my trade. The meals I prepared were simple, and I shudder now to think of the bully beef and other food with which I served our soldiers there. But then a revelation came. Perhaps you have heard of M. Alexis Soyer ? " Holmes and I both shook our heads. " He was the *chef de cuisine* at the Reform Club, and he came to the Crimea at his own expense to reform the food in our Army. I tell you, Mr. Holmes, it opened my eyes.

" I knew then that I should learn as much as I could about the art of gastronomy. I begged Soyer, though I was a mere corporal at the time, to give me an introduction to his French colleagues so that I might apprentice myself to them. He was kind enough to encourage me in my desire. I proved an apt pupil, and adopted a French name—François Lefevre is the French version of my English name, Frank Smith—as I learned the French language and adopted French ways.

" I wished to spend my old age in this country and accordingly applied for the post of *chef de cuisine* in the Club when it became vacant. It appears better in this profession for me to pass as French, though of course my employers are aware of my English origin."

" I see," said Holmes, obviously amused by this tale. " I am sure that this sort of *nom de cuisine*, as it were, adds a certain respectability to your reputation. But let us return to your tale of the birds. Surely you could have visited your friend, this M. Gérard, following your meal, to

enquire of him the meaning of this strange occurrence."

" Believe me, Mr. Holmes, that is exactly what I planned to do, once I had scanned the menu at the G— Hotel more carefully, and noticed two or three items on it that I had regarded as my personal property. Naturally, I did not order them to taste them, since I had already eaten my meal. Instead, I asked to see M. Gérard."

" With what result ? "

" This is what I cannot understand. I had arranged my visit for a Wednesday, as I usually do when dining at the G— Hotel. I know that M. Gérard is always present on that day, and after my meal, we usually sit together over a glass or two of cognac. When I had finished, I asked the waiter if I could speak with M. Gérard, and to my astonishment, I was informed that not only was he not present, but that he had not been present for the previous four days, without informing anyone that he was to be absent."

" Surely the hotel had attempted to locate him at his lodging ? "

" Indeed they had, but there was no answer when they knocked at his door, and his lodgings showed no sign of being occupied, according to the hotel manager with whom I spoke."

" And no-one else to whom you spoke could tell you of the appearance of the dish on the menu ? "

" No, they could not. I did, however, discover that it had only appeared one or two nights before— no-one seemed to be sure when this was. I appeared to be the only person who had ever ordered this meal. The hotel is not very busy at this season."

" I am somewhat ignorant of the workings of a hotel," said Holmes, " but it would seem to me that some training of the staff would be needed in order to produce an item so new to the menu."

The other shook his head. " While the *chef de cuisine* and the *sous-chef* may remain as a permanent member of the establishment's staff," he explained, " the *sauciers*, *entremetiers*, *poissoniers*, and so on may not work in one establishment for extended periods, and accordingly are used to working from written instructions to prepare the dishes. It is, I suppose, possible that one of my staff could have noted the instructions provided to them, copied the recipe, and passed it on to the G— Hotel. But in that case, they would have omitted the finishing touches that I myself add when certain of my original dishes are served."

" Where do you keep the written recipes ? " asked Holmes.

" They are in a book stored in a locked drawer of my office at the Club. I always keep the door to the office locked when I am not there. I will not say that it is impossible for anyone to have obtained access to them, but I have observed no signs that this has occurred."

" We will investigate," replied Holmes. " At what time would it be convenient for us to call on you at the Club ? "

" If you were to call at about four o'clock this afternoon, I would almost be certain to give you some time."

" Excellent. We will ask for M. Lefevre, rather than Mr. Smith, of course ? "

" Of course," replied the other, smiling. " One more question. Your fee ? "

" Have confidence that my services will be well within your financial grasp," Holmes assured him.

" That is some relief. And now I shall bid you adieu until this afternoon," he replied, rising from his seat and leaving us.

" PRETTY little problem," remarked Holmes. " Your thoughts, Watson ? "

But he was never to hear my incomplete musings on the matter. As I started to frame my reply, the door to our room burst open, and Inspector Lanner of the Metropolitan Police, a junior colleague of Inspector Lestrade, stood framed in the entrance, panting a little. His red face was covered with perspiration, and his entire body, which tended towards corpulence, shook somewhat as he panted heavily.

Sherlock Holmes had worked with Lanner on several cases before this, and on those occasions I had been struck by the contrast that I had observed between the brilliant amateur, constantly seeking and retaining clues to the solution of the problem, and the more pedestrian efforts of the professional.

" Mr. Holmes," burst out the police officer. " Forgive the intrusion, but I am at my wit's end, and I would appreciate your help in solving a crime that, quite frankly, horrifies and baffles me."

" Why the hurry, Inspector ? " replied Holmes, lazily stretching his legs towards the fender. " Sit down, catch your breath, and take your time."

" Thank you, Mr. Holmes, I will," replied the little man, accepting Holmes' invitation, and seating himself in an armchair. " Truth to tell, I have encountered a particularly horrid crime, and it has shaken my nerves not a little."

" Here, take this," offered Holmes, extending a glass of brandy and water to the Inspector who, in truth, did appear to be badly affected by whatever had occurred. His cheeks were heavily flushed, and his whole demeanour was one of a man who has been severely shaken by an event out of the everyday round of experience.

" Thank you," replied Lanner. " It goes against my usual habits to take a drink at this hour of the day, but in this instance..." He emptied the glass as if it were medicine, and his face resumed a more normal hue as his breathing slowed. " This is a murder, Mr. Holmes. A murder such as I have never seen before, and I pray God I will never again encounter."

Holmes lounged back in his chair, his keen eyes hooded, but keeping an alert watch on the official detective.

" We were called in," continued Lanner, " by a neighbour of the dead man, who had complained of the smell emanating from the room. He had complained to the constable on the beat, who smashed down the locked door, and encountered what can only be described as a charnel-house. The limbs of the victim had been severed from the torso, apparently with an axe or some similar implement, and the whole room was a mass of blood and flies. The insects had apparently multiplied in this recent warm weather we have been experiencing. On beholding this sight, the constable, not unnaturally, felt unwell, but had the presence of mind to summon the detectives of Scotland Yard. I tell you, Mr. Holmes, I have just come from

the place, and I cannot bring myself to remember it without a shudder."

" Is everything as it was when the constable opened the door ? " asked Holmes.

" Believe me, Mr. Holmes, there is not a man on the Force who would want to touch anything there. It is certain that this will have to be done, but I am unsure how and by whom this will be accomplished. I dare not invite any of my colleagues to share this horror, and I have some hesitation in requesting your assistance, but since you have been of some assistance to us in the past, I felt that perhaps you might be willing to..."

" Lanner, though we have not worked together on many occasions, I think you know my reputation well enough to know that I will be happy to assist you," answered Holmes.

" I warn you, it is pretty bad," said Lanner seriously. " Doctor Watson, will you come along ? I fear that the police surgeon may be somewhat out of his depth, and I hardly dare to call Sir Justin Thorpe-Monteith, the pathologist, to the scene of the crime."

" I have seen terrible things on active service," I replied. " I will come."

" My thanks for your assistance. I have ordered some long butcher's coats to be in readiness for us, which I recommend we wear at the location. I assume that neither of you has any wish to end up covered in blood. I confess I was confident enough of your assistance, Mr. Holmes, and that of Doctor Watson here, that I have ordered three such coats."

" Thank you for your consideration," Holmes replied. " Before we set off, I would appreciate your giving me any information about the man who has been killed and the place where we are going."

" We will be going to a boarding house in Dean-street in Soho," replied Lanner. " As to the man's identity, he is a Frenchman, according to his landlord, employed at the G— Hotel as the chief cook there— the *chef de cuisine* is his official title, I believe."

" That would be a Monsieur Gérard, I believe," remarked Holmes.

Lanner dropped his notebook, from which he had been reading these facts, in consternation. " You are correct there," he stammered. " How in the world could you possibly know that ? Do you have some sort of supernatural powers ? "

" I cannot deceive you, since the case is of such a serious nature.

The gentleman was the subject of a discussion held in this very room a matter of minutes before your entrance. There is nothing of the supernatural involved."

Lanner looked at Holmes quizzically. " In what regard was he mentioned ? " he asked.

" It was remarked by my client that he had been missing from his place of work for several days, and no-one was aware of his whereabouts."

" The poor devil was probably killed a few days ago," confirmed Lanner. " So your mystery seems to be solved."

" Not all of it," replied Holmes. " And it would appear that you are bringing us a new mystery of your own. Let us be off, then, and inspect the scene of the crime."

⋯⟫⊙⟪⋯

EFORE entering the room, Holmes, Lanner and I donned the white coats that had been provided. On opening the door, Lanner disclosed to us a scene of carnage and butchery that quite turned my stomach. The stench of decay was considerable, and it was all I could do to maintain my composure. The Scotland Yard detective, though he already knew of the horror within, was obviously likewise suffering, and even Holmes, whom I had thought impervious to such scenes, blanched and hesitated as he stepped across the threshold. A swarm of flies lifted themselves from the blood-soaked floor at the sound of our steps.

As we had been informed, the limbs had been savagely hacked from the naked body and distributed about the room, with gore staining seemingly every surface. The eyes of the corpse were still open, and appeared to be glaring at us with a ferocity that was almost inhuman. The face was livid, and appeared to be somewhat distorted in its expression, though it was possible to see that the dead man had been a handsome figure, somewhat stocky in build, aged about forty years, with dark hair cut short, and just beginning to turn grey at delay temples. A small goatee beard adorned the chin, and a neatly waxed moustache graced the upper lip.

Holmes, whose nerves seemed to have recovered from the initial shock caused by the sight of the horrendous contents of the room, stooped and examined the left arm, lying in the centre of the room. He withdrew a lens from the kit bag he carried, and peered through it at the severed shoulder joint. He then moved to the other arm, lying beneath a deal chair, and repeated the operation.

" I would draw your attention to the way in which these have been removed," he said to Lanner.

" I am no anatomist," replied the police detective. " Your observations are wasted on me."

" Watson, then," he replied.

I suppressed my disgust at the sight of the dismembered corpse, and examined the severed joint. " This hardly the way we learned the art of dissection at Bart's," I remarked. " For one thing, I would guess that the instrument was not a surgical tool of any description. It would seem to me that an axe or some sort of similar instrument was employed."

" I would concur with that judgement," said Holmes. " Is there anything else that you observe ? "

" The method of detaching the arm would appear to be the work of someone other than a trained surgeon. In fact, it looks almost like the work of a butcher."

" Bravo, Watson ! " exclaimed Holmes. " I think you have reached the same conclusion as myself."

" What do you mean ? " asked Lanner.

" Consider the dead man's occupation," replied Holmes, a little testily. " Come, man, think."

The policeman appeared to be somewhat discomfited by this, but nodded. " So you believe the dead man's killer was in some way connected to his work as a cook ? He was murdered by someone in the same line of business ? "

" The evidence I have observed so far would tend to argue that to be the case," replied Holmes. " Something of which you are not aware is the fact that the hotel kitchen supervised by the dead man served up a dish whose recipe up until that time had been regarded as a professional secret. The client who visited me just before your arrival claimed that the recipe had been stolen from him."

" You are now providing both a motive and means for your client," pointed out Lanner. " If he is a cook, and there was some sort of rivalry between him and the dead man, we only lack the opportunity."

" I trust that you are mistaken, but in any event, I would suggest searching the room now," commented Holmes. " It may be that we will discover something of interest here that will serve to confirm your theory—or otherwise. While you and I are thus engaged, Watson, if you have a mind to do so, will you examine the body and make any notes that may occur to you ? "

Lanner's face fell somewhat at this suggestion, and I have to admit that the prospect of conducting a search in that apartment of death would have filled me with a sense of disgust. " Could it not wait ? " he asked Holmes.

" Certainly it could wait," replied my friend equably. " If you are prepared to risk losing the scent in this case, naturally it can wait."

I considered Holmes' remarks regarding scent to be in poor taste, considering the reek that pervaded the room, but it appeared that he was unconscious of any play on words.

" Very good, then," Lanner grudgingly agreed. " Let us proceed with the search. I hope you will not withhold from us anything that you may discover."

" Inspector Lanner," retorted Holmes stiffly. " I trust that your colleagues with whom I have worked in the past, such as Lestrade and Gregson, have acquainted you with me and my methods sufficiently for you to be confident that I invariably share any clues that I may discover with you and your colleagues. Furthermore, in the event that I solve a case and the police, for whatever reason, fail to do so, I do not seek the public credit for the solution. I would remind you that it is you who sought my assistance on this occasion, and not I yours. Work with me in a spirit of cooperation, and not against me in a spirit of competition, and the business will proceed in a much smoother fashion."

Thus admonished, Lanner, drawing on a pair of fine rubber gloves which had been provided along with the white coats we were wearing, started to open drawers and search within. Holmes followed his example as I bent over the body.

" Here," called Holmes. " Do you see this ? " He pointed to the table, which he had been examining with a high powered lens.

" I see some breadcrumbs," replied Lanner.

" Ah, but that is where you are mistaken," retorted my friend. " Pray use my glass and then tell me if these are breadcrumbs."

With a bad grace, Lanner took the lens and peered through it. " Maybe not bread," he admitted.

" Certainly not bread," replied Holmes. " May I ? " he asked, retrieving a small envelope from his pocket, and making as if to sweep the crumbs into it.

" Why should I object ? "

" This, my dear Inspector, may prove to be evidence," said Holmes, shaking his head sadly. " I take it, then, that the Metropolitan Police will not concern itself with these trifles."

" You are welcome to whatever rubbish you may find," replied the other.

" Tut, man," said Holmes. " It is

evident that you have much to learn in your profession."

The police detective flushed, but said nothing in reply. The search continued, and I soon noticed Holmes stoop and use his forceps to pick up a small black object from under the table. " And this, Inspector ? "

" You may keep it," said the other, shortly, turning his back on Holmes.

Holmes gave me a glance, and once more shook his head in disgust, signifying his contempt for the lack of method he considered was being displayed by the official detective.

Once more the search continued, with Holmes moving to the drawers of the table.

" Aha ! " he cried, waving aloft a small black notebook which he had removed from the drawer. " This may prove to be of interest, I think, Lanner, even to your uncurious mind."

The Inspector and I moved to Holmes' side, as he slowly turned the pages.

" It's all in French," grumbled Lanner.

" What would you expect ? M. Gérard was, after all, a Frenchman. It appears to be some sort of account-book."

" The sums involved appear to be somewhat large for an individual's accounts," remarked Lanner.

" Perhaps they are for his work ? " I suggested, but Holmes shook his head at this.

" Hardly that, I think," he said. " See here. ' *Table et chaises*'—that is, table and chairs, and ' *Armoire*'— wardrobe." I see no table and chairs in this room that would seem to warrant such an expenditure as twenty-five pounds."

" And that wardrobe in the corner

is one for which I would not part with half a crown," added Lanner. " If he really gave thirty pounds for that, he was a fool."

" Indeed. We are therefore left with a number of possibilities. First, that this notebook is not the property of the late M. Gérard, and the entries herein were not made by him. That can easily be determined by comparison with other specimens of his writing. Next, that the items listed here do not correspond to the items we see here in this room. Again, that can easily be checked by reference to the sellers of the items, who are conveniently listed here. Maybe he was exporting furniture to France—for what purpose, I cannot tell. Lastly, and this I believe to be the most likely, the items in this book form a kind of code, representing items of a completely different kind, and ones which might attract the unwelcome attention of the authorities if they were accurately described and this book were to fall into their hands."

" By Jove, Mr. Holmes," cried the little detective, intrigued, despite himself, at Holmes' analysis. " I believe you have hit on the truth of the matter."

Holmes smiled. " We must continue our search," he said. " Maybe there is more here that can aid us in our quest for the truth."

It was Lanner who discovered the next item that appeared to be out of place in that chamber of horror. " What," he asked Holmes, " do you make of this ? " pointing to a pile of sawdust in one corner of the room, part of which had absorbed some splashes of blood. Beside the sawdust were a bradawl and a carpenter's brace and bit.

" Curious," replied Holmes. " Very curious indeed," as he once again brought his high-powered

lens into play over the pile of wood dust. " This would appear to be cherry-wood, or possibly pear- or apple-wood, and I see no article composed of that material in this room."

" You can distinguish the kind of wood from sawdust ? " laughed Lanner. " Come, Mr. Holmes, you cannot expect me to believe that. Even you with all your tricks cannot reconstruct a tree from dust."

" I care not if you believe it or not," replied Holmes stiffly. " As it happens, I am making my identification not so much from the dust as from the larger chips of wood contained in it. I would suggest, if you doubt me, to search the wooden objects in this room for a hole of half an inch in diameter, corresponding to the bit fixed in this brace, which has obviously been in use at a comparatively recent date. I wager you will find no such thing."

" And your no doubt ingenious theory concerning this ? " sneered Lanner.

Holmes drew himself up to his full height and glared down at the other.

" Inspector Lanner, I will remind you for the last time that it is you who requested my assistance and not the other way about. Should you decide that you are still in need of my help, I would be obliged if you would refrain from making remarks such as your last. Otherwise I will be happy to take myself elsewhere and leave you to attempt the solution of this problem alone."

" I beg your pardon," replied Lanner, obviously somewhat taken aback by the prospect of losing the observations of the distinguished amateur. " It is merely that your methods tend to differ from those employed by us at the Yard."

" I am well aware of that fact," Holmes commented drily. " But no matter. The fact remains that we have carpenters' tools here, a pile of otherwise unexplained sawdust, and a list of those from whom furniture has apparently been purchased in the past, from which we might expect the sawdust to have come. It would seem to me that your time when we leave here would be best spent in examining that list and making enquiries of those people."

"You may do as you wish, Mr. Holmes. As for me, I think that I will go to the heart of the matter and arrest your client, if you will tell me his name." Holmes looked at the Scotland Yard detective with an air of defiance. "I will remind you that I have the legal power to order you before a magistrate and compel you to give the information. I hardly feel that you would see that to be in your best interests."

"Very well," replied Holmes, reluctantly providing the name and address of our earlier visitor to the policeman. "I would ask you to refrain from arresting him until tomorrow morning at the very earliest. I will guarantee that should you still feel it necessary to arrest him, he will be there for you. I make no such promises regarding your ability to secure a conviction."

Lanner laughed unpleasantly. "Well, you may have your theories, Mr. Holmes, and I will deal in facts. I have no objection to delaying the inevitable as you request."

"In that case, you will have no objection to my retaining this?" asked Holmes, holding up the notebook that he had discovered.

"Please yourself," said Lanner. "I thank you for delivering the murderer into my hands."

The two men continued the search in an angry silence, and I was conscious of the tension between the detectives, one a brilliant amateur,

and the other an unimaginative official. Even allowing for Holmes' prejudices, I felt there was some justification for his condemnation of the Scotland Yard police officer. I was heartily glad when the task was completed, without anything else of interest being discovered, and we were able to leave the stinking room and strip off the overgarments that had protected our clothing.

"Can you let me have a report on the body soon, Doctor?" Lanner asked me.

"Certainly. I will be producing a neat copy this afternoon or early this evening and will have it sent to you as soon as I can."

"Thank you, Doctor. I think we have shared everything of importance," Lanner addressed Holmes.

"That depends on your ideas of what you consider to be of importance," retorted Holmes. "You seem determined to overlook the most important matters in this case."

"I am sorry that I ever brought you into this business," replied Lanner. "You have given me the name of the murderer, for which I thank you. Other than that, I fail to see that you have done other than waste my time."

I could tell that Holmes was angered at these words, but he maintained some control over his temper. "I bid you a very good day," he said stiffly to Lanner, whereupon he turned on his heel and strode off. I followed him as he walked down the street at a crisp pace.

"I was a fool to allow myself to be cajoled into helping that stiff-necked blockhead Lanner," he muttered to himself. "His single redeeming characteristic is that he is tenacious, and when he has been set on the right track, that is no bad thing, to be sure. But in a case like this, where he is facing in completely the wrong direction, it is a disaster."

" What makes you sure that our visitor is not the killer ? " I asked.

" For one thing, those cuts to remove the limbs were almost certainly made by a left-handed man, and Lefevre, as he calls himself, is right-handed, as you no doubt observed. For another, and more convincing proof, he told us that he was informed that Gérard had not appeared for some days before he consumed the meal concocted from the stolen recipe. It is easy for us to confirm the relevant dates, and Lefevre must know that. It would make no sense for him to lie about these things."

" Unless he had previous knowledge of the theft, murdered Gérard several days ago, and took his meal at the G— Hotel several days later as a subterfuge ? " I suggested.

" I think you and Lanner attach too much importance to the stolen recipe," replied Holmes. " He was most certainly aggrieved by its loss, but I really have my doubts as to whether he would kill for such a reason. What did you conclude from your examination of the body ? "

" There were few signs of violence other than the obvious post-mortem dismemberment," I replied. " The pupils appeared to be unnaturally dilated, from what I could tell. If I had to make any kind of conjecture, I would have to say that he was poisoned by some form of alkaloid. I will make a note in my report that the contents of the stomach should be analysed by the pathologist. I am curious, though, as to why the corpse was dismembered and then abandoned there."

" I consider it to be merely a matter of the time available to the murderer," replied Holmes. " Think

about what was missing from that room."

I racked my brains, but was unable to come up with an answer to the conundrum.

" Where were the clothes he was wearing ? " asked Holmes. " We came across many clean white outfits such as are worn by cooks, in addition to many freshly laundered undergarments in the drawers. But where were the clothes he was wearing when he died, eh ? "

I stopped in my tracks, struck by this fact. " I never considered that," I admitted.

" No more did that blockhead Lanner," replied Holmes. " I do not blame you for not remarking the fact, as you were otherwise engaged with the cadaver, but Lanner was meant to be seeking evidence and he should have been well aware of the simple fact of the missing clothes. My theory is that the murderer removed the dead man's clothes and disposed of them, prior to returning to the body and dismembering it in order to dispose of it. For whatever reason, he found he was unable to re-enter the room, and therefore decided on discretion being the better part of valour, and abandoned the attempt entirely."

" It seems plausible enough," I replied. " And now where do we go ? "

" To the first address in the book," Holmes replied, hailing a cab. " A Mr. Simon Oliphaunt, who would appear to reside in the Portobello Road."

The address turned out to be a shop specialising in the sale of fine old furniture. Mr. Simon Oliphaunt turned out to be an amiable man, who was happy to talk about his work.

" Do you remember selling," Holmes consulted the notebook,

"a gate-leg table and four spin-dle-backed chairs in September last year for the sum of thirteen guin-eas ? This notebook is written in French, but I trust that my extem-pore translation makes sense to you."

"It makes perfect sense, sir. Those are the correct terms. And yes, I remember that sale well. I was expecting a little more from those pieces, I must say, but Mr. Phillimore is a sharp man of busi-ness, and I was not able to realise the profit I had anticipated," he chuckled.

"Mr. Phillimore, eh ? " ask-ed Holmes. "Is he a regular customer ? "

"Indeed he is, sir. He tends to go for the slightly older pieces, of the time of Queen Anne or the first George. He has good taste."

"And this entry here ? " asked Holmes. "A large circular clawfoot table in November last year ? "

"That was a beautiful piece, sir, and to be fair to Mr. Phillimore, he paid what it was worth."

"What does he do with all these items, does he say ? "

"He dispatches them to France, to Toulouse, I believe, where there is a market for English furniture of that period. I must assume so, in any case, otherwise there would be little point in his taking this trou-ble, would there ? "

"Indeed it would seem to be pointless otherwise," agreed Holmes. "Could you describe Mr. Phillimore to us ? "

The shopkeeper frowned as he re-called the appearance of his custom-er. "A little shorter than yourself, sir, but only by an inch or two at the most. An elderly gentleman, thin, and perhaps sixty years old, I would guess, with white hair worn some-what long at the back."

"A moustache or beard ? " asked Holmes.

The other shook his head. "Nothing like that, sir. He is a clean-shaven man."

"Have you observed whether he is right- or left-handed, by any chance ? "

"No, sir, I have not. Though, now I come to think of it, perhaps he is left-handed. I have a vague recollection of his signing his name left-handed on one occasion."

"Thank you, Mr. Oliphaunt. That has been most illuminat-ing." Holmes replaced his hat and we walked out onto the Portobel-lo Road. "Well, Watson ? " he quizzed me.

"I am astounded."

"Oliphaunt has surprised me, I confess," he replied. "It would now appear that the man whom Ol-iphaunt knew as Phillimore was Gérard. If that is the case, the dead man whom we have just seen is not Gérard. The two descriptions cannot conceivably be of the same man. Was the dead man right or left-handed, in your opinion ? "

"I cannot tell. Remember that the limbs were not side by side for my comparison." I shuddered invol-untarily at the memory. "Though there was one fact that I noted. On the left hand, there were a number of knife scars and half-healed cuts on the fingers."

"From which I would deduce that the dead man was a right-hand-ed cook, who used a knife with suf-ficient frequency to cut his other hand, which is a common occur-rence in that trade."

"Oliphaunt has a memory of Phillimore writing his name with his left hand, and the murderer was left-handed, you judged," I remind-ed Holmes.

"Not strictly true, Watson. I

said that he who made the cuts to remove the limbs would appear to have been left-handed. The killer and the individual who performed the dismembering may not be the same individual," he corrected me. " Let us visit another name from the book. I fear that we will be told the same story as we have received just now from Oliphaunt, however."

In the event, Holmes' prediction was fulfilled. David Edwards, a furniture dealer in Paddington, gave a description of the man he had known as Phillimore which was almost identical with the one we had been given earlier by Oliphaunt.

" Let us now to Lefevre's place of work, and wait for him," suggested Holmes.

E were admitted to the Club, after some slight confusion at the door, where the porter seemed to have difficulty in believing that Holmes and I were seeking an interview with one of the Club servants, albeit one of the more senior of that number.

We were ushered to the Visitors' Room, and informed that Lefevre would be with us shortly, and invited to partake of tea and cake, which we accepted.

At four precisely, Lefevre entered. " I am sorry to have kept you waiting," he said. " I trust the refreshments were to your taste ? "

" Certainly," smiled Holmes. " And we were a trifle in advance of the appointed hour."

" Come, then, let us to my office." He led the way through the back corridors of the Club, and opened a door to a dingy small apartment chiefly occupied by a large desk. " This is where I am forced to spend too much of my time," he complained. " I would sooner be in the kitchen, but as you can imagine, there is more paper than pastry in my life. Still, I must not complain. To work here at the Club is one of the pinnacles of my profession. Now, have you discovered anything ? " he asked Holmes.

" I come as the bearer of bad tidings, I am sorry to say," answered my friend. " You may be expected to be arrested tomorrow morning."

The effect on Lefevre was electric. " On what charge ? " he asked. He had clapped a hand to his chest in alarm, and looked as shaken as I have ever seen a man.

" On the charge of the murder of M. Gérard," replied Holmes.

" Mon Dieu ! " exclaimed Lefevre, reverting to French, and a look of horror spreading over his face. " He is dead ? "

Holmes shook his head. " I have reason to believe not. However, the police seem to think so, and they also are under the impression that you are the killer."

" I swear to God that I did not even know that he was dead. I did not kill him, I give you my word."

" Do you know anything about a death at his rooms in Dean-street in Soho ? "

" His rooms in Soho ? " asked Lefevre. " You mean Gilbert Place in Bloomsbury, do you not ? He has rooms there above a bookshop. I have visited him at that address on two or three occasions."

" You have no knowledge of the rooms in Dean-street ? That is where the police have discovered a body which they believe to be his."

" I have no knowledge of this at all," the other replied simply. " I always knew his address to be number 10, Gilbert Place."

" I believe you," said Holmes, writing in his notebook. " Tell me more about M. Gérard, and your relations with him, if you would. First, give me a description of his appearance."

" Certainly. Jean-Marie Gérard is a tall man, maybe as tall as you, Mr. Holmes, and slightly built. My age or thereabouts, with grey, almost white, hair, somewhat longer than mine. Clean-shaven. A somewhat long face. I am sorry, but I do not consider myself to be an expert at this sort of thing. I hope this is of some use, though."

" No matter," replied Holmes. " That is most helpful. For how many years have you been acquainted with him ? "

" We worked together in the same restaurant in Paris some twenty years ago, and became friends at that time. Since then we have never lost contact with each other, and I would describe our relations as being friendly, though of course, the nature of our work and the times at which we are busy mean that we are unable to meet as often as we would like."

" You called on me earlier today, and informed me that M. Gérard's kitchen was serving up one of your recipes. You were never in the habit of sharing your professional secrets ? "

" No. As I say, in our profession we tend to be somewhat jealous of our skills and knowledge. It is a harsh world, Mr. Holmes. And I am convinced that Gérard would never have stolen the recipe from me, either directly or through the intervention of some third party."

" Where do you keep the recipes ? " asked Holmes.

" Here, in my office. They are written in a book kept in a locked drawer of my desk. Would you like to view it ? "

" Certainly."

Lefevere brought a bunch of keys from his pocket, and selected one before inserting it into the lock of the desk drawer.

" Is that the only key to that drawer ? " asked Holmes.

" There is one other. It is kept in the safe of the Club manager." He turned the key and opened the drawer triumphantly. As he looked into the drawer, his face turned ashen. " The book is gone ! " he exclaimed with a face of horror. " See for yourself." Indeed, the drawer was completely empty.

" Possibly you put it in another drawer ? " suggested Holmes. " Or you removed it and forgot to replace it ? "

" I fear that you do not understand the importance of this book to me. This is the culmination of my professional career. This is my life's work. I would never have placed the book anywhere but here, and I would certainly never have omitted to replace it." He placed his head in his hands, and appeared to be stricken to the point of weeping.

" Come, man," said Holmes. " Let us approach this problem rationally. When did you last see the book ? When do you last know that it was here ? "

" Let me recall." His voice was a little more steady as he considered the matter. " I would have to say somewhat less than a week ago. There were one or two suspicions that there was too much cinnamon for some tastes in one of my desserts, and I had occasion to modify the quantity. I do not remember opening the drawer again after I had locked the book away."

" Who else knew that the book was stored here ? "

" My *sous-chef*, who has been with me here for the past seven years, and the Club manager. That is all. Others may have suspected its presence, but it would be no more than a suspicion."

" Would M. Gérard have known of the existence of the book ? "

" He would certainly have been able to guess of its existence. Maintaining such a record is part of the duties of a *chef de cuisine*, after all."

" May I examine the desk ? " asked Holmes, bending and examining the lock with his magnifying glass. " Aha. It would appear that your lock has been recently opened by means of a picklock. You say that you always lock your office when it is unoccupied ? "

" Without fail. Apart from anything else, it is necessary for me to keep quantities of cash here for day-to-day expenses and the like."

" Have you noticed any money missing ? "

" No, not at all. Part of my daily routine is to count the money and balance the petty cash book."

" Let us look at your office door, then," replied Holmes, rising, and subjecting the door lock to the same scrutiny as he had previously done with the desk drawer lock. " Yes, this has also suffered the same fate. A picklock has been used at some time to gain entry. Is there any time when this could have been done without attracting attention ? "

" I would say that it could have happened at any time while I was working in the kitchen. This passage is not in frequent use."

Holmes appeared to be lost in thought as he pondered the matter. After a few seconds, he broke the silence with, " I have a few other other questions regarding Gérard.

Have you ever noticed whether M. Gérard is left-handed ? "

" Oh yes, most certainly he is. When we worked together in the kitchens in Paris, we had to arrange our *mises en place* to accommodate that."

" That is most interesting. One more question. Does he have an interest in older furniture ? "

" I did notice one or two fine pieces—tables, chairs, and the like—on the occasions when I visited his house in Gilbert Place. I never enquired about the interest, though. He was possessed of a certain taste in such things, I suppose."

" I suppose that you would have no knowledge regarding this man ? " asked Holmes, giving a description of the dead man whom we had left in the room in Dean-street.

" From your description, it sounds as though you might have encountered Jules Navier, who used to work for me here as a *patissier*, in charge of preparing desserts and the like, before moving to the G— Hotel to work for Gérard. I must confess that he and I parted on somewhat less than cordial terms. Did you happen to notice a tattoo inside his left wrist ? "

" A small bird, a swallow or some such ? " I asked.

" Yes, indeed. Then almost without a doubt, you encountered Navier. A skilled worker, but a man with a violent temper, and to be frank, I suspected him of some dishonesty with regard to the pantry."

" This is all gratifying," replied Holmes, rubbing his hands together. " It means that the police are on entirely the wrong track."

" Maybe this business is gratifying for you, but not for me, since you say that I am to be arrested in the morning. What should I do ? I must fly the country ! " replied the stricken *chef*.

Holmes shook his head once more. " No, you must not do that. Believe me, that is the worst thing you could possibly do, and would only serve to confirm your guilt in the eyes of the police. Trust me, and do what I tell you." Holmes' manner was impressive, and his presence commanding as he said these words. Lefevre nodded word-lessly. " When the police come for you, they will probably be headed by a blockhead named Lanner. This Inspector does not care to have his opinions contradicted, so my strong advice to you is to hold your peace, no matter what he says to you. Nei-ther confirm nor deny his accusa-tions, no matter how preposterous they may seem. Do you compre-hend me ? "

" I understand what you are say-ing, and I will endeavour to follow your instructions."

" Good. Have you a lawyer ? No ? I will ensure that you are pro-vided with a good lawyer who will be able to advise you in your deal-ings with the police. Indeed, I will ensure that he is with you from to-morrow morning. May I have the address of your lodgings ? "

" I have a room here at the Club."

" I will send him here the first thing in the morning so that he may be with you when the police arrive. I repeat that you have nothing to fear if you are innocent."

" May I ask why you are doing this for me ? " asked Lefevre. " I must warn you, I am unsure of my ability to pay your fees, or those of the lawyer."

" You requested my assistance, did you not ? " replied Holmes. " There is a mystery here that I in-tend to clear up, and I will not see the lumbering boots of the police trample over the truth of the matter, which is more complex than they would like to admit. As far as fees are concerned, I think we can cross that bridge when we come to it. Be-lieve me, the question of money in this case will be a relatively minor one as far as you are concerned. Do not worry about this, or indeed, about anything connected with this case. I can give you my word that you will emerge from this with your reputation unscathed."

" That is good to hear."

" At what time shall I arrange for the lawyer to call ? "

" Eight will be convenient."

" Very good, then. Believe me, your case has my full attention."

" E must act, and act fast," said Holmes. " My first task is to engage the lawyer whom I promised to poor Lefevre." So saying, we proceeded to Chan-cery Lane, where Holmes called at the offices of Joskin & Fitch, and engaged the services of Mr. Hubert Joskin, with whom he had done business in the past, assuring him that he, Holmes, would meet all the expenses incurred.

" And now back to the Portobello Road. With luck, we will discover Mr. Oliphaunt's shop is still open, and he will be willing to speak with us."

At the shop, Holmes was able to confirm that the furniture bought by " Phillimore" had been dis-patched to the Gilbert Square house mentioned by Lefevre.

" To Baker-street," commanded Holmes. " There is little else we can do today. Congratulations on your observation of the tattoo. That is the little detail that clinches the business." Holmes appeared to be in high good humour as we rattled through the London streets. " Not only will that fool of an Inspector arrest the wrong man, but he will arrest him for the wrong crime."

" Meaning that Phillimore and Gérard are one and the same person, and that the dead man is not Gérard ? "

" Precisely. Now, the questions we must ask ourselves are the following. First, why does Gérard appear to be leading a double life, in two establishments, with two names ? Obviously he has something to hide as Phillimore, since Gérard qua Gérard would appear to be completely without any secrets. And it is as Phillimore that he purchases this furniture. Therefore, we may conclude that the furniture is the key to the mystery."

" That seems clear enough," said I.

" If you remember, ' Phillimore' mentioned that he was sending the furniture to France. That may indeed be the truth of the matter. But why ? It would seem an odd way for him to supplement his income, and would hardly, if legitimate, seem to justify the duplicity of a second address and a second name."

" The apartment in Soho was hardly large enough to act as a furniture store," I pointed out.

" Then why does he trouble to maintain it at all ? Why not conduct all his business from Bloomsbury ? " objected Holmes. " No, there is something distinctly queer about this whole business that makes me believe that the furniture is a pretext for some other nefarious purpose."

" Perhaps the crates containing the furniture are also packed with whatever it is that he is exporting ? " I suggested.

" Hardly that. The Customs authorities in both countries would be sure to examine them, and any such attempt at smuggling would be doomed to failure on that account."

We rode in silence back to Baker-street, and I commenced writing the report on the corpse that I had promised Lanner.

" Omit nothing in the report," Holmes told me. " I do not wish it said that I was in any way responsible, either directly or through you, for withholding any information that could lead the police to an erroneous conclusion."

I soon discovered that my concentration was broken by the sound of Holmes' violin, which he had balanced across his knees, and was scraping away abstractedly as he sat, seemingly lost in thought.

" Holmes, the noise you are making is intolerable and is preventing me from working. I am tempted to fill your wretched instrument with stones in order to prevent your scratchings."

" I apologise, my dear fellow," he replied, putting aside the fiddle. " I was totally unconscious of the fact that I might be causing you some distress." He paused. " Watson ! " he fairly shouted. " You have solved the problem for me. What it is to have a friend such as you ! "

I was completely baffled by this outburst, and said as much.

" It all fits, Watson, it all fits ! You must be aware of the jewel thefts that have taken place over the past year. The booty has never turned up for sale in this country. Not a single stone has been recovered. However, several of the pieces have been offered for sale in the south of France and in northern Spain. Where were we told that Phillimore sends his furniture? Toulouse, was it not?" answering his own question.

" But how...?"

" You said it yourself, Watson. You threatened to commit sacrilege by filling my Stradivarius with stones, an act which I would have found hard to forgive, I assure you, had you carried it out in reality. But what if stones of a different type were introduced into the furniture being dispatched to France? You remember the carpenter's bradawl and tools and the pile of sawdust? It is my considered opinion that the legs and so on of the furniture have been hollowed out and the cavities filled with the stolen jewellery before being re-sealed."

" It would account for the secrecy and the false names," I agreed.

" I would guess that the Soho location is the place where the jewels are delivered to Gérard, and where he actually does the work. It also serves as his official residence as far as his employers are concerned. I would guess that he leads a perfectly respectable life in his Bloomsbury house, maybe as Gérard, or quite conceivably as Phillimore."

" And the stolen recipe and the dead man Navier?"

" They are important, I admit, but I think they are less so the gems being taken out of this country in this way. There may well be a connection, I admit it, but the common element of this puzzle we have here is the man Gérard. Maybe we can pay a visit to Gilbert Square tonight and discover a little more."

He rose to his feet and was actually in the act of reaching for his coat when there was a knock on the door, and Inspector Lestrade entered.

" What brings you here at this hour of the evening?" asked Holmes.

Lestrade appeared grave. " Mr. Holmes, you know that I am grateful to you for your assistance in the past, and I know that you have given generously of your time and energy to assisting us and providing hints for us."

" Yes?" replied Holmes. " I sense a ' however' coming. Am I correct?"

" I fear so," replied Lestrade. " Young Lanner is quite upset by your treatment of him in this Gérard murder case. He was actually asking me to arrest you on charges related to the obstruction of justice."

Holmes laughed. " My dear Lestrade, I trust that is not why you are here?"

" Naturally I refused his request," replied Lestrade. " However, I have to say to you that if you continue to exhibit this attitude toward senior police officers, any cooperation we may have extended toward you in the past will no longer be forthcoming."

" I see," replied Holmes, thoughtfully. " Sit you down there, Inspector, and have the goodness to accept a glass of something—a dry sherry, perhaps? —while I proceed to inform you of my discoveries in the case, and lay my theory before you."

" There can be no harm in my doing that," replied Lestrade, " and I accept your offer of a sherry with pleasure. Thank you, Doctor," he added, as I handed a glass to him.

Holmes outlined the discoveries of the day, and added his supposition that the furniture was being used to smuggle stolen gems out of the country. Lestrade listened in silence, and at the end of Holmes' recital, placed his glass on the table beside him.

" It is a fine set of facts you have discovered, Mr. Holmes, and Lanner would indeed appear a fool, if that is not too strong a term, were he to arrest the wrong man for the murder of a supposed victim who is in all probability still alive. I appreciate your frankness in letting me know these things."

" They would have been presented to Lanner along with the report of Doctor Watson here," Holmes replied.

" That would have been after Lanner had made the arrest," Lestrade pointed out.

" I had hoped to sow sufficient seeds of doubt in his mind to delay that eventuality, but no matter."

" The question now arises as to how we now proceed," Lestrade ruminated.

" You say ' we', Lestrade ? " asked Holmes, smiling.

" Yes, I do. I shall remove Lanner from the case, and take charge personally," replied Lestrade. " And despite any differences of opinion that you and we of the official police may have had in the past, I sincerely hope that you will be of assistance in helping to solve this mystery."

It was an offer graciously made, and Sherlock Holmes accepted it in the spirit in which it had been extended. " It will be my pleasure and privilege to work with you," he replied. " Another sherry, Inspector, while we discuss tactics ? "

 HERLOCK Holmes was awake and out of the house the next morning, before I had even opened my eyes. I had broken my fast and was settling down by the fireside (for it was a dismal, damp day), when my friend returned.

" A good start to the day," he remarked to me. " Lestrade has called off his dogs, and the imbecile Lanner is now a person of merely historical interest, at least as far as this particular case is concerned. My opinion of Lestrade is somewhat improved from what it has been. I see you have eaten, so if you are ready, we will depart for Bloomsbury."

" As you fixed with Lestrade yesterday ? "

" Indeed. We agreed, did we not, that the sight of Sherlock Holmes and John Watson would probably arouse fewer suspicions in the neighbourhood than would a

uniformed policeman, or even the plain-clothes detectives of the Metropolitan Police ? We are to spy out the land and determine more about our friend Gérard before Lestrade pounces."

" One moment, Holmes. There is something here in the newspaper, unlikely as it may seem, that may have a bearing on this matter." My acquaintance with Sherlock Holmes had taught me to scan the agony columns of the newspapers in search of subjects of interest. " See here. ' Commode now safe to move from 10GP. 1:30PM today. G.' "

" By Jove, Watson, I think you have it ! Excellent work. Maybe there is something to be said for staying in bed for an extra hour, after all. Yes, we may take G to be our friend Gérard, do you not think ? 10GP to be number 10, Gilbert Place, and the commode is now safe to move, perhaps since he feels that the murder in Soho, since it has not been reported in the newspapers, has as yet remained undiscovered. Let us look in the papers of the days before and see if there are any other such messages."

He seized the untidy stack of paper that comprised the previous week's journals and scanned them hastily. " Yes, we have it, Watson. Here we are, on the day following the day on which we may guess the murder to have been committed. ' Commode cannot be moved at this time. Watch here for further messages. G.' I am certain that G, should we take the trouble to look, will have placed many messages over the past few months. We are running out of time. Watson, may I impose on your good nature ? I must go and relieve Lefevre's mind, and assure him that he now runs no further risk of arrest and that he is in no danger, other than being called as a possible witness at some future date. At the same time I will inform Joskin that he no longer need shoulder the burden of standing guard over Lefevre. Now we know what we are looking for, may I trouble you to go to the offices of the *Daily Chronicle* and scan the agony columns over the past few months, working backwards from the present. You will do that ? Good man. I will join you there in an hour or so. Let us move fast. The game is afoot, Watson. The game is afoot," he repeated with relish.

The files of the *Daily Chronicle* were soon opened to me at the mention of Sherlock Holmes' name, and I pored over the printed pages, discovering several messages that appeared to be relevant to our case. I copied these down, together with the dates, and had a list of six or seven when Sherlock Holmes joined me.

" You have them, Watson ? " he asked. " Well done indeed," he exclaimed, looking over the list I presented to him. " Now to Scotland Yard."

" Not Bloomsbury ? " I asked.

" Not at present. Now we are dealing with a more reasonable colleague on the official side, I wish to make use of his cooperation."

Lestrade greeted us in his office. Holmes explained the messages in the agony column, and the events of the morning.

" This promises well, Mr. Holmes," said the Inspector. " What would you suggest now ? "

" I would ask you the same question," replied Holmes, his eyes twinkling.

" My next action would be to reconcile the dates of these messages with the dates of robberies that have been reported in the same period. But no doubt you have other plans ? "

" That is exactly what I would do myself, Inspector. Bless my soul, but if you continue in this way, I will be able to retire and keep bees in Sussex, or find some other equally preposterous and unlikely way of passing my time."

" Very good," replied Lestrade, calling for a clerk and giving instructions that the records of any robberies of valuables in the weeks previous to the dates of the agony column messages be fetched to him.

" And now," when the clerk had departed, " you believe that the commode, whatever that may be, will be despatched from this house in Gilbert Place this afternoon ? "

" I believe that to be the case."

" Then we can arrest the sender and the carrier at that time."

" Not so fast, Lestrade. I would have your men follow the carrier to his destination, then make the arrest. Two birds with one stone, and the sender will be none the wiser, still in the belief that the commode and whatever it may contain has been safely delivered, We may then leave the sender alone for the present. In any event, he appears to have deserted his post at the G— Hotel for the past few days, and we may well expect him to be occupying the rooms at Gilbert-street."

" That makes more sense," agreed Lestrade. " I will arrange for plain-clothes men and a hansom to watch and follow."

" Make sure you use discretion, Lestrade. Put your best men onto this. We are dealing with professional criminals here, I believe, and we may be playing for high stakes. When do you expect the results of the search of the records that you have just ordered ? "

" An hour, maybe a little more," replied Lestrade.

" Good. In that event, Watson and I will take ourselves to Blooms-bury in advance of your men, and make discreet enquiries."

Gilbert Place turned out to be a small side street near the Museum, and number 10 was a small book-shop, with the part of the building above the shop apparently used as residential accommodation.

We entered the shop, and Holmes enquired of the owner as to whether a Mr. Troutbridge was the occupant of the rooms above the premises.

" No, sir, I think you must be mistaken there. There's no Mr. Troutbridge in the rooms above, and I've never heard of the name in this area."

" Maybe I misheard the name," admitted Holmes. " The man to whom I was introduced, and who told me he lived here was a short dark man, with a heavy beard and moustache. He told me he was from

the North of England, where he has a business manufacturing cutlery, and was lodging at this address."

" There's no-one like that here, sir. The only man in the rooms above here is a Mr. Phillimore— that's Mr. James Phillimore, and he's a tall thin gentleman, with white hair and no beard or anything like that. I think there's something a bit foreign about him, but we don't see him that often, as he's got some job with old furniture, buying and selling it, that takes him out of Town at times, and he keeps odd hours as a result. Perhaps you misheard the address, sir ? Maybe you are thinking of Gilbert-street, off Oxford-street ? "

" I am sure you are right," replied Holmes, courteously lifting his hat and exiting the shop.

" Capital," he exclaimed, rubbing his hands together. " We have Mr. James Phillimore where we want him, and now we will be able to trap him at our leisure."

" Who is Troutbridge ? " I could not help but ask.

" I was not going to make the elementary mistake of asking for Phillimore by name or give any kind of description. Even if the shopkeeper is no confederate of his, it might come to Gérard's ears that someone has been making enquiries about him. I therefore enquired after a figment of my imagination, with a physical appearance totally unlike that of Gérard. Now, let us scout the area, and discover the most suitable points for Lestrade's myrmidons to station themselves later in the day." We strolled casually along the length of the street, and Holmes made notes on his shirt-cuff as we walked. " Scotland Yard now, Watson." As we turned to go, Holmes clutched at my sleeve.

" Look behind you, Watson, as discreetly as you can. It is he ! "

I bent, as if to adjust my bootlace, and shifted my gaze to the building that housed the bookshop out of which we had just come. I perceived a tall, slim, elderly man leaving the house, through a door at the side of the shop. He was immaculately, even foppishly, dressed, and corresponded in all respects to the description we had been given earlier. Carrying a tightly rolled umbrella, he sauntered leisurely down the road in the direction of the Museum.

" Excellent," exclaimed Holmes. " We now have proof, if any were needed, that Gérard and Phillimore are one and the same, and that he is currently occupying these premises."

Lestrade expressed his delight at Holmes' report, and his advice on the positioning of the police later that day. " Thank you for this information, Mr. Holmes. And I have information for you," he added, with some satisfaction, after he had given detailed orders to the police officers who were to watch the house and dispatched them. " In the week prior to all these announcements in the *Chronicle* discovered by Dr. Watson here, there was a robbery involving valuable pieces of jewellery. The victims were typically those in high society, as you might expect from the nature of the stolen items. All these recent jewel robberies were made from the houses of the victims, while the family was absent."

" So we may assume that the thief had knowledge that there would be no family at the house on those occasions."

" That was my thought also," replied Lestrade.

" Then we must search for a common thread, Inspector. Maybe the same servant moved between the different households, acting as a spy for the gang, or possibly even acting as the thief ? "

" I am afraid we have investigated that possibility," Lestrade answered, smiling ruefully. " The servants in the households in question seem all to have been trusted servants who had been in the employ of the families for many years. None of them left soon after the robberies, as that theory would seem to indicate. In any event, there was clear evidence that the burglaries were carried out by breaking and entering, not from within the household. Believe me, Mr. Holmes, that was an idea that we, too had considered, but were forced to reject."

Holmes shook his head. " Well, Inspector, you seem to have covered that ground pretty thoroughly. Please accept my congratulations on your efficiency. It is difficult to know, though, how a thief could come to learn of the absence of the family from the home in so many cases, unless a watch was set on the target, which would undoubtedly raise suspicion unless it were carried out skilfully. In any event, my experience with this class of criminal is that they have little patience with this sort of tactic."

" Maybe some cab driver in the thieves' employ ? " I suggested.

This time it was Lestrade who disagreed. " These were wealthy families with their own carriages."

" Wait ! " exclaimed Holmes, clapping his hands together. " What a fool I am. What a blind fool not to have seen this before ! " Lestrade and I could merely gaze at him in wonder. " Lestrade, look through those reports again. I will wager that the families who suffered these losses spent their evenings at the G— Hotel. As the *chef de cuisine* there, Gérard would be in a perfect position to learn of the reservations being made for dinner several days in advance, and could lay his plans accordingly."

" It would fit the facts," Lestrade agreed, drawing the file of papers to him and looking through them. After a few minutes he looked up. " The destination of the owners of the jewellery on the nights of the robberies is not always recorded," he confessed, " but in three of the cases here, they were attending a function at the G— Hotel. I think you have hit on it, Mr. Holmes."

" It would not surprise me in the least if the dead man, whom we suspect to be Jules Navier, were also involved somehow with this."

" Ah, yes," remarked Lestrade. " We have the Soho murder. I read your report, Doctor, and note your conclusion that the man was poisoned."

" I have my strong suspicions there," remarked Holmes. " While examining the room yesterday, I came across two highly suggestive pieces of evidence, which your man Lanner chose to ignore. First, we have this," producing an envelope from his pocket. " Your fool of an associate—and I make no apology at all for using that term, Lestrade— without bothering to examine them closely, first pronounced them as being breadcrumbs. When invited to examine them more closely, he went back on that opinion, but refused to commit himself to what they might be."

" Well, what is your opinion of these ? "

" I have no opinions on the matter, Lestrade, I am merely stating the facts as I perceive them. These are without the faintest doubt, crumbs of *choux* pastry. A confection which is chiefly the product of skilled *patissiers*, the trade that we consider the dead man to have followed."

" And the other envelope ? "

" Ah, this may prove the answer to the riddle."

" It looks like a bilberry," I remarked.

" I agree with you," said Holmes. " It does indeed resemble that fruit. I have every confidence, however, that it is a berry of *atropa belladonna*."

" Deadly   nightshade ? " I enquired.

" Yes, that is one of the English names it goes by," replied Holmes. " It resembles various edible berries, but is highly toxic. My guess is that when the autopsy is carried out, the dead man will turn out to have ingested some of the berries. As few as ten can cause death."

" How would he come to eat them ? " asked Lestrade. " I cannot imagine that he would make such an error of judgement as to mistake belladonna for some kind of fruit."

" I cannot at this moment say," replied Holmes. " This will, I am sure, be one of the details about which Gérard will enlighten us in due course. I am convinced that in some way this will turn out to be connected with the original problem with which I was presented— the stolen recipe for the *canetons à la mode russe*."

" We have an hour to wait before the time at which that message in the Chronicle tells us that the commode is to be picked up," said Lestrade.

" We will be ready," said Holmes.

N the event, it was some two hours before Lestrade received the message that the carrier of the furniture and the occupant of the warehouse to which it was delivered were in custody, and the commode itself was likewise in the possession of the police force.

" To Whitechapel, then," said Holmes.

We arrived at the address we had been given, which turned out to be a repository for bric-a-brac of all kinds, including some handsome pieces of furniture. The commode in question stood by itself, having obviously just been unloaded from the cart that had transported it there.

A brief conversation with the carter was enough to establish the fact that his services had been hired for the day, and that this was the first such occasion on which he had made such a delivery from Gilbert Place. After verifying and recording his identity, Lestrade was happy to let the frightened man return to his usual place of business.

The owner of the warehouse, a certain Alfred Vicks, to whom the delivery had been addressed personally, was a different matter. A small man, whose general appearance reminded me of some sort of small rodent, such as a mouse or rat, continually protested his innocence in an unconvincing whining tone following Lestrade's formal words of arrest.

" You've got nothing on me, so help me Gawd," he kept saying. " I'll see the whole b— lot of you in court before I'm through."

" Dear me. Such language will avail you nothing," said Holmes. " I believe you may be correct there, though. We may well have the pleasure of seeing you in court, but I fancy that you will be in the dock, and we will be in the witness box, giving evidence against you."

He moved to the commode and proceeded to examine it minutely, calling Lestrade and myself over after a few minutes. " Observe closely, Lestrade. The screws in this hinge are hand-cut, and are original with the rest of the piece. On this hinge, you can see clearly that the screws have been substituted with modern replicas, created by machine."

" I see what you mean," said Lestrade. " Your conclusions ? "

" My conclusion here is that the hinge was removed, and replaced. The original screws were damaged when the hinge was removed, necessitating their replacement. The lack of patina caused by years of polishing with wax is also absent in the gap between the wood and the metal of the hinge."

" To what end ? "

" Let us see," replied Holmes. From his pocket, he produced a folding knife of a curious design with many blades and attachments, out of which he produced a screwdriver. I was later to discover that this was a present from a Swiss client, whom he had assisted the previous month. " Ha ! These screws offer no resistance, which further confirms my conjecture that they were recently inserted. And here we are," removing the hinge and revealing under it, rather than the solid wood that might be expected, a cylindrical hole, about twice the diameter of a lead pencil, out of which protruded a length of gut fishing line. " This is what we have been seeking, I believe, Lestrade. Will you do the honours ? " taking the end of the line, and offering it to the police detective.

Lestrade took the line and pulled gently, extracting a small muslin bag attached to the other end, the mouth of which was secured by a drawstring.

" I think there may be something of interest in there," remarked Holmes, examining it. " Open it carefully, Inspector."

From the bag, Lestrade poured into his hand a stream of small brilliantly cut gems, chiefly diamonds and rubies, that sparkled in the sun filtering through the warehouse skylight. I could not help but let out a cry of astonishment at the sight, and Lestrade himself audibly caught his breath as he gazed at the priceless spoil nestled in his palm.

" They have been removed from their settings, but I would lay odds that these are the stones from the spoil of the Floughton robbery ten days ago. If I remember from the description, the settings were of far less value than these stones, which are all of the first water and cut."

The man Vicks had turned pale as Holmes did his work, and at the sight of the stones, he started to babble.

" It wasn't me who blagged them," he protested.

" You knew they were there, though, and you knew they were stolen," Holmes said firmly.

" I knew they was in that lumber somewhere, but Phillimore never said where they were. That was for them Frogs at the other end to find out. My lay was to take the lumber, send it on a ship, and keep Phillimore's name out of it. I reckon you've nibbed him already, since you've found the sparklers so quick ? "

" We have yet to arrest Phillimore," replied Lestrade. " You can thank Mr. Holmes here for the discovery of the stones."

" You're a smart one, and no mistake," Vicks said to Holmes. " We

reckoned no-one would ever twig the lay." There was no trace of mockery in his tone.

" Thank you," said Holmes. " Compliments are always welcome, no matter what their source. By the way, you know that Navier is dead ? "

" No, never 'eard of 'im. Who is 'e ? " Vicks' surprise and ignorance appeared genuine.

" Never you mind that, my lad," said Lestrade. " It's Bow-street for you in the morning. Take him back to the station," he said to the uniformed constables who had accompanied us.

" While we are here," said Holmes, " we should be looking for the other pieces, in case they are still here. We have the list written in the notebook."

Alas, our best efforts failed to discover any of the pieces listed in the notebook, and we were forced to abandon the search. On Holmes' recommendation, however, Lestrade gave orders that the warehouse be sealed off, pending a thorough search of the whole premises at some time in the near future.

Holmes and I returned to Baker-street, Holmes having obtained permission from Lestrade to analyse the mysterious berry that had been discovered in the room in Soho.

Once returned, he plunged into his mysterious world of retorts and reagents. After about an hour, he let out a cry of triumph. " I suspected it, but this is absolute proof of the presence of hyoscyamine, one of the poisons to be found in the berries of deadly nightshade, or belladonna."

" But how did he administer it, and why ? " I asked.

" There, I confess, I am still baffled, but I believe that we will discover the details in the immediate future."

At that moment, there was a knock on the door, and Mrs. Hudson, our landlady, handed a telegram to Holmes. He tore it open, and scanned the contents. " We have no need to make an early start tomorrow, Watson," he reported. " Lestrade has established for the past few days that Gérard has not stirred from his house till after ten o'clock, and therefore suggests that we wait outside the Gilbert Place house from half after eight. He has a magistrate's warrant, and is ready to arrest him at a moment's notice. I trust that his enquiries were discreet enough not to disturb the game before the time is ripe."

HE next morning saw Holmes, Lestrade and myself standing at one end of Gilbert Place, with two of Lestrade's colleagues having taken their place at the other end. It was a raw, chill morning, and a light rain had started to fall. Holmes was wearing his warm travelling ulster, but I was forced, being relatively unprepared, to share the shelter of Lestrade's umbrella, which he had fortuitously brought with him.

At length the door beside the bookshop opened, and the man we had come to know as James Phillimore stepped out into the street. As we had seen him on the previous day, he was smartly dressed, but after taking a few steps, he appeared to realise his lack of any protection against the rain, and turned to re-enter the house.

" Now ! " cried Lestrade, and dashed forward. As our quarry reappeared, this time holding an umbrella, he laid a hand on Gérard's shoulder. " Jean-Marie Gérard, I am arresting you on charges relating to the death of one Jules Navier, and others related to the theft of jewellery."

Somewhat to our surprise, the tall man's face appeared to take on a look of relief. " I thank you, sir," he replied. " The last few days have been a *cauchemar*—how you say, a nightmare, for me. Believe me, it is a weight from my mind that you have come."

Lestrade raised his eyebrows. " Then you will have no objection to telling us your story down at Scotland Yard ? "

" I will not say it will be a pleasure," replied the other. " But it will be a relief to do so."

Once at Scotland Yard, the Frenchman sat facing Holmes, Lestrade and myself, with a policeman recording his words.

" I understand that this will be evidence in the court," he began, " but I wish to make a clean chest of the facts and to lay them before you.

" First, I want to tell you that I am responsible for the death of Jules Navier, but I was sorely provoked, I assure you. Maybe you know something of him ? He was a *patissier* of genius—a true *artiste* of the dessert—but he was not a man to be trusted. Maybe you do not know this, but among those of us at the top of our professions, there is a great rivalry. My English friend, Francis Smith, who now styles himself as François Lefevre, which is the name by which I now think of him, once stole one of my creations when we worked together in Paris, and started to claim this recipe as his own. It was a mere trifle, an *amuse-gueule*, and it helped him in his career." He shrugged. " *C'est la vie*. It happens, and we live with it.

My friend Lefevre was a good friend in all other respects—he helped me when I was in trouble with my restaurant several times, and he helped me to obtain my present position at the G— Hotel. But still, the offence stayed inside me and I thought about it still.

" Navier was a gift from Heaven for my work at the Hotel. My previous *patissier* had left me to return to his home in Avignon some months before, and his replacement was far from possessing the same level of skill. So when Navier came to me, this reaffirmed my position as a true *chef de cuisine* in the Hotel. His meringues..." Gérard kissed the tips of his fingers. " His *profiteroles* and *éclairs*. Beyond compare." He seemed lost in a reverie before continuing. " He was the man, I was sure, who could help me obtain the famous recipe for *canetons à la mode russe* that Lefevre had devised in the past. That dish had won plaudits from the whole of the culinary world, and many had tried and failed to replicate it. I knew of Lefevre's habit of adding the final touches himself, which he kept as a secret, and I knew that his book of recipes was stored in his desk, from hints he had dropped, although he had never told me outright. I wished to serve the course at a special dinner to be given by the Russian Ambassador in honour of a visit by the Archduke Alexei next month, but I needed to perfect it before then, and accordingly determined to place it on the menu.

" I procured a skeleton key from a friend—I will tell you more of such friends in a little while—and gave it to Navier with my instructions. He was only to remove the single recipe and copy it onto a sheet of paper. However, when he delivered it to me at my rooms in Soho, he discovered me working on the commode which I have just sent to France."

" That commode will never reach France," Holmes told him. " It and its contents have been seized, and Vicks was arrested yesterday."

" I cannot pretend to be sorry," replied Gérard. " I have been living the life of a dog for too long. Let me explain the whole sorry business to you. In my youth, I did several bad things, and the results are still with me. There are two men in France. They do not bear my name—rather they bear that of a noble family— but they are my sons nonetheless. The powerful family whose daughter I seduced—I see no reason to hide this from you gentlemen—offered me the choice of death or making over to the family an annual payment of a large sum of money. Which would you have chosen ? By hard work, and with the help of my friends, I could scrape together the money, leaving me almost penniless at the end of each year. Lefevre helped me leave France—*mon Dieu*, I can almost say that I escaped the country—and come to England, where I believed I was safe.

" Then one day I had a visit from a Frenchman, who introduced himself as the attorney for the family I had wronged.

" ' Now you are here in this country,' he said to me, ' you are in a better position to make the payments. You will tell us the names of your wealthy patrons at the Hotel before they visit you. We have friends who will visit their houses, and deliver the proceeds to you. You must then send these to France, in whatever way you think best. Otherwise, steps of a kind described to you in the past will be taken.' You have no idea, gentlemen, how much that speech frightened me. I could read death in his eyes, and I knew that there were those, even in this city, who would take my life for a few sous.

" Well, I need hardly tell you that I complied. The first set of jewellery arrived as had been planned at my Soho lodgings."

" Excuse   me," interrupted Holmes, " but I am puzzled as to why you adopted two names and two addresses."

" It was because the name of Gérard had become hateful to me, though it was the name I used at the G—Hotel and was the name of my birth. And the Soho lodgings where I had been staying had likewise become a place where I could no longer live as I wished. I therefore adopted a new name and a new identity as James Phillimore.

" But to return to my story. I gazed at the trinkets that had been given to me by one of the lowest of the low, and asked myself how I was to send them to France without drawing the attention of the authorities to them. I could, of course, have carried them myself, but my work at the Hotel was too demanding to allow for that. It was then that I had my *coup de tête*, my brainwave. My father had been a cabinetmaker by trade, and before I apprenticed myself in the kitchen, I had received instruction from him in the art. It occurred to me that there are many possible hiding-places for small valuable objects in old pieces of furniture, and I accordingly arranged for the purchase of such pieces, to be delivered to me in my person as Phillimore at Bloomsbury. My background enabled me to choose fine pieces that would arouse no suspicion were they to be exported. There would be little point in my selecting rubbish to send to France, eh ?

" Once the first piece had been

delivered, I examined it closely to determine how best to secrete the gems. I removed the portion of the piece of furniture on which I was to work—the leg of a table, for example—and carried it to my rooms in Soho. There, I kept tools and materials allowing me to construct hollow hiding places and false bottoms to drawers and the like. I had no wish to do the work at Gilbert Place, feeling it safer to separate the furniture and the work I was doing on it, in order to remove suspicion.

" I communicated with the shipping agent, Vicks, through messages placed in the *Daily Chronicle*. He would send a carter to remove the furniture from Bloomsbury, and from then on, the matter was out of my hands. I explained to my neighbours who remarked this traffic that I was in the business of exporting old English furniture to France, and this seemed to be accepted as an explanation.

" About six or seven such deliveries had been made over the period of about a year, when it all came to an end less than a week ago. As I say, I had asked Navier to purloin the recipe, given his knowledge of the workings and the geography of the Club where Lefevre works, and so he did, but he went much further than I had instructed him, or indeed, than I would ever have desired.

" ' *Voici*, here you are,' he told me, handing over the whole book to me. I was completely flabbergasted, gentlemen. This was not what I had wished, and I told him so in no uncertain terms. There was no way that I could return the book to my friend without confessing my guilt in acquiring his recipe. I am afraid I lost my temper with Navier, and called him names which I will not repeat here, even though I have my doubts as to whether you would understand the French words involved.

" As I was berating Navier, I noticed his eyes stray towards the work I had been doing; boring a hole in the thickness of the wood into which I would insert a bag usually used for *bouquet garni* in the preparation of *bouillon*, but in this case stuffed with the jewels from the pieces that comprised the latest haul. Navier saw this, as I say, and also saw the gems, which I had foolishly left on the table beside the tools.

" ' I am sure the police would be interested in your new hobby,' he sneered. ' Maybe I can be persuaded to keep your activities a secret,' he added, with a meaningful leer. Needless to say, I was overcome with fear with the thought that I might be discovered. Navier and I haggled over terms, and we came to a financial disposition that, while satisfying his greed, was highly unsatisfactory to me. We arranged that he was to visit my Soho rooms the next night, and I would pay him the sum demanded in return for his silence.

" I returned to Bloomsbury that night, carrying the piece of wood in which I had concealed the bag containing the gems, and sick at heart. To be the victim of one blackmailer, Mr. Holmes, is a wretched state. To be the victim of two such rogues is to be placed in a condition beyond despair. I was at my wits' end. The next morning I was walking to my work at the Hotel, when I noticed a familiar plant growing in one of the London squares. I had been chastised by my mother as a child for attempting to eat the berries of belladonna, and it had remained as a strong memory throughout my whole life. The similarity of the

berries to some of those we used in our desserts struck me, and I swiftly denuded the bush of its fruits, placing them carefully in my handkerchief. I had no definite plan in my mind, other than that I knew that I could use these. Since I was alone in the kitchen, I swiftly concocted my plan, and produced some sweet tarts, which I decorated in the privacy of my office with the berries I had picked earlier.

" Later, Navier came in, and the scoundrel had the infernal impudence to wink at me as he settled down to work. I could bear his rudeness, as I knew what was in store for him later. I left the Hotel ay my usual time, and made my way to my rooms in Soho, carrying a large meat cleaver with me. When Navier arrived to demand his money, I offered him one of the tarts I had prepared previously, on the pretext that they had been presented to me by an applicant for a post in the kitchens as samples of his work. I told him that I wished to know his professional opinion, and played on his vanity. The fool took me at my word, and greedily devoured two, which, I felt, would ensure his demise.

" And so it transpired. Soon after eating the second, he started to sweat and breathe heavily. His eyes bulged, and he struggled for breath, as I watched him. Believe me, gentlemen, it gave me no pleasure to see him die, other than the fact that I was ridding my life of a poisonous reptile. In less than an hour, he was dead, and I was now faced with the prospect of disposing of the body.

" Navier's clothing was distinctive, marked with the name of the G— Hotel, and it was essential, I believed at that time, that the body and the clothing were separated. It disgusted me, but I stripped the body of its clothing. Then I turned to the business of dismembering the body. I had brought the heaviest butcher's cleaver I could find from the kitchen and a set of overalls, such as are used by those who clean the kitchens. I donned the latter to protect myself from the blood that I was sure would otherwise splash my clothes. It had been a long time since I had done any heavy butchering, and I was nauseated with my work and with myself. I had intended to dispose of the body in small pieces, but found myself unable to continue the ghastly work. Accordingly, I wrapped the cleaver in the clothes and the blood-soaked overalls, tied them into a bundle and made for the Embankment, where I hurled the package into the river."

" We will ask you to identify the place later," Lestrade broke in for the first time.

" I will be happy to oblige," replied Gérard. " Once I had disposed of the weapon and the clothes, I knew inside myself that I could never return to the room with the limbs and body of Navier. I could not force myself to enter, and I knew that for ever more that room of horror would be closed to me. I shut myself in my room in Gilbert Place, in my character of James Phillimore. I cared nothing for the kitchen at the G— Hotel. I cared nothing for anything in my life. I knew that the hotel would never connect James Phillimore with Jean-Marie Gérard, and I was safe from the direction of my work. I still had the gems and the commode in which they were to be delivered, so I made arrangements for their delivery, which it appears you intercepted."

" One thing," Holmes asked. " When did you become aware that you had left this," holding up the notebook, " in the room with Navier's body ? "

" I realised it as soon as I returned to Bloomsbury on that fatal night. I knew it was there in the drawer, and I had no stomach to return for it. The fact that it would be discovered filled my dreams, such as they have been for these past terrible nights."

" It is a sad tale, to be sure," said Holmes, " and I cannot but consider that you were provoked, but you are guilty of the most serious of all crimes—that of taking a human life."

" I am well aware of that," said the wretched man, " and I am now prepared to take whatever consequences may arise."

T was some two months later that Holmes put down the newspaper and sighed. " Life, Watson. How cruel it can be."

It was unlike Holmes to make remarks of this sort, and I enquired what had caused him to speak in this way. By way of answer, he passed over the copy of the newspaper, in which two items on the same page caught my eye.

The first told of the sentencing to death at the Old Bailey of Jean-Marie Gérard, who had been found guilty of the murder of Jules Navier. The other, a mere footnote at the bottom of the same page, told of the discovery of the body of one François Lefevre, alias Francis Smith, who had apparently hanged himself in his room at the Club where he was employed as *chef*. No note was found, and no motive could apparently be ascribed for the deed, but for my part, I put it down to his grief at the sentence passed on his friend, whose trial had been widely publicised, and for whose death he somehow felt at least in part responsible as the result of his past actions.

Sherlock Holmes
& The Case of the
Trepoff Murder

" THERE IS IN ODESSA A FLIGHT OF STEPS LEADING FROM THE WATER TO
THE CITY—THE PRIMORSKY STAIRS, SOME 200 IN ALL." (PAGE 324)

EDITOR'S NOTE

The Trepoff murder case is mentioned by Dr Watson in A Scandal in Bohemia. *In it, Holmes is described as travelling to Odessa, but it has never been clear from the brief description provided by Watson whether the murder took place in Odessa, or whether Holmes made his visit to discover new facts regarding the murder which took place in another location, whether he was required to make a report to the Russian authorities, or whether he was retained by the local police to investigate the murder.*

The second of those possibilities has always appeared to me to be the most likely, given the connections of Holmes' brother Mycroft with the Foreign Office and other British government institutions.

This suspicion was confirmed to some extent when I opened the deed box that had been sent to me from London, and came across the adventure entitled The Odessa Business, *which I have transcribed and published earlier.*

Though Holmes makes reference to "the Odessa business" in this case, there is no clue as to what that business might be, and I was beginning to despair of ever finding the answer to this riddle.

In Holmes' day, travel from London to Odessa would have involved much more time and effort than it does today in the age of airlines. Such a journey would almost certainly have occupied a number of weeks, and would hardly have been undertaken lightly. I therefore concluded that there was a very good chance that this adventure would

have been recorded by Watson, even if it was only in the form of rough notes, since it was of considerable importance in the development of Holmes' career.

I was therefore delighted when it became obvious that a sheaf of papers in the deed box, pinned together, formed the manuscript of Watson's relation of this case. This is interesting in that the manuscript has been annotated by another hand, which I have learned to recognise as that of Sherlock Holmes, making a few factual corrections and emendations, often acerbic, to Watson's original words. Wherever the original is still legible following Holmes' editing, I will endeavour to reproduce it, together with the notes that he added, which I have placed in square brackets and italicised. For example:

" Count Beloffsky was a middle-aged man *[hardly middle-aged !]* of florid appearance".

Since it is obvious that Watson did not accompany Holmes on this adventure and was forced to record the events from Holmes' own account, recorded on a number of different occasions (as is evident by the different inks and pens used throughout the narrative), it is likely that he passed his final draft to Holmes for correction and approval, almost uniquely, as far as I am aware. This adventure is therefore probably one of the most factually accurate of all of the cases described by Dr Watson.

The story was originally released in ten weekly instalments on the

Internet. This is the first time that it has appeared in print.

<hr />

OR some years now it has been my privilege to be the chronicler, and if I may be so bold as to say so, also the friend of the greatest detective of our age, Mr Sherlock Holmes.

For many of the adventures I have set forth, I was lucky enough to observe Mr Holmes' work at first hand, giving me an excellent opportunity to set forth his methods. For others, I was not present for all or some of the case, forcing me to rely on Sherlock Holmes' own testimony regarding his actions.

Here I might add that Holmes, whilst being an excellent raconteur and companion, regarded his adventures more in the nature of scientific studies, and his accounts were correspondingly dull. However, on some occasions, I was present for a part of the case, and I was therefore able to infuse sufficient interest into the accounts to hold the attention of the amateur or enthusiast of the detective art (or science, as Holmes himself would have it). Such an adventure was that of the Trepoff murder, which I present here.

<hr />

T was a bright clear morning in the Spring of 189– when Inspector Lestrade burst in on Holmes and myself as we were eating our breakfast.

" I am sorry to see you here in this state, Lestrade," remarked Holmes. " I take it that you are the bearer of bad news ? "

" From my point of view, it could hardly be worse," replied the policeman. " You are aware, of course, that Prince Mikhail Robinski, cousin of the Tsar, will be visiting London next week ? "

" I had heard the news," replied Holmes. " Do sit down, Lestrade, and take a cup of tea. Your constant hovering is an irritant to digestion."

Lestrade allowed himself to be persuaded to join us at the table, and continued. " The Prince will be staying at the Russian Embassy. He fears for his safety if he takes rooms in a hotel here, given the anti-Russian sentiment of many Britons at this time."

" Not to mention the Russian nihilists and anarchists who are rumoured to be in London," I added.

Lestrade nodded. " Indeed, I think they are more on his mind than our own enemies of Russia," he replied.

" And your problem ? " asked Holmes.

" The Naval Attaché, a Vice-Admiral Yevgeny Stepanovich Trepoff, was discovered murdered in his room at Chesham House, the Russian Embassy, last night," replied Lestrade, bluntly. " Prince Mikhail has a keen interest in his country's navy, and we had heard that he was especially looking forward to meeting Trepoff and discussing matters of naval import with him, particularly regarding the growth of our own Navy and the latest developments in battleships. The Prince's itinerary included a visit to Barrow-in-Furness in the company of Trepoff, to call on the shipyards there."

" You say the man was murdered," said Holmes. " Are you sure of that ? "

" When a man can shoot himself through the head in a manner that causes instant death, and then dispose of the weapon in such a way that it cannot be discovered, I will consider suicide. Otherwise, I will assume that it is a case of murder."

" It would seem likely, certainly," Holmes smiled in agreement. " And your problem ? I assume, naturally, that you have experienced a problem, otherwise we would not be enjoying the pleasure of your company at this moment."

" Of course. The description of the finding of the body was given to us by the Embassy staff. By the time our men arrived, we discovered that the doors were shut to us, and we were not permitted to enter."

Holmes frowned. " Where is the body now ? "

" It is still within the Embassy. We have no authority to enter and claim it, even for a post-mortem examination, without the permission of the Embassy staff. We need to investigate and clear up the matter before the Prince's visit."

" And why, my dear Inspector, do you believe that I will be able to gain access where you, with the full might of the Metropolitan Police behind you, have failed ? "

" Your brother..." began Lestrade, with some hesitation in his voice.

" Ah, I begin to take your meaning. You wish me to talk to Mycroft and ask him to apply some sort of pressure to make the Russians cooperate in the investigation ? "

" Precisely."

" I can but try. Mark you, Mycroft is his own man, and I have little influence over him."

" I thank you, anyway."

" It crosses my mind," mused Holmes, " that the Embassy staff, while averse to a visit from the official police, might yet allow me to work what little skill I have in the investigation. Would that be satisfactory to you ? "

" By all means," replied Lestrade. " Provided that you make your findings on the murder available to us."

" Naturally I will do that. You may depend on it."

" Very good," said Lestrade. He finished his tea, took up his hat and left us.

***

T seems we must make our way to Mycroft," Holmes said to me as the sound of Lestrade's footsteps down the stairs faded.

" Do you believe he can be of assistance here ? "

" He has some influence with the Tsar as a result of his work on the Polish question. I believe that influence could extend to the Embassy here if he so desired. Whether he will consider it politically expedient to interfere in this affair is another matter."

" So we are for the Diogenes Club ? " I spoke of that strange society of solitary men, where speech was forbidden, and the members sat in aloof splendour, magnificently unaware of their fellows in the same room.

Before Holmes could answer,

there was a thunder of feet up the stairs, and a furious knocking at the door.

" Halloa," exclaimed Holmes. " A client in trouble, by the sound of it. Enter ! " he commanded.

The man who stepped into our sitting-room was one of the most extraordinary personages ever to cross the threshold of 221B Baker-street. A true giant, clad in traditional Russian costume, he could have stepped out of the pages of a Tolstoy novel. From his felt boots to his peasant blouse and his full flowing beard, he was the epitome of what we have come in England to regard as a Muscovite.

" You are Holmes ? " he asked in heavily accented English. " You are man who saves innocents ? "

" I have performed that function on occasion," replied Holmes urbanely, and, realising that our visitor's command of English was far from perfect, added simply, " Sometimes."

" Good. I need your help. I am Golotsin, and I live here in London."

" And you are a sculptor, working in marble, but as yet your genius is unappreciated by those who determine such things in the art world," remarked Holmes.

The Russian screwed up his face in concentration as he attempted to discern the meaning of Holmes' words, but once comprehension had dawned, his eyes danced in his face, framed in that uncouth beard. " *Da, da,* yes, yes ! " he exclaimed. " You have heard of me, then ? "

" Not at all," replied Holmes. " I observe your muscular development and the callouses on your hands which could only have come from wielding a mallet and chisel. You could be a stonemason, but the chips of marble nestling in your hair and in the creases of your garments, as well as the garments themselves, would indicate a higher calling, as does the spirituality of the artist showing in your face. The fact that your clothes are not new and that you need new boots argues that your artistic labours have so far been in vain."

Again after an interval for thought and comprehension, the Russian broke into a broad smile. " You are wizard, Mr Holmes ! So please, I need your help. My political views are not that of Russian government. I am radical, and some might say anarchist but I love my country. I wish to rid Holy Russia of those at top who destroy our lives. Of those, one of those worst ones is Yevgeny Stepanovich Trepoff."

Holmes looked up at the mention of the name. " You are the second person today to mention his name. Why should you mention it now ? "

" He is in London, and my comrades in Petersburg have asked me to kill him here. I was sent a letter from them" (in truth his English now became so broken and halting that I have been forced to give a more complete rendering of his words) " instructing me to bring about his death. That letter was in Russian, but not in code. Last night, I know that agents of the Okhrana—the Russian political police—working from the London Embassy broke into my studio and took the letter. I am bound to be arrested or worse if any harm should befall Trepoff."

" Then you do not know ? " asked Holmes.

" Know what ? "

" Trepoff was killed last night."

The Russian crossed himself, and his head sank on his breast. " I did not kill him," he muttered sullenly.

" It was not I. I did not kill him," he repeated.

I looked astonished at our colossal visitor, who appeared to have shrunk into himself, huddled, with his arms wrapped around his body, and rocking gently back and forth.

I made as if to go toward him, but Holmes stopped me, his finger to his lips.

" Let him be," he said to me, so softly that I had to strain my ears to catch his words. " It is the way with these people, and he will cease soon of his own accord."

We waited in silence, watching the strange sight before us. Suddenly, with a mighty roar, the Russian leaped to his feet. " They will see my innocence ! " he bellowed, in a stentorian voice that made the very glasses on the dining table rattle. " You, sir, will assist me in my proof ! " pointing a long finger at Holmes.

" Very good," replied my friend quietly. " Leave me an address at which you can be contacted, and do not fail to let me know in the event of future developments."

The Russian broke into a broad grin, and spreading his arms wide, he advanced upon Holmes and embraced him in a bear-like hug before presenting him with a card on which was written an address in Aldgate. I was forced to submit to the same embrace myself before Golotsin let himself out of the door and thundered down the stairs to the street.

" Well ! " I exclaimed, laughing. " This is hardly your everyday client."

Holmes himself was obviously in high good humour, and laughed in his turn. " Indeed so. I value such differences in my fellow men, and in those who seek my services. Come, to Mycroft. We can hardly complain of a lack of variety in our lives, can we ? From the ridiculous to the sublime, Watson, or would you sooner have it the other way round ? "

REFRAINED from answering the question, and we soon found ourselves outside the Diogenes Club, where we made our enquiries regarding Mycroft Holmes, and were informed that he was not on the Club premises.

" Most unusual," said Holmes to me, pulling out his watch. " It is as if the bells at Westminster were suddenly to change to playing the tune of the National Anthem. Brother Mycroft runs on rails like a well-regulated tram."

" Ha ! I spy him coming now," I replied. Sure enough, the distinctive bulk of Mycroft Holmes could be seen approaching us from the direction of Whitehall. His eyes were cast down, and he was obviously in deep thought as he hastened towards his Club with all the speed of which he was capable. As he drew near, he raised his head, and perceived his brother and myself waiting on the pavement.

" I assumed you would be here," he called to Sherlock Holmes, waving his stick in greeting. " The Trepoff business, of course ? "

" Of course," replied my friend.

" Then come inside, both of you. Deuced annoying morning. I have just been spending time which I can ill afford in convincing the Foreign Secretary to let you deal with the Russians directly, hence the delay of," he pulled out his own watch, " four minutes and three quarters. Truly intolerable," he puffed, as we made our way up the stairs.

" How did you come to know that your brother was to visit the Russian Embassy ? " I could not forebear from asking. By now we were ensconced in chairs in the Strangers' Room of the Diogenes Club, the only place in that singular establishment where speech is permitted.

Mycroft slowly swung his massive head toward me, like the turret of some great warship. " It was simple," he smiled. " Given that the Metropolitan Police were called in, and subsequently refused entry, it was obvious that there was only one place where they could turn for help. It is Lestrade, so I hear, Sherlock ? "

" You are correct, Mycroft, as in almost everything." To my amusement, I detected a faintly malicious emphasis on the word ' almost'. " I would have preferred Stanley Hopkins to have had the case, however. He has a more delicate touch in these matters. But needs must..."

" And talking of delicate touches, you have met the good Ivan Gregorivitch Golotsin, I assume ? "

" We have just torn ourselves from his embrace. He wished to assure us that despite evidence to the contrary now in the hands of the Okhrana, he is innocent of the murder."

" His papers are not in the hands of the Okhrana," said Mycroft Holmes pleasantly. " They were removed by officers of the Special Branch, and are now in my desk at Whitehall. We did," and here an impish smile spread over his face, " leave some ends of Russian *papirosi* cigarettes at Golotsin's studio to give the impression that it was the Okhrana who were responsible.

I confess that your monograph on tobacco ashes gave me the idea, brother."

" I am glad to have been of service," commented Sherlock Holmes wryly. " I take it that Golotsin is not guilty of the murder ? "

" Of course not." Mycroft's chins wobbled as he considered the matter. " He is a wild-eyed dreamer, and as gentle as a lamb according to those who know him. A wild and shaggy lamb, maybe, but still a lamb."

" But he may lead you to those who are less peaceful, I assume ? " asked his brother.

" Indeed, and this is your task, Sherlock. As a result of the assistance I rendered the Tsar over the recent social reforms, I was able to persuade the Russian Embassy to allow you to enter and investigate the death of Admiral Trepoff. Thanks to your labours, Doctor," turning to me, " my younger brother is now famous, even in such remote locations as Omsk and Perm, let alone Petersburg and Moscow."

" When am I expected ? "

" As soon as is convenient. My final task, as I mentioned earlier, was to persuade the Foreign Secretary that you were to be allowed into the Embassy as the official representative of Her Majesty. Here," reaching inside his coat and withdrawing two thick envelopes. " One for you and one for Dr Watson."

I received my envelope and withdrew a sheet of thick paper, on which was written, in a florid hand, a request to those who read it to treat the bearer, John H. Watson, Esq., as an official diplomatic representative of Her Britannic Majesty.

Mycroft chuckled as he observed me take in its import. " Congratulations, Doctor," he said to me. " You may enjoy this status for the period for which is is valid—the next forty-eight hours."

" To the Russian Embassy, then," said his brother. " Come, Watson.

If your new-found dignity will permit your riding in a hansom cab, let us go into the street and hail such a common vulgar vehicle."

 E arrived at the Russian Embassy to be greeted by a heavyset man whose thin face was framed by a trim grey beard.

" Mr Holmes and Dr Watson," he greeted us in impeccable English, marred only by a slight guttural accent. " We were informed that you would be coming here. Your adventures, sir, as recorded by you, sir," bowing in turn to Holmes and myself, " have given many readers in Russia a great deal of pleasure. It is indeed an honour for us to have you here, but alas ! I wish it were under happier circumstances."

" Thank you," Holmes replied simply. " I appreciate the courtesy you have shown in allowing us here today."

" We had little choice," laughed the other. " A telegram arrived from Petersburg demanding that we open our doors to you. Not, of course," he added diplomatically, " that you would not be welcome in any event. Do you wish to view the body ? "

" First, I would like to examine the room where the body was discovered," answered Holmes.

" The body is still there. We have moved nothing."

Holmes rubbed his hands together briskly, always a sign that he was in high good humour. " Lead me," he commanded.

We were led up two flights of stairs to a small, meanly furnished room, containing an iron bedstead and a deal wardrobe and washstand. " This room is... ? " asked Holmes.

" This is the late Admiral's

bedchamber." On noticing Holmes' raised eyebrows, he explained, " The Admiral prides—rather he prided himself on his simple lifestyle and his piety." He pointed to an ikon painted in the barbaric medieval style, hanging over the bed. The gold was flecked with red, which had emanated from the hideous scene below. The corpse of a slightly-built man in his nightshirt lay on its right side on the bed. The head was shattered as by a blow, and the pillow's white linen cover was now a scarlet mess.

Seemingly unmoved by the ghastly sight, Holmes bent over the corpse and picked up the left hand. " Was Trepoff left-handed ? " he asked.

" He wrote with his right hand, but used a sword with his left."

Holmes had now turned his attention to a pair of pince-nez which had been lying by the side of the bed, peering first through one lens and then the other. " These were Trepoff's ? " he asked.

" Yes, they were."

Holmes hummed a little ditty to himself as he busied himself around the head of the corpse. " Doctor, come here, if you would," he addressed me. " If you can do so, please lift the body by its shoulders."

With some repugnance, and not a little difficulty, for *rigor* had not yet fully departed, I did so, while Holmes examined the blood-stained pillow. At length he signed that I could set down my grisly burden, and I did so with a sigh of relief.

" What did you find ? " I asked him.

" Nothing," he replied. " And that, to be frank, my dear Watson, is a mystery to me. From the angle of the head and the geometry of the wound, I was expecting a bullet, or at least the bullet's mark in the pillow."

" Which means ? "

" He was shot elsewhere and brought to die on this bed, without, however, leaving a trail of blood on the floor, while the ikon, as you can see, is spattered with blood. A pretty puzzle, is it not ? "

" That is impossible ! " exclaimed our Russian companion. " The room was locked. There were two keys only. Admiral Trepoff possessed one, and the other was kept with the porter. It was with this latter that we gained access to the room."

" Why did you feel the need to enter the room ? " asked Holmes, curiously. " Did you, or some other person, hear the shot that killed Trepoff ? "

" No, there was no shot heard. But one of the junior secretaries was passing on the way to his room— many of us find it more convenient to have lodgings within the Embassy itself—"

" Safer, too, no doubt," Holmes interjected drily, " given the number of those in London who are opposed to the current Russian government."

" Yes, yes, that too, of course. The secretary was passing, as I say, when he heard the sound as of a body falling and a groan. Naturally he was concerned, but there was no answer when he knocked on the door and called. Rather than break down the door, he roused me from my sleep and we collected the key to the room from the night porter. We entered at precisely 11:13—I made a note of the time."

" And you have left the room as you found it ? " asked Holmes.

" Other than to check the pulse, I have not touched the body or anything else in the room. The Embassy doctor made some examination before issuing the death certificate, a copy of which I have here."

Holmes scanned the document that was passed to him. " Cause of death, heart failure," he read.

" Heart failure ? " I asked, somewhat astounded.

Holmes regarded me steadily. " Ultimately, is that not the cause of all death ? " he enquired, but not without a certain sarcasm apparent in his voice. " As a doctor, surely you are aware of this simple fact ? "

I fell silent, abashed. [I had no intention of making Watson appear foolish here, whatever he may have felt at the time. I did consider, however, that this was not an appropriate occasion on which to be raising doubts as to the competence of the Embassy doctor.]

Holmes stood, regarding the ikon hanging above the bed, and slowly turning his head to and fro. Suddenly he stopped, and gazed fixedly at the ikon. " Aha ! " he exclaimed, bringing his lens to bear on a mark that did not appear to form part of the ikon's design. I also examined it, and saw that it was a hole, seemingly caused by a bullet or some similar projectile.

" With your permission ? " asked my friend, brandishing his penknife at the ikon. The Russian nodded, though it appeared with some reluctance, and Holmes began a careful excavation of the cavity. He gave a small cry of triumph as a small object dropped into his hand. " Your opinion, Watson ? " he asked, holding it out to me.

" It is a bullet, of course. An

expanding bullet such as is commonly used in revolvers," I replied.

" Excellent.   And the problem is ? "

" The problem, as I see it, is that there is no revolver in this room, and there is no sign of the bullet having entered the room through the window."

" No ? " smiled Holmes.   He pointed to the window of the room, which was slightly ajar.

" No-one could have fired a revolver through that," I objected. " It would be impossible to aim a pistol so accurately. Why, the nearest house must be over thirty yards distant."

" A touch over thirty-three, I would say," replied Holmes. " Mr. Lebed," he addressed the Russian, " how tall was Admiral Trepoff ? "

" A little taller than me. Perhaps the same height as Doctor Watson here."

" Excellent ! Watson, be so good as to stand just here and look out of the window, if you would," indicating a spot on the floor beside the bed. " Thank you. And now let us see. He stood behind me, and I could hear his movements. At one point, I detected the sensation of some cold object being momentarily pressed to the back of my neck, and I flinched instinctively. " My apologies," I heard him say, and in a second or two the cold feeling vanished. " You may move now. Thank you," were his next words. " Excellent," he said, with a satisfied smile. " Let us go now, Watson," as he picked up his hat and prepared to leave the room.

" You are leaving ? " asked Lebed, incredulously. " You know who killed the Admiral ? "

" I am reasonably certain that I know what killed him, even if I am still a little unsure as to the identity of the human agent," replied Holmes.   " There is no time to waste, though. Let us away."

FOLLOWED Holmes as he swept out of the Embassy, and made his way to the mews behind the building. " This one," he said, pausing before one of the houses facing the rear of the Embassy, and knocking on the door.

A surly-faced man, dressed as an ostler, with a strong odour of horse clinging to him, opened the door to us.

" What can I do for you gents ? " he asked in a none too gracious tone of voice.

" I wish to ask you some questions about the gentleman who used the front room on the second floor last night," Holmes stated.

" There ain't nobody living in that room, and there ain't been for a month or more," replied the other, truculently.

" Will you make a wager on that ? " Holmes absent-mindedly fingered a sovereign as he spoke these words.

" A quid it is, then. You can see for yourself," said the ostler. " Up those stairs."

" Thank you," replied Holmes, springing up the stairs. Once in the bare room, Holmes dropped to his knees and examined the floor through a lens. " Large square-toed boots," I heard him mutter. " A long military stride, and halloa ! " He pointed to a dent in the wooden flooring. " What do you make of that ? "

"I have no idea," I replied. "A heavy object has been dropped onto the soft wood at some time?"

"Recently, my dear Watson, not merely 'at some time'. The exposed wood fibres are still clean. And this is quite clearly more the result of steady pressure than it is of a falling object," he added with some asperity. *[Again, I may have been a little brusque in my attitude, having temporarily forgotten the advantage afforded to me by the use of my lens]* He moved towards the window. "And see here," pointing to the windowsill. "This window has been opened recently, and I see the mark of what is unmistakably an elbow in the dust."

"An elbow?" I asked.

For answer, Holmes took his walking-stick, pressed the handle to his shoulder, and aimed it as if it were a rifle, with the elbow of his left arm supporting the stick hovering a little way above the window-sill, sighting along the stick towards the Russian Embassy.

"I take your meaning," I replied. I looked out of the window, from which Admiral Trepoff's room, recognisable by the partly opened window, could clearly be seen. "It is possible that a marksman could aim through the gap in the window. He would have to be an excellent shot, though. And," as other objections crossed my mind, "not only was no shot heard, but the bullet you discovered in Trepoff's room could only have been fired from a revolver."

"As to the first of your objections, I have a man in mind who could accomplish the feat of marksmanship you have described. Not only is he skilled in the use of guns of all kinds, he is almost totally without fear, and equally devoid of morality. I may never be able to prove it, but I am certain this was his work. As to your other two objections, they are

definitely not without merit. However, I have heard reports from Germany that would definitely quash them." He would say no more, but we made our way downstairs where we confronted the ostler.

"Your money, I believe," said Holmes, handing the coin to him. "The room is indeed unoccupied. However, it would be in your interest, to the tune of a similar amount, were you to tell me of the man who was in that room last night."

The other's tongue played around his lips greedily. "I never saw him before yesterday, and that's the honest truth. He was a big sort of cove. Soldier-type, if you ask me. Blue eyes that look straight through you, and a big forehead with a lot of brains behind it, I reckon. Big nose, and a look to his mouth that showed you wouldn't want to cross him."

"How much did he pay you, Mr— ?"

"Lovatt. George Lovatt. He paid me two guineas."

"Then I can do no less," replied Holmes, reaching into his pocket and finding two companions to the sovereign he had donated earlier, and adding a florin.

"Why, thank you, sir," replied the now obsequious Lovatt.

We returned to Baker-street by cab, Holmes explaining to me how Trepoff had been shot. *[He had been standing in front of the bed. The soft bullet passed through his skull, spraying the wall and the ikon with blood and brains (Watson failed to notice this last, and I did not draw his attention to the fact). The victim's first instinct was to clap his left hand to the wound at the back of his head, as was shown by the hand being covered in blood. This accounted for the lack of bleeding on the floor. He then collapsed onto the bed, with the groan and sound that were heard from outside the room. He soon lost consciousness as the result of blood loss and died very shortly thereafter.]*

Holmes had hardly started to dictate to me the report that we were to present to Lestrade, when the little police inspector himself burst into the room.

" Another murder at the Embassy ? " Holmes asked with a smile.

" It is no laughing matter," replied Lestrade. " A man living near the Embassy has just been discovered dead—strangled, with his neck broken."

" Who was he ? " I asked, though some presentiment told me I already knew the answer.

" An ostler living in the mews behind the Embassy, who went by the name of George Lovatt."

Though Holmes appeared to be somewhat taken aback by the news, it was not in the way I had expected. " So soon ? " he exclaimed. " This becomes more serious, and more dangerous, than I had imagined."

Lestrade and I looked at him questioningly, but he provided no further explanation.

" It is time for me to reflect on this and consider our next move," he said, reaching into his pocket. His face expressed annoyance. " I must return to the Embassy," he informed us. " I remember removing my pipe from my pocket as we examined the body, and I must have forgotten to replace it. Do you remember where I placed it, Watson ? "

I shook my head, having no recollection of the incident.

" No matter. Typically, material possessions mean little to me, but a pipe is an old friend, and one should never desert one's friends, eh, Lestrade ? " Something in Holmes' manner gave me more than a little disquiet, but I offered to accompany

him on his errand, or to perform it on his behalf. " No, no," he protested. " *Mea culpa*, and I shall expiate the sin myself. Do you stay here, Lestrade, for as long as it pleases you. I feel somewhat soiled by my exertions this morning. Forgive me while I retire to wash and to change my shirt, at the least." He stepped into the bed-room.

" Thank you," replied the Scotland Yard officer, " but I must return to my duties soon." He sat in silence for a minute or two, presumably savouring this time of repose. " While you are at the Embassy," he addressed Holmes through the door, " I think you may advise them that the body may be moved and funeral rites may begin, if you are satisfied as to the cause of death, and have learned all that you can in this regard."

" I will certainly do that," replied Holmes as he returned to the drawing-room from the bed-room, sporting a fresh shirt, and pulling on his coat. " The full report will be with you soon, believe me, but in the meantime there is nothing of urgent import to communicate." With those words he departed, leaving Lestrade and myself somewhat perplexed.

" Well, Doctor," began Lestrade. " I have learned enough in my time to know that questioning Mr Sherlock Holmes as to his movements and actions almost invariably leads to frustration on my part. But I would give a week's pay to learn what he is up to now. There is more to this than meets the eye, I feel."

" I agree."

" But I must return now, as I said, and investigate this latest murder. What do you know about the man Lovatt ? "

" I really do not think I should

discuss the matter without Sherlock Holmes' permission."

Lestrade threw me a look which seemed to signify contempt. " You are becoming as mysterious as your friend," he complained with more than a touch of anger in his voice. " Do not abuse the trust that I and the police repose in him—and you."

" You will receive the report in good time, never fear, and it will include the details relating to George Lovatt," I assured him.

" I look forward to receiving it," he replied, with more than a touch of coldness in his voice. He collected his hat and stick, and left me to reflect upon my friend's peculiar relationship with the official forces of law and order. I cast around for the morning newspapers, and started to read them. One of the entries in the agony column of the *Times* caught my eye, thanks to the mention of Chesham. " JM - Chesham job complete - SM".

I was pondering the meaning of this, and the identity of the two individuals denoted by the initials, when Holmes returned, brandishing his favoured cherry-wood pipe. " It was where I knew it would be," he told me, in a kind of triumph that seemed to be somewhat excessive, given the trivial nature of the occasion.

I showed him the entry in the agony column, and he frowned. " As I suspected originally," he muttered. " But I can prove nothing."

" Then you do not wish to write the report you have promised to Lestrade ? " I asked, and informed him of my conversation with the little detective.

" At present, no. Events may preclude that, in any case."

Though Holmes' ever more mysterious pronouncements excited my curiosity, I bit my tongue, and forbore from further questioning. He, in his turn, lit his pipe and requested me not to speak to him for the space of at least one hour and a half. I was somewhat accustomed to these requests, and therefore felt no animosity or ill-will as a result.

※————————

HE appointed time for my silence had nearly elapsed, when Lestrade was shown into our room for the second time that day. Holmes spun to face our visitor, whose face was contorted in anger.

" Those wretched Russians ! " he exclaimed (in truth, the adjective he employed to describe the Muscovites was one that I have chosen not to use here). Such an open display of anger from Lestrade was unusual, and I asked him what had caused this outburst.

" It is not just them, but you, Mr Holmes ! " he fairly shouted in his excitement.

" Calm yourself, my dear man," replied Holmes, himself as cool as if nothing untoward had occurred.

" How did you come to overlook the revolver ? " asked Lestrade, angrily. " Or did you merely feel that it was beneath your dignity to mention it to the police ? Earlier, I was saying to the Doctor here that your ways are sometimes mysterious, but this beats the band."

" The revolver ? " I asked.

" Yes, the pistol that was lying under the pillow. When the Embassy staff moved the body, following the instructions of Mr Sherlock Holmes here, they discovered a revolver with one empty chamber under the pillow. The dead man had obviously shot himself and disposed of the revolver under his head as his last act. And you told me that there was nothing that needed to be communicated urgently ? I would put it to you that a proof of suicide would be a matter of some urgency, even to one of your remarkable talents, given that this was being investigated as a murder." The sarcasm in his voice was almost palpable.

I was certain that no such weapon had been present when I had lifted the dead man's head, and even if I had not been aware of its existence, I was convinced that Holmes would have been. I looked at his face, but it was an impassive mask and revealed nothing of his thoughts or emotions.

" There was also," added Lestrade, " an empty bottle which had once contained some Russian spirit—I believe the name is vodka—which was lying on its side under the bed. How did you come to omit telling us about that, Mr Holmes ? I cannot believe that you simply overlooked it. Or was this just another little detail that could have been left until later ? " The look he gave my friend was positively venomous.

" What can I do but offer my apologies ? " Holmes meekly replied. The answer did not seem to satisfy Lestrade, who continued to glower at him.

" This will be the last time that I, or any other officer of Scotland Yard, will call on your services," he finally spat out. " You are welcome to use your little tricks and methods to trace erring husbands and straying dogs in the future." Holmes' face flushed a little at these words, and the muscles in his jaw worked, but he refrained from giving an answer. " The most junior constable on the Force would have made a better job of it than you, Mr Sherlock Holmes, and shown a greater sense of public duty. And I thank you, Dr Watson, but the report you mentioned earlier will not be needed. You may save yourself the trouble of writing it. A good day to you gentlemen." With that, he swept out of the room, closing the door behind him sharply.

I turned to Holmes, interested to know his reaction to Lestrade's outburst, but to my surprise, he was laughing silently.

" Holmes ! " I admonished him. " I am surprised at your behaviour now, and and your lapses earlier. I hardly know what to say."

" It would be better to say nothing," he replied. [At this point, I was ready to add my explanation to this account, in order to provide the facts of the case in a logical progression. On reflection, however, I must admit that Watson's over-dramatic style makes for interesting reading, and I will permit him to tell the story in his own way.]

" In that case, I will indeed hold my peace," I retorted, annoyed with Holmes for having jeopardised his very career on account of either an inexcusable blunder, or, as seemed more likely to my mind, an excessive love of secrecy.

HE inevitable verdict, given the evidence that had been presented at the inquest of Admiral Trepoff, was *felo de se*. Neither Holmes nor I was summoned to attend, and we were forced to follow the case from the newspaper reports. Lestrade kept his word, and we received no further visits from Scotland Yard in any official capacity, though Inspector Stanley Hopkins, whom Holmes regarded as one of the more promising members of the detective force, occasionally visited us to gain some hints about cases on which he was working.

Meanwhile, as I have explained elsewhere, the joys of married life soon took me from Baker-street to my own establishment, and to some extent, I lost touch with Sherlock Holmes. I was therefore surprised one day to receive a telegram from his brother Mycroft, inviting me to the Diogenes Club for a meeting in the Strangers' Room.

I arrived at the appointed hour to find Mycroft Holmes ensconced in that large chair with which I will always associate him, leafing through a file of papers.

" Ah, Doctor," he greeted me, giving me his hand, which always somehow reminded me of a seal's flipper. " You have not seen my brother in some time ? "

It was not so much a question as a statement, and I assented. " I take it there was no—how shall I put it—rupture between you and him ? " he enquired.

" By no means. My recent marriage deprived me of his company and him of mine."

" Then you would have no objection to performing a small service on his behalf ? "

" None whatsoever. Would this also be on your behalf ? "

He smiled. " You are as sharp as ever, Doctor. Yes, I would take it as a great personal favour if you were to do this for me. You would also be rendering assistance to Her Majesty's Government, by the way. I merely require you to take up residence at 221B Baker-street for several days each week. I wish to give the impression that the rooms are tenanted."

I expressed my surprise. " Sherlock Holmes has moved away from there ? "

" Temporarily, yes. He is on his way to Odessa."

" Odessa ? " I exclaimed in surprise.

" At the request of the Russian government," continued Mycroft calmly. " It is necessary that this be kept a secret, and for that reason, the rooms at Baker-street must appear occupied. Three, maybe four nights every week, for the next two or three months."

" I must arrange these things with my wife."

" Of course. Send a telegram to me here at the Club when all is arranged. Here are the keys to the rooms and the house." He passed me the keys that I had relinquished when I had quitted the Baker-street rooms. " I am sure that Mrs Hudson will welcome the prodigal's return."

ARRANGED matters with my dear Mary, who professed to understand the situation in which I had been placed by my loyalty to my friend, though it was plain to me that she was somewhat distressed by this. I passed nearly three months dividing my time between my house and Baker-street, though the latter depressed me by its seeming emptiness without the vital presence of Sherlock Holmes to fill it.

One day, after a few nights' absence, I entered the familiar surroundings of Baker-street to be greeted on the stairs by the well-remembered sound of a violin, playing some tune of a somewhat barbaric and exotic nature.

" Holmes ! " I exclaimed with delight, flinging open the door to reveal my friend seemingly engrossed in the intricacies of his fiddling.

It was rare for Holmes to make a public show of his emotions, but it appeared that my arrival gave him genuine pleasure, as he immediately laid down his prized Stradivarius and advanced towards me, smiling. " How good it is to see a good honest English face such as yours," he remarked warmly, gripping my hand in greeting. " And in the old surroundings, too ! Mycroft has informed me of the generosity with which you have assisted me and him, and I assure you that this will not be forgotten." (I may add that Her Majesty's Government was kind enough, some months later, to make a small addition to my finances, in respect of the services I had rendered.)

" So," I replied, " you have been in the wilds of Russia. You look well, I must say." Indeed he did. His spare frame seemed to have gained sinew and muscle, and his visage had gained a healthy bronzed colour, unlike his usual London semi-pallor.

" It has been, I suppose, of benefit to my health. However, that was not the purpose of my journey to the shores of the Black Sea."

" Tell me all," I entreated him. " Your brother could not, or would not, tell me anything germane to the matter."

" Very well. Can you contain your curiosity until this evening ? I have several matters on hand about which I was cogitating while whiling away the time attempting to recall the Russian folk tunes to which I have so recently been exposed. Will seven suit you ? Good. I will ask Mrs Hudson to exert herself on our behalf."

RETURNED at the appointed hour, and Holmes and I sat down to supper. It was clear, from the production of one of the finest creations ever to grace the board at 221B Baker-street, that Mrs Hudson was delighted to see the return of her lodger. Not a word would Holmes vouchsafe regarding the purpose of his travels until we had done justice to the culinary masterpieces before us, preferring instead to talk of other matters.

At length, settled in our customary chairs, and smoking some fine cigars provided by Holmes, he began his story.

" I am sure that you noticed," he began, " that there was no revolver in Admiral Trepoff's bed-room when we examined the scene of the crime."

" I assumed that you had placed

it there when you returned for your pipe," I replied, " though I am puzzled as to why you would have done such a thing. It was a cause of great annoyance to Lestrade."

Holmes laughed in response. " Poor Lestrade. He did not deserve such a trick to be played on him. In my absence, though, Mycroft paid a call on him and explained the situation. My broken relationship with Lestrade and the detective force of Scotland Yard is now mended.

" As you so correctly deduced, it was I who was responsible for the placing of the revolver and the empty vodka bottle. By the by, I had never forgotten my pipe. That was merely my excuse for returning to the scene. The death of the ostler Lovatt had informed me that our adversaries were desperate men, who were anxious to guard the secrets of their misdeeds. I therefore wished to provide them with the impression that the death of Trepoff be officially recorded as a suicide, rather than as murder, in order to draw the danger away from us. Unfortunately, it was necessary to throw dust in the eyes of the official force while doing this, and thereby alienate Lestrade.

" I had heard rumours regarding the weapon by which Trepoff met his death which is, as you have no doubt deduced, no ordinary gun, and seems to have been made to order in Germany for the sole purpose of assassination. I have reason to believe that there is a man roaming London at this very hour whose infernal services are for sale to the highest bidder. His name is not one I wish to reveal to you at present."

I must confess that I was somewhat disconcerted to hear this, given that in the past, Holmes had freely shared such information with me. [My intention in keeping the name a secret from Watson was in no way intended as a slight on his character. There have been many times, though, that it has proved advisable for myself alone to be the bearer of dangerous knowledge, and it was for the safety of Watson, and that of his wife, that I refrained from giving the name of the assassin.]

" But who, I asked myself," continued Holmes, seemingly oblivious of my discomposure, " would hire an Englishman to assassinate a prominent Russian diplomat, and for what purpose ? In cases like this, it is to brother Mycroft that I turn, in the expectation that his knowledge and connections within this Government and those of other countries will prove of use.

" When I confronted him in his rooms in Whitehall, he was good enough to let me know details of a revolutionary movement here in London who seek the overthrow of the Tsar and his government. The existence of this was hardly news to me, but Mycroft possessed many more details of the movement and its members than did I, and further informed me that the particular branch of the revolutionaries suspected of hiring the assassin were based in Odessa, a town on the Black Sea. Naturally, the English murderer and his hiring by the revolutionaries here are an embarrassment to our Ministers. However, Mycroft made the suggestion that the information he had made available to me also be imparted to the Russian Embassy here, together with the suggestion that I be invited to Russia to assist with the destruction of this nest of vipers.

" At that time, I had few cases requiring urgent attention, and I confess that the solitude occasioned by your departure for the fresh fields and pastures new of married life was not altogether to my taste. I therefore assented to this, and in due course, I received a handsome epistle, with the double eagle of the Romanoffs at its head, inviting me to Odessa.

" I will not weary you with the details of the journey, other than to note that Constantinople, at which we stopped for a few days, is at once the most noisome and the most fascinating city that I have ever encountered. Odessa, when we arrived there, turned out to be a most beautiful city. Though my Russian was almost non-existent at the start of my stay, most of the high officials spoke French fluently, and some had considerable ability in speaking English, and there was therefore no difficulty in everyday communication.

" The hotel in which I was lodged was, while not up to the standards one would expect of an English hotel, at least equal to that which one might find in a provincial town in France. The deputy chief of the political police, to whom I was introduced on my arrival, was a Count Beloffsky, a middle-aged man *[he was hardly middle-aged—he was verging on the elderly !]* of florid appearance.

" It is seldom that I take an instant dislike to anyone, but in the case of Beloffsky, I found it hard to summon up any kind of sympathy for the man.

" ' I do not know why Petersburg has sent you here,' were his first words to me, spoken in fluent French, with a heavy accent, when I made my first call at his offices. ' We are perfectly capable of managing our own affairs.'

" As you can imagine, this hardly made me comfortable. I had been assured by the Russian Ambassador in London that my services were requested, and to receive this kind of welcome was scarcely an encouraging start to my stay in Russia. I replied as best I could, making some kind of promise that I was not about to interfere in the business of the local police, but he cut me off sharply.

" ' We will visit the Chief,' Beloffsky informed me. ' Prince Rostanoff has expressed some interest in meeting you.' This hardly sounded like the warm welcome of which I had been assured in London, but I was in no position to argue with this. I was escorted along the corridors of the police headquarters, which, I may tell you quite frankly, are a far remove from those buildings occupied by Lestrade and his men."

" In what way ? " I asked.

" They are closer to being a palace than a government building. Indeed, I believe that they served at one time as a residence for royalty. In any event, I was marched along—there really is no other way to describe it—to meet the Chief of the political police for Odessa and the surrounding area. The double doors were flung open before me, and I proceeded across the expanse of polished wooden floor to the desk at the other side of the room, with Prince Rostanoff sitting behind it. In contrast to his deputy, he rose at my approach, and extended his hand to me in a warm welcome.

" ' I am delighted you are here,' he greeted me. ' Beloffsky, I wish to speak with this Englishman. Leave us,' he commanded. Once we were alone in the room, he invited me to sit beside him on the sofa beside the desk, and I took the liberty of observing him closely. To my surprise, he was considerably younger than his deputy. My first thought was that he had attained his rank through his social connections, but a look at his face disabused me of that notion. He had the face of a thinker and one who is used to getting his own way through force of intellect. A certain amount of untidiness was observable in his dress, showing that he was somewhat careless as regards some of the social niceties. There was nothing but friendliness in his attitude as he addressed me.

" ' Mr Holmes, you must know that I am an admirer of your work,'—your little efforts, Watson, have borne fruit as far away as Odessa, it appears—' and it is an honour and a privilege to have you here. I must warn you that what I am about to tell you is to go no further. Have I your word that you will keep it a secret ? '

" I readily assented, and he continued, ' I am concerned by the death of Admiral Trepoff in London. He was a distant cousin of mine, but in addition, he was very much in favour of political reform, as am I, surprising as it may seem to you. Several of us were working together to change our country for the better, and this was well known to all. For this reason, I find it hard to believe that the anarchists and revolutionaries were behind his death. I have a strong suspicion that his assassin was hired by one of the reactionary party, and that his murder was masterminded from here in Odessa. Possibly even from within this very building.' "

" Naturally, this concerned me not a little. It was now obvious to me that I had been dispatched to Odessa to locate and track down this Russian traitor—a prospect that gave me some pause for thought. As you are no doubt aware, the average Russian felon is more desperate and more ferocious in his self-defence than is our average English criminal. He has, after all, more to lose,

as regards the severity of the punishment that will be meted out to him. It has always been my experience, Watson, that a cornered rat knowing its death is imminent will always fight harder than one expecting some chance of escape or reprieve.

" In addition, it was by no means certain that I could rely, as I do in London, on the good faith and efficiency of the authorities. Not only did the barrier of language erect itself between me and those with whom I was dealing, but I could not be sure that they and I would always be working towards the same ends.

" Also, and it in some ways it pains me a little to admit this, I missed your companionship, Watson. I fear that I have often failed to pay you your due, but your support is invaluable to me." I was touched by this tribute to myself, as who could not fail to be, and Holmes continued.

" My immediate puzzle was where to begin my enquiries. As you are no doubt aware, the trifling successes you have been pleased to record are not merely the result of my reasoning, but also of my knowledge of the city and the nation in which we dwell, as well as the inhabitants and their character. I was now placed in a position where both my surroundings, and those around me were likewise unknown. This was a case for pure deduction from first principles, with little in the way of *a priori* assumptions.

" The first step was, naturally, to ask my host what reasons he had for suspecting this.

" He answered me, ' We are, as your brother Mycroft, with whom I am in communication, no doubt informed you, provided with information by the political police—the Special Branch—of your country.

They are good enough to keep a close eye on those undesirables that we indicate to them, and let us know of their movements. They have even gone further on occasion by providing us with information about suspected anarchists and revolutionaries of whose existence we were previously unaware. We are unfortunately unable to return the courtesy, since your country does not seem to breed such exiles. The intentions of all those in England who wish harm to to Russia are therefore known to us.'

" ' And I take it that no such known revolutionaries were in contact with the assassin or his organization ? ' I replied.

" ' That is correct, to the best of our knowledge. By the way, I must thank you for your ingenuity in persuading the criminals that the police believe Trepoff's death to be a suicide.'

" I explained to him that, given the intelligence and the organisation of the criminals I suspected of having carried out the murder, it was unlikely that the deception would be maintained for long, especially since my name had been mentioned in connection with the investigation of the case, and he appeared a little crestfallen at my assessment of the situation.

" ' However,' I concluded, ' this does not preclude my investigating the case you have set before me. In the first place, what reasons do you have for assuming that the orders to murder Admiral Trepoff originated here ? '

" ' In the first place,' he replied, ' I should tell you that Admiral Trepoff, whatever his other qualities, was not a popular man within the Imperial Navy or within the government. There were those who whispered that he owed his position to

his association with certain ladies at the Petersburg court. For myself, I do not believe that. He was a highly competent officer, and served with some distinction in his brief time at sea. However, he was not liked by his officers or men, being at the same time puritanical in his views, and brutal in his discipline. He was known to beat the men with his fists, and it was rumoured that he had knocked down several officers who had disagreed with him.'

" ' I had remarked the ikons within his room in the Embassy in London,' I replied. ' We have officers in the Royal Navy who are unpopular, too, of course, but I hardly think that their rivals would stoop to assassination.'

" The Prince shook his head. ' The Royal Navy is a remarkable institution and one I wish we would emulate further. You must understand, though, that the upper ranks of our navy are not so much a collection of experienced seafaring men as of courtiers who have gained their position through means other than experience of commanding ships. We have too many parlour admirals, to be perfectly frank, and too few sailors. This leads to an unhealthy scramble for rank and position within our navy.'

" ' You mentioned that the order could have originated from within your own organisation,' I pointed out.

" ' Ah, this is truly sad. Family loyalty seems to count for much in Russia. My deputy Beloffsky, who brought you to this room, is related by marriage to one of these officers. I believe you were informed of Trepoff's planned visit to the shipyards in the North of England accompanying Prince Robinski ? '

" ' I was so informed.'

" ' I need hardly tell you that

Great Britain produces the world's most advanced warships, and that the purchase of some of the techniques employed in the construction of these, or even the outright purchase of such a vessel, would increase our naval strength considerably. If Trepoff were to be instrumental in the acquisition of the British skills and materials and thereby strengthened the Russian navy, it would definitely be to his credit, and he could expect promotion, which would cause considerable annoyance, not to mean financial embarrassment, to Beloffsky's kinsman.'

" ' I understand the annoyance,' said I, ' but I fail to perceive the financial aspect of the matter.'

" ' You should know,' said the Prince, and his voice sank to a whisper, ' that Beloffsky's kinsman is in debt to the tune of several hundreds of thousands of rubles as the result of his spending. He now expects the promotion that Trepoff would have obtained had his efforts with the English shipyard borne fruit. I therefore strongly suggest that you concentrate your initial investigations on Beloffsky.' As he said these words, an unpleasant smile spread across his face, which took on the character of some beast toying with its prey.

" ' I understand,' I replied." *[Indeed, I did begin to have some understanding of the situation in which I now found myself. It seemed clear to me that the Prince's position as chief of the police in Odessa was in some sort of jeopardy, being threatened by Beloffsky, and that I was to be the tool that would bring Beloffsky down from his current position.]*

" ' I would like you to start investigating Beloffsky in the way you think best. I have arranged for you to be provided with an office in which to work, and I will send one of my assistants to act as an interpreter and translator. In the meantime, I need hardly tell you that you should maintain a friendly attitude toward Beloffsky.' "

Here Holmes paused, stretched out his legs, and took a long drag at his pipe. He half closed his eyes, and gazed up at the ceiling.

" Your assignment would appear to have been perfectly straightforward, if not altogether what you expected," I remarked to him.

Holmes sat up with a jerk and fixed me with his gaze. " It would have been simple enough," he agreed, " had Beloffsky, who escorted me from my meeting with Prince Rostanoff, not then engaged me in conversation. From this, it was plain to see that while Rostanoff enjoyed the title and rank of chief, the bulk of the work carried out by the department, and the resulting decisions, were Beloffsky's."

" I begin to appreciate some of the difficulties."

" These were complicated by Beloffsky when he also informed me that he suspected that Trepoff's murder had been orchestrated from Odessa. However, he gave me to understand that a cousin of Rostanoff had been assaulted by Trepoff while a young naval lieutenant serving under him, and that Rostanoff had ample personal reason to wish revenge on Trepoff. I found myself truly trapped between two opposing forces, with no obvious means of escape."

"AS you can imagine, this left me in somewhat of a quandary. My position was precarious in the extreme. Other than Mycroft, I had no reason to believe that no-one in London had any knowledge of my whereabouts—he had not seen fit to let me know if he was about to inform you that I was in Odessa. It would be possible for either of the conflicting parties to dispose of me in such a way that I would simply seem to have disappeared from the face of the earth, and no-one in England would be any the wiser. Both parties had the ability to arrange such a circumstance, and I believed that both were ruthless enough to do so.

" My task seemed to have simplified itself into one of mere survival."

I broke in at this point. " Surely you could have set your course for London and left Odessa behind you ? " I suggested.

Holmes shook his head. " I would have done so, but for two factors. Firstly, travel in and out of Russia is a complicated matter, either for natives of the country, or for foreigners. I would have required official permits and the like, and I had no expectation that these would be forthcoming. Secondly, I wished to discover the truth of the matter. It is not in my nature, as you know, to leave such stones unturned.

" I returned to my hotel room to consider the matter in privacy, but was disturbed by a knock at the door, which I opened to discover a young lady, who introduced herself as Mademoiselle Orlova, a friend of Prince Rostanoff's, who had been sent by the Prince in order to show me the sights of Odessa.

" I had little doubt as to the intentions behind this visit. Though she expressed a strong desire to be with me, indeed, wrapping her arms around my neck and clinging to me, I sent the hussy packing, in order that there should be no breath of suspicion. I had already observed on my journey back to the hotel that I was being followed by two separate groups of followers, whom I could only assume were those of Prince Rostanoff and Count Beloffsky. The way in which I was followed was amateurish in the extreme, by the way, and makes even the efforts of our own Inspectors Lestrade and Jones appear polished and professional by comparison.

" In any event, I had to assume that I had to work almost entirely on my own. I had no doubt that I could slip the leash of my followers, but I was handicapped by my lack of ability in the Russian language. It was necessary for me to obtain an interpreter and translator for myself—one who was not liable to be interrogated by either of my so-called hosts.

" My luggage naturally contained some articles with which I could disguise my appearance, and I selected clothing that would not appear too obviously out of place in the Odessa streets. I therefore used these, and made my way out of the hotel through the doors at the back of the building." *[As it happens, Odessa is a less " Russian" and more cosmopolitan metropolis than many Russian cities, so the task of appearing inconspicuous was perhaps not so arduous as might be imagined.]*

" After checking several times to ensure that I had indeed shaken off my followers, I set my course for the Jewish quarter of the city, where many international merchants have their businesses, and where I might expect to discover a polyglot who was willing to help me. I had already learned the forms of the Russian alphabet on my journey, so I was able to recognise the word for "Great Britain" on the sign outside one of these houses. In any case, the familiar symbol of our Union Flag, alongside those flags of other major European nations, signified to me that there was at least a reasonable chance that some English would be spoken on these premises.

"I accordingly entered, and to my delight, the hall porter appeared to comprehend my wishes almost instantly, and bade me wait while he made enquiries. After a few minutes he reappeared with an elderly gentleman of obvious Hebrew extraction.

"Mr. Solomon Meyer proved to have an excellent command of English, and I have no doubt of many other languages, though I was unable to put this supposition to the test. I explained my situation to him as circumspectly as I could.

"'I require the services of a translator to put documents from Russian into English, and who can be relied on to keep the subject confidential,' I informed him. 'I should mention that I am being watched by the political police, but I can assure you that I am not engaged in any illegal activity.'

"He raised his eyebrows at this. 'Indeed, Mr Oliphaunt,' he replied, addressing me by the name by which I had announced myself to the porter. [It had suited my fancy to give another name. In the event that I was being followed, it might serve to throw pursuers off the scent, at least temporarily.] "May I enquire which of the political police are following you?'

"'I was under the impression that there was only one political police force in Russia,' I responded. 'Was I mistaken?'

"'By no means. There is indeed only the one such force in Russia. But in Odessa,' and here he shook his head sadly, 'we have two. That of Prince Rostanoff and that of Count Beloffsky. We citizens of Odessa must learn to balance ourselves between them.'

"'I am personally acquainted with both gentlemen,' I informed him, 'and I regret to inform you that it appears that I have aroused the suspicions of both of them.'

"'My congratulations, sir,' he responded. 'For a new arrival in this city, you seem to have adapted yourself to local customs remarkably quickly.' His sense of somewhat barbed wit appealed to me, and I found myself liking Mr. Meyer immensely. 'I take it that you were not followed here, of course?' I responded in the negative. 'Can I help you?' Meyer asked himself, smiling into his beard. 'The question really should be whether I will help you, is it not? You are able to pay for any services provided, of course?'

"By way of answer, I brought out a small purse containing some sovereigns, which I exhibited to him.

"'Very good. I will ask my son Jonathan to assist you. You will permit me to set the times and places for your meetings? I fear for your safety and that of my son should you be permitted to arrange these matters.'

"'How will you get word to me? I do not wish messages to be delivered to my hotel, where they will inevitably be intercepted.'

"'Have no fear of that,' he smiled, and proceeded to describe his plan.

"This was a most ingenious method of communication, Watson, and one worthy of note. There is in Odessa a flight of steps leading from the water to the city—the Primorsky Stairs, some 200 in all. As Meyer explained things, I was to walk past the top of these stairs every morning, and look for a child's toy—a doll, or some such, on one of the steps. The number of the step from the top on which the toy lay signified the hour at which we were to meet, with the day of the month added in minutes. Hence, if I were to see a doll on the fourth step down on the seventeenth of the month, I was to meet the younger Meyer at seventeen minutes past four o'clock in the afternoon. If there were no toy, no meeting would take place that day."

" Ingenious indeed," I agreed. " And for the place ? "

" That was again signified by the location and positioning of the toy. The toy was not to be in the centre of the steps, but at one side or the other. I was to descend to the bottom of the steps, and then make my way to either the left or the right— the opposite of the side on which the toy was placed—for a number of paces corresponding to the day of the week. Sunday would be one hundred paces, Monday two hundred, and so on. It is a system that I will almost certainly adapt and employ in my own investigations should I have need of something similar." *[As it happens, it proved that I had little need of such a system, but the details and the elegant simplicity of the scheme commended themselves to me.]*

" ' And now, since I have taken you somewhat into my confidence,'

continued Meyer, ' I would appreciate your confidences in return. You have probably not given me your true name, and I shall not seek that. However, I would like to know the reason why you are here.'

" ' You have heard of Admiral Yevgeny Stepanovitch Trepoff ? ' I asked him.

" ' My friend, Zhenya ? Of course. It was a shock when he died in London.'

" ' You knew him ? ' I asked, somewhat taken aback.

" ' Of course. We knew each other from childhood. My firm deals extensively with the requirements of the Imperial Navy, and my friend purchased many articles from England for the Navy's use. Nothing large, you understand—articles such as signal flags, and some items for the officers' wardrooms—but in quantities that required our services. It was a great loss to me personally, and somewhat of a loss to this firm commercially when he died. I do not believe his replacement will continue the business with us.'

" I was surprised at this reply. Mycroft had failed to inform me of this aspect of Trepoff's duties at the London Embassy. ' I am investigating his death,' I replied. Meyer showed no obvious sign of surprise at this announcement, but shook his head sadly, and hissed through his teeth. ' May I see a list of the items he shipped in this way ? ' I asked. I had no specific reason for making this enquiry, but it appeared to me that I might learn a little more about the man from these details."

ERE Sherlock Holmes paused in his narrative, and indicated that he wished to rest, and would continue his recital of events at some future date.

At least two weeks passed before a suitable opportunity presented itself. Holmes had been engaged on a number of cases—his absence had been remarked by the official police, and it appeared that every unsolved case in their books had been awaiting his return. On the occasion I mention, we had taken a train to investigate an incident some way outside London, which, although it had been the cause of some puzzlement to the local constabulary, had presented very few challenges to the detective skills of Sherlock Holmes. He was in an unusually talkative mood as we sat alone in our first-class compartment returning to the metropolis, and I begged him to continue with his Russian narrative.

" Meyer presented me with the records of Trepoff's shipments of materials from England," he began. " As I said on the last occasion, this was the first time that I had heard of such an arrangement. I could hardly credit the fact that Mycroft had omitted to inform me of this, assuming him to be aware of it, and I found it equally improbable that he should have remained ignorant of the matter. It seemed to me, therefore, that the existence of these orders and shipments had been withheld from me for some reason.

" In any event, this seemed to be the first solid evidence I had obtained regarding Trepoff since my arrival in Russia. It was my strong impression that the innuendos and charges laid against each other by the two heads of the political service were fictions motivated by spite and ambition, rather than being based on any firm evidence.

" My examinations of the shipments failed to provide me with any useful information. For the most part, the items ordered were those of a high quality of manufacture, presumably those where British standards were superior to those of Russia. Sheffield cutlery featured prominently in several shipments— and if the standard of the knives and forks supplied to the Russian Navy was equivalent to those which were on the table of the hotel where I was staying, this came as no surprise to me.

" Meyer had also mentioned signal flags as another frequently ordered item, and this, too, was confirmed by the receipts and bills of lading. Among the other items were pocket notebooks, presumably for the use of officers. This was somewhat of a surprise to me. I would hardly have imagined that English items of this nature were sufficiently superior to the native article to justify the expense and trouble of shipping them to Russia. Looking at the ledgers, I noticed that the last such shipment had yet to be delivered to the Navy, although they had been received from England just two days before.

" On a whim, I asked Meyer where these notebooks were to be found, and whether it was possible for me to see them. ' Of course you may,' he answered me, obviously a little puzzled by my request. ' Shall I have them brought to you ? '

" ' I would sooner see them *in situ*, if that is possible.'

" ' That will be easy. Since these are small articles, they are brought here, rather than remaining in the warehouse, where the damp and rats would affect their condition.'

" Accordingly he rose, and conducted me himself to a room at the back of the building which was filled with neatly stacked packages and boxes. He muttered to himself as he moved around, searching, referring to a list that he held in his hand. ' Ah ! Here we are,' he exclaimed, pointing to a small wooden crate. ' Of course, this contains more than just the notebooks that you remarked.'

" ' May I open it ? ' I asked.

" ' Do you feel that it may have some bearing on Zhenya's death ? '

" ' I do.'

" He gave his consent, and I set to work. As you know, Watson, it is my habit to carry with me a collection of small tools which may be used for a variety of purposes, and I now employed these to open the crate. Inside were a number of parcels wrapped in brown paper, three of which bore the mark of a famous London stationer. One of these had the appearance of having been opened. It was clear from my recent exertions that the crate had not been opened previously, and I therefore was forced to draw the conclusion that the package had been opened before it had been placed in the crate—in London.

" ' Since these packages and items come from different sources, would I be correct in assuming that Admiral Trepoff packed the crates himself before they were shipped here, do you know ? ' I asked Meyer.

" ' I believe that was generally the case.'

" At this point, Watson, matters took an interesting turn in my mind. It was clear to me that Admiral Trepoff had been a man who was neat and tidy in his habits, almost to the point of obsession. We had observed this together, had we not, when we visited his room at the Embassy ? This neatness was also present in the packing of the crate, and it seemed to me most unlikely that a man of Trepoff's apparent turn of mind would have allowed such a package to be dispatched, unless there were some ulterior motive. I thereupon removed the package of notebooks from the crate, and saw

that indeed the package had been opened at some time, and the paper re-folded, but in such a way that it was still obvious that it had been opened.

" On my carefully unfolding the opened package, it was immediately obvious to me that one of the notebooks had at some time been removed and replaced."

" How could you tell ? " I asked Holmes. " It was elementary, Watson. When the hand of a professional has been employed, even in such a trivial matter as the packing of notebooks in a package, the work of an amateur stands out by comparison. Just as if, to take an extreme example, I were to attempt even a simple surgical operation, you would know instantly from a mere glance at the sutures that it was not the work of a professional surgeon. In any case, there was no doubt whatsoever in my mind that this notebook had at some time been removed from the package and subsequently replaced. Indeed, the clumsiness of the replacement almost seemed deliberate, as if to draw attention to the fact.

" Meyer was looking out of the window, and I was confident that I would not be observed as I slipped the notebook into my inside pocket and refolded the package closed.

" I started to replace the items in the crate and secure the lid, and Meyer turned towards me. ' Did you discover what you were seeking ? ' he asked me.

" ' To be frank with you, Mr. Meyer, I am not sure that I know what I am seeking at this juncture.' I attempted to smile and to keep my words light as I spoke, but I was certain that the notebook currently reposing in my pocket held an important clue which would aid me in discovering the secret of who had procured the death of Admiral Trepoff. The jousting between two bureaucrats seemed to me to be a diversion—as much as that of that extraordinary Russian sculptor, Golotsin, who visited us. Did he call again while I was away, do you know, Watson ? "

" He died about a month after you had left England," I informed him. " It was reported in the newspapers."

" Indeed ? " said Holmes, his eyebrows raised in a characteristic arch of surprise. " Was it reported how he met his end ? "

" It was indeed. He died as the result of a freak accident involving a large sculpture on which he was working. Apparently he was in his studio alone late one night, and by all accounts, the props which secured the large block of marble from which he was carving his masterpiece gave way, and the marble toppled, crushing him to death."

" How unfortunate," mused Holmes. " Unfortunate for him, that is. Maybe fortunate for others, though."

" What in the world can you mean by that ? " I exclaimed.

" I have my theories, Watson, but I would prefer to keep them to myself until I have confirmation of their veracity."

" Then pray continue your account of what took place with the notebook," I replied, somewhat exasperated by Holmes' reticence.

" I continued to engage Meyer in conversation," Holmes resumed his story, " seeking additional information regarding the shipments made form London. It appeared that the shipments were made at relatively frequent intervals of a month or even less, and that they were never large items. One other remark of Meyer's puzzled me.

" ' I would be obliged, Mr Oliphaunt,' he said to me, ' if you could clear up a minor mystery in connection with this matter. Many of the items that were shipped by my friend are already available in Russia through regular channels. This silverware, for example,' and he pointed to the entry for Sheffield cutlery that I mentioned earlier, ' is readily available in the best stores in Moscow and Petersburg, and may be easily ordered from those places, at a lower cost than the total price displayed here.'

" At this, I became aware that something was amiss. I hurriedly steered our conversation to a close, and made my way back to the hotel, entering through the rear of the building. I was confident that I had not been followed. As soon as I entered my room, I took all reasonable precautions, such as locking the door, and drawing the curtains to prevent any eyes from the building opposite the hotel from watching my actions.

" On my examination of the notebook, I was initially disappointed. I was not sure what I had been expecting to discover, but every page of the notebook looked to be blank. I shook the book to ensure that I had not missed any paper tucked between the leaves. I examined the binding to ensure that it had not been slit open, and material inserted there, but this proved equally fruitless."

" Some sort of ink, invisible until heated or treated with a chemical compound ? " I suggested. Holmes smiled. " Naturally, that was my next thought. I held up the pages to the light, as sometimes traces of such an ink are visible in this way. I was astounded to see, on one of the pages I held up, not ink, but indentations, such as might have been caused by writing with a blunt lead-less pencil or similar implement. I used a soft lead pencil of my own to rub lightly over the page, as a child may do with a coin to take an impression, and read the following in our Latin alphabet:

" ' Majestic 12" x 4, 6" x 12, 12pdr x 16', followed by what I could guess was the Russian for ' torpedo' and 5. Then some Russian and '17kt' and some more Russian words, one of which translated to ' Harvey'. There were similar cryptic jottings on other pages, preceded by ' Caesar' and ' Illustrious'. Now, Watson, what would you make of that, eh ? "

As it happens, I was able to oblige Holmes with an answer. " They are the names of our latest battleships," I replied. " I am guessing that the figures refer to the guns with which they are armed, as well as details of their speed and armour—Harvey armour is the latest such development in this field—though to the best of my knowledge, this information has not been made public."

Holmes looked somewhat astonished. " I had no idea of the depth of your knowledge in these matters, Watson. It took me a little time to discover these things."

" I am naturally interested in those things concerning the defence of our Empire," I told him. " But what you had discovered obviously implied that Admiral Trepoff was passing on confidential naval secrets to his country."

Sherlock Holmes nodded in agreement. " Yes, he was a spy," he confirmed. " There is no doubt whatsoever of that fact."

HE next question I asked myself," continued Sherlock Holmes, " was how I should communicate this information to London, to alert them to the fact that important naval information was being passed to a potential enemy of our nation. There is, naturally, a British Consul in residence in Odessa, but Mycroft had particularly warned me against having anything to do with Ashcroft, claiming that his servants were in the pay of the Okhrana, and any matters that I imparted in confidence to him would soon find their way to Petersburg.

" The question also arose as to where the information was being passed. It had been unclear to me when I examined the package and the manifest what was the ultimate destination of the notebooks, and I would have to return to Meyer to obtain the information.

" Accordingly, having passed a somewhat sleepless night, during which I considered the various options open to me, I took a morning stroll along the top of the Primorsky Stairs, where I noticed a doll placed on the second step at the west side. I was therefore to meet Meyer's son at six minutes past two o'clock, the day being the sixth of the month. I need hardly tell you that my time until that hour hung heavy upon me. I had no fears that my discovery of Trepoff's espionage had, in its turn, been detected. That would only occur when the notebooks were delivered and the expected notebook was found to be missing. However, I had to make a pretence of investigation and appearing busy with a problem in which I felt I was wasting my energies.

" When the appointed hour came, I returned to my hotel, assumed my previous disguise, and, after assuring myself that I was not being followed, met Meyer's son at the appointed place. I asked him to meet me again at the same spot in two hours' time, bringing with him the details regarding the final delivery of the notebooks.

" He performed the task admirably. As we stood looking over the harbour, he informed me that the notebooks were scheduled for delivery in the next week, and they were to be delivered personally into the hands of Admiral Tyrtoff, the commander of the Black Sea Fleet.

" It was now apparent to me that I needed to make my way from Odessa as soon as possible. I had no idea whether either Rostanoff or Beloffsky was aware of Trepoff's operations, but I strongly suspected that one or maybe both of them would be privy to the secret, and that it would prove nearly impossible for me to obtain the papers that would allow me to leave the country legally. I would, after all, have to provide some plausible motive for my departure, and some credible account of Trepoff's death that would satisfy the parties involved.

" My only hope therefore lay in leaving secretly, and again, it appeared to me that approaching Meyer for help would be my safest course of action. I therefore asked Meyer's son to conduct me once more to his father's house. There was nothing in my hotel room of particular value, all my money and papers being carried on my person, and most importantly, the notebook in question was carried in my inside pocket and I was prepared to suffer the loss of a few garments for the sake of a whole skin.

" However, Jonathan Meyer, with a due regard for caution of which I heartily approved, told me that he would precede me, and let his father know that I would be following. He instructed me on the path I was to take to his father's house and gave me to understand that if I did not present myself there within forty minutes, some of Meyer's men would be sent to search for me.

" I waited for the agreed length of time, and took the approved route. It became apparent to me very quickly that I was being followed, and I recognised one of the men who had been following me at the start of my stay in Odessa.

" I was now, as you will readily perceive, in a quandary. I was reasonably certain that my follower had not been present during my meetings with Jonathan Meyer, but had only recently attached himself to me, possibly by chance. However, if I were to allow him to follow me to my destination, I would place Meyer and his whole establishment under suspicion, not to mention myself.

" There were two possible solutions to this problem. Firstly, I could abandon the attempt to reach Meyer, or alternatively, I could attempt to prevent my follower from tracking me to my destination."

" You were not seriously considering murder ? " I asked, a thrill of horror running through me.

" I was considering it as a last resort," he replied seriously. " I had little doubt that if I were to fall foul of the authorities, I would have little chance of ever seeing England again. However, the taking of a human life, unless my own is in immediate danger, is naturally repugnant to me. I had sized up my potential adversary, and was reasonably confident of my ability to incapacitate him in a way that would cause him temporary inconvenience. I therefore slipped into a space between two buildings on the otherwise deserted street along which we were walking, taking care that he observed my action.

" I had been fortunate enough to encounter a Japanese gentleman on the ship on which I had travelled to Nicosia. He was continuing to his home country by way of Suez, but before I left the ship I had many interesting conversations with him, and he taught me some of the holds and techniques of a Japanese system of wrestling, known as *baritsu*. It was one of these that I employed when my follower unsuspectingly entered the alley in which I was waiting. His revolver flew from his hand as I swept his feet from under him, and I swooped to pick it up and clapped it to his head. The poor wretch was obviously astonished at this turn of events and could only stare dumbly at me as I proceeded to deal with him.

" In a trice he was gagged with my handkerchief, and rendered immobile by the scientific application of a few feet of string that I happened to be carrying in my pocket, and my scarf, which I sacrificed in what I believed to be a worthy cause—that of my survival." Here Holmes smiled ruefully. *[I must confess that my success here is what is often termed " beginner's luck". The few techniques of* baritsu *that I had been taught were of limited use, and were only applicable to certain situations, one of which presented itself to me in the course of our brief struggle.]*

" I noted the place where he was lying, glaring furiously from above his gag, but I was unable to tell him that I had no intention of leaving him permanently in that state, as we had no common language.

" I slipped from the alley, and deliberately turned back along the way I had come, in the hope that he would notice this, and therefore would set his course in the wrong direction when he was eventually set at liberty. I discovered a network of side-alleys along which I could double back unobserved, and soon found myself outside Meyer's door.

" ' I require your assistance,' I told him when I was facing him, ' but if you do not care to provide it, I will leave you and think none the worse of you for your refusal.' I explained to him that I wished to leave Odessa quietly with as few as possible being aware of the fact.

" ' You can pay, Mr. Holmes ? ' he asked. " I was astonished to be addressed by my true name, and I confess that my surprise showed in my face.

" ' Do not worry,' he chuckled. ' Even if I am an avid reader of the *Strand Magazine* that reaches me from London, I do not believe that it is a journal that is commonly read here in Odessa.'

" ' Very good,' I replied. ' I have some money, and since I am known to you, should the fee you are requesting prove to be beyond my immediate means, you may be sure that I will pay the balance through your London agents on my return to England.'

" ' I am sure that we can come to some arrangement of that kind,' he smiled. He named a price which was considerably under that which I was prepared to pay, and I protested.

" ' No, no,' he explained. ' I would not dream of taking a kopek for myself to assist Sherlock Holmes. But there are those whose palms must be greased, you understand ? Any money you provide will not remain in my hands, believe me.'

" I was more than gratified

by this attitude, especially as he seemed anxious to expedite matters. ' Can you pass as a mariner ? ' he asked me. ' If so, the *Ivan Grozny* requires a deckhand. She sails to-night for Alexandria in Egypt.'

" As you know, I have never been one to shrink from a challenge of this nature. I accepted immediately, and paid him the previously mentioned fee. He led me to a closet, where a suit of somewhat disreputable clothes, such as those worn by Russian sailors, was presented to me. As I changed my garments to the somewhat noisome attire provided, I informed Meyer of the existence of the recumbent member of the Okhrana who was lying in an alley some few hundred yards away.

" ' I will take care of him—after your ship has sailed,' he told me. ' I have no love for that breed, but I cannot allow him to remain in the condition you describe.'

" Accordingly, I took ship in the *Ivan Grozny*, a filthy tramp steamer bound for Alexandria with a cargo which I am convinced was otherwise than was declared on the bill of lading. As we were leaving the port, a small steam-launch pursued us, and hailed to us, ordering us to heave to, but the captain of our ship refused to acknowledge the order, and we piled on a head of steam which gave the lie to the otherwise shabby and decrepit appearance of the ship, far outpacing the launch until we were well out of Russian waters."

" They knew that you were on board, then ? " I asked him.

" I think not. My guess is that when my absence from the hotel was discovered, the railways and all ships leaving the city were searched, as well as the city also being examined for my presence. In any event, Meyer had obviously given Captain Beloff his instructions, and we

ignored Russian officialdom with a fine disdain.

" I worked my way to Alexandria as a common deckhand, picking up a fair amount of nautical knowledge along the way. It may come in useful on some future occasion, I suppose. In any event, I was able to book a more conventional passage from Alexandria back to England, during which time I was able to consider the matter on which Mycroft had dispatched me."

" And did you reach any conclusions ? "

" I was forced to an extremely unpleasant conclusion. One which I had to force myself to accept."

" That being ? "

" I leave you to draw the final inferences, Watson. But I am convinced that Mycroft was not under the impression that the murder of Trepoff had been ordered by any Russian when he dispatched me to Odessa. I am sure that he had full knowledge of the identity of the murderer, and those who hired him. My being sent to Odessa was Mycroft's way of distracting me, and preventing me from making the investigation."

" Who, then, do you suspect of ordering Trepoff's murder ? " I asked him.

" I think it is somewhat obvious when one comes to consider it," he answered me. All good humour had left his face, and his expression was set and drawn. " It can be none other than the British government that was responsible for hiring the assassin and putting an end to Trepoff's activities."

" Holmes, you horrify me ! " I exclaimed. " I cannot believe that those in authority over us would ever countenance such an action."

My companion shook his head sadly. " I fear it is all too common.

Some of the actions taken by the Special Branch against the Fenians in recent years have been of much the same ilk. However, to my knowledge, in those cases they did not employ professional criminals such as I believe to have been used in this particular instance. That is a depth to which I would hardly have dreamed they could sink." He seemed lost in thought, and remained silent for a minute or so. "It is not so much the action that they have undertaken that offends me, so much as the fact that my own brother deliberately set me on the wrong trail."

"What you mean by that?" I asked him.

"Surely it is clear to you," he replied somewhat testily. "Had I remained in London, I was certain to discover not only the identity of the assassin, but also the identity of those who had employed him, which I would have been duty-bound to report to the police. It was therefore necessary for me to be moved away from the investigation until the affair had blown over and the lack of remaining evidence made it no longer possible for me to investigate the matter fully. Choosing Odessa as my place of exile was a logical step, given the political rivalry in that place, and the connections that the murdered man had with the city."

"What do you propose doing about this?" I asked him.

"The first thing we must do is to make our way to Mycroft and hear what he has to say for himself." Holmes' tone was cold and his eye piercing as he said this. I knew that this icy demeanour masked a fierce anger, which I had seen before, and I shuddered to think that it was now directed against his own flesh and blood. Holmes obviously had noticed the expression on my face. "Yes, Watson, I am indeed angry, but have no fear. I am not about to attempt violence. There has been quite enough blood shed already without my adding to it."

E made our way by hansom to Mycroft's office in a side street off Horse Guards Parade. It was the first time that I had visited his place of work, but was unsurprised when we entered a building which was obviously official, but which bore no sign or notice on its front door.

"The entrance at the rear of the building connects directly to Downing-street," remarked Holmes, after we had given our cards to the commissionaire on duty and were waiting for him to admit us to Mycroft's presence. "Given Mycroft's indolence, it is often easier for the Prime Minister to visit Mycroft here than it is to persuade him to rise from his seat and take a few steps to visit the Prime Minister."

The commissionaire returned and addressed us. "Mr Holmes and Dr Watson, Mr Holmes will see you now," ushering us to the rear of the building, where a large mahogany door bearing a brass plate on which "M. Holmes" was inscribed. He knocked, and Mycroft's well remembered voice invited us to enter.

As was usual in our meetings, Mycroft Holmes did not deign to move his massive bulk out of the chair in which he was sitting, but extended his hand across the desk, first to Holmes, and then to myself before waving us unto the chairs facing him.

"So you have solved the Odessa mystery?" he said to his brother.

"The mystery was born in London," Sherlock Holmes replied, with some heat in his voice. "And you know it well."

The other did not flinch at his sibling's attack, but continued to stare impassively at his younger brother with cold eyes. "How much do you know?"

"I believe I know all. The motive, the method, and the identity of perpetrator, as well as that of he who gave the assassin his orders. Why, Mycroft," continued Sherlock Holmes, "did you send me on that wild-goose chase to Odessa? Was it because you were worried that I would tell the world about the actions of our government?"

Mycroft's countenance remained unchanged. "Sherlock, you should know that I have a better understanding of your character than that. I have the utmost regard for your ability—and that of Dr. Watson here—to keep a secret. There were other diplomatic events of an extreme delicacy some months later than this—I will not reveal the details at this point—necessitating your temporary removal from London. It was inevitable that you would be drawn into the investigation of the Trepoff murder once again, and I was determined that you should not discover the whole truth. In a scandal such as this, it is best that as few people as possible were aware of the facts. Other than myself, and now you and Watson here, almost no-one else was aware of the arrangements that had been made for the removal of Trepoff when I sent you there."

Sherlock Holmes positively glared across the table at his elder brother. "You sent me to the other side of Europe, where my life was in danger, and I found myself caught in a battle between the interests of two extremely powerful men. If I had not taken matters into my own hands, I am reasonably certain that I would have been removed to the wilds of Siberia, never to be heard of more. Were you aware of the situation within the Odessa Okhrana when you sent me there?"

"I apologise, Sherlock. I had no knowledge of the state of affairs pertaining there. I may also add that I only discovered the truth regarding the murder after the event, and can assure you that I had no hand in Sir Robert's arrangements. Your discovery of them from across Europe is a testament to your skill. Quite frankly, I had underestimated your abilities."

"Sir Robert? You refer to Sir Robert Walstone, the chief of the Special Branch?"

Mycroft Holmes nodded his great head. "The same. He has a close personal acquaintanceship with the assassin. They hunted tigers together during the time that they served together in India, and he has a high regard for the old *shikari*'s skills with that peculiar weapon of Herr von Herder of which we are both aware."

Perplexed, I turned from one brother to the other in search of enlightenment, but found none in their blank faces.

"Mycroft, this is monstrous! Is he aware of the associations that Colonel—" Here Holmes checked his words, obviously not wishing to utter the name of the assassin in my presence, a reticence that, I confess, somewhat wounded me, since I had believed I had my friend's full confidence in such matters. "Is Sir Robert aware of these connections and associations ? If so, he is not fit to hold the position that he does. His duty is to enforce the law, not to encourage and reward those who break it."

" I agree, Sherlock," replied Mycroft Holmes. " I have had reason to reprimand him before with regard to similar incidents. The last straws on the camel's back in this case were the two murders committed which were, in my opinion, totally unnecessary. I refer, of course to the killings of the ostler who rented the room from which the fatal shot was fired, and that of the sculptor Golotsin."

" That was murder, then ? " I exclaimed. " I saw the notice of his death in the newspapers, but it was reported as an accident."

" Naturally it was reported as such," replied Mycroft Holmes calmly. " It was felt necessary by Sir Robert that he be silenced, so that he could not then deny the innocence of his revolutionary movement. He could have produced sufficient proof to show that he and the movement were guiltless of the murder of Trepoff, should the obvious objections against the verdict of suicide ever have been raised. If I had been consulted, I would have merely spirited him out of the country, out of the reach of the British press, and out of the reach of the Okhrana, but I was forestalled."

" And your solution to this, Mycroft ? " asked Holmes. " If I remember, it was on your recommendation that Sir Robert was appointed to his present position, and you are the only individual in a position of authority to set the matter right. It is your responsibility to ensure this never happens again. What steps will you take ? "

" I have already taken them. Sir Robert is to be promoted."

" Good Lord ! " I burst out, unable to contain myself. " I do not pretend to understand all the details, but for you to advance the career of a man who orders assassinations and consorts with a known criminal seems to me to be outrageous."

Mycroft Holmes waved a hand at me. " Doctor, your sentiments do you credit, but you do not seem to have a very high opinion of my abilities." I started to protest, but he interrupted me. " At the end of this week, Sir Robert will resign his current post, and will take up his new appointment as Governor of the Falkland Islands in the South Atlantic."

His brother clapped his hands together. " Capital," he exclaimed, smiling. " I think that will clip his wings a little."

" That is the general purpose of this particular exercise."

" And what of the other in the case ? "

" Ah, there we have a problem. We dare not arrest him and bring him into an open court. He knows too many secrets of the realm for that to be desirable, even if it were possible, which I doubt. He is, after all, a master of his damnable art, and could no doubt resist any attempt to apprehend him, or to silence him by other means."

" That last is hardly a road you should be pursuing," remarked Sherlock Holmes severely.

" I agree," replied his brother. " In any event, we have reason to believe that he has also been associating with Charles Augustus Milverton. I am certain that any attempt to curtail the Colonel's activities would bring down a plague on many houses." The name of Charles Augustus Milverton meant nothing to me at the time, but I was to be reminded of it some years later, when

Holmes and I went up against this poisonous serpent.

Holmes nodded thoughtfully. " I follow your reasoning. I trust you are keeping a careful eye on him."

Mycroft laughed ruefully. " As careful as we dare."

" In which case, there is no more to be said or done. Come Watson, it appears that we have been swimming in waters that are too deep for us."

" If it is any consolation," replied Mycroft, " it is a tribute to your skill that I sent you out of the country. And any information that you obtained in Odessa will be most welcome, should you care to pass it to the Admiralty or any other relevant authorities."

" Some small consolation," Holmes grudgingly admitted, taking his hat and stick, and rising to his feet. " You have a filthy trade at times, Mycroft. I wish you would join me in the clean air of crime and put away these intrigues."

" We will see about that," replied the other, enigmatically. " Maybe in due course. Now," looking at his watch, " I expect the Chancellor of the Exchequer to be visiting me in five minutes."

⊷⟫◉⟨⊶

 URING the ride back to Baker-street, Holmes said nothing, but remained grim-faced. Indeed, he refused to speak of the events of the Trepoff murder for many years. I did, however, set down the story, and passed it to him. He annotated it somewhat, and corrected some of my words, and then passed this manuscript back to me with the stern instruction that it was never to be made public.

In my opinion, this desire for the adventure to be kept hidden was as much a matter of Sherlock Holmes' personal vanity as of his wish to preserve secrets of state. Whatever the reason, I have respected his wishes, and will place this in the box with the other stories which are not to be revealed to the public, preserving it solely for my own purposes, to remind me of one of the stranger episodes in the life of my friend.

Colophon

E decided that these adventures of Sherlock Holmes deserved to be reproduced on paper in as authentic a fashion as was possible given modern desktop publishing and print-on-demand technology. We had already worked along these lines in *The Darlington Substitution*, but we felt that this volume required a slightly larger page size to accommodate the two-column layout we wanted to use here.

Accordingly, after consulting the reproductions of the original Holmes adventures as printed in *The Strand Magazine*, we decided to use the Monotype Bruce Old Style font from Bitstream as the body. Though it would probably look better letterpressed than printed using a lithographic or laser method, it still manages to convey the feel of the original.

The flowers are the standard Adobe Wood Type Ornaments, which have a little more of a 19th-century appearance than some of the alternatives.

Chapter titles, page headers, and footers are in Baskerville (what else can one use for a Holmes story ?), and the decorative drop caps are in Romantique, which preserves the feel of the *Strand*'s original drop caps.

The punctuation is carried out according to the rules apparently followed by the *Strand*'s typesetters. These include double spacing after full stops (periods), spaces after opening quotation marks, and spaces on either side of punctuation such as question marks, exclamation marks and semi-colons. This seems to allow the type to breathe more easily, especially in long spoken and quoted exchanges, and we have therefore adopted this style here.

Some of the orthography has also been deliberately changed to match the original—for instance, " Baker Street" has become " Baker-street" throughout.

Other Books by Hugh Ashton from Inknbeans Press:

Tales from the Deed Box of John H. Watson MD
The Odessa Business
The Case of the Missing Matchbox
The Case of the Cormorant

More from the Deed Box of John H. Watson MD
The Case of Colonel Warburton's Madness
The Mystery of the Paradol Chamber
The Giant Rat of Sumatra

Secrets from the Deed Box of John H. Watson MD
The Conk-Singleton Forgery Case
The Enfield Rope
The Strange Case of James Phillimore
The Bradfield Push

The Darlington Substitution

&

Tales of Old Japanese
Keiko's House
Haircuts
Click
Mrs Sakamoto's Grouse
The Old House

ABOUT THE AUTHOR

UGH ASHTON came from the UK to Japan in 1988 to work as a technical writer, and has remained in the country ever since.

When he can find time, one of his main loves is writing fiction, which he has been doing since he was about eight years old.

As a long-time admirer of Sir Arthur Conan Doyle's famous detective, Sherlock Holmes, Hugh has often wanted to complete the canon of the stories by writing the stories which are tantalizingly mentioned in passing by Watson, but never published. This latest brings Sherlock Holmes to life again.

More Sherlock Holmes stories from the same source are definitely on the cards, as Hugh continues to recreate 221B Baker-street from the relatively exotic location of Kamakura, Japan, a little south of Tokyo.

INKNBEANS PRESS

NKNBEANS PRESS is all about the ultimate reading experience. We believe books are the greatest treasures of mankind. In them are held all the history, fantasy, hope and horror of humanity. We can experience the past, dream of the future, understand how everything works from an atomic clock to the human heart. We can explore our souls, fight epic battles, swoon in love. We can fly, we can run, we can cross mighty oceans and endless universes. We can invite ancient cultures into our living room, and walk on the moon. And if we can do it with a decent cup of coffee beside us...well, what more can we ask, right?

Visit the Web site at www.inknbeans.com

Fresh Books Brewed Daily

MORE FROM INKNBEANS PRESS

If you enjoyed this book, you may also want to look at the following titles:

<hr/>

The Darlington Substitution (Book 4 of the Deed Box Series)

by *Hugh Ashton*. The deed box of Dr. John Watson, entrusted by him over a century ago to Cox & Co. of Charing Cross, and which made its way late last year to Hugh Ashton in Kamakura, Japan, continues to yield treasure. The box proved to have a false bottom, under which lay the manuscript of a full-length adventure of Sherlock Holmes, in which the great detective needs all his cunning and detective powers to unravel the mysteries at Hareby Hall. Mentioned in passing by Dr. Watson in his account of *A Scandal in Bohemia*, *The Darlington Substitution* is a tale of deceit, treachery, and murder most foul, set in the wild Border country of northern England. Holmes and Watson encounter a centuries-old legend which tells of the future extinction of an ancient noble family, and set themselves against one of the most ingenious and fiendish villains ever to cross the path of Sherlock Holmes.

<hr/>

Declaration of Surrender (Book 1 of the Nick West Series)

by *Jim Burkett*. Believing either Germany or Japan is about to win the war against the United States in early 1945, several members of Congress conspire to protect their own wealth by secretly creating a document that would give the rights of ownership of all U.S. properties and land over to the leading country before the end of the war is actually declared.

Signed by the President, the document is passed along underground to the Germans but is eventually confiscated back by U.S. Treasury agents along with account ledgers worth millions of dollars sitting in hidden Swiss bank accounts. Days later the agents are found murdered and the documents gone.

DHS agent Nick West is thrust into the world of government assassins and sought after for treason by his own country when he discovers the location of the missing sixty-five year old document but refuses to disclose its whereabouts in order to protect his own men.

<hr/>

Out of Touch

by *Rusty Coats*. Coats' debut novel, *Out of Touch*, follows a reluctant psychic who feels more burdened than gifted: able to see the past, present and future of those who touch an object before he holds it in his hand. Most of the events and emotions that pass through him like electricity are insignificant and benign, but there are those moments when he experiences the fear, horror and pain of catastrophic events, and even knowing when, where and how these catastrophes occur, his knowledge is useless to prevent them, pointless to protect the victims, nothing but pain and guilt for him. Until now.

An Unassigned Life

by *Susan Wells Bennett*. Frustrated novelist Tim Chase just thought of the best plot idea he has had in three years. The problem is he's dead.

Now he's stuck in the afterlife as an unassigned soul with two goals in mind: getting his last and greatest novel published and moving on.

Why can George see me? he thought. Pulling the El Pad from his pocket, he read the answer:

Some living humans, particularly those suffering from a chemical imbalance of the brain, are able to see and interact with you. Unfortunately, this imbalance frequently leads others to label these individuals as insane.

Great, he thought. If I want to hang out in an asylum, I can have all the company I want.

Yes, answered the El Pad.